GW01159339

The Recipe for Us

Ariana Monroe

Published by Ariana Monroe, 2024.

This is a work of fiction. Similarities to real people, places, or events are entirely coincidental.

THE RECIPE FOR US

First edition. October 8, 2024.

Copyright © 2024 Ariana Monroe.

ISBN: 979-8227999290

Written by Ariana Monroe.

Chapter 1: A Taste of Freedom

The golden light spilled across the hardwood floor, illuminating the cozy clutter of my apartment: an assortment of cookbooks teetered on a shelf, a collection of mismatched mugs filled the cupboard, and herbs sprouted in window boxes, their vibrant greens a testament to my attempts at gardening. I stretched languidly, feeling the weight of my cozy blanket slide away, and swung my legs over the edge of the bed, where my slippers lay like eager companions ready for adventure. As I shuffled to the kitchen, I could hear the soft chime of the café's doorbell below, signaling the arrival of regulars craving their morning fix. I poured myself a cup of that rich, dark brew, its warmth seeping through the ceramic mug and into my hands.

The barista, Ethan, always seemed to have an infectious smile, as if he had been personally chosen by the universe to make every morning a little brighter. "Ready for another food adventure, Ella?" he asked, wiping his hands on a flour-dusted apron.

"Every day is an adventure, Ethan," I replied, taking a sip and letting the flavor wash over me like a familiar hug. "But today feels especially promising. I'm off to 'Il Sogno.'"

His eyebrows shot up, and he leaned closer as if sharing a secret. "You're going to love it. I hear their carbonara is life-changing."

"Life-changing? That's quite the claim. I hope I can keep my expectations in check." I chuckled, envisioning a plate of creamy pasta so good it might just send me into a gastronomic epiphany.

With a wave to Ethan, I stepped out into the crisp mountain air, feeling the cool breeze tangle my hair, which I had tossed into a messy bun. The streets of Asheville were alive with the vibrant chaos of morning: the whir of bicycles, the laughter of tourists clutching oversized maps, and the soft strumming of a street musician playing a jaunty tune. I adored this city—the quirky shops, the artsy vibe, the people who wore their eccentricities like badges of honor. Every

1

corner seemed to tell a story, and today, mine was about to unfold in a cozy Italian eatery.

As I walked, the anticipation danced in my chest, a light fluttering that was as addictive as the coffee I'd just savored. The restaurant was a quaint little place nestled between a flower shop and an art gallery, its windows framed with lush green vines that whispered of Mediterranean summers. The door creaked softly as I entered, the scent of garlic and simmering tomatoes enveloping me like a warm embrace.

"Welcome to Il Sogno!" A cheerful voice called out from behind the counter. It was Mia, the owner, whose enthusiasm lit up the space. "You must be Ella! I've heard so much about you from the locals."

I grinned, feeling both flattered and slightly embarrassed. "All good things, I hope?"

"Only the best! Here, let me show you to your table." She led me through the rustic dining area adorned with exposed brick walls and soft, flickering candles that added a warm glow to the atmosphere. I settled into a cozy nook by the window, where I could observe the bustling street outside while enjoying my meal.

Mia handed me the menu, her eyes sparkling. "We have a special today—truffle risotto that melts in your mouth. And don't miss the tiramisu; it's made with a family recipe passed down for generations."

I nodded, taking in the menu filled with tantalizing options. My mouth watered at the thought of homemade pasta and rich sauces. It was like stepping into Italy itself, where every bite could tell a story.

As I waited for my meal, I pulled out my notebook, the pages filled with scribbles and sketches from previous culinary journeys. I often felt like a culinary historian, preserving the flavors and stories that unfolded before me. I loved capturing the essence of a dish—its appearance, aroma, and the sensation it evoked.

While lost in thought, a couple at the next table caught my attention. They were animatedly discussing their recent trip to Florence, their voices rising and falling like a well-rehearsed duet. "And the gelato! I swear I had the best chocolate of my life," the woman exclaimed, her eyes wide with nostalgia.

I smiled to myself, a wave of familiarity washing over me. Food had a remarkable way of weaving connections, threading experiences together in the most unexpected ways.

When Mia returned, she placed a beautifully plated dish in front of me, the risotto gleaming under the soft light. "Bon appétit!" she chirped, stepping back to allow me a moment of reverence.

I took my first bite, and the world faded away. Creamy, rich, with a hint of earthy truffle that danced on my palate, it was nothing short of heavenly. I could feel the flavors swirling together in perfect harmony, each bite a celebration of Italy's culinary mastery.

Just as I jotted down notes in my notebook, a loud crash broke my focus. I looked up to see a young man—his hair tousled and his cheeks flushed—gathering the scattered contents of his bag, which had exploded like a piñata all over the floor. He glanced up, our eyes meeting for the briefest moment, and I was struck by an unexpected spark of recognition.

"Sorry about that," he muttered, a sheepish grin breaking across his face. "This is what happens when you try to carry the world in your bag."

I laughed, the sound ringing out like a chime. "It's a brave choice. What were you carrying, a small village?"

He chuckled, rubbing the back of his neck. "I think I had every intention of bringing the whole Italian countryside with me."

We exchanged a playful glance, and in that moment, I felt an unexpected connection. In the midst of my culinary exploration, a small, unexpected thread of humanity had woven itself into my day.

The young man finally managed to gather his scattered belongings, his flustered demeanor only endearing him further. I had never been one for clichés, but if there were ever a moment where fate decided to play matchmaker over a table of risotto, it was then. He chuckled, his laughter ringing out like a bell as he secured a wayward notebook, the spine cracked and clearly well-loved.

"See? This is why I stick to my backpack," he said, plopping down across from me, his energy a whirlwind that seemed to pull in the warmth of the café. "Less chance of becoming a human confetti cannon."

"Human confetti cannon?" I repeated, my eyebrows raising. "Now that's a title I'd love to have. Just imagine the parties!"

His grin widened, and for a moment, the restaurant blurred into a backdrop of warmth and laughter, our impromptu exchange creating a bubble that felt refreshingly intimate. "Well, it's good to know someone appreciates my unique skill set. I'm Jake, by the way."

"Ella," I replied, and there was a flicker of recognition in his eyes, as if he'd heard my name before. "Food critic extraordinaire, at your service."

"Extraordinaire, huh? No pressure there," he said, feigning mock concern. "So, what's the verdict on 'Il Sogno' so far? Have they managed to snag your coveted 'seal of approval' yet?"

I lifted my fork, the glossy risotto glistening under the soft light. "Well, if this risotto is any indication, they're well on their way. It's like a hug from an Italian grandmother—warm, comforting, and slightly overwhelming in the best possible way."

He raised an eyebrow, leaning in closer as if he were about to be let in on a grand secret. "Are you saying you've had actual hugs from Italian grandmothers? Because that sounds like an experience worth writing about."

"Only in my dreams," I admitted, laughing at the ridiculousness of it all. "But I can assure you, I'm collecting plenty of culinary memories."

Our conversation flowed effortlessly, a delightful dance of banter that felt both familiar and thrilling. I learned that Jake was visiting Asheville for a few days, chasing the elusive dream of experiencing the city's famed food scene before heading back to his desk job in Charlotte. He mentioned his own obsession with food, though he considered himself more of a weekend warrior in the kitchen than a critic.

"I once tried to recreate a classic lasagna, but I accidentally used powdered sugar instead of flour for the béchamel," he confessed, shaking his head in mock horror. "Let's just say it was a sweet disaster."

I burst out laughing, the image of a sugary lasagna making my mind reel. "Well, at least you weren't trying to impress a date or anything. That could've turned into a romantic horror story."

"True! But wouldn't it have made for a great first date story?" he retorted, a twinkle of mischief in his eyes. "Imagine sitting across from someone, trying to act all sophisticated, and then dropping the bomb about your 'dessert lasagna.'"

The easy chemistry between us was intoxicating, and I could feel the café bustling around us, the clinking of cutlery and low murmur of conversations forming a comforting backdrop. I was lost in the moment, savoring the delightful tension that buzzed between us. Just as I was about to ask him what else he'd been exploring in the city, Mia swooped in with my next course.

"Just wait until you try the polpette," she announced, placing a steaming dish of meatballs and marinara sauce before me. "It's a family secret recipe—well, as much as I can share. My Nonna would have my head if I revealed everything."

Jake's eyes lit up, and he leaned closer, almost conspiratorially. "Is this where you reveal that you have a secret Italian grandmother too?"

I grinned and took a forkful, the rich sauce bursting with flavor. "Perhaps I do. Perhaps I don't. But if I did, I'd make sure she lived right next door for quick access to homemade pasta."

"Smart thinking," he nodded, visibly impressed. "A girl after my own heart. I'm just trying to find my own Italian matriarch in the area."

"Oh, good luck with that. You might end up with someone who insists on feeding you her entire pantry every time you visit," I teased, before taking another bite of the tender meatballs. "It's a tough job, but someone has to do it."

Just then, a commotion erupted at the front of the restaurant. A man burst through the door, a small boy clinging to his leg. "I'm telling you, we'll be late!" the man insisted, clearly frazzled.

"Not my fault! You took too long!" the boy yelled back, his face a mix of determination and rebellion.

The scene unfolded like a slapstick comedy. The father's desperate attempts to wrangle the child while simultaneously managing a phone call seemed like a performance piece. The boy, however, had clearly decided that today was not the day for adult supervision.

"Now, that's a duo," Jake said, his voice low and conspiratorial. "I'd pay to watch them navigate a restaurant."

"Maybe they're scouting for the best meatballs," I suggested, stifling a laugh. "Who knows, they could end up at my table next."

As the man finally coaxed his son toward the counter, I turned back to Jake, the warmth of our earlier conversation still radiating between us. "So, what's your favorite food?" I asked, curiosity piquing my interest.

"Honestly? It's like picking a favorite child," he replied, his expression serious yet playful. "But if I had to choose, I'd say tacos. There's just something magical about a perfectly crafted taco. It's like a flavor party that fits in your hand."

I nodded, appreciating the sentiment. "You can't go wrong with a good taco. But why tacos? What makes them so special?"

He leaned back, considering. "Maybe it's because they're versatile. You can dress them up or down, and they always manage to surprise you. Kind of like life, right?"

I couldn't help but smile at the depth hidden beneath his casual tone. "Life is like a taco. You never know if it's going to be stuffed with gourmet fillings or a random assortment of leftovers."

We both laughed, the playful tension hanging thick in the air, as if the world outside had dimmed, leaving just the two of us to bask in the burgeoning connection. In that bustling Italian eatery, surrounded by the scents and sounds of something truly delightful, I felt a spark of something unexpected—a sense of freedom in this charming, serendipitous moment that was tantalizingly beyond just food.

The laughter from our earlier exchange still hung in the air as I leaned back in my chair, trying to savor the last bites of my meal, but Jake's easygoing presence kept tugging at my attention. He was charming in a way that felt effortless, like a well-worn pair of shoes—comfortable yet somehow exhilarating. The warmth of the risotto had settled in my stomach, giving me a sense of contentment, but it was the shared humor that electrified the atmosphere between us.

"You know," he said, eyeing my nearly empty plate, "I might just have to order that polpette myself. If only to confirm that I've made the right decision by sitting here. It seems like you've got the best taste around."

"Flattery will get you everywhere, Jake," I replied, twirling my fork playfully. "But I promise you, my taste is not that remarkable. I just have a tendency to fall for good food and good company."

He raised an eyebrow, leaning forward with genuine interest. "So you're saying I'm just a pleasant afterthought to your meal?"

I feigned a gasp, placing my hand over my heart in mock outrage. "How could you say such a thing? You, my dear sir, are the unexpected dessert to my savory main course."

"Dessert, huh?" he shot back, a teasing smirk playing on his lips. "I'll take that as a compliment, though I'd prefer to be the cherry on top instead of some melted ice cream left to melt into a puddle."

"Fine, you can be the cherry, but I'm not promising you won't end up in someone's stomach later," I quipped, reveling in the light-hearted banter.

Just then, Mia reappeared, her hands cradling two steaming dishes. "Just in time! Here are our famous meatballs. And a little something extra for the cherry," she said, setting a slice of tiramisu down in front of us. The layers of coffee-soaked cake and mascarpone looked like a dream come true.

"Now that's a masterpiece," Jake said, his eyes widening at the sight. "You might need a bigger table if you're going to keep treating me like this."

"Next time I'll bring the entire Italian feast," I promised, eyeing the tiramisu with determination. "But for now, I'd say we have enough to keep us entertained."

Jake took a forkful of meatball, his expression transforming into pure delight. "You were right. This is definitely a hug from an Italian grandmother. I can feel the love radiating from the sauce."

"Now you're just trying to win me over," I teased, savoring my own bite. The richness of the sauce, the tenderness of the meat—it was a culinary hug indeed.

As we continued to share bites of food, the world around us faded further into a gentle hum, and it felt like time stood still. Conversation flowed freely, ranging from our favorite foods to the quirks of Asheville's food scene, and I found myself entranced by the ease with which he shared his thoughts. There was a depth to him, a subtle vulnerability that drew me in closer, as if he were revealing layers of himself with each anecdote.

"I've always found that food can be a bridge," Jake mused, his tone turning more serious. "You can share a meal with a stranger and suddenly, you're no longer strangers. You're part of something bigger."

"Absolutely. It's like an unspoken pact. You break bread, and suddenly the walls come down," I agreed, leaning in, intrigued by this unexpected side of him.

He nodded, his gaze earnest. "I've moved around a lot, but every new city feels like a chance to start fresh. And every meal becomes an opportunity to connect."

"Sounds romantic," I said lightly, trying to keep the tone casual, but my heart raced at the thought of such an unrestrained approach to life.

"Maybe it is. Or maybe I'm just a hopeless idealist," he replied, his smile playful, but there was an edge to his words.

Before I could respond, the bell above the restaurant door jingled, snapping our moment. In walked a woman, her presence commanding as she swept in like a gust of wind, dark hair cascading around her shoulders. She wore an outfit that screamed 'sophistication'—tailored, sleek, and somehow out of place in our cozy eatery. I couldn't help but notice the way she scanned the room with an intensity that sent a shiver down my spine.

"Is this the new hotspot?" she called out, her voice smooth and confident. "I've heard rave reviews."

Mia approached her, all professional cheerfulness. "Welcome! We'd be happy to accommodate you. Are you looking for a table?"

The woman's gaze flickered toward Jake and me, and I felt a sudden wave of protectiveness wash over me. Was it just me, or did she seem too calculating? Like a predator sizing up her next meal? I tried to shake the feeling, focusing instead on the delightful tiramisu before me.

"Actually, I was hoping to join the food critic," she said, her tone dripping with allure. "I'd love to hear about your experience, Ella."

I exchanged glances with Jake, who seemed equally taken aback. "Uh, well..." I stammered, unsure of how to respond to this unexpected intrusion.

"Sorry, I'm a little busy at the moment," I managed, forcing a smile as I waved my fork, half-heartedly gesturing to our half-eaten meal.

"Oh, don't mind me," she said, her smile unwavering. "I just figured I'd introduce myself. I'm Veronica—food enthusiast, connoisseur of all things delicious."

"Charmed," Jake chimed in, his voice light but edged with a hint of wariness. "But we were just discussing the fine art of human connection through food."

Veronica tilted her head slightly, a bemused expression crossing her face. "And what do you know about that?" she asked, her tone playful yet challenging, as if daring him to continue.

I felt the tension in the air shift, the bubble of our cozy conversation pricked by her sharp presence. "A lot, actually," I replied, my voice firming. "Food can bring people together, but it can also drive them apart. Depends on how you use it."

Veronica's eyes narrowed ever so slightly, a flicker of something dangerous sparking behind her cool demeanor. "Interesting take, Ella. Let's see how it plays out, then."

The challenge hung heavy in the air, a thread of uncertainty weaving through the warm atmosphere of the restaurant. Just as I was about to say something—anything—to cut through the tension, the door swung open again, and in walked a familiar face: my editor, Margaret, the one person I hoped to avoid in the middle of this culinary adventure.

"Ella! There you are," she called out, her voice slicing through the moment.

My heart sank. It was hard to tell whether this was a stroke of bad luck or something more. As Margaret approached, her eyes darted between me and Jake, then settled on Veronica, her expression unreadable. I was caught in a web of culinary intrigue, with an unexpected twist lurking just around the corner, waiting to unravel everything I thought I knew.

"Mind if I join you?" Margaret asked, pulling out a chair without waiting for an answer.

The world around me held its breath, and I felt the tension coiling tighter, like a spring ready to snap. Just when I thought the day had already served up all the surprises, it seemed life was determined to throw in one more. And as I glanced between the three of them, I couldn't shake the feeling that I was right on the edge of something profound, something that might change everything I thought I wanted.

Chapter 2: Culinary Sparks

Walking into Il Sogno was like stepping into a romantic dream, where the air was thick with the scent of garlic and rosemary, weaving a spell that wrapped around my senses like a favorite old sweater. The warm, golden lighting bathed the rustic wooden tables, each adorned with tiny vases of fresh basil, their vibrant green leaves promising the taste of summer in every bite. I inhaled deeply, savoring the fragrant perfume of culinary delights wafting from the kitchen, where the rhythmic clang of pots and pans mingled with laughter and the gentle hum of conversation.

Settling into my seat, I couldn't help but feel an unexpected thrill race through me, an electric buzz that sent shivers down my spine. My gaze wandered across the room, landing on a tall, dark-haired man whose laughter resonated like a warm melody. He sat surrounded by a group of friends, a glass of deep crimson wine in his hand, his smile easy and genuine, effortlessly charming in a way that made my heart flutter. I felt a slight blush creep up my cheeks as I quickly averted my gaze, pretending to study the menu as if it held the secrets of the universe. But curiosity gnawed at me, pulling my attention back to him, as if he were a magnet drawing me in.

I ordered the truffle pasta, its rich, earthy aroma promising to envelop my taste buds in a luxurious embrace. A glass of Chianti followed, its ruby hue glistening under the warm lights, inviting and bold, just like the man across the room. As the waiter placed my dish in front of me, the intoxicating aroma wafted upwards, teasing my senses. I took my first bite, the creamy sauce enveloping the al dente pasta in a velvety blanket of flavor that sent my mind into a state of bliss. Each mouthful was a decadent indulgence, an explosion of taste that danced on my tongue.

And then, as if conjured by the very essence of the dish, he appeared at my table, his confident stride matched by an easy grace.

"I hope you don't mind me interrupting," he said, a playful glint in his dark eyes. "I had to see who was brave enough to order the truffle pasta on a night like this. It's our special, and I always like to meet the connoisseurs."

Surprise fluttered in my chest, quickly replaced by intrigue. "Well, it seems I have excellent taste then," I replied, summoning the bravado that had been lying dormant within me. "Or perhaps just a reckless sense of adventure."

"Adventurous eaters are the best kind," he said with a smirk, leaning casually against the table as if he belonged there, as if we had known each other for ages. "I'm Marco, by the way. Head chef here. It's my job to ensure that your meal is nothing short of spectacular." His voice was warm, with a hint of an accent that curled around the words like a silk ribbon.

"Nice to meet you, Marco. I'm Emma," I replied, fighting the urge to fidget under his gaze. "And I have to say, so far, you're succeeding wildly."

"Flattery will get you everywhere," he said, grinning. "But I prefer to earn my praise. Tell me, what do you think of the dish?"

"It's divine," I replied, savoring another mouthful, the taste exploding with earthy truffle notes. "You must be the reason for this little piece of heaven."

His laughter was like a melody, rich and infectious, and I felt the tension in my shoulders melt away. "You have a way with words, Emma. But I assure you, the true magic happens in the kitchen." He paused, leaning closer, lowering his voice as if sharing a secret. "I actually invented that recipe during a late-night session after a particularly stressful dinner service. It became a hit, and now it's the one dish I refuse to take off the menu. I have a reputation to uphold, after all."

"I can see why," I said, feigning seriousness. "You've created a culinary masterpiece. I'm sure your other dishes are just as amazing, right? Or do you reserve all the best ideas for the truffle pasta?"

"Touché," he laughed, his dark eyes sparkling with mischief. "I suppose I'll have to prove myself. You should come back and try the seafood risotto. I swear it will change your life."

"Is that a promise?" I challenged, my heart racing with the thrill of playful banter, the air around us charged with an exhilarating tension.

"Absolutely," he said, a grin spreading across his face. "But I'll expect a review, of course. Only honest feedback, no sugarcoating."

"Deal," I said, extending my hand, the gesture both formal and absurdly flirtatious. As our hands met, an electric current shot through me, igniting something I hadn't anticipated. I wondered if he felt it too or if I was simply projecting my overactive imagination.

"So, Emma, what brings you to Il Sogno?" he asked, leaning back in his chair, his expression shifting from playful to genuinely curious.

I hesitated, the truth dancing on the tip of my tongue. "Just a little escape from reality," I admitted. "I'm in town for a few days, trying to find a spark in the chaos of my life. It's been... a lot lately."

His brow furrowed slightly, concern etched on his face. "A lot can weigh heavy on a person. Sometimes we need a little indulgence to remind us of life's pleasures. You chose wisely."

I nodded, feeling a strange bond forming, as if we were coconspirators in this quest for indulgence. "You have no idea how true that is. I could use all the indulgence I can get."

"Then you're in the right place," he said, his voice dropping to a conspiratorial whisper. "This restaurant isn't just a business; it's a sanctuary for food lovers. I like to think of it as a place where the mundane melts away, and we celebrate flavors that make us feel alive."

Our conversation flowed easily, weaving in and out of playful banter and deeper musings on life, food, and everything in between. Each word exchanged felt like a thread stitching together a tapestry of connection, and I found myself drawn to him in a way that was both thrilling and terrifying. Just as I started to lose myself in his charm, the unmistakable sound of glass shattering interrupted our moment.

My heart raced as I turned to see the commotion at the bar. A couple had been celebrating too enthusiastically, their laughter abruptly giving way to shock and a flurry of movement as waitstaff rushed to clean up the mess. Marco stood up instinctively, glancing back at me. "Let me take care of this. I'll be right back."

As he walked away, I felt a strange sense of longing, a mix of anticipation and anxiety swirling in my stomach. I took a sip of my Chianti, savoring the robust flavor, but I couldn't shake the feeling that this night had only just begun.

The sound of shattered glass echoed through the restaurant, cutting through the warmth and laughter like a sudden chill. I watched Marco rush toward the bar, his tall frame moving with a fluid grace that caught the attention of several diners, including me. The moment felt suspended in time, like one of those dramatic slow-motion scenes in a movie. I couldn't help but feel a pang of disappointment, the kind that comes when you realize that magic can't be bottled and preserved; it's a fleeting moment, delicate and ephemeral.

A waitress bustled past me, her arms laden with a colorful assortment of dishes that seemed to float above her head. I couldn't help but admire her efficiency as she navigated the chaos with a practiced ease. My attention turned back to Marco, who was now expertly helping the bartender sweep up the remnants of the broken glass while still managing to smile and reassure the shaken patrons. I had a strange urge to get up and help, to contribute to the dance of recovery, but I was rooted to my chair, captivated by the effortless way he commanded the room.

As I took another sip of Chianti, I realized how much I was enjoying the quiet moments between the clamor. There was a kind of magic in the air, something that seemed to linger just beyond reach. I could feel the anticipation building again, the promise of something unexpected hanging like a ripe fruit, just waiting to drop.

After what felt like an eternity, Marco returned to my table, wiping his hands on a kitchen towel, his smile sheepish yet charming. "Sorry about that," he said, his eyes dancing with mischief. "You know how it is—one minute you're serving delicious food, and the next, you're playing janitor. But enough about broken glass. Let's talk about your dinner. How's that truffle pasta treating you?"

"It's fantastic," I said, the words tumbling out with genuine enthusiasm. "I can see why you're so proud of it. It's definitely the highlight of my night, and I'm not just saying that to flatter the chef."

"Flattery might work on some, but I appreciate the honesty," he replied, leaning back in his chair, a glimmer of intrigue in his gaze. "So, tell me, what else do you enjoy besides indulging in fine cuisine?"

I pondered for a moment, relishing the question as if it were a delectable dish in itself. "I love exploring new places. I feel like every city has its own flavor, its own rhythm. I've found that food often tells the best stories about a place. It's like you can taste the history, the culture, and sometimes even the heartaches."

"Now that's a perspective I can get behind," he replied, nodding thoughtfully. "Travel can be a balm for the soul. What's been your favorite adventure so far?"

"Honestly? A little beach town in Italy. It was one of those places that felt untouched by time. The food was simple but bursting with flavor, and I spent lazy afternoons just sipping wine while watching the waves crash on the shore. It was bliss."

Marco leaned forward, his expression earnest. "Bliss is important. We need those moments to remind us why we do what we do. And what about you? Why are you in town?"

I hesitated, the weight of the question pulling at my heartstrings. "I'm trying to figure things out, you know? Life can sometimes feel like a recipe gone wrong. Too much salt, not enough sweetness. I just needed a break from everything."

His gaze softened, and for a brief moment, I felt as though he could see through my bravado to the tangled mess of emotions underneath. "I get it. Life has a way of throwing curveballs. But sometimes, we find what we need in the most unexpected places."

His words resonated with me, a soothing balm to the chaos I felt within. Just then, the waiter returned with a plate of dessert—a slice of rich tiramisu dusted with cocoa, the layers of cream and coffee calling to me like a siren song. I grinned at Marco. "Is this your doing as well?"

"Guilty as charged," he said, his grin widening. "It's a classic, but I like to add a little twist. A hint of orange zest in the mascarpone, just to keep things interesting."

"Interesting is good," I replied, scooping up a forkful and savoring the flavor explosion in my mouth. "Oh wow, this is incredible! You really know how to elevate a classic."

"Thanks, but I can't take all the credit. Tiramisu has a mind of its own," he laughed. "Like people, it can be unpredictable. One day it's fluffy and delightful; the next, it's flat and sad. You never know what you're going to get."

"Kind of like dating," I quipped, a playful smirk on my face. "Some days, it's a delicious experience, and others, you're left with stale bread and regrets."

"Exactly!" He threw his hands up in mock exasperation. "And don't even get me started on the occasional glass of red wine that turns out to be vinegar. What a disappointment!"

I laughed, feeling the connection deepen between us, each exchange like a note in a symphony that was beginning to crescendo. Just then, my phone buzzed on the table, breaking the spell. I glanced down at the screen to see a text from my best friend, the sudden reality of my life creeping back in.

"Uh-oh, duty calls," I said, my heart sinking slightly. "I should probably check in with my friend."

"Of course," he said, his tone shifting slightly. "But if it's about where you're going next, I hope you're not planning on leaving just yet. We have so much more to talk about."

His eyes held a challenge, and I felt an unexpected thrill. I typed a quick reply, trying to shake off the impending sense of obligation. As I set my phone down, Marco leaned closer, his voice lowering conspiratorially. "What if I told you that I have a secret stash of limoncello in the back? It's the good stuff—family recipe. Perfect for celebrating impromptu culinary adventures."

The way he said it made me feel like a child being offered a taste of forbidden candy. "Is that legal?" I teased, my heart racing at the prospect of breaking the rules just a little.

"Only if you promise not to tell the health inspector," he replied, his grin wide and inviting. "What do you say? A quick taste? No commitments."

For a moment, I hesitated. My mind flickered to the reality waiting beyond the restaurant doors—responsibilities, unanswered questions, and the reality that I was supposed to be figuring out my life. But then I looked into his eyes, filled with mischief and warmth, and suddenly, all I could think about was the tantalizing prospect of adventure.

"Why not?" I said, my voice firm with resolve. "Let's break some rules."

His laughter filled the air as he stood, extending a hand to help me rise. "That's the spirit! Just remember, once you step into the kitchen, the world outside fades away."

I felt a spark of exhilaration as I took his hand, letting him lead me into the heart of Il Sogno. The clamor of the restaurant faded, replaced by the rhythmic sounds of the kitchen—a symphony of sizzling pans, bubbling sauces, and the faint whispers of culinary secrets waiting to be discovered.

As Marco led me deeper into the heart of Il Sogno, the vibrant atmosphere of the dining area faded into a bustling kitchen filled with the intoxicating aromas of simmering sauces and freshly baked bread. The air was thick with anticipation, and I could feel the energy crackling like static electricity. Chefs moved with a synchronized precision, each one focused on their task, a choreography of culinary artistry that I had only ever seen on television.

"Welcome to my realm," Marco declared, spreading his arms wide as if he were presenting a stage. "This is where the magic happens, and where my little culinary secrets are kept." His eyes sparkled with mischief, and I couldn't help but smile at his enthusiasm.

"Is this where you keep the limoncello?" I asked, feigning seriousness, while my heart raced at the idea of breaking into the inner sanctum of a chef's domain.

"Ah, you caught me," he replied, laughter bubbling from his chest. "But only for special guests. Come on, I'll give you a taste that will make you forget your worries."

He ushered me to a corner where an elegant glass bottle glimmered in the soft light, nestled between jars of spices and dried herbs. "This," he said, pouring a generous splash into two small glasses, "is my family's recipe. A little slice of sunshine."

I took the glass from him, the chilled liquid glistening like liquid gold. "You know, I'm starting to think you're more of a magician than a chef," I teased, raising my glass in a mock toast. "To culinary sorcery!"

"To culinary sorcery," he echoed, clinking his glass against mine. We took a sip, the limoncello bursting with brightness and zest, a perfect balance of sweetness and tartness that danced on my tongue. "Told you it would lift your spirits," he said, his eyes searching mine. "How's that for a little escape from reality?"

"Better than I could have imagined," I admitted, savoring the moment, the warmth of the drink spreading through me like sunshine on a cold day. I felt emboldened by the sweet nectar, my worries slowly dissolving in the atmosphere of the kitchen.

As we stood there, amidst the chaos of sizzling pans and clattering utensils, our conversation shifted to a more intimate tone. "You know, Emma," Marco began, leaning in slightly, his voice lowered as if sharing a secret. "I've been in this business long enough to know that food is only part of the experience. It's the connections we make that truly matter. Moments like this, they're rare and precious."

I felt a flush rise to my cheeks, caught off guard by the sincerity in his words. "I couldn't agree more. It's easy to lose sight of that in the everyday grind. But tonight... it feels different."

"Different how?" he pressed, his curiosity evident.

"It feels... alive," I said, choosing my words carefully. "Like anything is possible, and maybe I can be whoever I want to be in this moment."

"Then let's embrace that," he replied, the corners of his mouth curling into a devil-may-care grin. "What would you do if you could be anyone tonight?"

I thought for a moment, the question hanging in the air like a tantalizing aroma. "I'd be an explorer, uncovering the hidden gems of this city. Trying everything I can—food, adventure, maybe even a little mischief."

"Now you're speaking my language," Marco said, his eyes lighting up with mischief. "Why don't we make that happen? After this, I'll take you to my favorite little spot—a hole-in-the-wall that serves the best pizza in town."

The thrill of spontaneity washed over me, and I felt a sense of exhilaration I hadn't experienced in ages. "Count me in! But if we're doing this, I demand a pizza topped with your most outrageous combination. No holding back!"

Marco threw his head back and laughed, the sound rich and infectious. "I love your spirit! Prepare yourself for a flavor explosion you won't soon forget." He reached for the limoncello bottle to refill our glasses, but just then, a shout erupted from across the kitchen.

"Marco! We need you at the grill!" A frantic sous chef waved him over, the urgency in her tone unmistakable.

"Duty calls," Marco said, a flash of disappointment crossing his features before he turned back to me. "Stay right here. I'll be back in a flash."

I nodded, trying to mask the disappointment I felt at his abrupt departure. I watched as he darted back into the fray, his presence quickly absorbed into the rhythm of the kitchen. I stood alone for a moment, surrounded by the clamor of culinary creation, my heart racing not just from the limoncello but from the anticipation of what was to come.

Suddenly, the kitchen door swung open, and a woman I hadn't noticed before stormed in, her eyes wide and panicked. "Marco!" she called out, her voice slicing through the noise. "You need to come see this—now!"

My heart sank. Something in her tone sent a wave of tension crashing through the room, and I felt an inexplicable urge to follow. The bustling kitchen, once filled with lighthearted banter, now hummed with an undercurrent of urgency. I sidled up to the edge of the action, straining to hear what was happening. Marco turned to the woman, his expression shifting from jovial to concerned as he approached her.

"What is it?" he asked, his voice steady but laced with an edge of anxiety.

"There's a problem with the delivery," she said, urgency tightening her features. "The ingredients for tomorrow's special never arrived, and the vendors are refusing to answer. We're going to be in trouble if we can't figure this out."

Marco's face hardened, the carefree demeanor evaporating as he took in the weight of the situation. "Alright, let's gather the team and brainstorm a solution. We can't let the customers down."

As he hurried away, I felt a pang of concern. The vibrant energy of the kitchen shifted, the lively chaos now punctuated by a frantic seriousness. I stood on the sidelines, torn between the thrill of the adventure we had planned and the reality unfolding before me.

I hesitated, unsure of whether to intervene or simply remain a spectator to the brewing storm. Just then, Marco glanced back at me, his eyes searching mine for a sign of support. "Emma," he called, his voice cutting through the din. "Stay close. I might need your help."

Help? I hadn't signed up for this. My heart raced, torn between the allure of the unexpected and the fear of stepping too far into his world. But before I could think, I found myself moving toward him, drawn in by the urgency of the moment.

"Okay, what do you need?" I asked, my voice steady despite the chaos around us.

He looked relieved, a flicker of gratitude in his gaze. "We need to come up with a backup plan, and fast. If the delivery doesn't show up, we'll have to create a new special for tomorrow. Something that's quick to prepare and still wows the customers. Do you have any ideas?"

My mind raced, flashes of flavors and combinations swirling in my thoughts, yet I was acutely aware of the clock ticking down. "What about a seafood linguine? It's simple but can be elevated with a good white wine sauce and some fresh herbs. Or we could do a seasonal risotto with whatever fresh vegetables we have left."

"Linguine could work," he replied, a spark of hope igniting in his eyes. "Let's gather the ingredients and see what we have on hand."

As we moved through the kitchen, gathering vegetables and spices, the tension hung thick in the air, a stark contrast to the carefree atmosphere just moments before. Suddenly, just as we were beginning to assemble our makeshift special, the front door burst open. A delivery driver stood there, looking frazzled but triumphant. "I've got your order!" he shouted, waving several boxes in the air.

Marco and I exchanged glances, relief washing over us. But as I stepped forward to greet the driver, my phone buzzed again, and I felt an uncomfortable twist in my stomach. I glanced down to see another text from my best friend, but before I could read it, I felt the world around me shift.

"Wait—what's that?" I heard someone shout, followed by the sharp crack of glass. I turned just in time to see the delivery driver stumble backward, the boxes tumbling from his hands. And as they fell, a strange glint caught my eye—a flash of something metallic slipping free, spinning in the air before landing with a resounding thud on the kitchen floor.

Everything went silent, the chaos of the kitchen falling away as the reality of what lay before me sank in. The atmosphere shifted again, tension crackling like static as Marco's face paled, his expression darkening with concern.

"What the hell is that?" he murmured, stepping closer to inspect the object now lying ominously among the fallen boxes.

I took a cautious step forward, my heart pounding in my chest. And just as I leaned down to get a better look, the weight of uncertainty settled over me like a dark cloud, and I knew that whatever this was, nothing would ever be the same again.

Chapter 3: A Recipe for Disaster

The golden light of late afternoon filtered through the arched windows of Il Sogno, casting an ethereal glow on the rustic wooden tables and the vibrant red and green accents of the decor. Each time I stepped inside, it felt as if I were entering a cherished painting—an idyllic snapshot of life steeped in rich flavors and hearty laughter. The air was laced with the aroma of simmering marinara and freshly baked focaccia, teasing my senses and tugging me closer to the source of my recent obsessions: Marco.

Marco had become the culinary magician I didn't know I needed in my life. His laughter rang through the restaurant like a cherished melody, the kind you replay in your mind long after the song has ended. With dark curls that framed his face just right and eyes that danced with a mischievous glint, he had a way of turning the simplest exchange into something exhilarating. Conversations that had once circled around the origins of caprese salad evolved into earnest discussions about our families, our dreams, and the little quirks that made us who we were.

Yet, the closer I got to him, the more I felt the heavy weight of my own apprehension settling over me like a thick fog. It was as if every shared laugh and lingering gaze served as a warning, reminding me of my deep-seated fear of commitment. Love, I had learned through experience, was a recipe fraught with the potential for disaster, and I was determined to keep my distance from the ingredients that could cause my heart to burn.

One evening, as I took a seat at my usual spot by the window, I noticed Marco behind the counter, focused and deftly preparing a batch of tiramisu. I watched as he whipped the mascarpone, a gentle smile playing on his lips as he hummed a tune that danced on the edges of familiarity. It was infectious; I found myself grinning, entirely captivated by the man who could coax sweetness from simple ingredients.

"Hey, Chef!" I called out, unable to resist the urge to tease him. "Do you always wear that apron, or is it just for show?"

His head snapped up, surprise quickly morphing into delight. "Ah, you caught me! This apron is my armor. You see, without it, I'm just Marco. With it, I'm Marco, the tiramisu warrior."

"Warrior?" I chuckled, leaning back in my chair. "More like a pastry prince with that flourish."

He placed a hand over his heart in mock offense. "You wound me! I'll have you know that my flourishes are legendary in this town."

"Legendary? Really?" I leaned in, a playful smirk dancing on my lips. "Tell me, does that come with a cape?"

"Only on weekends," he replied, deadpan, before his grin broke through. "What can I get for you today? A taste of my legendary warrior skills?"

"Surprise me," I said, feeling a rush of excitement that momentarily pushed aside my fears. "I trust you."

As he turned to the kitchen, I felt that familiar mix of exhilaration and anxiety swirl within me. The intimacy of sharing a meal crafted with care was something I had never shied away from before, but this—this was different. There was a level of vulnerability in trusting someone else with my tastes, my desires, and maybe even a piece of my heart.

"Hey, ready for some magic?" Marco returned, his hands expertly balancing a plate of spaghetti alle vongole, glistening with garlic and white wine, accompanied by a side of fresh-baked bread.

"Wow," I breathed, mesmerized by the vibrant colors and the intoxicating aroma. "This looks incredible!"

"Just wait until you taste it." He set the plate before me, leaning on the edge of the table as I took my first bite. The flavors exploded in my mouth—rich, salty, and utterly divine. I felt a moment of bliss, the kind that could only come from truly savoring something delicious.

"This is phenomenal!" I exclaimed, my eyes widening with delight. "How do you make it taste like sunshine?"

Marco chuckled, a low and warm sound that wrapped around me like a soft blanket. "It's all about the ingredients. You have to choose the best clams, and the rest just follows. Kind of like relationships, don't you think?"

His words sent a shiver of awareness down my spine. Could I really compare cooking to love? I contemplated his analogy, the very thought stirring up a storm of unease within me. Ingredients were essential, but so was timing, trust, and perhaps most daunting of all, vulnerability.

"Yeah, relationships can be tricky," I replied, trying to keep my tone light while the weight of my confession hung heavy in the air. "You can start off with the best intentions but end up with a recipe for disaster."

"True, but without taking a chance, you might miss out on something extraordinary." His gaze held mine, a silent challenge flickering between us.

I wanted to argue, to retreat back into my fortress of solitude, but something in the intensity of his expression tugged at me. Perhaps it was the way he spoke, the way he truly believed in the magic of connection. Yet that very belief filled me with trepidation. I wasn't ready to risk everything for the chance of a beautiful dish, no matter how enticing the menu looked.

"Life is messy, Marco," I said, my voice barely above a whisper. "I've seen what happens when you get too close to the flames."

He leaned back, arms crossed, studying me with a mix of curiosity and concern. "And yet here you are, at Il Sogno, partaking in the chaos. Maybe it's time to embrace the mess instead of running from it."

The challenge in his voice hung between us, an unspoken dare that made my heart race. As I stared into his eyes, I realized this was more than just about pasta or desserts; it was about peeling back layers I had spent years building. The thought terrified me, yet a small part of me longed to dive into the unknown.

But as the evening wore on and laughter filled the air around us, I felt the tension tightening in my chest. How could I allow myself to trust, to open up, when I had spent so long constructing walls? With each moment spent in his presence, I felt like a time bomb, ticking down to an inevitable explosion that would shatter whatever fragile connection we had begun to build.

I knew I couldn't stay indefinitely on this path, even if every part of me yearned to linger just a little longer. A recipe for disaster indeed.

The weeks slipped through my fingers like grains of sand, and each visit to Il Sogno began to feel like an intricate dance where I was both leading and following, caught in a rhythm I couldn't quite control. My heart was a hesitant partner, stepping back while my mind insisted on taking a leap forward. It wasn't just the food—though I could wax poetic about Marco's ravioli for days—it was the undeniable connection that was weaving itself into the fabric of my daily life. I was enchanted, yet terrified, as if I were standing at the edge of a cliff, peering into the unknown below.

One Thursday evening, I entered the restaurant with an anxious flutter in my chest. The place buzzed with the low hum of chatter and the clattering of cutlery, but all I could focus on was the familiar sight of Marco moving about the kitchen. He was a maestro conducting a symphony of flavors, effortlessly tossing ingredients together while cracking jokes with the kitchen staff. As I took my usual seat, he caught my eye and flashed that contagious grin, lighting up the dimly lit room like a match striking against the dark.

"Ah, my favorite customer! Here for your daily dose of culinary euphoria?" he called out, setting down a glass of sparkling water with a flourish.

I laughed, feeling a flush creep up my cheeks. "Daily? I'd say it's more like weekly, but I'm certainly not complaining."

His expression turned mock serious as he leaned against the counter, arms crossed over his chest. "Weekly? We need to change that. I'd hate for you to miss out on the delicate dance of flavors that await you. Are you ready for a night of gastronomic exploration?"

"Gastronomic exploration sounds exciting, but I'm afraid I might just get lost," I replied, trying to keep my tone light despite the weight of my apprehensions.

"Lost is just another word for 'discovered,'" he quipped, leaning in slightly. "Besides, I'll be your guide. Just trust the process."

His words sent a shiver of warmth through me, and I found myself nodding, swept up in the moment. "Okay, then. Lead the way, oh wise one."

Marco disappeared into the kitchen, leaving me in a state of heightened anticipation. I glanced around, noticing the other patrons immersed in their meals, laughter ringing out like the sound of clinking glasses. The atmosphere was rich with comfort and familiarity, yet I couldn't shake the gnawing sensation that accompanied the idea of letting someone in.

Moments later, Marco returned, balancing a plate piled high with colorful bruschetta, each piece a canvas topped with vibrant tomatoes, basil, and a drizzle of balsamic reduction. "First up, a classic! Tell me how it makes you feel."

I took a bite, savoring the burst of flavors that danced across my palate. "It's like a summer picnic in my mouth—refreshing and joyful," I declared, unable to hide my enthusiasm.

"Joyful, eh? I'm putting that on my menu. 'Bruschetta della Gioia.'" He grinned, jotting it down on a notepad that had clearly seen better days, filled with doodles and messy handwriting.

"More like 'Bruschetta della Delizia' if you ask me," I countered, unable to resist the urge to tease. "You know, you could make a killing with your menu as long as you don't let it get too, um, adventurous."

"Adventurous?" He arched an eyebrow. "What's wrong with a little excitement on a plate? If we didn't push boundaries, we'd all be stuck eating plain pasta and cold sandwiches. Besides, life's too short for boring food—or boring company."

The moment hung between us, charged with a tension that had been building for weeks. His gaze held mine, searching, as if daring me to step closer to the edge of that metaphorical cliff. My heart raced, caught between the thrill of the challenge and the deep-rooted urge to retreat.

"You're right, of course. But boundaries exist for a reason," I said, trying to inject levity into the conversation while my voice wavered slightly. "What if the adventure turns sour?"

"Then we adjust the recipe," Marco replied easily, leaning in closer. "And sometimes, the messiest dishes turn out to be the most memorable."

"Is that your philosophy for everything?" I asked, half-joking but genuinely curious.

"Absolutely. Life is one big kitchen experiment, and I'm just trying not to burn the soufflé." He chuckled, a melodic sound that warmed me from the inside out.

Before I could respond, a loud crash broke through the cozy ambiance, pulling my attention to the far end of the restaurant. A server had dropped a tray laden with glasses, the sound of shattering glass echoing like a gunshot through the laughter. Conversations halted, and the air thickened with tension as everyone turned to the scene unfolding.

"Looks like we have a little drama unfolding," Marco remarked, his brow furrowed slightly. "I better go help."

As he dashed away, I was left with the remnants of our conversation swirling in my mind. Was I really prepared to embrace the chaos of life? To risk that which felt so beautiful yet so perilous? I stirred my drink, the bubbles fizzing up like my tumultuous thoughts.

After a few moments, Marco returned, a small smile breaking through the cloud of concern etched on his face. "All hands on deck, but the drama's been quelled. The glasses have been swept away, and the chaos will soon be forgotten."

"Just like that?" I quipped, hoping to lighten the air. "You can't just sweep away chaos like a few spilled drinks."

"Ah, but sometimes you can," he said, his eyes sparkling with mischief. "Especially when you have the right tools. Just look at me—I'm practically a chaos-conquering superhero."

"Superhero, huh? What's your superpower?" I asked, feigning seriousness.

"Charming my way through life while serving pasta," he replied with a theatrical flourish. "And if that doesn't work, I've been practicing my superhero landing." He paused, then mimicked the pose, legs spread and hands on his hips, pretending to be a comic book character in all his exaggerated glory.

I burst into laughter, the tension from moments before dissolving into the air. "Now that's a sight I'd pay to see! But seriously, what if the superhero life doesn't suit you?"

"Then I'll just pivot to my backup career as a pastry chef," he replied, his tone light but his gaze serious. "Every hero needs a fallback plan."

I studied him, the playful banter weaving a thread of connection between us, each word a step toward breaking down the walls I had built. "You really have thought this through."

"Of course! Who wouldn't want to be a superhero with a bakery? It's the ultimate dream," he said, his laughter infectious.

I chuckled softly, feeling lighter. "A superhero who bakes. You should add that to your résumé."

"Right next to 'Gastronomic Explorer,'" he shot back, his eyes alight with humor.

As our laughter mingled with the chatter of the restaurant, I felt the fissures of my defenses begin to crack ever so slightly. Maybe chaos wasn't something to fear. Maybe, just maybe, it was the spice of life, the very ingredient that could elevate even the simplest of moments into something unforgettable.

And there, amidst the camaraderie and the comforting scents of olive oil and garlic, I pondered the thought of letting the walls come down, of truly savoring the flavor of a shared life, one dish at a time.

The evening air was thick with anticipation as I walked through the familiar wooden door of Il Sogno. The soft chatter of patrons mingled with the clinking of wine glasses, creating a symphony of comfort that wrapped around me like a warm embrace. I had arrived early, a rarity in my recent routine, needing a moment to gather my thoughts before Marco entered the scene. He was a force of nature, his energy infusing the restaurant with life and warmth. The thought of seeing him set my heart racing, yet a knot of anxiety tightened in my stomach, a familiar reminder of my reluctance to embrace the complexity of what we were building together.

Settling into my usual seat by the window, I caught a glimpse of Marco bustling about in the kitchen, his laughter echoing above the sizzling pans. The sight alone filled me with a blend of joy and apprehension. Here was a man who made pasta feel like poetry, yet every time I engaged with him, I felt the weight of my own fears crashing against the bright facade of our connection. I was determined not to let the fear of intimacy dictate my actions tonight.

When Marco finally emerged, a generous smile stretched across his face. "Look who decided to grace us with her presence! Have you come to save me from my own culinary madness?"

I raised an eyebrow, crossing my arms in mock indignation. "You make it sound like I'm your only hope. I'm merely here to sample your latest creations."

"Oh, but you bring the sunshine!" He leaned against the counter, effortlessly charming as he feigned deep thought. "And I need all the sunlight I can get in this kitchen of chaos. What's the plan today? Something adventurous?"

"Something simple," I replied, trying to keep my tone light despite the undercurrent of tension. "I don't want to overwhelm your culinary genius."

"Simple? I think you underestimate my ability to elevate the mundane!" he declared, spinning away with a flourish. "I'll whip up something that will have you begging for the recipe."

The banter flowed easily between us, wrapping around my anxieties like a comforting blanket. Yet, as he returned with a plate of truffle-infused risotto, rich and decadent, the lingering doubts crept back into my mind. "You really do have a way with flavors," I admitted, savoring the creamy texture and aromatic depth. "But can I ask you something?"

"Always," Marco replied, leaning closer, his eyes glinting with curiosity. "Hit me with your best question."

"Why do you put so much passion into your cooking? Isn't it just food?"

He paused, his playful demeanor shifting to something more earnest. "Food is never just food. It's an experience, a memory, a bridge between people. When I cook, I share a piece of myself, hoping to spark joy in others."

"Beautifully put," I said, genuinely impressed. "But doesn't that make it harder? To share so much and risk getting hurt?"

His gaze turned serious, a flicker of understanding passing between us. "Sure. But wouldn't you rather feel deeply than live a life on the surface? The joy is worth the risk."

His words hit me like a splash of cold water, and I struggled to hold his gaze. This was the crux of my dilemma—my fear of diving headfirst into the depths of emotion. The idea of exposing my heart was paralyzing, yet here was Marco, unfazed by vulnerability, daring me to join him in this dance of authenticity.

"Easy for you to say," I murmured, pushing a grain of risotto around my plate. "You're the master of your own kitchen. What's to stop you from shutting the door and cooking alone?"

"Ah, but then I'd miss out on your sparkling company!" he shot back, the corner of his mouth quirking up. "Besides, what's a chef without patrons to appreciate the meal?"

I laughed, shaking my head. "You have a knack for turning every conversation into a philosophical debate. You must be a hit at dinner parties."

"Dinner parties?" He feigned shock, placing a hand over his heart. "I prefer intimate gatherings. Besides, I'm already the life of the party in my kitchen. The truth is, I need to share my food to feel fulfilled."

"And you believe that translates to relationships?" I probed, feeling emboldened by the rapport we had built. "Sharing your life with someone can feel riskier than serving a meal."

"True, but wouldn't it be worth it to find someone who complements your flavor? Someone who enhances your experience?"

His words struck a chord, resonating in the depths of my guarded heart. As I chewed on the idea, a pang of longing washed over me. What if I did let someone in? What if I allowed Marco to be that person? The thought flickered in my mind like a candle in the dark, flickering but not extinguished.

Suddenly, the kitchen door swung open, and a figure stepped inside, catching both of us off guard. It was a woman, tall and poised, her blonde hair cascading in perfect waves. She exuded confidence, a quality that was both captivating and intimidating. I felt a twinge of unease, a sense that this unexpected arrival was an unwelcome intruder in our bubble of warmth.

"Marco!" she called, her voice smooth yet commanding. "I hope I'm not interrupting."

"Actually, we were just..." Marco began, but the woman cut him off, her focus narrowing on me.

"Ah, and you must be the infamous 'favorite customer' I've heard so much about," she said, extending her hand with an air of superiority.

I hesitated, shaking her hand reluctantly, feeling as though I were being sized up. "Infamous? I'm not sure if that's a compliment or a warning."

"It's a bit of both, really," she said, her smile faltering only slightly. "I'm Sophia, by the way. I'm here to discuss an important opportunity with Marco."

My heart sank at her words, the implication hanging in the air like an unwelcome cloud. "An opportunity?" I echoed, trying to keep my tone neutral.

"Yes, a collaboration," Marco interjected, his eyes darting between us as if gauging my reaction. "Sophia is a food critic for the local magazine and wants to feature Il Sogno in a special segment."

"That sounds amazing!" I forced a smile, but inside, I felt a storm brewing. "Congratulations, Marco."

He returned my smile, but his eyes were troubled. "It is a big deal, but it will require a lot of work. We'll need to showcase the best of what this restaurant has to offer."

"And I'm sure it'll be a hit," Sophia added, her gaze still fixed on Marco. "With your talent and my connections, we could turn this place into a must-visit destination."

I could feel the tension coiling between us, the easy banter of moments before slipping away like water through my fingers. The ease I had felt with Marco began to crack under the weight of this unexpected development. "So, you'll be working closely together then?" I asked, my voice steadier than I felt.

Marco shifted, the slight tension in his shoulders evident. "Sophia and I have worked together before. She knows how to promote a restaurant effectively."

"Oh, I'm sure she does," I replied, my tone slightly sharper than intended. "So this is how it works—she comes in, takes over, and you get to play the part of the genius chef?"

"Wait," Marco interjected, looking genuinely perplexed. "It's not like that. I want to showcase the restaurant and..."

"And make a name for yourself," Sophia finished, her tone cutting through the tension. "Marco, darling, this is your chance. Don't let anything—or anyone—hold you back."

I felt my heart drop, the prospect of losing the intimacy we had shared in favor of a professional partnership sending shockwaves of jealousy coursing through me. This was a recipe for disaster, one I had tried so hard to avoid. As I glanced between them, the realization hit me like a slap: what if this was the moment where everything I had built began to crumble?

Suddenly, the cozy ambiance of Il Sogno felt claustrophobic, the walls closing in around me. I needed to escape, to gather my thoughts and regain control before the fear I had tried to push aside consumed me entirely. "Excuse me," I said, my voice barely above a whisper as I rose from my seat. "I need a moment."

"Wait, where are you going?" Marco called after me, his voice laced with concern, but I didn't look back. I pushed through the restaurant door and stepped outside, the cool night air wrapping around me like a balm, but the knot in my stomach tightened.

I paced the sidewalk, my thoughts swirling as I fought against the sudden rush of emotions. How could I have been so naive? The vulnerability I'd started to embrace now felt like a foolish gamble. Just as I began to collect myself, I heard the door swing open behind me.

"Hey! Wait!" Marco's voice sliced through the stillness, and I turned to face him, the anger and confusion battling within me.

"What was that about?" I asked, trying to keep my voice steady as he approached. "You didn't tell me you were looking for a partnership with Sophia."

"I didn't know she was coming tonight! I swear, it's not what it seems." He reached for my arm, concern etched on his face, but I pulled away.

"Not what it seems?" I echoed, frustration boiling over. "It looks pretty clear to me. You're on the brink of a career breakthrough,

Chapter 4: A Culinary Competition

The scent of roasting garlic and fresh basil mingled in the air, wrapping around me like a warm embrace as I stepped into Il Sogno, the restaurant that had become my sanctuary over the past few months. The golden light from the chandeliers flickered softly, illuminating the deep burgundy walls adorned with artful photographs of Marco's culinary creations. Each image told a story of flavors and textures, a testament to the love and labor that poured into every plate. Today, however, the atmosphere buzzed with a different kind of energy, a thrilling concoction of excitement and anxiety that permeated the air.

I slipped into a corner table, the perfect vantage point to witness the unfolding culinary drama. The annual culinary competition was not just any event; it was the heartbeat of our little town, drawing in a crowd eager to witness local talent and, of course, to indulge in some gastronomic delights. I had volunteered to cover the event, penning an article that would celebrate the spirit of the restaurant and its chef, but little did I know that Marco had other intentions simmering beneath the surface.

As I sipped my sparkling water, I watched Marco, his dark hair tousled in that effortlessly charming way. He moved with a grace that belied his towering frame, gliding from station to station as if the kitchen was a dance floor. Every now and then, he'd throw a glance my way, a flicker of something deeper glimmering in his eyes—an unspoken connection that had thrummed between us since I first set foot in his restaurant. Yet, as the competition loomed closer, I could feel that connection stretching, straining against the weight of my insecurities.

"Care to share what you're writing?" Marco called out, his voice smooth, teasingly casual as he prepped a delicate sauce, a symphony of flavors coming to life under his deft hands.

I grinned, trying to mask the nervous flutter in my stomach. "Just a little piece on how Il Sogno is the heart of the town's culinary scene. You know, capturing the spirit of community."

He chuckled, a low, melodic sound that made my heart race. "It sounds nice, but I have a feeling you're hiding something. Is this about me?" His eyes sparkled mischievously, making it difficult to maintain my composure.

"Don't let it go to your head," I shot back, forcing a playful tone. "I'm merely a humble food writer observing a local chef's humble journey."

With a dramatic sigh, he placed his hands on his hips, mockingly puffing out his chest. "Ah, the humble journey of a culinary genius! Do you think I'll win them over with my dazzling charisma or my knife skills?"

"Definitely the charisma," I quipped, biting my lip to stifle my laughter. But deep down, a part of me felt the weight of his talent. I had always admired Marco's culinary artistry, but today, watching him in his element, I couldn't shake the creeping doubt. What did I have to offer someone so talented? I was merely a writer, a girl who had wandered into his world and found it intoxicating yet terrifyingly out of reach.

As the competition kicked off, judges strolled through the room, sampling each dish with a critical eye. The sound of clinking glasses and enthusiastic chatter blended into a harmonious backdrop, but my focus remained on Marco. He was a maestro, commanding the kitchen with a blend of precision and passion. Each plate he presented was more than just food; it was a part of himself, an invitation to experience his world.

Then it hit me. This wasn't merely about culinary skills; it was a performance, a showcase of dreams and desires. I leaned in closer, captivated as Marco plated his signature dish—a vibrant risotto, bursting with the colors of summer vegetables. The judges tasted it, their expressions shifting from skepticism to delight, their smiles wide as if they'd discovered a hidden treasure. I could see Marco's confidence swell, a beam of pride illuminating his face.

But the longer I watched, the more the shadows of my own self-doubt loomed larger. Here was a man whose life was a canvas painted with ambition and success, while I felt like a scribble on a forgotten notepad. What could I bring to his table? As he expertly drizzled a balsamic reduction over the risotto, I couldn't help but imagine him with someone more accomplished, someone who could match his zeal with equal fervor.

"Hey, are you okay?" Marco's voice cut through my spiraling thoughts, his brow creased with concern as he wiped his hands on a towel and approached me. "You look like you just watched a horror movie."

I forced a smile, but I knew it didn't quite reach my eyes. "Just thinking about how much I want to impress the judges too," I said, injecting a lightness into my words, even as my heart felt heavy. "I mean, you're setting the bar pretty high."

"Forget the judges. What matters is what you think," he said, leaning closer, his breath warm against my cheek. The intimacy of the moment sent a shiver down my spine. "I'm cooking for you. You're my muse, remember?"

At that, I felt the heat rise in my cheeks, a rush of warmth flooding me as I caught his gaze. It was both thrilling and terrifying, a reminder of the connection we had formed, one that I had longed to explore but had always been afraid to fully embrace.

With the first round nearly over, I took a deep breath, willing myself to push past the shadows of my insecurity. "Alright, Chef Marco," I said, trying to rally my spirits. "Show me what you've got. I want to see that culinary genius in action."

His smile widened, a hint of mischief dancing in his eyes. "Now you're talking. Just wait until you see what I have planned next."

And with that, the competition moved forward, and I resolved to let go of my fears, at least for a little while. I would cheer him on, savor every moment, and perhaps, just perhaps, find the courage to believe that I belonged in this vibrant tapestry woven with dreams, food, and a budding romance that was as intoxicating as the dishes Marco created.

The competition roared to life, the din of excited chatter and clinking utensils filling the air as each chef prepared their masterpieces. I watched from my little perch, the energy around me electrifying as I scribbled notes about the vibrant atmosphere, the creativity unfolding before my eyes. Marco's focus was palpable, and as I observed him dance through the chaos of his kitchen brigade, I marveled at the way he could command a room filled with frenetic energy.

As the second round began, Marco had his sights set on an ambitious dish that would showcase his Italian roots and a sprinkle of local flair. He was a whirlwind of movement, expertly chopping vegetables, stirring sauces, and sending out playful banter to his team that made everyone chuckle. It was infectious, a reminder of the warmth that lay at the heart of Il Sogno. Yet, as the clock ticked down, I felt an unexpected knot forming in my stomach.

"What are you making, Chef?" I called out, my curiosity piqued. I'd seen glimpses of his culinary creations in the past, but today, I craved a deeper understanding of the man behind the food.

"Something inspired by the seasons," he replied, a grin spreading across his face as he whisked a mixture of cream and parmesan, the thickening concoction clinging to the edges of the bowl. "This is my take on a seafood risotto, with a twist of lemon and a touch of saffron."

"Lemon and saffron? I can practically taste the Mediterranean sun," I said, leaning forward, eager to savor every detail. The way he spoke about food ignited a flicker of passion within me, and for a moment, I forgot about my insecurities.

"Just wait until you see it plated," he said with a wink, as if he knew the effect his culinary magic had on me. "You'll wish you had a fork and knife."

"Or a whole dinner party!" I shot back, my playful banter hiding the vulnerability that lurked beneath the surface. Watching him in this setting, surrounded by flames and flavors, stirred something deep inside me—a yearning to be part of his world, yet I feared the chasm that lay between us.

As the competition continued, I could see Marco's spirit shine. He moved seamlessly from task to task, a maestro conducting a culinary symphony, yet my own thoughts remained discordant, a cacophony of doubt. I watched as he presented the seafood risotto, garnished with fresh herbs and edible flowers that looked like tiny bursts of joy. The judges leaned in, their faces a tapestry of concentration and pleasure as they tasted his creation.

"This is exceptional, Marco," one judge said, his eyes lighting up as if he'd just discovered gold. "The balance of flavors is impeccable."

I beamed with pride, my heart swelling at his success. Yet beneath that swell, a nagging thought resurfaced: Did he really want to be with someone who couldn't bring the same passion to the table? The noise of the crowd faded into a dull hum, and I was left grappling with the weight of my own insecurities, spiraling as I mulled over what a relationship with someone like Marco would entail.

Suddenly, a voice jolted me back to reality. "Hey, what's wrong with you?" Emma, my fellow writer and friend, plopped down in the seat across from me, her auburn curls bouncing energetically. "You look like you've seen a ghost."

"Just thinking," I replied, forcing a smile. "You know, about the competition and how Marco is killing it."

"Thinking, or overthinking?" She arched an eyebrow, that knowing look in her eyes that only a true friend could possess. "You're worried he'll find someone better, aren't you?"

I shrugged, attempting nonchalance, but Emma saw right through it. "Girl, you've got to stop comparing yourself to him. He's a chef, and you're a fantastic writer. You each bring something unique to the table—literally."

"Maybe," I said, glancing back at Marco, who was chatting with the judges, his hands animatedly illustrating his culinary philosophy. "But he's not just a chef. He's a star."

"And you're his biggest fan," Emma said, her tone a mix of sincerity and playful sarcasm. "If he's impressed with your writing, you should be impressed with yourself too."

The competition raged on around us, but her words resonated, sparking a flicker of hope amidst my doubts. Perhaps it was time to stop viewing myself through the lens of inadequacy. I could be a writer who supported a talented chef without feeling overshadowed.

As if on cue, Marco returned, his face flushed with excitement, a triumphant smile gracing his lips. "Did you see their faces?" he asked, breathless, as he slipped into the chair beside me. "They loved it! I think I might actually have a shot at this."

I leaned in closer, heart racing. "You were incredible, Marco. Your passion just shines through every dish."

He glanced at me, the intensity of his gaze sending a thrill through me. "Thanks to you, you know. Your support means everything."

Just then, the announcer's voice boomed over the crowd, calling the competitors to the front. "We're ready for the final round, and it's going to be a showdown!" The anticipation in the room swelled, and I could feel the tension in the air as we all shifted forward, eager to witness the culmination of Marco's hard work.

He grinned at me, the corners of his mouth pulling upwards, igniting something in my chest. "Are you ready for the grand finale?"

I took a deep breath, nodding, excitement flooding through me. "Absolutely. Show them what you're made of."

As he stepped back into the chaos of the kitchen, I couldn't shake the feeling that something more than just culinary skills was unfolding before my eyes. This competition was becoming more than just a test of talent; it was revealing layers of ambition, desire, and the hope that maybe, just maybe, I could fit into this beautiful mess of flavors and dreams that Marco had created.

The clock ticked down, and as I watched him work, I realized I didn't just want to support him—I wanted to be part of his story. The tension thickened in the air, a mix of anticipation and unspoken words hanging between us like the fragrance of fresh herbs. Whatever the outcome, this moment felt pivotal, a crossroads where our paths could intertwine or diverge. I held my breath, not just for the competition, but for what lay ahead for both of us.

The tension in the room was palpable as the final round of the competition approached, each tick of the clock a drumbeat underscoring Marco's rapid movements in the kitchen. He was a blur of confidence, his brow furrowed in concentration as he meticulously assembled his last dish. With each clink of metal utensils and soft sizzle from the pans, I could almost hear the narrative he was crafting—a narrative that had me teetering on the edge of exhilaration and anxiety.

"Okay, time for the grand reveal," Marco said, wiping his hands on his apron, a flourish of dramatic flair that made me laugh. "Get ready for the pièce de résistance."

"Should I brace myself?" I quipped, leaning forward, my heart pounding in rhythm with the competition's frenzy. "Or should I bring a bib?"

He shot me a look, half-amused and half-serious. "You might need both, especially when I unleash my secret weapon."

"Secret weapon? Now you have me intrigued," I said, genuinely curious. The way he spoke about food was akin to storytelling, a hint of mystique woven through his words. It was easy to get lost in that charm, easy to forget the doubts simmering in my mind.

As he turned back to his station, I could feel my own insecurities creeping in again. What was I even doing here? While he crafted edible art, I was just a writer desperately hoping to capture a piece of his brilliance on paper. The walls felt closer, and the laughter of the crowd faded into a distant murmur as I watched Marco whisk together a bright green pesto, its aroma rich and inviting. I had never seen someone command ingredients with such passion, each movement a testament to his love for cooking.

"Last chance to ask for a taste test!" he called over his shoulder, a playful glint in his eye. "I promise not to tell the judges if you 'accidentally' get a little extra."

"Only if I can hide behind your apron while I do it!" I shot back, trying to shake off the weight of my thoughts. He grinned, and I felt my heart skip. The chemistry between us simmered just below the surface, like a pot about to boil over.

With a final flourish, he plated his dish, a stunning creation that was a vibrant array of colors—seared scallops perched atop a bed of saffron-infused risotto, adorned with delicate microgreens and a drizzle of his signature pesto. The judges gathered, their expressions turning serious as they prepared to taste the culmination of Marco's work.

"Remember to breathe," I whispered, a mix of encouragement and sympathy coursing through me. I felt the weight of the moment, the culmination of all his hard work, riding on this very presentation.

"Breathe? What if I hyperventilate instead?" Marco quipped, his voice barely concealing the nervous energy bubbling beneath his facade.

As the first judge took a bite, silence enveloped the room. Time seemed to stretch as the flavors danced on the judge's palate, and for an excruciating moment, I thought I could hear my own heartbeat. Then, as if struck by lightning, the judge's eyes widened, his mouth twisting into an impressed smile.

"This is extraordinary! The scallops are perfectly cooked, and the risotto is a dream!" His enthusiasm ignited a ripple of applause, lifting the tension in the air. I felt my heart swell with pride for Marco, a sense of belonging washing over me. Maybe I could be more than just a passive observer in his world.

"Now that's what I'm talking about!" Marco replied, a boyish grin spreading across his face, his confidence returning with each approving nod from the judges.

But the moment was short-lived. Just as the applause settled, a shadow flickered across Marco's face. The second judge, a stern woman with sharp features, took her turn, but her expression was far from impressed. She chewed thoughtfully, her brow furrowed as if she were deciphering a complex riddle.

"This is quite rich, perhaps too rich for my taste," she remarked, her voice devoid of the enthusiasm that had just moments ago ignited the room. "I expected more balance."

The air thickened with tension, my heart sinking as Marco's expression faltered. "Balance?" he echoed, the hint of disbelief in his tone.

"Precisely," she replied, looking almost accusatory. "A dish of this caliber should dance on the palate, not overwhelm it."

I could feel the world around me blur as I focused on Marco's face, the storm of emotions swirling within him. For a moment, he stood frozen, a man caught between the elation of a compliment and the sting of critique.

"What do you suggest?" he finally asked, his voice steady despite the tremor of vulnerability beneath the surface.

The judge leaned forward, her gaze penetrating. "Less richness, perhaps? Focus on highlighting the seafood. It's supposed to be the star, after all."

As she spoke, I noticed a flicker of irritation behind Marco's eyes, a fleeting moment where his confidence seemed to waver. My heart twisted for him, the urge to leap up and defend his artistry surging within me. "What does she know?" I wanted to shout. "She's not the one slaving over a hot stove!"

But I remained still, tension thrumming in my veins. Marco's face was a canvas of composure, though I could see the fire of determination brewing beneath the surface. "Thank you for the feedback," he said, his voice cool. "I appreciate it."

Once the judges had finished their tasting, Marco stepped back from his station, the adrenaline still coursing through him. "It's just one opinion, right?" he murmured, more to himself than to me.

"Exactly! You've already won them over once today; you can do it again," I encouraged, hoping to reignite that spark.

"Yeah, you're right," he replied, though I could see the doubt still flickering behind his eyes. "It's just—"

Before he could finish, the announcer's voice cut through the air again. "And now, the final dish from our very own Marco, a true contender!"

As Marco hurried back to his station, I felt an unexpected surge of protectiveness for him. This was not just about cooking anymore; it was a glimpse into who he was. A man shaped by both triumphs and doubts, wrestling with his own expectations.

Then it hit me—was I becoming a part of his journey, or was I simply a spectator? The question gnawed at me, its implications hanging heavy in the air.

With one last glance, I locked eyes with him, silently promising that I was in his corner, no matter what happened. He nodded, and for a moment, everything else faded. The world around us, the judges, the competition—none of it mattered as long as we stood together.

Marco began assembling his final creation, a dish that combined bold flavors and delicate presentations, each element a testament to his culinary evolution. The crowd watched with bated breath, their excitement palpable. I could sense the shifting energy, and with it, the stakes of our unspoken connection.

Just as Marco completed the last touches, a loud crash erupted from behind the judges' table. My heart lurched as I turned to see one of the judges accidentally upend a glass of red wine, the crimson liquid cascading like a waterfall across the pristine white tablecloth, splattering onto the floor and sending shards of glass flying.

"Oh no!" I gasped, but my concern quickly turned to dread as I noticed Marco's reaction. He froze, staring at the chaos, his eyes wide with disbelief. The commotion shifted the atmosphere, pulling the focus away from his masterpiece and into the fray of a rising panic.

"Marco!" I shouted, my voice barely slicing through the din of chaos. But as he turned, his face morphed from confusion into something darker—a storm brewing behind those expressive eyes.

The judge struggled to regain composure, scrambling to clean the mess while murmurs spread through the crowd. Suddenly, I sensed a shift, an undercurrent of tension that coiled tightly around us. Just as Marco opened his mouth to respond, a strange figure slipped into the chaos, a woman in a sharply tailored suit with an air of authority.

"Stop!" she commanded, her voice slicing through the noise like a knife through butter. All eyes turned to her as she surveyed the scene, and I felt an electric pulse of uncertainty ripple through the crowd.

"What is happening here?" she continued, her gaze landing on Marco. "I need to speak with you immediately. It's urgent."

Panic coursed through me as the gravity of the moment settled. Marco glanced at me, and in that instant, everything shifted. The culinary competition, the accolades, the connection we'd begun to forge—it all hung precariously in the balance as I held my breath, uncertain of what would come next, terrified that this woman's intrusion could change everything.

Chapter 5: The Taste of Regret

The bell above the café door chimed like a distant echo, ushering in the scents of freshly baked goods and the comforting hum of casual chatter. I sank into the worn leather of my favorite booth, its creases familiar beneath me, a small fortress against the world outside. The place was vibrant, draped in string lights that twinkled with an almost mischievous energy, like they were in on a joke I hadn't yet figured out. The barista, with her lavender hair and a smile that could spark joy in even the grumpiest soul, was busy crafting an elaborate matcha latte for a customer with an Instagram account that was practically a food blog in its own right.

I flipped through my notes, the pen dancing between my fingers, but the words refused to come. Each review I scribbled felt hollow, lacking the zing that usually accompanied my thoughts. It was as if the very essence of my inspiration had fled, leaving behind a cavernous void. My mind drifted to Marco, and the memories rushed in like waves, crashing against my resolve.

The way he'd leaned across the table at Il Sogno, his laughter warm and infectious, had felt like a secret. He had a way of turning mundane moments into treasures, weaving his passion for food into every conversation. I recalled the taste of that truffle risotto—silky and rich, with an earthy undertone that lingered on the palate like a sweet goodbye. How could I have pushed him away so easily?

From the corner of my eye, I spotted a couple sharing a plate of colorful vegan nachos, their delight palpable as they savored every bite. The woman tilted her head back, laughing, and her joy seeped into the air, swirling around me like the steam from the coffee machines. It stabbed at my heart, each laugh a reminder of the connection I had let slip through my fingers, and the sharp pang of longing sliced deeper with each joyful sound.

I couldn't just sit here drowning in nostalgia, I told myself. My phone buzzed, jolting me from my reverie. A notification from one of the food festivals I had signed up for flashed across the screen: "New Competition! Showcase Your Culinary Review Skills!" My heart raced at the thought of competing again. Perhaps this was my chance to reclaim a bit of that lost spark, to channel my energy into something that might help me forget—or at least redirect—my thoughts of Marco.

As I sipped my lukewarm coffee, the rich bitterness mingling with the sweetness of the coconut milk, I felt a flicker of determination ignite within me. What was it that they said? The best way to get over someone was to get under someone new? I could not only write my way through the memories but also emerge stronger on the other side. It was time to stop living in the shadow of my regrets and start tasting the moments that were still waiting to be savored.

I signed up for the competition, my fingers flying over the keyboard as I crafted a snappy entry that captured my excitement. Just as I hit send, a familiar voice cut through the air, rich and melodic, sending a jolt of surprise racing through me.

"Didn't expect to see you here, alone," Marco's voice teased, laced with that same playful edge that had always made my heart flutter.

I turned, the surprise freezing my thoughts momentarily. He was leaning against the counter, his hands casually tucked into his pockets, a familiar smirk playing on his lips. The sunlight streamed through the window, catching the flecks of gold in his hair, and I suddenly felt a wave of warmth wash over me.

"Just my luck, right?" I replied, trying to sound nonchalant, though my heart was pounding in my chest. "Isn't this café supposed to be the hottest spot in town?"

"Apparently. I'm just here for the pastries," he said, his eyes sparkling with mischief. "They say the croissants are life-changing."

A chuckle escaped my lips before I could stop it. "Life-changing? Is that a promise, or a claim you've taken on as a personal challenge?"

His grin widened, the warmth of it melting the distance I'd so desperately tried to maintain. "Why not both? I could use a partner in crime for this culinary adventure. You up for it?"

The air between us crackled, a subtle tension threading through our playful banter. I wanted to say yes, to dive headfirst into the moment and let the world around us fade away. But the weight of my choices lingered, and I hesitated. "I don't know, Marco. We've got a complicated history, don't we?"

He stepped closer, his expression earnest. "Complicated doesn't have to mean bad. Sometimes it just means we have a story worth telling."

His words hung in the air, echoing with unspoken possibilities. My mind raced as I considered the weight of his offer. Could we navigate this newfound connection, the uncharted waters of our relationship? Would I be able to let go of my fears and embrace whatever was still simmering beneath the surface?

As if sensing my internal struggle, he leaned closer, lowering his voice to a conspiratorial whisper. "Come on, let's rediscover the joy of food together. Besides, what's the worst that could happen? You'll either have a great time or you'll have a story to tell. Either way, you win."

His playful challenge hung between us, tempting me like the sweetest of desserts. I took a deep breath, the aroma of fresh pastries enveloping me, and nodded. "Okay, let's go for it. But I warn you—I'm a tough critic."

"Perfect," he said, his smile widening into a grin that could light up the dimmest room. "Just what I need. Someone to keep me on my toes."

With that, I took his outstretched hand, and as he pulled me toward the counter, the weight of my regrets began to lift, leaving behind a flicker of hope that maybe, just maybe, this could be the start of something new.

The café buzzed with life as Marco and I navigated through the assortment of pastries, a vibrant display that felt like an artist's palette. Croissants, danishes, and tarts were all vying for attention, their golden crusts glistening under the soft lights. I caught a glimpse of his face as he scanned the selection; his expression was a mix of delight and mischief, a look that tugged at something deep inside me. Perhaps it was nostalgia, or perhaps the faintest echo of something that might still be possible between us.

"What's your weakness?" he asked, his voice barely rising above the sound of an espresso machine grinding beans into submission.

"Definitely anything chocolate," I replied, glancing at a dark chocolate mousse cake that looked like it could bring about world peace. "But I have a soft spot for fruit tarts, too. They remind me of summer."

Marco raised an eyebrow, intrigued. "So, you're a sucker for nostalgia? I can work with that. What's your favorite summer memory?"

I hesitated, momentarily caught off guard. Memories of my childhood summers—sunshine-drenched days spent picking berries with my grandmother—flashed in my mind. "My grandmother had a garden filled with the most beautiful strawberries. We'd spend hours picking them, and then she'd make the best shortcake. It felt like magic, you know?"

"Magic, huh?" he mused, as if savoring the idea. "Maybe we should recreate it. A little shortcake for our taste test."

"Only if you promise not to burn the kitchen down."

He chuckled, a low, rich sound that made me smile despite myself. "I can't make any promises, but I can definitely make a mess. That's part of the fun."

As we settled at a table by the window, the outside world felt like a distant whisper, and all that mattered was this moment—two people reclaiming a spark that had almost fizzled out. Marco picked at a flaky croissant, the buttery layers crumbling at his touch. He glanced up, his eyes sparkling with mischief. "So, what's the deal with you and writing? I mean, aside from the obvious obsession with food."

"Obsession? That's a strong word," I said, smirking back. "I prefer 'passionate devotion.' Writing is like cooking; you have to blend the right ingredients to create something delicious. Sometimes it's a recipe for success, and sometimes, well, it's a burnt soufflé."

He nodded thoughtfully. "I get that. It's about the journey, not just the end product. What if we applied that to our lives? No more burnt soufflés, only delectable dishes."

I couldn't help but laugh. "You mean, no more second-guessing every move? That sounds terrifying and liberating all at once."

"Exactly!" he exclaimed, leaning forward as if sharing a secret. "Let's throw caution to the wind. You and me—no regrets. We'll make the mess and see what comes of it."

His suggestion hung in the air, enticing and terrifying. Could I really embrace this reckless spirit? The past few months had been an exercise in caution, a careful dance around my own fears. But as I stared into his earnest gaze, something began to shift. Maybe it was time to step out of my carefully constructed bubble.

"Alright, let's do it," I declared, feeling an unfamiliar thrill coursing through me. "We'll take this culinary journey together. But you have to promise to share the credit equally. I don't want you hogging all the glory."

"Deal," he said, extending his hand across the table. "May the best chef win."

I shook his hand, a bolt of electricity passing between us, as if the universe had conspired to nudge us back together.

Over the next hour, we nibbled on pastries, discussing everything from the most outrageous food trends to our childhood food failures. It felt like an easy rhythm, laughter punctuating our words as if we were sharing an inside joke. The taste of fresh fruit mingled with the buttery sweetness of our treats, each bite evoking memories that made the world outside fade into insignificance.

"Okay," Marco said, setting down his fork with an exaggerated sigh. "I have to ask. What was your worst food-related experience?"

I thought for a moment, then grinned. "I once tried to impress a date by making a homemade lasagna. I mixed up the measurements, and instead of two cups of flour, I accidentally put in two cups of powdered sugar. The result was a sweet, gooey monstrosity that could've been mistaken for dessert."

He threw his head back and laughed, the sound ringing like a bell. "That's brilliant! You could have called it 'Sweet Surprise Lasagna' and made a fortune."

"Or ruined my reputation in the culinary world," I shot back, laughing at the thought. "Not exactly the impression you want to make on a first date."

Marco leaned back, eyes glinting with an idea. "We should have a contest: the best food fails. Whoever can come up with the most ridiculous disaster gets a prize."

"And what would the prize be? A date with the best chef in town?" I teased, raising an eyebrow.

"Not a bad idea," he said, leaning closer, a teasing smirk playing on his lips. "But I was thinking more along the lines of a homemade dinner. My kitchen's not nearly as terrifying as it sounds, I promise."

"Are you sure you want to risk it? I have a reputation to uphold here," I replied, my heart racing at the thought of spending more time together.

"Trust me, I'm up for the challenge," he shot back, his confidence infectious. "Besides, what's a little kitchen chaos between friends?"

"Alright, I'm game. But if it turns into a disaster, I'm blaming you," I said, half-serious, half-laughing.

As we finished our pastries and lingered over the last sips of coffee, the warmth of our conversation began to fill the space where uncertainty had once resided. I felt lighter, like a weight had been lifted from my shoulders. Maybe this was the first step in reclaiming the vibrant world I had once inhabited—a world where food and friendship intertwined, where laughter could banish the shadows of regret.

"Shall we get to planning our culinary escapades, then?" Marco asked, his eyes sparkling with mischief.

"Let's," I replied, my heart racing at the prospect of what lay ahead. As we left the café, the air felt charged with potential, and for the first time in months, I was eager to taste the moments that awaited us.

The afternoon sun bathed the city in a warm glow, illuminating the vibrant streets as Marco and I wandered toward the farmers' market. Our culinary contest was officially in full swing, each moment infused with a sense of playful competition and budding excitement. I had never felt so alive; it was as if the world was holding its breath, waiting for us to take the next step.

"Okay, strategy time," Marco declared, glancing around at the stalls bursting with colorful produce. "We need to gather the best ingredients if we're going to impress anyone—especially ourselves."

"Are you sure you're ready for this? I mean, we might have to actually cook," I shot back, feigning a look of horror. "What if we burn the place down?"

He chuckled, a low rumble that sent a thrill down my spine. "That's the spirit! Embrace the chaos! But let's start with something simple, like a killer sauce. The secret is in the layers."

"Layers, huh?" I mused, pretending to take notes. "What are we making, a lasagna?"

"Ha! No. I was thinking more like a piquant tomato basil sauce. But if you want to recreate your infamous 'Sweet Surprise Lasagna,' I'm game."

"Very funny," I retorted, nudging him playfully. "But let's focus on not sabotaging our dinner first. Lead the way, chef."

We meandered through the market, stopping to sample fresh fruits, aromatic herbs, and artisanal cheeses. The air buzzed with laughter and the sound of vendors calling out their wares, creating a rich tapestry of life that enveloped us. Marco picked up a ripe heirloom tomato, holding it up like a trophy.

"Look at this beauty!" he exclaimed. "It practically screams summer. It's begging to be turned into something delicious."

"It does look promising," I admitted, feeling a twinge of excitement. "What else do we need?"

He furrowed his brow in thought, a playful seriousness overtaking his features. "We'll need garlic, fresh basil, and—oh! What about some red pepper flakes for a kick?"

I nodded, catching a glimpse of the vendor's stall overflowing with fragrant herbs. "Let's get the basil, then we'll scour the place for garlic. Can't have tomato sauce without garlic."

We wandered over to the stall, and I couldn't help but admire how Marco interacted with the vendor. His charm was effortless, disarming even. They bantered back and forth, and I found myself laughing along, feeling warmth blossoming in my chest as I watched him.

"Are you always this charming?" I asked when he returned, a small bouquet of basil in hand. "It's like you've got a secret spell or something."

He shrugged, feigning modesty. "It's all part of the package. Good looks, culinary skills, and a way with the local merchants."

"Oh, please," I scoffed, rolling my eyes playfully. "I think you've been watching too many cooking shows."

As we continued our adventure through the market, I felt a growing sense of comfort in our banter. Each teasing remark and shared laugh built an invisible bridge between us, and with each step, the worries that had once weighed me down began to dissipate. Maybe it was the thrill of competition or perhaps just the joy of rediscovering each other, but I felt a warmth blooming in the pit of my stomach.

With our basket full of ingredients, we finally headed back to my apartment, where the real fun would begin. I set up the kitchen with a slight twinge of anxiety, half-expecting disaster to strike at any moment. Marco, however, was unfazed. He began by washing the tomatoes and chopping the basil with a precision that reminded me of a practiced artist.

"Okay, chef, what's next?" I asked, pretending to take notes as he worked.

"Now we dice the garlic," he said, glancing over his shoulder with a grin. "But first, you should know that the key to great cooking is to taste as you go."

"Sounds dangerously fun. What do I get to taste first?"

He paused, leaning in with a mock-serious expression. "How about some olive oil? Just drizzle a bit on your finger and give it a whirl."

I did as he suggested, the rich flavor enveloping my senses, and Marco's eyes lit up with approval. "Perfect. Now you're starting to get it. But we can't just snack all day; we actually have to cook something."

"Fine, fine! I'm on it," I replied, but the thrill of the moment made it hard to focus. I began chopping the garlic, a rather messy endeavor, but I was determined to not let my clumsiness ruin our creation.

"Careful, you might chop your way into culinary history," he teased, watching me with a mix of admiration and amusement.

Just then, my phone buzzed on the counter, pulling my attention away from the chaos of our cooking adventure. I glanced at the screen, the message stopping me in my tracks. It was a notification from a food festival I had entered weeks ago: "Congratulations! You've been selected for the finals! Details to follow."

My heart raced, excitement mixed with anxiety. "Marco, I—"

"Whoa! What's with the sudden panic? Did you find a bug in your garlic?" He glanced over, but his expression shifted when he saw my face. "What's going on?"

"I got into the finals for that food festival competition!" I exclaimed, the thrill of the news bubbling up, but with it came a wave of uncertainty. "This is a big deal, Marco. I don't know if I'm ready for this."

"Of course, you're ready! You're a culinary genius!" he said, his enthusiasm infectious. "This is your moment to shine. We'll prepare together; you'll crush it."

I couldn't shake the nagging worry in my stomach. "What if I mess up? What if my dish flops?"

"Hey!" he said, stepping closer and placing a hand on my shoulder, grounding me. "This is about having fun, remember? You're not just competing; you're sharing your love of food. You've got this."

His support wrapped around me like a warm blanket, easing the knots of tension. I smiled, but then my phone buzzed again. I glanced at the message, and my heart dropped. It was from a number I didn't recognize, a sharp contrast to the warmth I had just felt.

"I know where you are. I'm watching."

I froze, staring at the screen as dread curled in my stomach. The kitchen, once filled with laughter and the heady aromas of fresh ingredients, suddenly felt suffocating. I could barely process the words. Marco must have sensed my change in demeanor because he stepped back, concern shadowing his face.

"What's wrong?" he asked, peering closer at my phone.

I couldn't tear my gaze away from the message. "I— I don't know. This message... it's from someone I don't recognize. They said they're watching."

"Watching? What do they mean?" Marco's brow furrowed, his playful demeanor evaporating, replaced by genuine worry.

I took a breath, trying to steady myself, but my heart raced as the weight of the message settled in. "I don't know, Marco. I don't know who this is."

The atmosphere shifted, the kitchen suddenly feeling too small, too constricting, as reality crashed back in. Marco's hand found mine, the warmth grounding me in a moment that felt like it was spiraling out of control. "We'll figure this out together," he said, determination etching his features. "But first, let's finish this sauce. No one's going to ruin our day."

As he turned back to the stove, the tension hung in the air, unspoken and heavy. I knew that the fun we were having was now tinged with uncertainty. But with the adrenaline pumping through my veins, I also knew that I couldn't let fear dictate my next move—not when everything was finally starting to come together.

Yet, as I glanced back at my phone, the weight of that message loomed larger than any culinary disaster could. And just as I opened my mouth to share my concerns with Marco, the doorbell rang, slicing through the tension like a knife. The sound echoed ominously, and I exchanged a wary glance with Marco.

"Who could that be?" he asked, eyebrows knitting together in confusion.

"I have no idea," I whispered, heart racing as I moved toward the door, my gut churning with an unsettling mix of anticipation and dread. As I reached for the doorknob, my mind raced with possibilities. Would it be a delivery? A friend? Or something more sinister, lurking just beyond the threshold?

With a deep breath, I turned the knob and swung the door open, bracing myself for whatever lay on the other side.

Chapter 6: A Dinner Invitation

The air inside Il Sogno was a heady mix of rich aromas—fresh basil, garlic, and something sweet, like the lingering essence of vanilla in the air. I stepped through the heavy wooden door, my heart a tambourine beating a frenetic rhythm against my chest. The soft glow of the candles cast a warm halo over the tables draped in deep red cloth, each one adorned with a delicate vase holding a single white rose, which seemed to whisper secrets of romance. I could already feel the cozy embrace of the restaurant wrapping around me, pulling me away from the chilly evening outside.

Marco was waiting, leaning casually against a tall table, his dark hair tousled just so, like he'd been running a hand through it absentmindedly while thinking of me. He looked up, and for a moment, the world narrowed to just the two of us. His smile was a gentle curve, inviting yet layered with a hint of something unspoken, and I couldn't help but smile back, even if my heart was a mess of conflicting emotions.

"Hey," he said, his voice warm like the wine he was holding, "you made it."

"I wouldn't miss it for the world," I replied, trying to keep my tone light, even as I felt the weight of everything we hadn't said hanging between us like a shimmering thread, pulling tighter with each passing moment.

He gestured for me to join him, and as I settled into my seat, I noticed how the candlelight danced in his eyes, giving him a glow that was almost otherworldly. "You look stunning," he said, his gaze sweeping over my dress—a deep emerald green that hugged my curves and made my skin feel luminous. I felt my cheeks warm at the compliment, an instant flush of color igniting beneath my foundation.

"Thanks, I thought I should make an effort," I replied, my fingers fiddling with the silver necklace resting against my collarbone, a nervous habit I hadn't quite managed to shake. "It's not every day I get a dinner invitation from Marco."

He chuckled, the sound rich and genuine, sending a ripple of warmth through me. "I can see that you're still quick with the comebacks. I was hoping you wouldn't have forgotten about me."

"Forget about you? Not a chance," I said, the words slipping out before I could stop them. There was a slight edge of seriousness in my tone that startled me, but Marco only raised an eyebrow, intrigued.

"Good to know. I might have to start charging you for my charm, though," he said with a wink, leaning closer, and for a moment, the world outside ceased to exist.

As the waiter approached, I was grateful for the distraction, a chance to collect my thoughts. I ordered the seafood risotto, the signature dish that I had heard so much about, while Marco opted for the osso buco. We fell into easy conversation, the kind that felt both natural and thrilling, as if we were tiptoeing along the edges of a cliff, teetering on the brink of something exhilarating.

"So," I began, keeping my tone playful, "tell me all about your new life. Have you joined a cult yet? Or are you just still charming everyone at the coffee shop?"

"Ah, the coffee shop," he sighed dramatically, raising his glass as if toasting to a long-lost friend. "I still work there, but I might have started a cult of my own—one devoted to coffee and pastries. Membership is free, but you have to endure terrible puns."

"Count me in," I laughed, my heart lifting a little more. With every shared smile, every playful jab, the weight of our past began to dissipate, replaced by the thrilling prospect of reconnecting. Yet, a small, nagging voice in the back of my mind whispered doubts—what if this was just a temporary illusion? What if I had built up a fantasy around our past that had no foundation in reality?

Before I could spiral too deep, the waiter returned with our plates, and the intoxicating aroma enveloped us. Marco's eyes widened in delight as he leaned in, his excitement contagious. "This, my dear, is what life is all about. Good food and even better company."

I looked down at my plate, a swirl of creamy risotto glistening like a golden treasure, and felt a rush of appreciation for this moment—here, at Il Sogno, I was reminded that life could still surprise me. I took a bite, and the flavors exploded, sending my taste buds into a frenzy. "Oh my god," I said, my eyes lighting up. "This is incredible!"

As we savored our meals, the conversation flowed like the wine, each word unlocking another layer of connection between us. We shared stories about our childhoods, our dreams, and the misadventures that had colored our recent years. I was entranced, laughing at his animated retellings, the way he gestured with his hands as if painting the scenes in the air between us.

But as the evening wore on, I couldn't ignore the shadow lurking at the edges of my mind. With each laugh and shared secret, I felt the specter of past pain lurking just out of sight. How easy it was to slip back into this familiarity, to bask in the warmth of his presence. Yet I was acutely aware of the fragile nature of our reconnection.

"Okay, so I have to ask," Marco leaned forward, his eyes narrowing with mischief. "What's the craziest thing you've done since we last saw each other? Spill the beans. I promise I won't judge."

"Just one?" I teased, feeling a daring thrill course through me. "You have no idea how crazy I've been. I took a salsa dancing class once. Almost took out a light fixture."

His laughter filled the space, bright and unguarded, and I felt my pulse quicken. "Please tell me you have photographic evidence of that," he said, leaning back, arms crossed over his chest, his smile never wavering.

"Sadly, no. I live to tell the tale, but that's about it," I said, my heart racing with the promise of more laughter. But behind the fun, a part of me braced for the inevitable question about why we had drifted apart in the first place, about the heartache that had once tied us up in knots.

Before I could second-guess myself, I said, "What about you? You must have some wild stories up your sleeve."

He paused, the lightness in his gaze flickering momentarily, like a candle threatened by a sudden breeze. "Nothing quite so spectacular, I'm afraid. Just working, keeping busy. You know how it goes."

There it was. The delicate barrier between us, a moment of honesty tinged with the unsaid, and I felt the air thicken as the laughter faded, leaving only the weight of what we had lost hanging in the air.

I took a deep breath, attempting to capture the fleeting warmth of the moment. The intimate atmosphere of Il Sogno surrounded us, but it was Marco's presence that truly enveloped me. We had laughed and shared stories, but now there was a silent pause, a pregnant moment where the laughter faded and the weight of unspoken truths lingered like the last note of a favorite song.

"So," he said, breaking the silence as he leaned forward, his expression shifting from lightheartedness to something more serious, "what are you really doing with yourself these days?"

I opened my mouth, ready to rattle off the usual rehearsed lines about work and life, but then I hesitated. What was I doing? It was a simple enough question, yet it felt layered with complexity. "You mean besides dancing my heart out like a deranged flamingo?" I replied, trying to keep the tone light, but there was a slight tremor in my voice.

He chuckled, though there was an edge of seriousness behind it. "Okay, fair point. But seriously, I want the real answer. The last time we talked, it felt like we were both stuck in a holding pattern."

The way he said it made my stomach churn with the truth. I didn't want to admit how lost I'd felt, how each day had blended into the next with a mundane rhythm that felt unbreakable. "It's been a bit of a slog, to be honest. Work is fine, nothing groundbreaking, and my social life... well, let's just say it's taken a bit of a nosedive."

"Still avoiding the crowds then?" he asked, a hint of understanding in his voice.

"More like dodging awkward small talk and the inevitable questions about my love life," I admitted, my heart racing as I waded into deeper waters. "You know, it's almost comical how people think their opinions on my romantic choices matter."

Marco's expression softened. "You don't have to justify anything to anyone. Your life is your own."

His words wrapped around me like a warm blanket, and for a fleeting moment, I felt seen. But the nagging uncertainty crept back in, the shadows of doubt lurking just outside the glow of our connection. What if this was all just a temporary reprieve? What if, as soon as I left this restaurant, the world would snap back into focus, reminding me of all the things I wished I could forget?

"So what about you?" I asked, shifting the focus back to him, trying to shake off the heavy cloak of vulnerability. "What's been keeping you busy besides the coffee cult?"

He smirked, leaning back in his chair, clearly enjoying the change in topic. "Well, the coffee cult is thriving, and I'm the high priest of caffeine, but outside of that... I've been working on a side project."

"Do tell." My curiosity was piqued, and I leaned in, hoping for a glimpse of that passion I remembered from our past.

"It's a little insane, actually," he began, rubbing the back of his neck as he searched for the right words. "I've been tinkering with the idea of opening a mobile coffee cart. Something whimsical—like a traveling café that pops up at different spots around the city. You know, in parks, at festivals, maybe even outside some popular art gallery."

"Wow, that actually sounds amazing! I can totally see you whipping up lattes and charming the masses with your dazzling smile," I said, my enthusiasm bubbling over. "Do you have a name yet?"

"Not yet. I'm still workshopping it, but I thought something like 'Wanderlust Brews' might work," he said, his eyes lighting up with excitement. "The idea is to create a space where people can gather, share stories, and enjoy coffee that's just as adventurous as they are. Plus, I'd like to incorporate local artists to showcase their work at each stop."

"That's brilliant! It's like a coffee festival on wheels. I can picture it now—people gathering around, laughing, sharing stories. You should definitely go for it," I encouraged, feeling a spark of inspiration ignite within me.

"Thanks! Hearing you say that means a lot." His gratitude shimmered in the air between us, but as he spoke, I could sense the hesitation lurking beneath his words. "I just hope I can actually make it happen. You know how easy it is to let fear creep in."

"Fear is the thief of joy," I said, recalling a quote I had once read, trying to dismiss my own anxieties in the process. "But you've always been the kind of guy who takes risks. You left your corporate job for this, didn't you? You can do it again."

He smiled, but it didn't quite reach his eyes. "Yeah, I suppose. But it's different now. I have more to lose." His voice lowered, and the shift in tone sent a shiver down my spine.

"What do you mean by that?"

He hesitated, glancing down at his half-empty glass of wine. "It's just... I guess I've realized that pursuing your passion is a double-edged sword. It can either liberate you or drown you if it doesn't go as planned."

I nodded, sensing the gravity of his words. "It's terrifying to put yourself out there, to risk everything for a dream."

"But what's the alternative?" Marco looked back up, his gaze fierce and determined. "Staying stuck in a safe bubble? I've done that for too long, and I'm tired of feeling like a ghost in my own life."

The honesty of his admission resonated within me, and the air crackled with unspoken understanding. Here we were, two souls fumbling through the dark, yearning for light, yet afraid of the path to get there.

"Okay, here's the deal," I said, half-jokingly. "If you start this coffee cart, I'll be your first customer. No, wait—your first regular."

He chuckled, and the momentary levity helped to lighten the air. "Deal! And in return, you have to promise to come to one of my events. I'll make you my special customer of the month, complete with a personalized drink."

"Can I be a judge? Like a coffee critic?" I proposed, a glimmer of mischief lighting up my eyes.

"Only if you promise to wear a beret and use phrases like 'notes of blackberry with a hint of despair,'" he shot back, and we both burst into laughter.

The tension that had held us captive began to dissipate, replaced by the playful banter that had once defined our relationship. But just as I started to feel a sense of comfort, a shadow passed over Marco's face, a flicker of something darker. I wondered what ghosts still haunted him, what struggles lurked behind that charming smile.

The waiter returned with our desserts, and I tried to shake off the unease curling in my stomach. A rich chocolate mousse and a delicate panna cotta graced our plates, tempting and indulgent. As we savored the desserts, the conversation flowed back to lighter topics, but I couldn't help but steal glances at him, watching as he became animated once more.

Yet, beneath the laughter and delicious food, the reality of our situation loomed. The laughter was a temporary balm, a soothing lull in the storm, but what awaited us when the evening ended? As Marco gestured dramatically about his plans for the future, I felt the tug of impending farewells settling heavily in my heart. Would this be another fleeting moment, or could it signify a deeper reconnection?

As the final bites of dessert lingered on our plates, the air thickened with an electric tension that made my heart race. Marco's laughter faded into a thoughtful silence, and I could feel the gears turning in his mind, as if he were wrestling with something significant, something that wanted to break free. I couldn't help but lean in closer, drawn to him like a moth to a flame.

"Do you remember that time we tried to bake that ridiculous soufflé?" I asked, desperate to pull him from whatever shadow loomed over us.

"Of course! We nearly set your kitchen on fire," he chuckled, the warmth returning to his voice. "That was the moment I knew we'd never make it as chefs."

I laughed, the memory bright and vivid, yet the laughter felt like a mask, a thin layer protecting us from the deeper truths we had yet to confront. The restaurant around us hummed softly, couples sharing intimate whispers while the waitstaff flitted about like busy little bees, but within our little bubble, the warmth was palpable, mingled with something bittersweet.

"Do you ever think about what could've been?" Marco asked suddenly, the question hanging in the air like the scent of cinnamon from the dessert menu, tantalizing yet unsettling.

The weight of his words settled over me, and I felt my heart leap into my throat. "All the time," I admitted, my voice barely above a whisper. "But then I remind myself that we're here now, and that has to count for something."

He nodded slowly, the flickering candlelight casting shadows across his face, illuminating the uncertainty etched on his features. "It does. But I can't help but wonder if we're just skimming the surface. What if we're too afraid to dive deep?"

"Are you suggesting we should start swimming lessons?" I joked, hoping to lighten the mood, but the nervous smile I wore didn't reach my eyes.

Marco's gaze turned serious. "No, I'm serious. I feel like we've both been treading water, avoiding the big waves. There's so much we haven't talked about."

"Like the fact that you left without saying goodbye?" I countered, unable to suppress the defensive edge creeping into my voice.

"Touché," he replied, his lips quirking into a half-smile. "But you know it wasn't like that for me. It was more about trying to find my footing."

"Footing?" I echoed, the word resonating with a deeper truth that I wasn't ready to confront. "Or was it running away?"

The light in his eyes flickered again, a shadow passing over his expression. "Maybe a little of both," he said quietly. "I think we both needed some space to figure things out. But now, sitting here with you, I realize how much I've missed this—us."

His admission sent a rush of warmth through me, a reminder of everything I had tried to bury. I wanted to reach out, to bridge that invisible gap that still lingered, but something held me back, a whisper in my mind cautioning against vulnerability.

"What if we've both changed too much?" I asked, letting the words slip through my defenses. "What if we can't go back to what we had?"

"Maybe we shouldn't go back. Maybe we should build something new," he said, and the earnestness in his voice struck a chord within me, resonating with both hope and fear.

"Build something new?" I mused, tilting my head as I contemplated the enormity of his suggestion. "That's a tall order."

"Tall orders are my specialty," he replied, his eyes glinting with mischief. "Besides, we've already weathered a storm together. What's a little rebuilding?"

As I looked at him, the candlelight catching the warmth in his eyes, I felt a surge of longing mixed with apprehension. There was so much unspoken between us, a lifetime of memories and heartaches intertwined, and yet here we were, flirting with the idea of something more.

Just then, my phone buzzed, slicing through the tender moment like a sudden gust of wind. I pulled it out, my heart sinking as I saw the name flashing on the screen. It was my mother, her name a familiar weight that brought with it a rush of obligations and expectations.

"Sorry, I should take this," I said, the urgency of her call threading through the air between us.

"Sure, go ahead," Marco replied, his smile softening, but I could see the flicker of concern behind it.

I stepped outside, the cool night air wrapping around me like a shawl as I swiped to answer. "Hey, Mom."

"Sweetheart, I need to talk to you about something important," she said, her voice tight, almost brittle.

"Is everything okay?" My heart raced, the familiar knot of anxiety tightening in my stomach.

"Not exactly. I was hoping you could come over tomorrow. We need to discuss your future—specifically, the plans for your career."

"Mom, we just had this conversation last week," I replied, my frustration bubbling over. "I'm still figuring things out!"

"Figuring things out? Honey, you're not a child anymore. You need to start making decisions. What about that law school application we discussed?"

"I've told you—law isn't for me!" I snapped, catching myself as I realized the edges of our conversation were beginning to fray.

"Then what is? Because I can't keep watching you drift through life. You need a plan, and fast," she insisted, her voice unwavering.

I opened my mouth to argue, but the words caught in my throat as I glanced back into the restaurant through the glass doors. Marco sat alone, his gaze turned toward me, expression unreadable. Suddenly, the stakes felt higher, the weight of expectation pressing down on me.

"Fine. I'll come over," I said, my voice deflated, devoid of the conviction I had hoped to convey.

"Thank you. We'll discuss everything then. And I expect you to take this seriously." Her tone softened slightly, but the urgency remained.

"Yeah, sure," I mumbled, my heart sinking further as I hung up, the call leaving me unsettled.

As I stepped back inside, the warmth of the restaurant washed over me, but the buzz of the conversation that had felt so promising moments ago now seemed to hang like a fragile web between us. Marco looked up, his brows knitting together with concern.

"Everything okay?" he asked, his voice laced with genuine worry.

"Just my mom being... well, my mom," I said, forcing a smile that felt more like a grimace. "She's on about my future again."

"That sounds... fun," he replied, though his tone hinted at something deeper.

"Yeah, you know how it is. Pressure to get it all figured out," I shrugged, trying to brush it off, but the frustration bubbled just below the surface.

"Do you feel pressure to follow a certain path?" Marco pressed, his gaze steady.

"I don't know," I admitted, frustration creeping back in. "Sometimes I feel like I'm being pushed down a road I didn't choose. It's exhausting."

"Then maybe it's time to take a detour," he suggested, leaning forward as if sharing a secret. "Life's too short to let someone else drive your narrative."

His words struck a chord within me, igniting the spark of courage I had buried beneath layers of doubt. But just as I opened my mouth to respond, the restaurant door swung open, and a familiar face stepped inside, the rush of cool air following her in like an unwelcome breeze.

"Marco!" she called, and I felt the blood drain from my face as recognition struck. It was Chloe, his ex-girlfriend.

"Of all the nights..." I murmured under my breath, my heart plummeting as she strolled in, a confident smile on her face that radiated trouble.

"Fancy seeing you here!" she exclaimed, her eyes lighting up as they landed on Marco, and suddenly, the warmth of our moment flickered, leaving a chill in its wake.

I felt the weight of the world shift, the delicate balance we had found moments ago teetering dangerously. Marco's expression morphed from warmth to something akin to panic, and the tension in the room crackled like static electricity.

Chloe approached our table, her gaze flitting between us, curiosity mingled with mischief. "What a cozy little dinner you two have going on. Mind if I join?"

"Actually—" Marco began, but I cut him off, sensing the impending chaos.

"Of course! The more, the merrier," I forced out, my heart racing. The evening had just taken a turn I wasn't prepared for, and as I looked at Marco, the questions in his eyes mirrored my own. What was about to unravel?

Chapter 7: Cracking the Shell

The warmth of candlelight flickered between us, casting playful shadows on the rustic wooden table that had seen better days. The restaurant hummed with the sound of laughter and clinking glasses, the air rich with the mingling scents of garlic and rosemary. I leaned back in my chair, a vibrant red wine swirling in my glass, contemplating the man across from me. Marco's dark hair fell in soft waves, a few errant strands brushing against his forehead as he concentrated on the plate before him, his brow furrowing in that adorable way that made my heart flutter.

"Here, try this," he said, a hint of mischief dancing in his hazel eyes as he slid a forkful of his signature risotto across the table. The creamy concoction glistened under the soft lighting, speckled with vibrant green peas and slivers of parmesan. Hesitantly, I took the fork and raised it to my lips, the warmth of his gaze igniting an ember of boldness within me.

I had spent so long building walls around my heart, convinced that love was a fire that would only leave me burned. But here I was, leaning into the warmth of his attention, allowing the layers I had wrapped around myself to peel away—slowly, tentatively, yet undeniably. The risotto was a revelation, rich and satisfying, and I couldn't help but smile as I savored the first bite.

"Delicious, right?" Marco grinned, his smile brightening the room more than the candlelight ever could. "I used a little secret ingredient."

"Let me guess—your heart?" I teased, and he chuckled, the sound deep and soothing, like the rich notes of a jazz melody echoing in the background.

"Close! But no. Just a pinch of saffron. Adds that extra kick," he replied, leaning forward, resting his chin on his hand, captivated by my enjoyment. "But I think you just give it a different flavor altogether."

The compliment slipped under my skin, warming me from the inside. I felt the flutter of vulnerability rise within me again, ready to burst out. "You know," I began, my voice a touch shaky, "commitment scares me. It always has. I worry it's a straight shot to heartbreak."

Marco's smile faltered for just a heartbeat, but then he nodded, his expression earnest. "I get that. Being a chef, I've felt that pressure, too. Every dish is a gamble. You pour your heart into it, hoping it turns out right, but sometimes... it just doesn't."

His admission lingered between us, heavy with shared understanding. I watched as his fingers tapped nervously on the table, a reminder that behind the confident exterior was a man grappling with his own uncertainties. "It can be a lonely pursuit," he added quietly, his eyes darkening. "You chase this dream, but sometimes, it feels like you're just running away from everyone else."

The honesty of his words struck me. Here we were, two people trying to bridge the gap between our fears and desires. My heart thudded against my ribcage, and for the first time, I felt the walls I had so carefully constructed begin to crack. "So what do we do?" I asked, my voice barely above a whisper, as if speaking too loudly would shatter this moment.

"Maybe we take things slow," he suggested, his gaze unwavering. "Let's explore what this is without the weight of expectations. Just... see where it goes."

I nodded, feeling a mixture of relief and exhilaration. The idea of treading lightly, of navigating the unknown without the fear of failure clinging to my back, was a concept I could embrace. "Like a culinary experiment," I said, allowing a wry smile to dance on my lips. "Only this time, we're the ingredients."

He laughed, the tension breaking like a wave crashing on the shore. "Exactly! Just two people trying not to burn the kitchen down."

The conversation flowed effortlessly after that, like a well-practiced duet. We talked about everything and nothing—his dreams of opening a restaurant with a menu that mirrored the seasons, my aspirations of starting a small bakery that captured the essence of my grandmother's recipes. The more we spoke, the more I found myself wrapped in the vibrant tapestry of his dreams, the colors bright and bold, each thread pulling me closer to him.

Yet, even amidst the joy, a shadow lingered in my mind, whispering warnings of past heartbreaks and missed connections. I had never let anyone this close; it was terrifying yet intoxicating. I was dancing on the edge of a cliff, the wind pulling me toward the precipice, but Marco's laughter grounded me, tethering my fears to the warm, sturdy earth.

As the night wore on, our conversation veered from dreams to lighthearted banter, our laughter melding with the sounds of clinking glasses and the distant strum of a guitar. "Okay, one more question," Marco said, leaning back with a playful glint in his eyes. "What's your guilty pleasure?"

I smirked, thinking of my well-honed secrets. "Well, there's this reality show about competitive baking..."

"No!" he exclaimed, feigning horror. "Not the one with the overly dramatic judges who throw shade like it's confetti!"

"Exactly that one!" I grinned, reveling in the shared absurdity. "I'm a sucker for the tension and the over-the-top critiques. It's like a train wreck I can't look away from."

Marco shook his head in mock disapproval, his laughter infectious. "We are going to need to watch that together, but I might judge you for it."

I raised an eyebrow, pretending to be scandalized. "Judge me? You're the one who serves up food with a side of 'I hope you like it,' every time. How about we make a pact? You cook, I critique—just like the show!"

He chuckled, and for a moment, the world around us faded into a blur. It was just Marco and me, two souls finding solace in each other's presence, laughter blending with the rich aroma of the food that surrounded us. The night seemed to stretch infinitely, each moment a delicious morsel that I wanted to savor.

And so we sat, the candles flickering, the air thick with the scent of potential, and I couldn't shake the feeling that perhaps this was the beginning of something remarkable—an unexpected dish of two hearts daring to dance in the flames of uncertainty.

The laughter and chatter of the restaurant faded into a comfortable background hum as Marco and I continued to explore this newfound connection. I couldn't help but marvel at how a simple dinner had transformed into an intimate dance of words and shared vulnerabilities. Each moment felt like an uncharted territory, ripe with potential, and my heart raced with the thrill of the unknown.

As the server cleared our plates, Marco leaned back, his gaze steady on me. "You know, the last time I felt this comfortable with someone was in culinary school. It's like we've skipped all the awkward small talk and just jumped into the good stuff."

"I think we're both just too stubborn to beat around the bush," I replied, swirling my wine again. "Why waste time pretending we're anything but the wonderfully flawed people we are?"

His grin broadened, revealing a hint of mischief. "Exactly! So, what's next on the agenda for this culinary critique club? We have to step up our game."

I tapped my chin, feigning deep thought. "How about a bake-off? You can try your hand at pastry, and I'll show you what a real dessert looks like."

"Please," he scoffed, crossing his arms dramatically. "Do you really think a bakery can compete with my Michelin star-worthy cuisine?"

"I'll have you know," I shot back, leaning closer with a teasing glint in my eye, "that my chocolate éclairs have brought grown men to tears. You might want to rethink that bravado."

He laughed, the sound deep and inviting, echoing around us like music. "Challenge accepted. But you do realize that I'll have to bring my A-game, right?"

"Let's make it interesting, then. Loser buys dinner at the winner's restaurant of choice."

"Oh, it's on!" He leaned forward, enthusiasm lighting up his features. "And when I win—and I will win—you'll have to endure my relentless critique of your technique."

"Fair warning: I don't take criticism well," I replied, shooting him a playful glare.

"I'll keep that in mind while I critique your soufflé," he shot back, his eyes sparkling with mischief.

The playful banter spun between us, drawing us closer with each witty exchange, but beneath the surface, I felt the lingering threads of my vulnerability tugging at my consciousness. Each laugh we shared was a step deeper into uncharted territory, a place where I would need to decide if I was willing to risk my heart again.

Just then, the server returned with dessert—a decadent chocolate molten lava cake that practically glowed under the restaurant's soft lights. It was practically an advertisement for indulgence, the rich aroma wafting through the air as it was placed in front of us.

"I'm not even sorry for what's about to happen," I declared, diving into the cake with my fork, taking a generous bite and closing my eyes as the warm chocolate enveloped my senses.

"Wow," Marco said, his eyes wide. "I think you've just gone to another dimension."

I chuckled, half-heartedly pointing my fork at him. "And here I thought you were going to critique me on my choice of dessert. You, of all people, should appreciate the artistry behind a molten cake."

"Artistry?" he scoffed. "This is more like a religious experience." He took a bite, his eyes widening in delight. "Okay, I concede. You might have just set the bar impossibly high."

"And don't forget it!" I grinned, taking another indulgent bite. The dessert was blissful, but as I savored the rich, velvety chocolate, I felt the gnawing uncertainty creep back in. I could see the future unfolding before me—each laugh shared, each moment of connection also opening the door to possible heartbreak.

As if sensing my sudden change in mood, Marco set down his fork. "Hey," he said gently, "what's going on in that beautiful head of yours?"

I hesitated, the weight of my thoughts pressing down like a heavy blanket. "It's just... all of this feels too good, you know? I've been burned before, and I'm terrified of getting my hopes up."

His expression softened, and he reached across the table to take my hand again, the warmth of his palm grounding me. "I get that. Believe me, I do. But we can take our time. No pressure, just... enjoy this moment."

I nodded, taking a deep breath, grateful for his understanding. "You're right. I just need to remember that we're both here, and we're both trying. No expectations, just a genuine connection."

"Exactly." He squeezed my hand lightly, a gesture that sent a flutter of warmth coursing through me. "And let's be honest; I'm kind of enjoying this whole flirty baking war thing. It makes for a much more interesting evening."

"True, I can't argue with that," I said, a smile creeping back onto my face. "Who knew culinary rivalries could be this thrilling?"

We shared another laugh, and I leaned back in my chair, feeling lighter. The conversation shifted to our favorite baking memories, and I recounted the time I had tried to bake a cake for my best friend's birthday, only to accidentally mix up the sugar with salt. Marco listened, rapt, his eyes gleaming with laughter as I described the horrified faces of my friends and the laughter that had ensued.

"You're a braver soul than I am," he said, shaking his head in disbelief. "I wouldn't have even attempted that."

"Bravery or stupidity? Sometimes it's a fine line," I said with a wink.

"True. I'll have to remember that if you ever try to pull a stunt like that on me," he replied, leaning closer, the space between us growing charged with an energy I hadn't expected.

Just then, a group of patrons burst into the restaurant, laughter echoing off the walls. One of the women, unmistakably tipsy and boisterous, slipped and nearly collided with our table. "Whoa, sorry!" she exclaimed, righting herself with exaggerated flair, as though she were on a stage.

"Just testing the floor, making sure it's not made of ice," she quipped, her friends laughing behind her.

Marco and I exchanged amused glances, and I couldn't help but grin at the interruption. The energy was infectious, a reminder of the chaotic beauty of life. The woman turned to us, eyes sparkling. "What are you two lovebirds up to? Planning a bake-off, I see!"

Before I could respond, Marco leaned in, his expression playful. "Oh, you have no idea. I'm about to win the biggest culinary challenge of my life."

"Love and food? Count me in!" she said, clinking her glass against ours in a toast. "To new beginnings!"

"To new beginnings," I echoed, feeling a rush of warmth as the clinking of glasses merged with laughter, the chaos around us fading into a delightful background hum.

As the night wore on, I felt a palpable shift in the air. The laughter and camaraderie lifted my spirits, and with every smile exchanged with Marco, the weight of my past began to feel less like a burden and more like a stepping stone toward something new. I was discovering that maybe, just maybe, opening my heart wouldn't be a catastrophe after all; perhaps it could lead to something sweet—like a perfectly baked dessert, waiting to be savored.

The night unfolded like a delicate pastry, each layer revealing something richer than the last. As the laughter of the tipsy woman faded into the background, I felt a surge of warmth wash over me. The restaurant, with its soft glow and rich scents, transformed into our own little world where worries seemed to drift away like the last wisps of a summer breeze. I watched Marco, the way his eyes sparkled when he laughed, and the way he effortlessly navigated the ebb and flow of conversation. There was a buoyancy to him, a lightness that contrasted sharply with the weight of my past.

"Alright, so now that we've both officially declared war in the kitchen, what's our first move?" Marco asked, leaning forward, his elbow resting on the table. His playful smirk was infectious.

I thought for a moment, then replied, "We should probably start with the basics. Like, what's the worst thing we could bake? You know, to build character."

"Ah, the 'What's the most ridiculous thing we can do and survive?' approach," he said, nodding with mock seriousness. "I like it. How about soufflé? The enemy of many a home cook."

"Oh, that's brave," I laughed, my heart fluttering at the thought of battling the infamous culinary beast. "But we need a real plan.

What if we decide to get fancy and end up with a disaster? I could ruin our chances of a friendly rivalry!"

He leaned back, crossing his arms, a mischievous grin spreading across his face. "Disaster is half the fun! Besides, if we both end up in a culinary emergency, we can call for takeout."

The banter flowed easily, yet beneath the surface of our light-hearted exchange, I felt an undercurrent of tension, a mix of excitement and apprehension swirling within me. As the dessert plates were cleared, Marco reached for my hand again, the warmth of his palm sending delightful shivers up my arm. "Can I confess something?"

I tilted my head, intrigued. "Always."

"I'm really looking forward to this little competition. But part of me is terrified," he admitted, his voice softening. "It's like I'm walking into the lion's den and hoping not to get eaten alive."

"Same," I replied, squeezing his hand, relishing the connection that seemed to tether us together. "We're both stepping outside our comfort zones. But maybe that's the point. We can't grow if we stay in our safe little bubbles."

He nodded, his expression serious. "Exactly. And honestly, I think that's what makes this even more exciting. The possibility of failure, of making mistakes, is what makes it all worthwhile."

As we exchanged nervous smiles, the energy in the restaurant shifted. A group at the next table erupted into a round of cheers, drawing our attention. It was a celebration of some sort—a birthday, perhaps, the bright red balloons bobbing above their heads confirmed my suspicion. A slice of cake was paraded through the room, the flickering candles casting a soft glow on the jubilant faces.

"Imagine that," I said, watching them with a sense of longing. "Cake. The ultimate symbol of celebration, but it also reminds me of all the times I tried to bake one for a birthday and ended up with a catastrophe."

Marco chuckled. "What happened? Was it a 'volcanic eruption' cake or a 'falling apart' cake?"

"Both, actually. It was my sister's birthday, and I had this grand vision of a three-tiered masterpiece. Instead, I ended up with a lean-to of cake layers and frosting sliding off like it was auditioning for a role in a disaster movie," I confessed, shaking my head at the memory.

"Now that sounds like a story for the ages," he said, laughing. "But that's part of what makes it special, right? The memories? Even the disasters."

"True," I said, pondering his words. "At least we can look back and laugh, right?"

As if on cue, the group at the next table began to sing "Happy Birthday," their voices harmonizing in a cheerful cacophony. I joined in, my voice a little louder than intended, and Marco's laughter rang out beside me, a beautiful melody that blended perfectly with the joyous chorus. It was moments like these that felt so liberating, where the barriers I had built started to feel like memories of a distant past.

Once the song ended, I turned to Marco, who was still chuckling softly. "Okay, since we're doing confessions, here's another: I'm not the best baker in the world. I'm more of a 'wing it and hope for the best' type."

He leaned in closer, his eyes sparkling with mischief. "Good. That makes it more of a challenge. I'll be your sous chef and we can just wing it together."

"Deal," I said, the prospect of facing the kitchen with him felt exhilarating. "But just remember, when I set the oven on fire, it's totally your fault."

"Only if you bring the marshmallows," he shot back, laughter bubbling between us.

As the night progressed, we shared more stories, each laugh creating a tapestry of connection that felt both exhilarating and daunting. The more I revealed, the more I wanted to share. He made it easy to lower my defenses, and the way he looked at me made me feel seen in a way I hadn't experienced in years.

But just as I was beginning to let myself believe that this connection could lead somewhere beautiful, the door swung open, and a chilling draft swept through the restaurant. I shivered, rubbing my arms as I turned to see a woman enter. She was striking, with long dark hair that cascaded down her back and an air of confidence that commanded attention. Her gaze swept across the room, landing on our table, and the instant I saw the flash of recognition in her eyes, my heart dropped.

"Ella?" she called, her voice cutting through the hum of the restaurant.

I froze, the warmth of the moment dissipating as the familiarity of her voice washed over me. It was a voice I hadn't heard in years, a voice I had hoped to leave behind. My pulse quickened, and I exchanged a glance with Marco, who looked equally bewildered.

"Do you know her?" he asked, concern etched across his face.

"Yeah," I whispered, my throat dry. "That's my ex."

The air thickened, and I could feel the tension crackling between us like static electricity, pulling me back to a past I thought I'd finally moved beyond. As she approached, I could feel the weight of unresolved feelings and unspoken words swirling around us, threatening to engulf the fragile connection Marco and I had just begun to build.

"Surprise, surprise," she said, a wry smile playing on her lips as she took in the scene before her. "Didn't expect to find you here."

Just then, my phone buzzed on the table, the screen lighting up with a message that made my stomach drop even further. "We need to talk."

The room spun around me as I faced the familiar specter of my past and the unpredictable future that lay ahead. The stakes were suddenly raised, and the question lingered in the air: could I navigate this new chaos without losing everything I had just begun to embrace?

Chapter 8: A Stormy Encounter

The rain hammered against the windows like an impatient guest, demanding entry into our candlelit refuge. Marco and I sat at a corner table in the small, eclectic restaurant, the kind where every wall had a story etched in mismatched frames, and the air was thick with the aroma of roasted garlic and fresh herbs. A sudden flicker of the overhead lights sent a shiver through the room, and the soft glow of the candles became our only guide through the encroaching darkness.

"Guess this is one way to get a table for two," Marco quipped, a playful smirk tugging at the corner of his mouth. His voice, smooth like the bourbon he had just poured for us, wrapped around me like a warm blanket on a chilly night. I couldn't help but laugh, the tension from earlier dissolving into the shadows.

"You do realize that a power outage isn't the romantic backdrop they advertise in movies, right?" I shot back, feeling bold. The storm outside seemed to echo our playful banter, the wind howling as if it, too, was caught up in our back-and-forth.

"Maybe not, but it's definitely more interesting than the usual dinner date," he replied, leaning back in his chair with a relaxed confidence that made me lean in closer. The flickering candlelight danced in his deep-set eyes, revealing a warmth that made my heart flutter with unexpected excitement.

I glanced out the window, the sheets of rain obscuring the view, transforming the street into a murky canvas of darkness. The storm had arrived without warning, a wild beast unleashed upon the city. Just moments ago, the skies were a serene blue, and now they churned with menace, turning the world outside into a blurry watercolor painting.

"Do you think we'll be stuck here all night?" I asked, half-joking, but a flicker of anxiety gnawed at my insides.

He shrugged, a playful twinkle in his eye. "Would that be so bad? Just you, me, and an endless supply of breadsticks?"

"Don't tempt me. I could make a meal out of those," I teased, my stomach grumbling in agreement. It was one of those moments when laughter felt like a lifeline, pulling us both from the swirling chaos outside.

The atmosphere shifted as the wind picked up, rattling the windows. My laughter faded, replaced by a thick tension that clung to the air. Marco leaned closer, and the space between us felt electric, charged with an unspoken connection that was both thrilling and terrifying. The playful banter transformed into something more profound, a deeper exploration of who we were beyond the confines of the restaurant walls.

"So, what's your story?" he asked, his voice low, almost intimate, as if sharing a secret with the flickering flames. "What brings you to Asheville?"

I hesitated, glancing down at the remnants of my meal, my fork tracing circles in the half-eaten pasta. "Honestly? I thought it would be different," I admitted, the weight of my words hanging between us. "I wanted to escape. The city life felt too... constricting. I needed a change, something more... me."

"Me too," he said, his expression growing serious. "I moved here a year ago, chasing dreams and running from my past. The mountains felt like a fresh start."

Our eyes locked, and I felt a wave of understanding wash over us. It was a connection I hadn't expected to find on a stormy night, and yet here we were, two souls caught in a tempest of our own making. Just as the atmosphere began to feel ripe with possibility, a loud crash outside shattered the moment, reverberating through the air like a gunshot.

"What was that?" I gasped, instinctively leaning toward him.

Marco was already on his feet, rushing to the window. The light from the candles flickered ominously as he peered outside. "Oh no," he muttered, his voice tinged with urgency. "A tree just fell. It's blocking the road."

I scrambled to my feet, joining him at the window, our shoulders brushing in the tight space. Sure enough, a massive oak lay sprawled across the street, its roots exposed and flailing like the limbs of a giant. The rain poured relentlessly, and I could see branches splintering in the gale, adding to the chaos that now enveloped us.

"Looks like we're stranded," he said, glancing back at me with a mixture of concern and mischief in his eyes.

"Fantastic," I replied, a smirk breaking through my anxiety. "Stuck in a candlelit restaurant with a handsome stranger during a storm. What a cliché."

He chuckled, shaking his head. "Not the worst way to spend an evening, though."

"Depends on how well you can hold a conversation," I shot back, but the playful retort was laced with an undercurrent of nervousness.

As the storm continued its assault on the world outside, we settled back at our table, the flickering candlelight now a sanctuary from the raging tempest. The shared moment of fear transformed into an opportunity for intimacy, a chance to strip away the facades we wore in the bustling world.

We traded stories, secrets spilling forth like the rain against the windows. I spoke of my dreams and my struggles, my desires for a life that felt genuine, not just a series of expected checkmarks. Marco listened intently, his gaze unwavering, and for the first time in a long time, I felt seen.

"What about you?" I asked, the curiosity bubbling inside me. "What dreams did you chase here?"

He leaned back, his expression thoughtful. "I wanted to be an artist," he said, his voice filled with a quiet intensity. "I've always painted, but it took moving to a new place to really find my voice."

"Show me," I urged, the words slipping out before I could think.

"Tonight?" he replied, a playful glint in his eyes.

"Why not? We have all night."

He grinned, that charming, disarming smile that sent a thrill through me. "Okay, but don't blame me if it's terrible."

"I promise, I'll only judge you a little," I laughed, feeling lighter, the weight of the storm outside now a distant memory as we began to create our own little world within the restaurant's cozy embrace.

He returned to the table, his expression a mix of exhilaration and apprehension. "Well, I suppose the universe really wants us to have this moment, doesn't it?"

"Or it's playing some kind of cosmic prank on us," I countered, a grin stretching across my face. "This could be the world's worst blind date."

"True," he said, laughter bubbling in his throat. "But at least we have each other and a decent selection of breadsticks."

With a theatrical flourish, he gestured to the basket of untouched breadsticks on the table. I couldn't help but giggle, imagining a future where this night would become an anecdote, a charming story to recount over future dinners.

"So, show me your art," I prompted, leaning forward, excitement dancing in my chest.

Marco hesitated, a flicker of vulnerability crossing his face. "I'm not a professional or anything. Just... a guy with a paintbrush and too much time on his hands."

"Which is exactly why I want to see it. I want to know the guy behind the charming smile and killer breadstick jokes."

He studied me for a moment, gauging my sincerity, then relented. "Alright, but it's just sketches. Nothing grand."

"Just sketches? Show me!" I insisted, my curiosity bubbling over like the remnants of our dessert wine.

With a reluctant smile, Marco reached into his backpack, which had been lying inconspicuously at his feet. He pulled out a worn sketchbook, the edges frayed and the cover adorned with flecks of paint, a testament to the journeys it had taken. He placed it on the table, and a sense of anticipation washed over me.

As he opened it, the soft rustle of the pages filled the air, mingling with the distant sounds of the storm. The first few sketches were simple, portraits of strangers he'd encountered—a woman with a bewitching smile, a man lost in thought. Each drawing captured a fleeting moment, imbued with life and depth.

"Wow, you're really talented," I breathed, tracing the lines with my finger as if I could summon the essence of the people he'd immortalized on paper. "You should have more confidence in your work."

"I don't know about that," he replied, a hint of embarrassment tinting his cheeks. "They're just... observations. More like doodles than anything significant."

"Observations are significant. They reveal how you see the world." I met his gaze, my voice steady. "And how you see the world matters."

The atmosphere shifted, charged with something unspoken. The air between us felt thicker, heavier with possibility, and I could see a flicker of realization in his eyes. Just as I thought he might respond, a loud crash echoed from outside, shattering the fragile moment.

"What now?" I exclaimed, instinctively grabbing his arm.

Marco rushed to the window once more, his expression shifting from curiosity to concern. "It looks like another tree fell. The power lines are down."

"Fantastic. We really are trapped," I said, the weight of the situation pressing down on me like the storm clouds overhead.

He turned to me, his eyes serious yet mischievous. "I think it's time to embrace the chaos, don't you? I mean, we're in a restaurant with no power, a storm raging outside, and a barrel of laughs waiting to happen."

I couldn't help but smile at his optimistic spirit. "You make it sound so romantic."

"Hey, if you can't find romance in a blackout, when can you?"

With a playful roll of my eyes, I leaned back in my chair, trying to shake off the lingering unease. "Fine, let's embrace the chaos. What's next, a game of charades?"

"Actually," he said, his eyes lighting up with a spark of mischief, "I was thinking of a storytelling contest. We each tell a story from our past, and the other has to guess if it's true or fabricated."

"That sounds dangerously fun," I replied, my heart racing at the thought of revealing parts of myself. "But be warned, I'm a professional fibber."

"Bring it on," he challenged, leaning forward, the candlelight flickering across his handsome features. "You go first."

"Alright," I began, weaving a tale of my childhood where I claimed to have once rescued a baby bird that had fallen from its nest, only to realize it wasn't a bird at all but a particularly feisty squirrel.

"Please tell me this is true," he said, chuckling, clearly amused.

"Maybe it is, maybe it isn't," I replied with a mischievous grin. "Your turn."

He launched into a story about a summer camp experience where he had accidentally set off a fire alarm while trying to impress a girl with his nonexistent cooking skills. As he animatedly recounted the chaos that ensued, I found myself hanging on every word, enthralled not just by the story but by the man telling it.

"True," I declared after he finished, unable to resist his infectious laughter.

"Of course, it's true. I'd never make something that ridiculous up," he replied, shaking his head. "Your turn again."

I leaned back, contemplating my next tale, when suddenly the lights flickered back on, bathing the restaurant in a warm glow. A chorus of cheers erupted from the kitchen, and I couldn't help but laugh at the abruptness of reality crashing back in.

"Looks like the spell is broken," Marco said, glancing around as the world re-entered our intimate bubble.

"Not necessarily," I insisted, refusing to let the moment slip away. "We were just getting started."

"Then let's not stop. We can always pretend the power went out again."

"You have a flair for the dramatic, don't you?" I said, smirking as I picked up a breadstick and waved it like a wand.

"Only when the occasion calls for it," he replied, eyes sparkling with mischief.

We fell into a rhythm, exchanging stories and playful jabs, the noise of the restaurant fading into a soft murmur. The world outside may have been raging with storm and chaos, but here, with Marco, it felt like we had created our own sanctuary. A place where the storm couldn't touch us, where laughter and connection wrapped around us like a warm embrace.

Just when I thought the night couldn't get any better, he leaned in, his voice dropping to a conspiratorial whisper. "Okay, but what if I told you that I'm actually a secret agent? You know, working undercover to save the world?"

"Please," I laughed, shaking my head. "With your cooking skills, I'd say you're more of a danger to yourself than a hero."

He feigned offense, his hand clutching his chest. "Ouch! That stings!"

"Good. It's meant to."

We continued to banter, the storm outside fading into a distant memory, replaced by the warmth of our connection and the thrill of shared secrets. The world may have been chaotic, but in this moment, nothing else mattered.

The hum of conversation around us had shifted into a low murmur, the laughter and chatter of other diners fading into the background as Marco and I wove our own tapestry of connection. The sudden flicker of the restaurant lights felt like an uninvited reminder of the outside world, but we had both decided, in our own unspoken way, that we weren't done yet.

"So, if you're a secret agent," I said, folding my arms playfully, "does that mean I can never tell anyone about you? This could be a real conundrum for my social life."

He leaned in, eyes gleaming with mischief. "You could always spin it as an exhilarating love story. You know, the girl who falls for the mysterious stranger with a double life."

"Except for the part where I'm just here for the carbs and the ambiance," I retorted, a laugh bubbling up. "It's not quite the dramatic plot twist you might be hoping for."

"Hey, carbs are essential for maintaining the energy needed to save the world," he shot back, gesturing grandly with his hands as if conducting an invisible orchestra. "And this ambiance? Top-tier. I mean, have you seen how well this candlelight flatters my jawline?"

I couldn't help but roll my eyes, but there was a genuine warmth blooming in my chest, the kind that made it hard to focus on anything else. "True. It's doing wonders. I should really invest in a few candles for myself."

Just as I was about to launch into my next quip, the lights flickered again, and then—silence. The power cut out entirely, plunging the restaurant back into darkness. Gasps erupted from a few patrons, followed by a chorus of nervous laughter. I felt a jolt of adrenaline rush through me, but before I could react, Marco's hand found mine beneath the table.

"Don't worry, it's just a blackout," he reassured, his voice a low murmur in the enveloping dark. "I've got you."

His grip was warm and grounding, and my heart raced not from fear but from the thrill of uncertainty that surrounded us. It was one thing to bond over stories and laughter; it was another entirely to share this moment of vulnerability, cloaked in the shadows.

"Is this your secret agent training kicking in?" I joked, trying to keep the mood light.

"Absolutely," he replied, squeezing my hand. "I'm trained for all scenarios, including candlelit dinner emergencies."

We both laughed, the sound echoing in the now-quiet room. The flickering flames of the candles created a dance of shadows on the walls, transforming the restaurant into a cozy hideaway that felt like it belonged to us alone.

"Should we just declare this a romantic escapade?" I suggested, half-seriously, my heart pounding in anticipation.

"Why not?" Marco replied, his voice suddenly serious, thick with something I couldn't quite place. "We could be the star-crossed lovers in a romantic comedy where everything goes hilariously wrong."

I looked at him, really looked at him, and felt a rush of something potent—an intoxicating blend of excitement and trepidation. "And if it all goes wrong?"

"Then at least we'll have a great story to tell," he said, his gaze locking onto mine.

Our faces were only inches apart, and I could feel the air crackling between us, charged with a tension that seemed to pulse with every beat of my heart. Just as I was about to respond, the front door swung open, and a gust of wind rushed in, bringing with it the unmistakable scent of rain-soaked earth and the tumult of the storm.

"Hey! Anyone in here?" called a voice from the doorway, pulling me from the moment.

"Just us," Marco called back, his tone half-joking.

The figure stepped into the dim light, revealing a young woman soaked to the skin, her hair plastered to her forehead. "I was looking for my friends. We got separated in the storm."

"I'm sure they're safe," I said, feeling a pang of disappointment at the interruption. "Why don't you join us? We're just... enjoying the ambiance."

The newcomer's face lit up with gratitude. "Thank you! I thought I'd be stuck outside forever." She settled into the empty chair at our table, shaking her head as if to dislodge the raindrops clinging to her like unwelcome memories.

"Now you're trapped in a cozy candlelit dinner," Marco said, flashing her a charming smile. "How lucky are you?"

"Very lucky," she replied, her eyes glinting with mischief. "I hope you don't mind sharing your evening. I have some great stories myself."

Just as she settled in, the power flickered back to life, the overhead lights illuminating the restaurant in harsh fluorescent glow. It was as if a spotlight had shone down on our little group, but the magic had shifted.

"Looks like the universe wants to keep us company," Marco said, his tone now teasing as he gestured to the newly illuminated space.

"Or it wants to ruin our romantic moment," I shot back, half-jokingly.

"Not a chance!" he declared, giving me a conspiratorial wink.

The woman laughed, but there was a glimmer of something else in her eyes, a hint of curiosity as she observed the interplay between us. "You two seem quite the pair. What's the story?"

As I opened my mouth to respond, I felt a sharp jolt in my chest, an instinctual awareness that this was not just an ordinary night.

Something about the newcomer felt... off. She was too eager, her smile a fraction too wide, as if she was absorbing every detail of our conversation for her own purposes.

"Just sharing some tales," I said, trying to keep my tone light, but a sense of unease began to settle in the pit of my stomach.

"Well, I hope you don't mind me joining," she replied, her voice dripping with sweetness that felt more like syrup than sincerity.

The tension shifted again, thickening the air around us. Marco's brow furrowed as he glanced between me and the newcomer, sensing my hesitation. "Actually, we were just getting into some interesting topics. How about you share your best story?"

"Oh, I have a great one," she said, leaning in closer, her eyes glinting in the candlelight. "But I'm not sure if you're ready for it."

I felt Marco tense beside me, and instinctively I squeezed his hand tighter, drawing strength from him as I prepared to navigate this new dynamic.

"Try us," I said, my voice steady despite the storm brewing inside me.

As she began her tale, I couldn't shake the feeling that this night was turning into something entirely different. My heart raced not just with the thrill of connection but with the lingering uncertainty of the unknown, a shadow creeping closer as the storm outside subsided, leaving us all at the mercy of the words that hung in the air.

Just then, the restaurant door swung open again, revealing a familiar figure soaked to the bone, his expression one of urgency. I froze, recognition crashing over me like a wave.

"Wait, what are you doing here?" I gasped, heart pounding as the realization hit me like lightning splitting the sky.

Chapter 9: The Taste of Commitment

The soft glow of dawn filtered through the sheer curtains, casting delicate patterns on the walls of Marco's bedroom, the remnants of last night's storm whispered away by a gentle breeze. I stirred, nestling deeper into the warmth of his embrace, the comfort of his presence wrapping around me like a favorite blanket. It felt surreal, waking up like this—dreamlike yet undeniably real. The quiet hum of the world outside mingled with the rhythmic sound of his breathing, creating a lullaby that kept the edges of reality at bay. I could smell the faint scent of rain mingling with the rich aroma of the coffee that I knew would soon fill the air, and the thought made my heart flutter with something I hadn't expected: hope.

Turning slightly, I peeked at Marco. His hair was tousled, and his lips were slightly parted in a peaceful slumber, the faintest hint of a smile playing on his face. I couldn't help but trace the outline of his jaw with my eyes, the way it caught the light just right, making him look both rugged and tender. It was in these small moments that I found myself grappling with the vulnerability that love demanded. My heart, once fortified behind high walls, was now a fragile thing, exposed to the possibility of being hurt—or worse, abandoned.

As the memories of the previous night came rushing back—our laughter, our shared stories, the way his gaze held mine like it could anchor me to this moment forever—I felt a surge of clarity. I had taken that leap of faith, declaring my feelings as if they were the most natural thing in the world. The surprise in his eyes had mirrored my own, but it had quickly melted into something more profound. When he had smiled, I had felt the weight of my own fears lift. We had made a promise—unspoken yet palpable—to navigate the labyrinth of our lives together, arms linked as we faced the uncertainties of what was to come.

My mind wandered back to the kitchen, where the sounds of sizzling bacon and the bubbling of a pot filled with water would soon beckon us. Food had always been my language, my way of expressing love and care. It was an art I had mastered in the solitude of my small apartment, an escape from the chaos of my thoughts. I could already envision the breakfast we would share: fluffy scrambled eggs, the sweetness of fruit, and perhaps, a decadent stack of pancakes drizzled with maple syrup. I smiled at the thought, knowing that breakfast had a way of breaking down barriers and fostering intimacy.

Just as I contemplated slipping out of bed, the warm weight of Marco's arm tightened around my waist, pulling me back into his warmth. "Where do you think you're going?" he murmured, his voice still thick with sleep, laced with a playful lilt that made my heart skip.

"Just to make us breakfast," I replied, my tone teasing. "Unless you're planning on starving me?"

He chuckled softly, a deep sound that vibrated through me, igniting that familiar flutter in my stomach. "I could survive on your smile alone, but breakfast sounds nice too." He opened his eyes, and when they met mine, there was a spark, a knowing that made my heart race.

"Okay, chef," I grinned, "you can help. I could use a sous chef."

"Oh, I don't know. I might just distract you with my dazzling personality," he said, feigning modesty while his eyes danced with mischief.

"More like your ridiculous charm," I shot back, laughing as I nudged him playfully. "But I could use the help—unless you plan on just standing there looking handsome."

With a dramatic sigh, he rolled out of bed, a playful glint in his eye. "Well, if it involves food, I suppose I can manage."

We moved to the kitchen, the air thick with an electric energy that felt like the promise of a new beginning. The sunlight streamed through the window, illuminating the small space where we had spent countless hours cooking together, sharing stories, and peeling back the layers of our lives. As I rummaged through the fridge, I felt Marco's gaze on me, a warmth that was almost tangible.

"What are you thinking about?" he asked, leaning against the counter, his arms crossed casually, yet I could sense the intensity of his focus.

"I was just thinking how different things feel now," I admitted, glancing over my shoulder. "Like, I never expected to wake up here with you, feeling this... content."

He smiled, that slow, genuine smile that made my heart do a little dance. "Life has a funny way of surprising us, doesn't it? Just when you think you have everything figured out, it throws a curveball. But I wouldn't trade this for anything."

The sincerity in his voice sent a shiver down my spine. We moved seamlessly through the motions of preparing breakfast, banter flowing like the syrup I planned to pour over the pancakes. I was chopping fruit, and he was whisking eggs, our movements synchronized in a comforting rhythm.

"You know," I said, pausing mid-chop, "I used to think I was perfectly fine being alone. It was easier to build walls than to let anyone in."

"Walls are a double-edged sword," Marco replied thoughtfully, his eyes flickering with understanding. "They keep the bad out, but they also keep the good at bay."

His words struck a chord deep within me, resonating with the truth I had been too scared to acknowledge. I glanced at him, the warmth of our shared vulnerability wrapping around us like a cozy blanket. This was new, this was exciting, and above all, it was terrifying. But in that moment, I felt ready to embrace it all.

The aroma of sizzling bacon filled the kitchen, mingling with the sweet scent of fresh fruit, creating an intoxicating blend that felt like an embrace. I stood at the stove, flipping pancakes with a flourish, relishing the sound of batter sizzling against the hot griddle. Marco leaned against the counter, casually twirling a fork in his fingers, his gaze fixed on me with an intensity that made my heart race. It was as if he were trying to memorize the way I moved, the way I laughed at my own jokes—something I was entirely too good at.

"Do you think the pancakes are jealous of the bacon?" I mused, trying to break the tension that crackled between us like static electricity. "I mean, bacon gets all the love, but pancakes are so fluffy and sweet."

Marco chuckled, his laughter like music in the otherwise cozy chaos of the kitchen. "Nah, the pancakes are too busy being delicious to worry about that. Besides, I think they know they're the real stars here." He nodded solemnly at the pancakes, as if they were his long-lost friends.

"Well, if the pancakes are the stars, then we're the supporting cast," I replied, flipping another one with a flourish, the golden-brown surface glistening under the kitchen light. "Ready for your Oscar-winning performance?"

"Only if I can accept the award while holding a piece of bacon," he replied, his eyes sparkling. "You know, to really sell the moment."

We both laughed, the sound ringing through the small space and washing over me like a balm. This was the kind of morning I had dreamed of—one filled with laughter, warmth, and the occasional witty repartee that felt like a dance. I poured syrup over the pancakes, the thick liquid cascading down like a sweet waterfall, and set the stack on the table. The vibrant colors of the fruit I had arranged beside them popped against the white plate, and for a brief moment, I felt like I could conquer the world.

"Breakfast is served!" I announced, setting the table with a flourish, feeling like a queen in my own little kingdom. Marco followed me, his steps light and playful, and as we settled down, I noticed the way his eyes lit up with anticipation.

"Just so you know," he said, picking up a fork and eyeing the pancakes, "I've been known to have an insatiable appetite. So, if I eat all the pancakes, don't take it personally."

"Good luck with that," I teased, rolling my eyes. "I have a strategy. I'll just make more if you try to pull a fast one on me."

"Challenge accepted," he shot back, a mock-seriousness taking over his expression.

We dug into breakfast, each bite bringing forth an array of flavors that danced on my tongue. The pancakes were fluffy and warm, while the bacon added that perfect crunch, each piece perfectly salty. Marco watched me, a bemused smile on his lips as I savored the food like it was a work of art.

"Do you always eat like it's your last meal?" he asked, amusement etched across his face.

"Only when I'm sharing it with someone worth my culinary efforts," I replied, winking at him.

"Oh, so I'm just a means to an end? A way to get through breakfast?" he countered, feigning hurt.

"Don't flatter yourself. You're the main course," I shot back, unable to suppress a grin.

Just then, my phone buzzed on the table, shattering our playful banter. I glanced at the screen, my heart sinking as I saw my mother's name. It was a call I had been dreading, one that brought with it the weight of expectations and the suffocating pressure of her well-meaning but often intrusive nature.

"Hey, you okay?" Marco asked, sensing the shift in my mood.

"Yeah, just... it's my mom. I should probably answer," I muttered, my voice barely above a whisper.

"Do you want me to leave the room?" he asked, his brow furrowing with concern.

"No, it's fine. I just... I wasn't expecting her to call today," I said, forcing a smile as I swiped to answer.

"Hi, Mom," I said, trying to inject cheerfulness into my tone.

"Sweetheart! I've been meaning to call. I wanted to check in on you. Are you still seeing that boy?" she asked, her voice laced with that familiar curiosity that often felt more like an interrogation.

"Yes, Mom, Marco and I are still seeing each other," I replied, glancing at Marco, who was now holding back laughter, his expression somewhere between entertained and sympathetic.

"That's wonderful! You know, your father and I were just discussing how important it is to settle down. You're not getting any younger," she continued, her tone casual yet pointed.

"Mom, we're just enjoying each other's company," I said, trying to keep my voice steady. "I'm not looking for a wedding ring just yet."

"Oh, honey, but think of the future! You have so much potential, and I want to see you happy," she insisted, her words weaving through the air like a fine silk thread, pulling at my insecurities.

"Of course, I appreciate that, but—"

"I'm just saying, you should really consider where this is going. It's not enough to just have fun," she interrupted, her voice firm yet laced with affection.

I glanced at Marco again, and he raised an eyebrow, silently urging me to stand my ground. "Mom, I'm not rushing into anything. I want to take my time to really understand what I want. Just because I'm dating doesn't mean I'm looking for a life plan."

There was a beat of silence on the other end, and I could almost hear her processing my words, her vision of my future clashing with my desire for independence. "Well, I just want what's best for you, you know that," she finally said, her voice softer now.

"I know, Mom. I promise I'll figure it out," I replied, determination threading through my voice. "I really have to go now, though. Marco and I were in the middle of breakfast."

"Alright, darling. Just remember what I said," she said, her tone hinting at an underlying concern that never truly faded.

"Of course. Love you," I said before hanging up, the weight of our conversation lingering in the air like a storm cloud.

I took a deep breath, setting my phone down with a mix of relief and frustration. Marco watched me, his gaze steady, and I could feel his presence like a soothing balm.

"Family dynamics?" he asked, breaking the silence, a knowing smile creeping onto his lips.

"Something like that," I replied, rolling my eyes. "Mom's on a marriage mission."

"Ah, yes. The 'let's settle down' speech. I remember mine well," he said, feigning a dramatic sigh. "You'd think they'd take a hint."

"It's like they think they can just draft up our future on a napkin," I muttered, my fingers tapping restlessly against the table.

"Hey," Marco said softly, leaning closer, "it's your life, not theirs. You get to decide how it unfolds."

His words settled over me like a warm blanket, igniting a spark of defiance within. For the first time, I felt ready to embrace the chaos of my family while carving out my own path. In that moment, surrounded by the remnants of our breakfast and the warmth of his gaze, I realized that perhaps love wasn't just about the big gestures or grand plans. Sometimes, it was about the simple act of being present, of sharing pancakes and laughter, and navigating the messy intricacies of life together.

The sunlight streamed through the window, illuminating the kitchen with a warm, golden glow as I leaned back in my chair, allowing the weight of the morning's conversation to settle. I could still taste the sweetness of the pancakes on my tongue, but the lingering shadow of my mother's call hovered nearby, a constant reminder of expectations and the future that loomed over me like an unwelcome guest. Marco, ever the perceptive one, watched me with an expression that was both tender and understanding.

"Still with us?" he asked, breaking into my thoughts, his voice light but laced with concern.

"Just contemplating the mysteries of the universe," I replied with a smirk, trying to brush it off. "You know, things like why my mom thinks my life needs a timeline."

"Ah, the age-old question of parental timelines," he mused, leaning back in his chair with a playful air of mock seriousness. "I think the answer lies somewhere between their hope for grandbabies and their fear of being left behind in the social media age."

I laughed, the tension in my chest easing slightly. "If they only knew I can't even keep a houseplant alive, let alone a human."

"Plant parenthood is a lot of pressure, I hear," he said, his eyes sparkling with mischief. "But in all seriousness, do you want to talk about it?"

I bit my lip, contemplating how to articulate the whirlwind of emotions inside me. "I don't know. I love my parents, but sometimes it feels like they don't see me for who I am. They have this picture of me that doesn't include late-night ice cream binges or a proclivity for spontaneous road trips."

"Yeah, well, we can't blame them for wanting to plan the perfect version of you. It's way less messy," he replied, waving his fork theatrically. "But messy can be fun."

"Fun, or an absolute disaster waiting to happen?" I shot back, feeling emboldened by our banter.

"Disasters make for the best stories," he countered, leaning forward, his gaze earnest. "I mean, look at us! We went from being strangers to practically living together in less than a week. That's a rom-com in the making."

The thought of our whirlwind romance made me smile, but it also sparked a little flicker of fear. How fast was too fast? Just as I opened my mouth to respond, the shrill sound of my phone chimed again, interrupting our moment. This time, it was a text—a simple notification, but my heart raced as I saw it was from my brother.

"Need to talk. Can't do this anymore."

I frowned, glancing at Marco. "It's my brother. Something's wrong."

"What's going on?" he asked, his expression shifting from playful to serious in an instant.

"I don't know," I replied, frustration bubbling inside me. "He never texts me unless it's urgent."

"Want to step outside? We can talk while getting some fresh air," Marco suggested, standing up and offering me his hand.

I took it, feeling the warmth of his palm against mine as we stepped onto the small balcony that overlooked the quiet street below. The fresh morning air enveloped us, crisp and tinged with the scent of blooming flowers. I scrolled through my brother's message, my heart sinking further.

"Can you call him?" Marco asked, his voice gentle yet insistent.

I nodded, hesitating only a moment before dialing my brother's number. The ringing filled the silence between us, each tone echoing my mounting anxiety. When he finally answered, his voice was strained, and I felt a chill creep down my spine.

"Hey, it's me," I said, forcing a calmness I didn't feel. "What's wrong?"

"I can't do this anymore, Kay," he said, his voice barely above a whisper. "I'm sorry, but I need to come home."

"Home? What do you mean?" I asked, my pulse quickening. "You just started college, everything seemed fine."

"It's not," he admitted, and I could hear the break in his voice. "I feel so lost. I don't think I can keep pretending everything's okay when it's not. I... I'm struggling."

Panic surged within me, but I kept my voice steady. "You're not alone. We can figure this out together. Just give me a minute, okay? I'm here for you."

There was a pause, the weight of his silence heavy. "I don't think I can do this anymore. I need to come home and take a break from all of it. Please."

"Whatever you need, I'm here," I said, trying to soothe him, my mind racing with the implications. The uncertainty, the worry—it all coiled tightly around my heart, making it hard to breathe.

"Thanks, Kay. I'll explain everything when I get there. I just can't stay here," he replied, his voice breaking.

I ended the call, a sense of dread pooling in my stomach. "He wants to come home," I said, turning to Marco, who was watching me with concern etched across his features. "He's struggling with school, and I don't know how to help him."

"Hey," he said softly, stepping closer and resting his hands on my shoulders, grounding me. "You'll figure it out. You're stronger than you think, and you've got me, remember?"

His words wrapped around me like a lifeline, but the shadow of my brother's despair loomed over my thoughts. I wanted to help him, to support him, but the weight of his struggles felt heavy on my chest.

"Maybe I should go back home with him," I said, my voice trembling slightly. "He might need me there more than I realize."

"Are you sure that's what you want?" Marco asked, his brow furrowing. "I mean, we just had this amazing moment, and now—"

"I know! I just..." I sighed, frustration bubbling to the surface. "I can't just ignore him. What if he really needs me? What if I'm his only lifeline right now?"

"Then you should go," he said, his tone unwavering. "But don't forget what you have here, too. You're not obligated to carry everyone else's burdens alone, especially not at the cost of your own happiness."

I stared into his eyes, searching for the right words, my emotions swirling like the autumn leaves that danced in the breeze. "I just don't know how to balance it all, Marco. My family, my life, us—"

Before I could finish, the distant sound of sirens echoed through the street, cutting through the air like a knife. My stomach dropped as I turned to look, and my heart raced when I saw a police car pulling up across the street, lights flashing.

"What's going on?" Marco asked, his voice rising with concern as we moved to the railing for a better view.

I squinted, trying to see what was happening. A group of people had gathered, murmuring among themselves, pointing toward a building down the block. The sight made my pulse quicken, and an uneasy feeling settled in my gut.

"I don't know," I said, anxiety tightening my chest. "It doesn't look good."

As I watched the officers step out, my heart began to race even faster. My brother had mentioned something about a student from his school recently going missing. Could this be related? The questions tumbled through my mind like a raging river, each one more disconcerting than the last.

Just then, Marco's phone buzzed in his pocket. He pulled it out and glanced at the screen, his expression shifting from concern to shock. "It's my mom," he said, frowning. "I've got to take this."

"Okay," I replied, feeling a knot form in my stomach as I watched him step away, anxiety creeping back in as I turned my attention back to the scene unfolding below.

But before I could even process the sight of flashing lights, my own phone buzzed again. I glanced down, my heart plummeting as I read the name flashing across the screen.

It was my mother.

Taking a deep breath, I swiped to answer, fully expecting the usual lecture about life plans and timelines. But the moment I heard her voice, something felt off.

"Kay, you need to come home. Right now," she said, her tone urgent, almost frantic.

"Mom, what's wrong?" I asked, my pulse racing, the world around me fading into a blur.

"I can't explain everything over the phone. Just... please, you need to come home," she insisted, and the panic in her voice sent a chill down my spine.

"I'll be there," I said, already moving toward the door. But as I glanced back at Marco, the urgency in my mother's voice echoed ominously in my mind, leaving a sense of foreboding hanging in the air.

The cliff's edge loomed closer, and I felt the ground beneath me shifting, threatening to unravel everything I thought I knew.

Chapter 10: A Taste of Tradition

The morning sun bathed the market in a golden hue, casting playful shadows as I weaved through the stalls, my fingers brushing against the rough wooden surfaces, the scent of freshly baked bread mingling with the sweet notes of honey and the sharp tang of homemade pickles. I turned to Marco, who was kneeling in front of a stall, examining a mound of shiny, red cherries as if they held the secrets of the universe. "What do you think?" I asked, nudging him gently. "Do you think they'll taste as good as they look?"

He looked up, his face lighting up with that irresistible smile that made my knees weak. "Only one way to find out." His voice, low and playful, had a way of wrapping around me like a soft blanket. He picked one cherry and offered it to me, our fingers brushing together, sending a jolt of warmth through my body. I bit into the fruit, its sweetness exploding in my mouth, and I closed my eyes momentarily, relishing the burst of flavor. "Oh wow, that's like summer in a bite!" I exclaimed, and Marco chuckled, a deep, warm sound that made my heart race.

"Summer in a bite sounds like a good name for a restaurant," he mused, clearly lost in thought. "Or maybe a cocktail." He straightened, and his gaze shifted to the vibrant colors around us, as if he were seeing the world anew through my eyes. The farmers' market was alive with laughter and chatter, the sound of children playing in the background mingling with the soft strumming of a guitar nearby. I spotted a couple dancing to the music, their movements carefree, and I felt an unexpected flutter in my chest—a longing for that same lightness in my own life.

"Are you planning on opening a restaurant someday?" I asked, half-jokingly. "Because I'd happily be your sous chef."

He laughed, a sound so rich and warm it felt like a sunbeam piercing through the cool morning air. "I don't know about that," he replied, shaking his head. "I think I'd need someone with a bit more skill than I have. I mostly just throw things together and hope for the best."

"Then you're doing a hell of a job," I said, nudging him playfully with my shoulder. "I've never tasted anything like those stuffed peppers you made last week."

His cheeks flushed, and he waved a hand dismissively, but I could tell he was pleased. "Well, maybe I'll take you up on that sous chef offer," he said, his eyes sparkling with mischief. "As long as you promise to chop things properly and not make a mess."

"Deal!" I grinned, feeling a warmth that reached deep into my chest. These moments—simple, unguarded—had started to fill the spaces in my life I didn't even realize were empty. They reminded me of why I had fallen for him; it was his genuine spirit, his passion for food, and the way he made me feel—alive, vibrant, and entirely myself.

As we strolled further, we reached the cheese stall, where a burly man with a bushy beard offered us samples of a sharp, tangy goat cheese. Marco leaned in, his eyes widening in delight as he tasted it. "This is incredible!" he exclaimed, turning to me with a look of pure joy. "You have to try it."

I hesitated. I loved cheese, but I wasn't sure if I was ready for the sharpness. I watched him, though, that look of unadulterated enthusiasm was infectious. I took a slice and popped it in my mouth, and the flavor hit me—bold, tangy, and somehow comforting all at once. "Okay, that's amazing," I admitted, nodding enthusiastically. "What do you think about mixing it with the heirloom tomatoes? A little basil and balsamic glaze, and we've got a summer salad that'll knock anyone's socks off."

"Now you're talking!" Marco said, his eyes gleaming with inspiration. "We could even grill the tomatoes a bit. I can see it now—smoky, tangy, with a touch of sweetness."

Our conversation flowed easily, and it felt so natural, like we were two parts of a whole. As we moved from stall to stall, the atmosphere around us pulsed with life—friends meeting, families sharing laughter, the playful bickering between vendors and customers. Each interaction reminded me of a quilt made of small, vibrant patches; together, they formed something beautiful and warm.

Yet, amid the vibrant market and our lighthearted banter, a shadow of doubt crept in. It was subtle but persistent, like a fly buzzing around a sunny picnic. What if I got too attached? What if this slice of happiness crumbled under the weight of reality? I glanced at Marco as he admired a vibrant bouquet of sunflowers, his eyes wide with appreciation. Could I risk losing this feeling, this connection?

Before I could spiral further into my thoughts, Marco turned to me, his expression suddenly serious. "You know, I really enjoy these moments with you," he said, his tone gentle, yet heavy with unspoken meaning. "I feel like I can be myself around you."

My heart stuttered for a moment, caught between the vulnerability of his admission and my own swirling fears. I wanted to say something profound, something that would assure him of my feelings, but all that came out was a soft, "Me too."

We stood there, surrounded by the vibrant chaos of the market, the laughter and music swirling around us like a warm embrace. In that moment, everything else faded away, and it was just the two of us—lost in the colors, the scents, and the unspoken possibilities stretching out before us like the infinite blue sky above.

The rhythm of laughter and chatter filled the air, and the sun continued its ascent, casting a warm glow over the bustling market. I took a moment to observe Marco as he chatted animatedly with the cheese vendor, his hands animatedly gesturing while he detailed the perfect pairing of cheese with a rich Merlot. I couldn't help but marvel at how effortlessly he drew people in. His enthusiasm was like a flame, brightening everything around him, and in that moment, he was nothing short of captivating. The vendor nodded, clearly taken by Marco's passion, and I felt a swell of pride.

"Do you think they'll ever let you host a tasting here?" I teased, sidling up next to him. "You'd put half these vendors out of business with your cheese wisdom."

He shot me a mock-serious look, his brow furrowed as he adjusted an imaginary pair of glasses. "Ah, yes. Let me put on my sommelier hat. Pair the goat cheese with an oak-aged cabernet—an absolute delight!" His voice dropped to a conspiratorial whisper, "And a dash of panache, of course."

I couldn't hold back a laugh. "Panache? Now that's something I could get behind." I watched as he threw an arm around my shoulder, pulling me close, the warmth of his presence wrapping around me like a comforting blanket. Just then, a child nearby stumbled, her strawberry basket spilling its contents onto the ground. Marco's grip tightened on my shoulder, and without hesitation, he released me to help the little girl gather her precious fruit.

I watched as he knelt beside her, picking up the strawberries and placing them back in the basket, his gentle smile coaxing a giggle from her. There was something beautiful about how he interacted with people, the way he took the time to connect, even in such a small moment. I felt an unfamiliar warmth pooling in my chest—a mixture of admiration and a flutter of something deeper.

"Here you go!" he said, handing her the last berry, his eyes crinkling with genuine joy. The girl beamed up at him, her smile radiant, and it struck me how naturally he elicited happiness in others. "Remember, don't forget to wash them before you eat," he added playfully, straightening up.

"Good advice!" I chimed in as he returned to my side, grinning ear to ear. "Not all heroes wear capes, you know."

"Some wear aprons," he said, gesturing to the nearby food stall that specialized in artisan sandwiches. "Speaking of which, I could definitely go for one of those infamous Caprese sandwiches right about now."

My stomach grumbled in agreement, and I glanced at the stall, its colorful display of fresh bread, mozzarella, and basil promising something delightful. "Lead the way, chef," I quipped, and he dramatically gestured for me to follow, striding toward the stall as if he were the star of a culinary show.

Once we reached the sandwich stand, I was struck by the array of ingredients displayed like a painter's palette. A handsome man behind the counter wore a smile that could charm the socks off anyone, expertly assembling sandwiches as he tossed ingredients around with the flair of a seasoned chef.

"What can I get you two lovebirds?" he asked, winking as he eyed us. Marco, unperturbed, leaned over the counter with a conspiratorial grin.

"Two Caprese sandwiches, please. And don't hold back on the balsamic glaze. It's the secret to love, you know."

The vendor laughed, and I raised an eyebrow at Marco. "I didn't know you were such an expert on love," I teased, folding my arms. "Should I be taking notes?"

"Absolutely," he replied, his eyes sparkling with mischief. "First note: always add extra balsamic. It makes everything better, even relationships."

As we waited for our sandwiches, the vendor continued to banter, and I couldn't help but appreciate the effortless rhythm of their conversation. It was easy to lose myself in this moment, wrapped in the simplicity of good food and laughter.

After what felt like an eternity, our sandwiches were ready, the scent alone making my mouth water. We settled on a nearby bench, the wood warm beneath us as we unwrapped our meals, revealing layers of fresh mozzarella, basil, and the juicy slices of tomato that seemed to glisten under the sun. Marco took a hearty bite, and I watched, curious about his reaction.

"Oh, wow," he exclaimed, his eyes widening in surprise. "This is like a hug in sandwich form!" He held it up in a toast, and I clinked mine against his, grinning at the absurdity of it all. "To hugs, sandwiches, and summer!"

"To all of the above!" I laughed, biting into my own creation. The flavors danced on my tongue, and I couldn't help but close my eyes for a moment, letting the taste transport me. "This is incredible!"

As we savored our meal, a sudden flash of a memory drifted through my mind—Marco and I on a similar bench in a different city, our laughter echoing through the streets as we shared a ridiculous dessert that was far too sweet for two adults. It felt as though the universe was pulling threads together, weaving our moments into something larger.

But then, amidst the joy, I felt that familiar tug of uncertainty. I swallowed hard, trying to push the thought aside, but it was there, lurking like a shadow. "Hey, Marco," I began, my voice a touch hesitant. "What do you think makes a good relationship?"

He paused, the sandwich halfway to his mouth, and his expression turned serious. "Honestly? I think it's about finding someone you can be completely yourself around. Someone who challenges you but also makes you laugh." His gaze held mine, piercing and earnest, making my heart race. "And, of course, sharing food is key. It creates this bond, you know?"

"Bonding over food?" I echoed, a playful smirk on my lips. "So, you're saying if I burnt dinner, you'd still love me?"

He chuckled, the tension breaking, and I could see the warmth in his eyes again. "Absolutely! Just think of it as a culinary adventure. I'd definitely be there to help you clean up the mess."

We both laughed, but I felt an undercurrent of seriousness in his words. It was an unspoken promise wrapped in jest, and I found myself clinging to it. But as the laughter faded, a weight settled in the pit of my stomach, as if the universe was preparing to toss us an unexpected curveball.

The atmosphere around us shifted slightly, a tension I couldn't quite place creeping into the air. A woman, elegantly dressed with an air of authority, approached us, her eyes scanning our table with an intensity that felt unsettling. My stomach dropped as I recognized her—a figure from Marco's past. The kind that often carried the scent of unresolved emotions.

"Marco?" she said, her voice smooth yet firm. My heart pounded as I glanced at him, searching for clues in his expression, which shifted from relaxed to guarded in a heartbeat.

Marco's expression shifted, a slight furrow forming between his brows as the woman approached us. Her polished appearance and confident stride made her stand out like a beacon against the rustic backdrop of the farmers' market. I could feel the atmosphere crackle with unspoken tension, an electric charge that turned the vibrant colors around us into a dull haze.

"Marco?" she said again, her tone firm but laced with an undertone of something I couldn't quite place. I watched as his smile faded, replaced by a look of apprehension that knotted my stomach. "It's been a while."

"Yeah, it has," he replied, his voice low and steady, but I could hear the barely concealed edge of surprise in it. "What brings you here?"

Her gaze flicked to me, assessing, and for a moment, I felt like a child caught eavesdropping on a conversation between adults. "I was just passing through," she said, her eyes narrowing slightly as she registered my presence. "But I'm glad to see you're doing well."

The unease washed over me like cold water, and I instinctively leaned in closer to Marco, seeking comfort in his presence. The warmth that had enveloped us moments before was now replaced by an uncomfortable chill. I studied her closely, trying to decipher the unspoken history that lingered in the air between them.

Marco cleared his throat, trying to shift the focus. "What about you? Still working at the magazine?" He was trying so hard to keep his tone light, but the undercurrent of tension was palpable.

"Yes, still there," she replied, her lips twisting into a small smile that felt more like a smirk. "I actually came across some exciting stories that I thought you might be interested in. You know, if you're still writing."

"I've been a bit busy lately," he said, the corner of his mouth twitching, but it was a half-hearted attempt at levity. The way her eyes sparkled with something unnameable sent a shiver down my spine.

"You could say that," I interjected, attempting to lighten the mood. "He's too busy saving the world one sandwich at a time." I shot him a teasing grin, but it felt forced, my nerves simmering just below the surface.

The woman's gaze flicked back to me, her expression shifting into something inscrutable. "Is that so?" she asked, her tone as sweet as the honey being sold a few stalls down, but I sensed the sting lurking just beneath. "What's your name?"

"Ella," I said, forcing the word out, my heart pounding in my chest. "And you are?"

"Lila," she replied, a hint of superiority creeping into her voice. "Nice to meet you." But the way she said it felt anything but sincere, and the tension hung in the air like a thick fog.

Marco shifted uncomfortably, his gaze darting between us as if trying to navigate a minefield. "Lila and I go way back," he said, attempting to diffuse the situation. "We were... friends in college."

The word "friends" hung awkwardly in the air, and I felt my stomach churn. I studied him closely, searching for signs of discomfort, but he was a master at masking his emotions. Lila, however, wasn't so subtle. There was a glimmer in her eye that hinted at deeper layers of their history, and I couldn't help but wonder what secrets lay beneath her polished surface.

"Ah, college friends," I echoed, a hint of sarcasm slipping into my voice. "Always an interesting dynamic, aren't they?" I glanced at Marco, trying to gauge his reaction. He caught my eye, his expression pleading for me to keep it light, but it was hard to ignore the tension that swirled between the three of us.

"Anyway, I should get going," Lila said, her gaze lingering on Marco a moment too long. "Just wanted to say hi. Let's catch up sometime?"

"Sure," Marco said, his voice strained, as if the word was a reluctant promise.

Lila smiled—an expression that held too much, too many unsaid things—and turned to leave. As she walked away, the space between us felt heavy, laden with questions I was too scared to voice.

"Wow," I said, trying to catch my breath as I turned to Marco. "What was that about?"

He rubbed the back of his neck, a gesture I recognized as a sign of his discomfort. "She's... someone from my past. We had a brief thing back in college."

"Brief?" I asked, arching an eyebrow. "That looked a little more than just a casual fling."

"It was complicated," he said, his tone clipped, as if he was trying to shut down the conversation before it could spiral.

"Complicated how?" I pressed, feeling the heat rise in my cheeks. "Because right now it looks like she still has a hold on you."

Marco sighed, looking at me with an expression that mixed frustration and sincerity. "It wasn't like that. We were young and stupid, and it ended for a reason. I moved on."

"Did you?" I challenged, crossing my arms as I leaned back, trying to mask the swell of insecurity. The brightness of the market began to dim, the cheerful colors transforming into an ominous backdrop.

"I did," he insisted, his voice steady but tinged with urgency. "Ella, you have to believe me. You mean something to me. This—" he gestured around us, "this is real."

But as he spoke, the doubt slithered in, and my heart raced in response. "How can I believe that when she looks at you like that? Like you're her unfinished business?"

Marco took a step closer, his eyes earnest, almost pleading. "That's not what I want. I'm here with you. I want to build something with you."

I studied his expression, searching for truth in the shadows of uncertainty. "Then why does it feel like we just got tangled in something I wasn't prepared for?"

Just then, my phone buzzed in my pocket, slicing through the heavy atmosphere like a knife. I fished it out, glancing at the screen, and my heart dropped. The message was from my sister, and the words blurred momentarily as a chill shot through me: "Ella, I need you. It's urgent."

"Is everything okay?" Marco asked, concern flooding his voice as he noticed my sudden shift in demeanor.

"I—" I started, my heart pounding, feeling the weight of the world press down on my chest. I couldn't shake the feeling that something was about to change, something I couldn't control. "I have to go."

"Now?" he asked, a flash of confusion on his face. "Can't it wait?"

I shook my head, the urgency in my sister's message igniting a fierce instinct within me. "I don't know what's going on, but it feels serious."

"Let me come with you," Marco said, stepping closer, his hand reaching out to grasp my arm.

"No," I replied, pulling away gently. "I need to handle this. I'll be back."

The words slipped from my lips, but even as I said them, I felt the knot in my stomach tighten. I turned and walked away, my heart racing not just from the impending sense of dread but also from the unresolved tension that lingered between us.

As I stepped into the throng of the market, the colors blurred, and the laughter faded into an echo. Behind me, I could feel Marco's gaze, a mix of concern and something else—something deeper that I couldn't yet grasp.

And as I hurried away, I couldn't shake the feeling that I was leaving behind more than just a simple afternoon at the market; I was stepping into a storm that would change everything.

Chapter 11: Unraveled Threads

The café was a sanctuary of soft murmurs and the heady aroma of freshly brewed coffee, a world that felt miles away from the chaos of my thoughts. Sunlight spilled through the windows, draping everything in a golden hue, transforming ordinary pastries into delectable treasures. I had nestled into my usual spot, a weathered wooden table that bore the scars of countless writers before me. The clattering of cups and the gentle hissing of the espresso machine created a symphony that usually inspired my words. Today, however, it felt like a dissonant chord, the pleasant sounds wrapping around me like a noose.

As I tapped away on my laptop, I couldn't shake off the words from the table beside me. Two women were engaged in animated conversation, their voices rising and falling like the waves of an uncertain tide. They discussed a food critic whose glowing reviews had led me to many a memorable meal, but now those memories felt tainted. He had been outed for leveraging his influence, using his reviews as bargaining chips, shaking down restaurants for exclusive perks. My heart raced as their words echoed in my mind, each one striking like a cold gust of wind. Had I been unwittingly stepping onto the same path?

I remembered my last review of Marco's restaurant, where I had poured my heart into praising not just the food but the man behind it. The way he had presented the dish, his passion bubbling over like the sauce simmering on the stove, had been captivating. I had written about his late-night inspirations and the early morning grind, every detail soaked in the tenderness that had sprung up like wildflowers in my heart. But as I sat there, the reality of that affection tightened around my chest. Was I, too, indulging in a self-serving agenda, allowing my feelings to blur the lines between objective critique and personal favoritism?

The barista, a friendly soul with ink-stained fingers and a bright smile, approached my table, her tray wobbling under the weight of my favorite caramel macchiato. "You look like you're wrestling with something fierce today," she said, setting the drink down with a practiced ease. I glanced up, attempting to muster a smile, but it fell short, a mere shadow of the joy I usually found in this place.

"Just pondering life and its many delicious complexities," I replied, the words spilling out more than I intended. She raised an eyebrow, a playful glint in her eyes. "Well, don't let it get too complicated. You know, coffee is great for clarity, or at least for keeping the caffeine jitters at bay."

"Or for making one's heart race out of control?" I quipped back, earning a laugh from her. It felt good, that momentary release, yet the laughter faded like the steam curling from my cup, leaving behind the weight of my thoughts.

I took a sip, letting the sweetness wash over my tongue, but even the comforting warmth couldn't stave off the chill of uncertainty. As I refocused on my screen, the cursor blinked back at me, a reminder that I needed to write something meaningful. But the words felt like unspooled yarn, tangled and impossible to weave back together. I closed my eyes, inhaling the scent of roasted beans mixed with cinnamon, attempting to ground myself.

The sound of the doorbell chimed, pulling me from my reverie. I opened my eyes just as Marco stepped inside, his presence illuminating the room. He looked effortlessly charming, his hair a tousled mess that somehow fit him perfectly, a few strands falling across his forehead. His eyes, a rich brown, scanned the café until they found me, and a smile broke across his face like sunlight breaking through the clouds. I felt the heat rise in my cheeks, a warmth that battled against the cold dread that had nestled in my stomach.

"Fancy seeing you here," he said, making his way over, a relaxed confidence in his stride. "What's got you so deep in thought? Planning your next scathing review?"

"Hardly," I replied, my tone laced with mock seriousness. "More like contemplating the nature of integrity in the culinary world. You know, the usual light reading."

He laughed, a sound that danced between us, warming the chill that had settled around my heart. "I've never been accused of integrity myself. I just make food and hope people enjoy it. That's all I can control, right?" His words hung in the air, light yet heavy with implications.

"Control is an illusion," I mused, not quite believing the wisdom of my own words. "But we all want to hold onto it, don't we?"

Marco's gaze shifted, an understanding passing between us, a flicker of something deeper. I wanted to dive into that current, to explore the implications of our conversation, but my mind swirled back to the women's conversation. Would I ever be able to separate my feelings from my critiques? What if my next review turned into nothing more than a love letter, a piece drenched in bias rather than the honest portrayal I prided myself on?

The café hummed around us, a vibrant backdrop to the brewing storm within me. Marco leaned in slightly, his smile turning conspiratorial. "So, tell me, if you could review any meal right now, what would it be?"

His question caught me off guard. I glanced around, the vibrant pastries and steaming plates of brunch flooding my senses with possibility. "I'd say a croissant from here paired with the perfect cup of coffee. Simple, but executed flawlessly."

"An excellent choice," he replied, a playful glint in his eye. "You know, I make a mean croissant. Maybe I should bring you one sometime. Just to ensure your review is entirely accurate, of course."

The banter flowed, but beneath it lay the tension of unspoken truths. I could feel the weight of my revelations, the threads of my life slowly unraveling, and I wondered if I had the courage to weave them back together before they completely fell apart. As we laughed and shared stories, the stakes felt higher than ever. The delicious warmth of connection battled against the gnawing fear of what it could all mean, and I found myself suspended in that moment, longing for clarity yet terrified of the answers that might come to light.

The conversation with Marco danced around us, a lighthearted veneer covering the deeper, more complicated emotions simmering beneath the surface. His laughter rang like a bell, slicing through my spiraling thoughts, and I wondered if he noticed the tension in my smile. We joked about the absurdities of the food industry—how a truffle oil shortage could cause a meltdown of epic proportions among chefs, or how a single bad review could send a restaurant spiraling into oblivion. But with each quip, my mind was a chaotic jumble, trying to distinguish between genuine camaraderie and the unsettling fear that I might become just another player in this disingenuous game.

"Okay, I'll admit it," Marco said, a playful glint in his eye. "I might have leveraged my culinary talents for the sake of free meals on occasion. But what can I say? I'm a starving artist, and free food is my muse." He leaned back, arms crossed, feigning an air of dramatic seriousness that made me laugh despite myself.

"And here I thought chefs were supposed to be above all that," I shot back, eyes twinkling. "How the mighty have fallen!"

"Hey, I'm just saying, a well-placed compliment can go a long way—especially when there's a lobster bisque involved," he countered, a conspiratorial smirk playing on his lips. I couldn't help but admire how effortlessly he turned a serious topic into playful banter. Yet, beneath the laughter, the question loomed larger: What did I truly believe in anymore?

As I sipped my macchiato, I caught sight of the two women at the neighboring table, still animatedly discussing the food critic. Their opinions on integrity and ethics floated over to us like unwelcome smoke, wrapping around my thoughts. It became harder to dismiss my growing doubts. What if I was so wrapped up in my feelings for Marco that I couldn't see my own biases? What if, in my pursuit of love, I was sacrificing my journalistic honesty?

The door swung open again, and a gust of autumn air rushed in, stirring the aromas of the café. A familiar face caught my eye: Judith, my longtime mentor and a fierce advocate for ethical reporting in the culinary world. She strode in with her usual flair, her silver hair catching the light, a sharp scarf tied around her neck like a badge of honor. Her gaze zeroed in on me, and I felt an involuntary wave of anxiety crest within me.

"Ah, if it isn't my favorite critic!" she called, her voice rich and full of authority. I offered a wave, my stomach flipping as she approached. Marco's eyes flickered with curiosity, and I could feel the unspoken questions building between us. Judith was a force of nature, and her straightforward approach could cut through my clouded thoughts like a hot knife through butter.

"Judith! What brings you here?" I asked, desperately trying to maintain an air of casualness.

"Just wrapping up a meeting with a client," she said, sliding into the chair beside me with practiced ease. "And I couldn't resist the siren call of a good espresso." Her gaze shifted to Marco, a discerning glint in her eye. "And who might this be?"

"Marco," he said, extending a hand, his easy charm palpable. "I'm the one responsible for getting her hooked on lobster bisque and late-night kitchen escapades."

"I see," Judith replied, her tone shifting slightly, an almost imperceptible glimmer of intrigue. "You've made quite an impression, then. Just be careful—she's a fierce one, our Bella."

The way she said my name made me cringe slightly, the weight of her expectations settling on my shoulders. I had fought long and hard to earn my place in this world, yet I felt myself teetering on the edge of a precipice. Marco turned to me, his expression shifting from playful to serious. "Is that so? You must have some wild stories up your sleeve, then."

"Oh, plenty," I replied, my voice slightly shaky. "But they're mostly about misadventures in the kitchen and the occasional disastrous review." I tried to lighten the mood, but I could feel Judith's keen eyes boring into me, as if she could sense my internal turmoil.

"Speaking of reviews," Judith said, her tone growing serious, "I hope you're being cautious, Bella. The last thing this industry needs is another critic embroiled in controversy." Her words wrapped around me, tightening like a vise. I forced a smile, but inside, my heart raced. The women's conversation echoed in my mind, feeding into my anxiety.

"I'm always cautious," I said, though my voice felt unsteady. "You know me—I believe in integrity." But even as I said it, I couldn't shake the gnawing doubt. What if I wasn't living up to that promise? What if my affection for Marco had already compromised my values?

Judith's gaze softened, sensing the turmoil beneath my bravado. "Just remember, Bella, it's essential to hold onto your principles. The moment you start letting personal feelings dictate your work is the moment you lose credibility."

Her words landed like a weight, anchoring me to the moment. I had built my reputation on honesty and transparency, yet here I was, teetering dangerously close to the edge of a moral abyss. I felt the urge to push back, to argue that feelings and criticism could coexist. But the truth was, I was scared. Scared that the threads of my carefully woven life were unraveling, and I might not be able to stitch them back together.

The café buzzed around us, but inside my mind, the noise grew louder, drowning out the chatter. I forced a smile, trying to shake off the weight of my thoughts, but the doubt hung heavily over me. I glanced at Marco, who was deep in conversation with Judith, laughter spilling from his lips, oblivious to the turmoil raging inside me.

"Bella?" His voice broke through the fog, pulling me back into the present. "You okay?"

"Yeah, just—thinking," I replied, my voice barely above a whisper. I caught Judith's watchful gaze, her expression a mixture of concern and expectation. "You two continue; I'll be right back."

As I excused myself, I slipped away to the restroom, needing a moment to collect my thoughts. The fluorescent lights buzzed overhead, stark against the warmth of the café. I splashed water on my face, the coolness shocking me back to reality. Staring into the mirror, I questioned the reflection staring back at me.

Who was I becoming? Was my heart leading me astray, or was it simply guiding me to a more profound understanding of what I truly valued? I felt like a jigsaw puzzle missing vital pieces, and I knew I had to confront the chaos within me before it consumed everything I had built.

Taking a deep breath, I stepped back into the café, my resolve solidifying. I was determined to find clarity, to reclaim my integrity. No matter how tangled the threads became, I needed to weave them back together. My heart raced with the anticipation of what lay ahead, and I resolved that no matter the outcome, I would face it head-on, ready to embrace whatever truths awaited me.

Emerging from the restroom, I took a moment to gather myself, pushing aside the swirling thoughts that threatened to consume me. The café felt alive, its walls buzzing with laughter, clinking cups, and the aromatic perfume of pastries mingling with coffee. I could feel the weight of Judith's expectations still hanging in the air, and the ease with which Marco and she engaged only added to my unease. I wanted to join their laughter, but a part of me felt tethered to the edge of a precipice, my heart thrumming in a disjointed rhythm.

"Everything alright?" Marco asked as I slipped back into the chair across from him, his brow furrowed with concern. "You disappeared like a soufflé in a too-warm oven."

"Just a bit of a reality check," I said, forcing a grin that didn't quite reach my eyes. "You know how it is—sometimes the truth is a bit too...raw."

"Raw, huh?" He leaned in, eyes twinkling. "Is this about your next review? Because if it is, I can help. I've got a killer recipe for a five-star lobster bisque that might just make the cut."

"Oh, you'd like that, wouldn't you? Just a delicious distraction while I wallow in my existential crisis." I shot back, my tone playful but laced with honesty. He paused, his expression shifting as if he could see through my facade.

"Hey, we all go through those moments. What's the worst that could happen? You find out your culinary crush isn't who you thought he was?" His voice dropped, sincerity threading through his words. "Or maybe you find out he's even better?"

The way he said it made my stomach twist in a delightful, terrifying knot. Did he suspect how deep my feelings for him ran? The tension between us crackled, thickening the air, and I found myself wanting to bridge that gap. Yet, the fear of complicating everything held me back. I was grappling with my integrity, and entangling my emotions with Marco's felt like navigating a minefield.

Judith interjected, her sharp voice cutting through the haze. "It's not just about culinary integrity, Bella. It's about who you want to be in this chaotic world. Are you comfortable blending personal feelings with professional critiques?"

Her probing gaze bore into me like a spotlight, forcing me to confront my wavering convictions. "I don't know," I admitted, my voice barely a whisper. "I want to be authentic, but what if my authenticity gets muddied by my feelings?"

"Then maybe it's time to examine those feelings," Judith replied, her tone even but firm. "What's so wrong about being in love with a chef? Or have you fooled yourself into thinking it's something to be ashamed of?"

"Being in love with a chef isn't the issue," I shot back, the words spilling out before I could filter them. "It's about whether I can separate that love from my work. What if I'm not as good as I think I am?"

"Then you find a way to be better," Judith said, her resolve unwavering. "But don't let fear hold you back from something wonderful. I've seen countless critics fall victim to their insecurities. Don't be one of them."

Marco watched us, a mixture of confusion and intrigue etched on his face. "Okay, I'm lost. Are we discussing food or feelings here? Because I can whip up a soufflé if you need a metaphor."

"Just trying to help Bella sort through her thoughts," Judith replied, a hint of exasperation in her tone. "It's a process, Marco. It's not as easy as a recipe."

He leaned back, crossing his arms, his expression shifting to one of playful defiance. "Fine, but if we're talking recipes, I'm bringing the wine."

"Not a bad idea," I said, chuckling despite the heaviness in my chest. The laughter came as a brief reprieve, but I could feel the conversation threading back toward deeper waters. I needed to change the subject, to redirect the energy back to something more lighthearted. "So, Marco, what's the craziest dish you've ever attempted?"

He grinned, a spark igniting in his eyes. "Oh, that would have to be my attempt at making a deconstructed tiramisu. Let's just say it didn't end well. The layers ended up in a heap that resembled more of a chocolate bomb than a dessert. It was like a sweet disaster, but at least it was tasty."

"Sounds like a metaphor for your love life," I teased, but my heart raced as I said it. "Messy, but delicious?"

"Touché," he replied, leaning forward, a newfound intensity flickering in his gaze. "But the trick is to keep trying until you get it right, Bella. Don't give up just because the first attempt fails."

His words hung in the air, a challenge wrapped in encouragement. As I contemplated the layers of meaning, Judith's phone buzzed, pulling her attention momentarily. She glanced at the screen, her brows knitting together, a hint of concern crossing her features.

"I need to take this," she said, rising from her seat, her tone shifting as she stepped away. "Just think about what we discussed, Bella. You're on the brink of something important."

Her departure left a void, the air thick with unsaid words. I turned to Marco, trying to regain my earlier lightness. "So, what's next on your culinary agenda? An epic dessert to redeem your tiramisu, perhaps?"

"Maybe I'll invite you to my kitchen for a crash course," he said, mischief dancing in his eyes. "You know, to keep you from becoming a food critic who can't separate love from critique."

I felt the heat rise in my cheeks, caught off guard by the invitation. "You really think I'd survive in your kitchen? I'd probably burn the place down."

"Then it'll be a memorable date," he quipped, his smile infectious, a teasing challenge that made my heart flutter with possibility.

But just as I was about to respond, Judith returned, her expression grave. "I need to go, Bella," she said, her voice low, almost urgent. "There's something I have to handle."

The abrupt change in her demeanor sent a chill through me. "What's wrong?" I asked, concern creeping into my voice.

"It's about the food critic—the one we were discussing earlier."

My pulse quickened. "What about him?"

Judith hesitated, her gaze darting around as if she were weighing the risk of her next words. "There's a chance he's connected to a larger issue in the industry. Something that could impact your next review. You need to be careful."

"What do you mean connected?" I pressed, heart racing at the implication of her words.

"There are whispers, Bella. I can't say much now, but this isn't just about bad reviews or ego. It's more dangerous than you think."

As the weight of her words settled in, I glanced at Marco, whose expression mirrored my concern. I felt the fabric of my reality shift, the threads of my personal and professional lives intertwining in a way that threatened to unravel everything I thought I understood.

"Wait," I said, my voice shaky. "You can't just drop that and walk away. What's really happening?"

Judith stepped closer, lowering her voice. "I'll reach out when I know more. But for now, trust your instincts. And whatever you do, keep your distance."

With that, she was gone, leaving me with a storm of uncertainty swirling in my chest. The air in the café felt charged, the laughter and chatter of patrons fading into a distant hum. I turned to Marco, who looked equally unsettled, his brow furrowed in concern.

"What just happened?" he asked, leaning forward, his intensity matching my own.

"I don't know," I admitted, feeling the ground beneath me shift. "But I think things are about to get a lot more complicated."

Just then, my phone buzzed on the table, breaking the tension like a glass shattering on tile. The screen lit up with a message that made my heart stop: We need to talk. It's about the critic. Meet me at the old pier at sunset.

The world outside faded into a blur as I stared at the message, realization dawning on me with the weight of a thousand possibilities. I had to decide. Did I follow this thread, even if it meant plunging into the unknown, or did I pull back and protect myself? The answer was hanging in the air like a ripe fruit, tempting yet dangerous, and I was left teetering on the edge, not knowing which way to fall.

Chapter 12: Sweet Temptations

The air inside "Sweet Temptations" wrapped around me like a warm hug, rich with the mingled scents of fresh pastries, butter, and a hint of vanilla that lingered in the corners like a fond memory. The sun streamed through the windows, illuminating the delicate dusting of powdered sugar that adorned the countless baked goods on display, each one more inviting than the last. I stepped further in, feeling the soft crunch of flour beneath my shoes—a testament to the bakery's relentless dedication to perfection. A bell tinkled above the door, its cheerful chime cutting through the ambient sounds of soft laughter and the rhythmic whir of the coffee grinder.

As I took in the scene, my heart raced with excitement. A chocolate croissant caught my eye, its flaky layers glistening as if begging to be devoured. I approached the counter, and as I lifted the pastry to my lips, the rich, buttery flavor melted like a dream on my tongue. Just as I settled into this moment of bliss, I caught a glimpse of a familiar figure behind the counter. There she was—Lily, my best friend from culinary school, her hair pulled back into a messy bun adorned with a few rebellious strands that framed her face. It was like a jolt of electricity surged through me, awakening a thousand memories of late-night study sessions and frantic baking marathons.

"Is that you? I almost didn't recognize you!" I exclaimed, my voice bubbling with excitement as I set my croissant down.

Lily looked up, her face lighting up with recognition. "Oh my gosh! It's been ages! You haven't changed a bit!" She came around the counter, enveloping me in a warm embrace that smelled faintly of cinnamon and sugar.

Pulling back, I marveled at her. "You look incredible! This place is amazing. I didn't know you were running it. It's like stepping into a pastry paradise!"

"Thank you! It's been a whirlwind since we graduated. I'm actually the head pastry chef here now. Can you believe it?" Her eyes sparkled with pride as she gestured around the bakery. "We've got everything from éclairs to tarts. What do you think?"

"I think you need to start feeding me pastries for old times' sake," I replied, grinning. "So, what's the secret? How did you land this gig?"

We settled into a corner booth, steaming mugs of coffee in hand, the clatter of dishes and laughter enveloping us in a comforting cocoon. As she recounted her journey from culinary school to this little haven of sugar and spice, I could see the fire in her eyes. "Honestly? I just kept trying. I applied for every position I could find, even the ones I didn't feel qualified for. Eventually, I landed an internship here, and the rest is history."

I nodded, savoring her words as they rekindled something deep within me. "That's so inspiring, Lily. I've been feeling a bit lost lately—like I've been wandering through a fog. Maybe I need to take some of your advice. Just dive in."

"Absolutely! You've always had the talent; you just need to believe in yourself. Remember that time we nearly burned down the kitchen trying to make those soufflés?" She laughed, and I joined in, the memory flooding back with clarity.

"How could I forget? I swear, the smoke alarm still has nightmares about that day," I chuckled, shaking my head. "We were so convinced we could make it work. What a disaster!"

"Right? But look at us now. You're going to figure it out; you just need a little nudge, a bit of sweetness." Her words hung in the air, a reminder that I wasn't alone in this culinary labyrinth.

As we reminisced, I couldn't shake the feeling of longing that tugged at my heart. I missed the thrill of creating something delicious, the sense of accomplishment that came with a perfectly baked pastry. But the shadows of self-doubt loomed large, whispering that perhaps I wasn't cut out for this anymore.

"Lily, what if I told you I've been thinking about opening my own place?" The words slipped out before I could catch them, igniting a flicker of hope in my chest.

"Are you serious? That's amazing! You absolutely should! What's stopping you?" Her enthusiasm was infectious, and I felt the familiar warmth of my old dreams flooding back.

I hesitated, the shadows creeping in. "I guess... I've just been afraid. What if I fail? What if it's not as great as I envision?"

"Failure is part of the process! You can't have sweet without a little sour, you know? Just look at me—I've messed up countless times, but that's how I learned!" She leaned in, her eyes narrowing playfully. "Besides, if it turns out to be a complete disaster, I'll help you eat your mistakes."

The laughter that bubbled up between us chased away the lingering doubts. I could almost see the outline of my dream kitchen, the vibrant colors, the joyful chaos of baking, all within reach if I just dared to grab it.

Just then, the door swung open, a gust of crisp autumn air sweeping in. I glanced over my shoulder to see a figure stepping inside—a tall man with tousled hair, his coat wrapped tightly against the chill. I felt an unexpected jolt, a sense of familiarity that twisted in my stomach.

"Didn't know they were serving eye candy today," Lily quipped, her gaze dancing between the man and me. I rolled my eyes, trying to dismiss the flutter in my chest. "No, really! That's Ethan, isn't it? From our culinary class?"

I turned back, catching his gaze as he scanned the room, a fleeting smile flickering across his lips when our eyes met. He approached the counter, a faint crease of surprise marking his brow as he recognized me.

"Is that you, Mia?" His voice, warm and rich, wrapped around me like a cozy blanket.

"Ethan! Wow, it's been forever!" I exclaimed, the weight of the past rushing back with the sweetness of nostalgia.

We exchanged pleasantries, and as he settled into the seat across from us, the conversation flowed with ease, weaving memories and laughter into a tapestry of shared experiences. Yet, beneath the surface, a current of tension hummed—both exhilarating and nerve-wracking. I had never anticipated that this day, meant to reinvigorate my passion for baking, would also spark feelings I thought were buried deep.

As Ethan recounted tales of his culinary adventures, I felt the spark of inspiration reignite within me, twinkling like the first stars of evening. Perhaps, just perhaps, this was the nudge I needed to step out of my shadows and embrace the sweet temptations life had to offer.

The scent of cinnamon mingled with the robust aroma of freshly brewed coffee, creating an atmosphere that felt like home. I watched as Lily moved behind the counter, her hands expertly assembling an intricate pastry, her focus razor-sharp. It was as if time had melted away, leaving us in a bubble of laughter and delicious pastries. Ethan settled into the booth across from us, and I could hardly concentrate on the buttery delights as I replayed our shared memories in my mind—our kitchen disasters, the late-night study sessions, and all those moments where we believed we were destined for greatness.

"So, Mia," Ethan began, leaning back comfortably, his presence magnetic. "What have you been up to since culinary school? Last I heard, you were planning to conquer the world of food blogging."

"Ah, yes," I chuckled, twirling my coffee cup between my fingers. "I guess you could say I'm more of a conqueror of procrastination at this point. The blog is still gathering dust, while I sort through the chaotic mess of life."

"Procrastination is a universal art form," Lily chimed in, smirking playfully. "We all have our masterpieces, right?"

"Right! Mine just happens to feature an alarming number of unfinished recipes and a backlog of half-hearted food photos." I grinned sheepishly. "But enough about my culinary disasters. What about you, Ethan? Any grand plans on the horizon?"

He shrugged, a half-smile playing at the corners of his mouth. "I'm working at a restaurant downtown. It's intense, but I love the pace. The pressure is exhilarating. You know, it's like one long, chaotic ballet where you're both the dancer and the stagehand."

"That sounds both thrilling and terrifying," I replied, captivated by the passion that flared in his eyes. "I can hardly keep my houseplants alive, let alone manage a full restaurant."

"They probably just need more love," he quipped, tilting his head to the side. "Or less water, depending on how you look at it. But hey, maybe you should give it a shot! I can see you dancing through flour and sugar with a flair of grace."

The banter flowed naturally between us, laughter bubbling up like a pot on the brink of boiling over. As we swapped stories, the initial awkwardness of our reunion faded, replaced by an easy camaraderie. The warmth of connection enveloped me, nudging the self-doubt to the periphery.

Lily glanced between us, a smirk playing on her lips. "You two are adorable. It's like watching a rom-com in real life. I half expect a montage of you baking cookies together or something."

I rolled my eyes, laughter spilling forth as I teased back, "And then we'd burn the cookies and cry over them while eating ice cream straight from the tub."

"Now that's a movie I'd watch," Ethan replied, his voice light with amusement. "But seriously, Mia, you should channel all this energy into something tangible. You've got talent. I remember the way you turned a simple cupcake into a culinary masterpiece."

"Back when I had the courage to try," I admitted, feeling a flicker of vulnerability seep through the jovial atmosphere. "It's been hard to shake off the feeling that I've lost my spark."

Lily reached across the table, her hand landing gently on mine. "You haven't lost it, Mia. It's just been buried under a pile of self-doubt. Just like these pastries," she said, gesturing to the display case filled with golden treats. "They don't start out perfect; they're crafted and shaped. Just like us."

Ethan nodded, a thoughtful look crossing his features. "And just like good dough, sometimes you need to knead through the resistance to rise." His words struck a chord deep within me, resonating with the truth I had been too afraid to confront.

Before I could respond, a loud crash erupted from the kitchen, drawing all our attention. The clatter of metal hitting the floor echoed through the bakery, causing a ripple of startled laughter. A frazzled baker stumbled out, flour covering her apron and a sheepish grin plastered across her face.

"Nothing to see here!" she exclaimed, waving her hands dramatically as if to dismiss the scene. "Just me trying to catch a rogue soufflé before it makes a break for freedom."

"Good luck with that!" Lily called out, laughter dancing in her voice.

I watched the scene unfold, the chaos a reminder that even in the most meticulously crafted environments, things could go awry. Life had its way of throwing curveballs—much like my attempt to reclaim my passion. It was messy, unpredictable, and sometimes downright ridiculous.

As the laughter subsided, I turned my attention back to Lily and Ethan. "Maybe you're right," I said, my voice firmer now. "Perhaps it's time for me to reclaim my place in the culinary world. To at least try."

"Absolutely!" Lily beamed, her enthusiasm infectious. "Start small. Maybe a pop-up shop or a special dessert menu? You could use this very bakery to showcase your creations."

"Lily's right," Ethan added, leaning forward, excitement glimmering in his eyes. "Your passion for food deserves a stage. It's just waiting for you to take that leap."

The idea hung in the air, tantalizing and terrifying all at once. Could I really do it? Could I bring my dreams back to life? I felt the weight of uncertainty pressing against me, yet there was a spark of hope flickering within.

"I'll think about it," I said slowly, allowing the idea to settle into my mind like the rich chocolate in my croissant. "But first, I need to taste more of what you've been creating, Lily. Let's get serious about dessert."

"Oh, you're in for a treat," she replied, her eyes gleaming mischievously. "Just you wait. I've got a new recipe I've been dying to test. It's an experiment, but I promise it'll be delicious—or at least entertaining."

As she disappeared into the kitchen, Ethan turned to me, a playful grin on his face. "So, how's it feel to be back in the game? Are you ready for some delicious experiments of your own?"

I chuckled, feeling lighter than I had in a long time. "Bring it on! If nothing else, I'll have a front-row seat to watch my dreams either rise beautifully or flop spectacularly. I'm hoping for the first option, of course."

With that, we settled into a comfortable rhythm of conversation, punctuated by Lily's joyful exclamations from the kitchen. I felt like I was standing on the edge of something beautiful and messy, the kind of adventure that called for both courage and humor. With each laugh, I felt a little more of my former self coming back to life—a reminder that while the path ahead might be uncertain, it was also ripe with possibilities, ready to be filled with sweet temptations.

The aroma of fresh pastries swirled around me, enveloping my senses in a sweet embrace as Lily reemerged from the kitchen, carrying a gleaming plate adorned with colorful treats. "Prepare yourself for a culinary adventure!" she announced, her enthusiasm bubbling over like the whipped cream she'd so expertly dolloped atop a tart.

As she set down the plate, my eyes widened in delight. Each pastry was a work of art: a golden lemon tart with a swirl of meringue that beckoned to be devoured, éclairs filled with rich chocolate cream, and delicate raspberry macarons glistening like little jewels. The vibrant colors contrasted beautifully against the rustic wooden table, a feast not only for the palate but for the eyes as well.

"Lily, this is stunning!" I exclaimed, feeling a childlike excitement bubbling inside me. "You've really outdone yourself this time."

She beamed, a flush of pride creeping into her cheeks. "I've been experimenting with flavors. It's all about balancing sweetness with a little tang—like life itself, right? Sometimes you need a little tartness to appreciate the sweet."

"Truer words have never been spoken," I said, picking up a macaron and savoring the explosion of flavor. The sweet almond shell crumbled delightfully, revealing a rich raspberry filling that danced across my taste buds. "This is perfection!"

Ethan, who had been watching us with an amused smile, leaned in, his voice teasing. "I see you're both food critics now. Should I be worried about my culinary reputation?"

"Only if you plan to cook with that questionable knife skills from culinary school," I shot back, a playful grin plastered on my face.

"Hey, I was young and reckless!" he protested, mockingly placing a hand over his heart. "I've evolved since then. My kitchen is a temple now, not a battlefield."

"I'm sure the smoke alarm has a different opinion," Lily interjected, stifling laughter.

The banter flowed freely as we indulged in the assortment of pastries, each bite igniting memories and laughter that wove us closer together. With each taste, I felt the initial flicker of self-doubt begin to melt away, replaced by a determination that surprised even me.

"Have you thought about what you want to create for your own menu?" Ethan asked, genuine curiosity etching his features.

"Not really," I admitted, my brow furrowing as I contemplated the question. "I guess I've been too busy wallowing in uncertainty to really dream."

"Then let's change that! Why not brainstorm some ideas right now?" Lily suggested, her eyes sparkling with excitement. "What flavors do you love? What makes your heart sing when you think about baking?"

I paused, allowing my mind to wander through the landscape of my culinary memories. "I've always loved the contrast of flavors. Maybe something that combines the warmth of spices with unexpected elements—like a cardamom-infused cake with a citrus glaze."

Ethan nodded, his expression thoughtful. "I can see that. Something that surprises and delights, much like you. You've always had a knack for mixing things up."

"Now I just need to find a way to make it work without burning my kitchen down," I said, chuckling as I imagined myself engulfed in flames, the fire department arriving to extinguish my culinary ambitions.

Just then, a sudden clang from the kitchen sliced through the cheerful chatter, sending a ripple of confusion through us. We turned in unison to see Lily's assistant, a young woman named Jenna, emerge from the kitchen, her face pale and wide-eyed.

"Lily! We have a problem!" she exclaimed, her voice barely above a whisper, but the urgency in her tone sent a shiver down my spine.

"What is it?" Lily's playful demeanor vanished in an instant, replaced by a sharp focus.

"There's a delivery issue with the chocolate shipment for the special event next week. The truck broke down, and they said it could be hours before we get more," Jenna said, panic threading through her words.

My stomach sank. "The chocolate shipment? That's crucial for your upcoming launch!"

Lily's brows knitted together in deep concentration. "We can't have that. What's the alternative?"

"We could use the chocolate we have, but it's not enough for the entire batch," Jenna replied, biting her lip anxiously.

A heavy silence filled the room, tension creeping into the atmosphere like a dense fog. My heart raced as I watched the gears turning in Lily's mind, and I suddenly felt the urge to step in. "What if I helped? I could work on a different dessert that doesn't require as much chocolate. Maybe a fruit tart or something with a rich vanilla base?"

Lily's gaze flickered with hope. "That could work. It would be a departure from what I had planned, but if you're willing to give it a shot, I'd be all in."

"Of course! Let's turn this into a challenge," I replied, adrenaline pumping through my veins. "Nothing like a little chaos to inspire creativity, right?"

"Exactly! And you know what they say about the best-laid plans," Ethan chimed in, his eyes sparkling with mischief. "They often lead to the most delicious accidents."

"Let's make some magic happen!" I declared, determination surging through me as I rose from my seat. The kitchen, once an intimidating realm of chaos, now seemed like a canvas waiting to be painted with flavors and colors.

Lily and Jenna rushed into the kitchen, their movements frantic yet purposeful, while I began rummaging through the ingredients, piecing together what I could. I felt an electric thrill coursing through me; it was exhilarating to dive back into the world of baking, the rhythm of measuring and mixing drawing me back to a place I had almost forgotten.

As I whipped the cream and mixed in fragrant vanilla, I could hear snippets of conversation from the kitchen, Lily directing Jenna with the precision of a seasoned conductor. With each passing moment, I felt my confidence swell, drowning out the lingering doubts that had clouded my mind for far too long.

Just as I finished assembling the tart, the door to the bakery swung open again, a gust of wind carrying in the crisp autumn air, mingling with the heady scents of vanilla and fruit. The familiar tinkle of the bell signaled the arrival of new customers, but this time, a chill ran down my spine as I noticed a figure lingering just outside the door.

A tall man, cloaked in shadow, stood watching us with a penetrating gaze. There was something about him—an unsettling aura that made the hairs on the back of my neck stand up.

"Who's that?" I whispered to Lily, who was still deep in conversation with Jenna.

"Not sure," she replied, her voice trailing off as she turned to look.

The man stepped forward, the light illuminating his face, and I felt a rush of recognition flood over me. I couldn't shake the feeling that this was someone from my past—someone whose presence could either ignite a spark or unleash a storm.

"What do you want?" I found myself asking, the tension thickening in the air, drawing everyone's attention to the stranger at the door.

His lips curled into a smirk, and in that moment, I knew nothing would be the same again.

Chapter 13: A Fork in the Road

The evening air wrapped around us like a warm embrace, carrying the fragrant notes of rosemary and garlic from the bustling kitchen of Il Sogno. Marco's laughter mingled with the soft strumming of a distant guitar, creating an ambiance that felt almost sacred. He sat across from me, his dark curls catching the glow of the candlelight, making him look impossibly charming. It was hard to believe that just a few months ago, I had been convinced that love was an overhyped fairy tale, best left to those brave enough to risk the heartbreak. Now, here I was, nervously stirring my wine and watching him talk animatedly about his latest culinary creation, a vibrant saffron risotto that danced on the tongue like a sunny day.

But as he described his plans for the upcoming culinary summit in San Francisco, a knot tightened in my stomach. This was it—the moment I'd been dreading. It wasn't just the idea of him traveling across the country; it was what that distance could mean for us. His dreams were as vast as the ocean, and I felt like a tiny boat tethered to a shore that could soon vanish into the waves. I had spent my entire life keeping people at arm's length, convinced that vulnerability was a trap. Now, with Marco, I was teetering on the edge of something beautiful but terrifying.

The stars overhead twinkled mischievously, their brilliance a stark contrast to the unease swirling in my chest. I cleared my throat, and the world around us faded. "So, San Francisco, huh?" I said, my voice a little unsteady. "That sounds... amazing."

He leaned in, a spark of excitement in his eyes. "It is! I've dreamed about this for years. It's a chance to show my work to some of the best chefs in the world. Can you imagine?"

I could see the enthusiasm radiating from him, his passion for food and the artistry of cooking spilling over like a pot left too long on the stove. It was infectious, and for a moment, I let myself bask in the glow of his excitement. But reality crept in like an unwelcome guest. "But what about us?"

His smile faltered slightly, and I could almost hear the gears turning in his mind. "Us? What do you mean?"

I took a deep breath, the weight of my words heavy on my tongue. "I mean... what happens when you're gone? You know, long-distance relationships can be tricky."

Marco's brow furrowed as he processed my concerns. "Are you worried I'll choose the summit over you?"

My heart raced at the thought. "It's not that simple. You have this incredible opportunity, and you deserve to chase it. But what if we can't make it work?"

He reached across the table, his fingers brushing against mine, grounding me in the moment. "Hey, it's just a few days. I'll be back before you know it. We can do this."

The sincerity in his voice was soothing, but my mind was a whirlwind of doubt. I had seen too many relationships crumble under the weight of distance and ambition, and I wasn't sure I had the strength to hold ours together if it came to that. "What if it turns into something more?" I asked, my voice trembling. "What if it becomes too easy to forget about each other?"

A shadow flickered across his face, a fleeting glimpse of something I couldn't quite place. "You really think that?"

"I don't know," I confessed, the vulnerability making my cheeks flush. "It's just... I've always kept my heart locked away, and now I feel like I'm standing at a cliff, staring down into the abyss. It's terrifying."

He leaned back, his expression shifting to one of contemplation. "You know, I get that. I've been there too. But love is a risk, isn't it? We can't predict the future, and we can't control everything. All we can do is hold on to what we have and trust it's enough."

His words hung between us like a promise, a delicate thread that tied our fates together. But the uncertainty remained, like a thick fog that refused to lift. "And what if it's not enough?" I asked, my voice barely above a whisper.

Marco sighed, his gaze steady and unwavering. "Then we'll figure it out together. But I don't want to walk away from what we have just because of a few miles. You mean too much to me."

A swell of emotion surged within me, filling the hollow spaces that my fears had carved out. "You really mean that?"

"More than you know," he said, squeezing my hand gently, the warmth of his touch sending a ripple of comfort through me.

The night wore on, the world around us slipping into the background as we navigated the landscape of our hearts. I wanted to believe him, to embrace the leap of faith he was offering, but the lingering doubts whispered insidiously at the edges of my mind. It felt like standing at a fork in the road, with one path leading toward the familiar comforts of my solitary life and the other toward a vibrant chaos that could either bring me joy or break me completely.

As we finished our dinner, the waiter brought out a decadent chocolate torte, rich and indulgent, a perfect symbol of the night. I watched as Marco savored each bite, the delight on his face lighting up the dimly lit restaurant. I wanted that joy for myself. I wanted to share it with him, but the specter of my fears loomed larger than the dessert itself.

"Hey," he said, breaking into my thoughts, "let's not dwell on the 'what-ifs' tonight. Let's enjoy this moment. We can talk more when the time comes."

I nodded, but my heart was still racing, caught between the sweetness of chocolate and the bitter taste of uncertainty.

The days after that fateful dinner at Il Sogno felt suspended in time, each sunrise greeted with the same gnawing anxiety that had gripped me under the stars. Marco's departure date loomed closer, the tension between us thickening like a well-reduced sauce. Our mornings began to shift; I found myself waking before the sun, the light creeping through the window like an unwelcome reminder of my tangled emotions. I could almost hear the clock ticking down the moments we had left together.

One Saturday morning, I decided to put my anxiety aside—at least for a few hours—and tried my hand at recreating Marco's saffron risotto. If I couldn't be near him, I could at least channel my thoughts into something productive, something that might even impress him. The kitchen quickly turned into a battleground of spices, broth simmering on the stove, and my courage wavering with each passing minute.

As I stood over the bubbling pot, I thought about how Marco had masterfully coaxed each flavor out of the ingredients, creating harmony where I felt only chaos. I stirred the rice, willing it to absorb the golden broth, but all I could think of was how every stir felt like a countdown. Each grain seemed to mock me, reminding me of how he would soon be showcasing his talents to the world while I remained here, battling my own insecurities.

Suddenly, the door swung open, and Marco strode in, his face flushed from the autumn chill. "What is that glorious smell?" he asked, dropping his bag by the entrance as if the world outside didn't exist. His eyes sparkled with intrigue, and I felt a mix of relief and dread wash over me. Relief, because he was here. Dread, because I knew I had to confront the questions swirling in my mind, like the steam rising from the pot.

"Just trying to channel my inner chef," I replied, a feeble attempt at humor as I attempted to remain nonchalant. "Thought I'd impress you with a little homemade saffron risotto."

Marco crossed the kitchen in a few quick strides, his eyes widening as he peered into the pot. "Homemade? You're brave. I should've known better than to underestimate you."

I feigned a smile, but my heart wasn't in it. "Brave or foolish, depending on how this turns out."

He leaned against the counter, arms crossed, a playful smirk dancing on his lips. "Or it could be a delicious masterpiece. Do you need me to step in and save the day?"

"Don't you dare," I shot back, my competitive streak flaring. "This is my moment. I can do this."

"Oh, I have no doubt," he said, the admiration in his voice warming my resolve. "But remember, cooking is as much about the love you put into it as the ingredients."

"Deep, Marco. Very deep. Is this one of those culinary mantras you picked up along your journey?"

"Absolutely. It's in my 'Cooking 101' book right next to 'Always keep your knives sharp and your heart sharper.'"

We laughed, and for a moment, the tension dissolved into the air, replaced by the familiar ease we shared. I could almost pretend that the upcoming summit wasn't looming like an ominous cloud. But as I stirred the risotto, the weight of reality settled back in. "So, about the summit..." I began, my voice quieter now.

He raised an eyebrow, the playful banter evaporating as he recognized the seriousness in my tone. "Are we really going to have this conversation while you're cooking?"

I nodded, my heart pounding. "Yes, because it's better than letting it hang between us like an uninvited guest."

"Fair enough. But I can't promise I'll be able to focus on your culinary genius if we dive into heavy topics."

"Priorities, Marco." I huffed, trying to keep my voice light despite the gravity of my thoughts. "I just need to know how you see us fitting into all of this."

His expression shifted, becoming more thoughtful. "I want to be here, with you. This opportunity is huge for my career, but it doesn't mean I'm choosing it over you."

"Are you sure?" I asked, my voice trembling slightly. "Because it kind of feels like you're about to be swept off your feet by the culinary elite, and I'll be here, in the shadows, hoping you'll remember me."

He stepped closer, a hand resting on the countertop beside the simmering pot. "You're not in the shadows, and I don't want to be the guy who forgets about the person who made me want to be a better chef in the first place."

My heart fluttered at his words, but the doubt still lingered. "You say that now, but what if it gets hard? What if I start to fade?"

"Then I'll remind you of your worth. I'll send you ridiculous texts about everything I miss—like the way you burn toast and somehow make it adorable."

I laughed, the image of me burning toast surprisingly comforting amidst my swirling thoughts. "Ridiculous texts? Great. That sounds like a perfect way to keep the romance alive."

"It's the modern age, darling. We have to adapt."

The risotto was coming together, the rice plump and creamy, but my mind was racing in a different direction. "You know, it's not just about missing each other. It's about the fear of being replaced. Of finding someone who's closer, who can share the small moments with you."

"Do you really think I'd find someone who understands my culinary genius better than you?" He raised an eyebrow, his voice dripping with sarcasm. "Let's be real. Who else is going to put up with my obsession with sous-vide?"

I rolled my eyes, unable to hide my smile. "Okay, valid point. But the whole world of food is at your fingertips—fancy chefs with Michelin stars. I'm just... me."

"Exactly," he said, crossing his arms and leaning against the counter like he was about to make a profound statement. "And you're the only 'you' there is. So if I ever seem to forget, just remind me that you're a rare spice that can't be replicated."

The kitchen filled with a warmth that had nothing to do with the stove. I felt the tension in my chest begin to ease, even if just a little. "So, you're saying I'm special? Like saffron?"

"Exactly! You're my secret ingredient."

I couldn't help but laugh, the sound ringing through the kitchen, mixing with the aroma of my almost-successful risotto. "I'll take that compliment, chef."

He stepped closer, taking a spoon from the counter and dipping it into the pot. He tasted the risotto, then grinned. "Not bad, chef. It might even compete with the summit dishes."

"Just wait until you taste the magic of my dessert," I teased, feeling buoyed by the exchange.

"Dessert? You mean your famous ice cream sundae?"

"Of course. What did you think? I was going to make something complicated?"

His laughter filled the space, echoing like a cherished memory. "You keep it simple and sweet, just like you."

In that moment, surrounded by the warmth of our laughter and the scent of saffron, I realized that love didn't need to be perfect. It just needed to be honest, messy, and filled with a sprinkle of humor—like the best recipes.

The days melted into a blur of preparation, with Marco's departure edging closer like the climax of a simmering pot. I found myself oscillating between moments of anticipation and waves of dread, my heart a pendulum swinging wildly between excitement for his opportunity and the fear that it would create a chasm between us. Each time I caught his eye, the tenderness radiating from him reminded me of the warmth we shared, but those moments were often chased away by the gnawing anxiety that simmered just beneath the surface.

The morning of his flight dawned crisp and clear, sunlight streaming through the windows like a spotlight on the impending departure. I busied myself with last-minute packing, rearranging a set of clothes that would be left untouched for days, while my mind swirled with a thousand "what-ifs." Every time I glanced at Marco, busying himself in the kitchen, the familiar tingle of love intertwined with a bitter thread of uncertainty.

"Are you sure you don't want to come with me?" Marco asked, stirring a pot of coffee as he leaned against the counter, his gaze steady and inviting. "It'll be a whirlwind, but it could be fun."

"Oh, sure. I can just sneak into a culinary summit under the guise of your plus-one. What's the worst that could happen? A five-star chef catches me licking the plate after the tasting?" I rolled my eyes, attempting to lighten the mood even though my stomach was tied in knots.

"Exactly! I can already hear the headlines: 'Mysterious Woman in Apron Creates Culinary Scandal.'" He chuckled, his laughter brightening the space like a burst of confetti.

"While I'd love to be an international fugitive, I think I'll sit this one out," I replied, forcing a grin that didn't quite reach my eyes. "I'd rather not make a fool of myself in front of the likes of Gordon Ramsay."

"Fair enough," he said, the teasing glint in his eyes fading slightly. "But don't think you're off the hook for keeping in touch. I expect daily texts, photos of whatever you cook, and maybe even a video call if you're feeling brave."

"Deal. But you know, if my culinary creations go awry, I'm blaming it on your absence."

"Just think of me as your inspiration. Every dish will taste better because of my incredible coaching skills." He puffed out his chest dramatically, causing me to giggle despite my anxious heart.

As we gathered his belongings, an uncomfortable silence crept in, thickening the air around us. I felt the shift as the moment grew heavier, a bittersweet anticipation tinged with the uncertainty of what lay ahead. "Are you sure you'll be okay?" I asked, my voice softer now. "I mean, the world will be pulling you in so many directions. What if it all becomes too much?"

He turned to me, his expression serious for a heartbeat before the corners of his mouth turned up. "If it becomes too much, I'll call you. You know, I'd rather share a panic attack with you than anyone else. You've got a PhD in overthinking. You could probably teach a masterclass."

I snorted, a laugh escaping me, but my heart was still tethered to the uncertainty that loomed. "Don't think I won't take you up on that. I'm great at convincing people that their worst fears are a reality."

With a lingering kiss that felt both like a promise and a farewell, he pulled back, eyes searching mine. "You'll be okay. We'll be okay."

The door closed behind him, and suddenly, the silence of our apartment felt deafening. I stood there, heart pounding against my ribs, wrestling with the void his absence left. In that moment, I had never felt more alone or more afraid.

The next few days unfolded like a poorly scripted romantic comedy. I immersed myself in work, throwing myself into my projects with a fervor that surprised even me. I tried to maintain normalcy—shopping for groceries, experimenting with new recipes, texting Marco incessantly about the mundane details of my day, from my attempt at baking to my emotional breakdown over a stubborn avocado.

He was sweet, responding with encouragement and playful banter, but the time zone difference soon began to feel like a chasm. Each message that pinged my phone was a lifeline, yet the distance left me feeling unmoored. I missed the rhythm of our daily interactions, the shared laughter, the unspoken understanding that accompanied our togetherness.

One evening, I decided to host a small dinner party for a few close friends, hoping the laughter and camaraderie would distract me from the growing void. I donned my apron with renewed purpose, pouring my energy into preparing an impressive spread. As the aroma of roasted vegetables filled my apartment, the sound of laughter echoed against the walls, creating a temporary haven against the bittersweet ache of longing.

But as the night progressed and the chatter grew, I found myself glancing at my phone more than I intended, hoping for a glimpse of Marco's name lighting up the screen. The more I tried to engage, the more the gnawing emptiness tugged at my heart.

"Okay, who's the sad sap?" one of my friends, Amy, nudged me playfully, noticing my distracted demeanor. "You've barely touched your wine."

"Just... missing Marco, I guess," I admitted, taking a sip of my glass as I tried to shrug off the sentiment. "It's hard to celebrate when he's not here to share it with me."

"Ah, the classic long-distance love conundrum," she said with a knowing smile. "Just don't let it turn into a Hallmark movie, okay? No one needs that much melodrama."

I chuckled, but the laugh felt hollow. "Thanks for the vote of confidence."

As the evening wore on, we settled into the couch, a smattering of leftover plates and empty glasses surrounding us like the remnants of our laughter. I tried to engage, but each passing moment was like a countdown, and my phone was the metronome ticking steadily toward disappointment. I could feel the weight of my longing pressing down on me, and I found myself spiraling deeper into my thoughts.

Then, as if the universe was listening to my turmoil, my phone buzzed with a notification that sent a thrill racing through me.

Marco's name lit up the screen, and I snatched it up with a breathless excitement. "Finally!" I exclaimed, the warmth of hope flooding me.

But as I read his message, my heart sank. "Hey, babe! Everything is amazing here. I just met Chef Rivera! I can't wait to tell you about it. But... there's something I need to talk to you about. Can we FaceTime tonight? I'll be free around 10 PM your time."

An icy dread crept into my veins, twisting my stomach into a tight knot. The tone of his message felt too formal, too distant. What could he possibly need to talk about that couldn't be shared through text? My pulse quickened, and as I looked around the room, the laughter of my friends faded into the background, replaced by the hollow thrum of anxiety.

"Everything okay?" Amy asked, catching the sudden shift in my demeanor.

I swallowed hard, my heart racing. "Yeah, it's just... Marco wants to FaceTime later."

"Sounds serious. Are you alright?"

"Honestly? I don't know."

With each tick of the clock, the minutes seemed to stretch endlessly, the impending conversation casting a long shadow over the evening. My friends began to trickle out, the laughter slowly fading until it was just me, alone with my racing thoughts and the flickering screen of my phone. I wanted to believe it was just nerves, that everything would be fine, but deep down, a gnawing fear began to blossom.

As the clock struck ten, I perched on the edge of my couch, my hands clammy and my heart a cacophony of anxious beats. I hit the call button, the screen lighting up with his handsome face, the familiar smile fading as he saw my expression.

"Hey," he said softly, but there was something in his tone that made my heart drop.

"Hey," I replied, trying to keep my voice steady.

He took a deep breath, his eyes searching mine, and in that moment, I felt a world of uncertainty loom before us, one that could tip the delicate balance of everything we had built.

Chapter 14: Waves of Change

The buzz of the city swirled around me like a familiar embrace, the kind that buzzed in your ears and filled your lungs with the scent of roasted coffee and warm pastries. I thrived on this vibrant energy, drawing strength from the rhythm of the streets as I made my way to the café that had become my second home. The bell above the door jingled, and I stepped into the comforting cocoon of chatter and clinking dishes. Soft jazz floated through the air, wrapping around me like a well-worn scarf.

Taking my usual seat by the window, I pulled out my notebook, its pages filled with half-formed thoughts and scattered ideas. My heart raced with the thrill of creation, a euphoric rush I hadn't felt in a while. I ordered my favorite: a vanilla latte, with an extra shot of espresso, because today was the day I would write something extraordinary. The summit was approaching, a tantalizing chance to prove myself, and I couldn't let the specter of Marco's absence overshadow my ambition.

As I scribbled the opening lines of my next piece, a reflection of my journey through culinary highs and lows, the warmth of the café seeped into my bones. The smell of fresh bread mingled with the sweet scent of pastries, each whiff a reminder of the comfort food that once filled my childhood kitchen. My mother used to say that cooking was like love—you had to pour yourself into it, or it would never taste quite right. I smiled at the memory, letting it bolster my determination. This was my time, and I would embrace it fully, even if it meant navigating the turbulent waters of my emotions alone.

Mid-sentence, my phone buzzed, breaking my train of thought. A quick glance revealed a notification from my favorite food magazine, the subject line teasing an exclusive interview with Marco. My heart skipped, both at the sight of his name and the realization that he was still out there, thriving, even as I felt like a ship adrift.

The article promised to showcase not only his culinary skills but his vision for the upcoming summit—a stage I had once imagined sharing with him. My fingers trembled as I opened the link, eager to immerse myself in his words.

As I read through the interview, I could almost hear his voice, animated and passionate, as he spoke about his inspirations. He described the summit as a celebration of creativity, a melding of cultures through food, and I felt a spark of excitement ignite within me. It wasn't just about recipes; it was about connection, emotion, and the stories we tell through what we serve. A small sigh escaped my lips, the bittersweetness of nostalgia washing over me like a wave. I missed him fiercely, yet I couldn't help but feel a surge of pride. He was chasing his dreams with unyielding fervor, and I had to respect that.

The ringing of my phone pulled me back to reality. It was my best friend, Lena, her voice bright and teasing, cutting through the haze of my thoughts. "Hey, you! Are you still sulking in that café? I swear, if I have to hear you mope about Marco one more time, I might just throw a scone at you."

"Very supportive, Lena," I replied, rolling my eyes though I couldn't suppress a grin. "I'm not sulking; I'm brainstorming. Besides, I'll take my chances with the scone. I could use some carbs."

"Good! You need to fuel that creative engine of yours. But seriously, you need to put your big girl pants on and figure out what you want. Are you going to wallow in the past or step up and show the world what you can do?" Her tone shifted to one of mock seriousness. "And if you're going to choose the wallowing option, I'll need a scone on hand to throw at your head."

Her words struck a chord, echoing in my mind long after the call ended. I stared out the window, watching the world bustle by, people lost in their own lives, each with a story and a purpose. The sun peeked through the clouds, casting a warm glow over the street, and I felt a flicker of determination. The culinary summit was not just Marco's stage; it was mine too. I could either stand back and let him shine or rise to the occasion, embracing my voice and creativity.

With newfound resolve, I reached for my pen, the tip poised above the paper. I would write something bold, something that would resonate with the world and remind me of my passion. I could support Marco, even from afar, and in doing so, maybe I'd rediscover what I loved about food and writing—the joy of sharing, of bringing people together through flavors and stories. It was a small step, but it felt monumental, like taking the first stride on a path I had almost forgotten.

The next few hours flew by, the words pouring from me like a waterfall. Each sentence was infused with the energy of the café, the clatter of cups and the laughter of patrons fueling my creativity. I lost myself in the process, crafting vivid descriptions of culinary delights and weaving in my experiences of love and loss. The characters sprang to life on the page, each with their dreams and desires, echoing my own.

When I finally looked up, the sun had dipped low in the sky, casting long shadows across the room. I felt a sense of satisfaction, a buoyancy I hadn't felt in weeks. As I packed up my things, my heart raced with the thrill of creation, a warmth blooming in my chest. I had found a way to embrace my aspirations without completely letting go of what I had with Marco. There was hope in the chaos, and I was ready to dive into it, one word at a time.

The following days blurred together in a whirlwind of scribbled notes and frantic edits. My laptop hummed with activity, a faithful companion as I transformed chaotic thoughts into coherent sentences. The summit drew closer, its promise like a bright star on the horizon, illuminating the path I was determined to forge. Yet, each evening, as the sun dipped below the skyline and painted the city in hues of gold and purple, I found myself retreating into an ocean of solitude. My apartment, once a sanctuary, now felt like a hollow shell echoing with memories of laughter and shared dreams.

One particular evening, my phone chimed with an unexpected message from Marco. My heart raced as I opened it, each word charged with the electric thrill of uncertainty. "Hey! Hope you're doing well. I just wanted to check in. The summit is almost here, and I'm super nervous! How's everything with you?" The casual tone felt dissonant against the backdrop of my swirling emotions. I could almost hear the warmth of his voice, that playful lilt that had always made my heart skip a beat. I hesitated, my fingers hovering over the keyboard, battling the urge to pour out my fears and frustrations.

Instead, I typed a simple reply: "Things are good! Just busy with work. Can't wait to see you shine at the summit!" With that, I hit send and felt an odd mix of relief and regret. I had avoided diving into the emotional depths, but perhaps that was for the best. I needed to focus on myself—on my own passions—without getting swept away in the currents of his world.

The next day, fueled by a renewed sense of purpose, I decided to visit the local farmers' market. The air was crisp, laced with the scent of ripe tomatoes and freshly baked bread, and the colorful stalls pulsed with life. Each vendor boasted their wares with enthusiasm, and I wandered among them, absorbing the vibrant sights and sounds. I couldn't help but smile as I picked up a basket of plump strawberries, their sweetness bursting like tiny fireworks in my mouth.

"Are you a secret food critic, or are you just here to sample every fruit known to humankind?" a voice called out, breaking through my reverie. I turned to find a tall man with tousled hair and a mischievous grin, leaning against a stall brimming with fresh herbs.

"Just a humble admirer of fresh produce, thank you very much," I retorted, a playful edge to my tone. "Besides, how can I resist? This place is a paradise for food lovers."

"True, but you look like you've got more than a little appetite for adventure," he said, arching an eyebrow. "I'm Oliver, by the way. I run the herb stall. If you're not careful, I might just recruit you as my taste tester."

His confidence was infectious, and I found myself grinning. "I'm not sure I have the qualifications, but I'll take a free sample any day."

As we chatted, Oliver's enthusiasm for his craft was palpable. He spoke about growing herbs, experimenting with flavors, and the magic that happened when ingredients came together in unexpected ways. The conversation flowed effortlessly, a refreshing breeze that pulled me from the heavy thoughts that had been clouding my mind. I felt lighter, unburdened by the weight of my worries.

"What about you?" he asked, tilting his head curiously. "What's your passion?"

"I'm a food writer," I admitted, my heart swelling with pride as I spoke. "I love exploring the stories behind the dishes and the people who create them."

"Ah, a wordsmith! You must have a way with flavors, then. Maybe we should collaborate. I could provide the herbs; you could bring the words. Together, we'd be unstoppable."

The suggestion caught me off guard, yet a spark of intrigue ignited within me. "You think we could create something worthy of the culinary summit?"

"Why not? Who says you need to be there physically to make a splash? We could showcase a unique recipe that highlights your style and my herbs," he proposed, his eyes shining with excitement.

I considered it, my mind racing with possibilities. This unexpected partnership could be just what I needed—a chance to blend my skills with someone else's creativity, to create something entirely new. "I'm in," I declared, a rush of exhilaration flooding through me.

As the sun climbed higher in the sky, casting a warm glow over the market, we exchanged contact information and made plans to meet again. My heart danced with anticipation, the idea of collaboration providing a welcome distraction from the emotional turmoil surrounding Marco. I felt like a phoenix, rising from the ashes of my self-doubt, ready to embrace this new adventure.

That evening, I returned home, the energy of the market still buzzing in my veins. I settled down at my kitchen table, a blank page before me, and let the ideas flow. I envisioned a dish that intertwined Oliver's vibrant herbs with my narrative style, a piece that would sing of flavor and passion. I wanted it to capture the essence of what I had learned, the connections forged through food, and the stories that lingered long after the meal was finished.

The following days were a whirlwind of creativity, my life revolving around Oliver's herbs and my passion for storytelling. We met frequently, experimenting with flavors and ingredients, blending our ideas until they became something rich and beautiful. His laughter was a balm for my spirit, and I found myself looking forward to our time together more than I had anticipated.

One evening, as we chopped herbs side by side, I couldn't help but tease him. "You know, if we actually win something at the summit, I'll probably have to start calling you 'Chef Oliver' or something equally pretentious."

"Only if you promise to wear a beret when you introduce me," he shot back with a grin, his eyes sparkling with mischief. "But honestly, I'm just thrilled to be a part of this with you. You bring a different flavor to the table."

The banter flowed easily, each jab and comeback building a bridge between us. But just as I felt myself sinking deeper into this new connection, a pang of guilt tugged at my heart. I was building something beautiful with Oliver, yet Marco's presence lingered like a ghost in the background. The culinary summit loomed ever closer, and with it came the question of where my loyalties truly lay.

As the days unfurled into a delicate tapestry of anticipation and creativity, I found myself increasingly enmeshed in my partnership with Oliver. Each afternoon, we gathered in my kitchen, the atmosphere crackling with a mix of laughter and the aromatic perfume of herbs that wafted through the air like a savory symphony. With every slice of garlic and sprinkle of basil, I felt the heaviness of my previous anxieties begin to dissipate. Oliver had this uncanny ability to make even the most mundane moments sparkle with possibility.

One day, while we were crafting a dish that featured a daring combination of strawberries and rosemary—an audacious twist on a classic—Oliver leaned against the countertop, wiping his hands on a dish towel. "You know," he mused, "if we pull this off at the summit, we might just set a trend. Imagine it—strawberry-rosemary salad gracing menus everywhere. Food critics will be begging for our secrets!"

I couldn't help but laugh. "Oh, absolutely! And we'll be chased down the street by desperate chefs hoping to steal our genius. You'll need to start wearing sunglasses and a disguise."

"Maybe I'll grow a handlebar mustache," he grinned, twisting his face into a mock expression of sophistication. "That'll throw them off the scent."

The ease of our banter felt refreshing, a welcome distraction from the emotional tug-of-war I was experiencing with my feelings for Marco. While Oliver's humor brought a lightness that I relished, the thought of Marco loomed like a storm cloud in my mind, threatening to overshadow everything I was building with Oliver.

The culinary summit was just days away, and I could hardly contain my excitement mingled with anxiety. My laptop pinged with a new email notification, and my heart jumped when I saw the sender's name: Marco. A pang of guilt sliced through me, but curiosity won out. I clicked it open.

"Hey! Just checking in. I can't believe the summit is almost here! How have you been?"

His words echoed with the warmth and familiarity I missed so dearly. I could almost hear his voice, infused with that playful charm that made every mundane conversation feel significant. My fingers hovered over the keyboard, torn between a casual response and the desire to pour out my heart. Instead, I settled for something light. "Busy with work! Can't wait to see you up there."

As I hit send, I was struck by the weight of my own words. Did I really mean that? Did I want to see him again, or was I simply caught up in the whirlwind of nostalgia? A knot formed in my stomach, twisting tighter with each thought.

Later that evening, Oliver and I sat together on the balcony of my apartment, the city sprawled out beneath us like a shimmering canvas. The fading light cast golden hues on the skyline, and I couldn't help but feel a sense of peace. We sipped herbal tea infused with lemon balm and mint, the refreshing taste mirroring the buoyancy of the moment.

"I think we're ready," Oliver said, his eyes bright with determination. "Our dish is going to be the star of the summit."

"Or the laughingstock," I teased, feigning a dramatic gasp. "Imagine the headline: 'Local Food Writers Create Abomination with Strawberries and Rosemary!'"

"Now that's a twist," he said, chuckling. "But I have faith in our culinary genius. We'll just have to wow them with our presentation."

We spent the rest of the evening discussing our vision, lost in a world of flavors and culinary dreams. The laughter came easily, but as we plotted our next steps, an underlying tension simmered in my chest. My feelings for Marco felt tangled with my burgeoning connection with Oliver. I had finally stepped out of my shell, yet the thought of Marco's impending arrival left me questioning everything.

The day of the summit dawned bright and clear, the excitement in the air palpable. My nerves fluttered in my stomach like a swarm of butterflies as I prepared. Dressed in a crisp white blouse and tailored black pants, I looked in the mirror, taking a moment to appreciate my reflection. Confidence was an elusive trait, but today, I needed it more than ever.

Arriving at the venue, a sprawling hall filled with tantalizing aromas and vibrant displays, I felt the energy envelop me. Chefs and food enthusiasts buzzed about like bees, each corner alive with creativity. My heart raced as I spotted Oliver setting up our station, his face alight with enthusiasm.

"Ready to rock this?" he called, grinning as he adjusted the arrangement of our herbs.

"Absolutely!" I responded, trying to match his excitement, though the nerves twisted my stomach in knots.

We worked swiftly, laying out our dish with precision. The strawberries glistened like jewels, and the rosemary danced in the light. I could see the judges strolling through the room, their expressions serious yet curious, and with each passing moment, I felt a mix of thrill and anxiety.

Just as we finished, I turned to catch my breath, only to find Marco entering the hall, looking every bit the culinary star I remembered. My heart raced at the sight of him. He was dressed sharply, the confidence radiating from him like a beacon. He spotted me and made his way through the crowd, his eyes locking onto mine with an intensity that made the world around us fade.

"Hey," he said, his voice a blend of surprise and warmth. "I didn't expect to see you here."

"Surprise!" I replied, forcing a smile as I fought the tumult of emotions swirling within me. "I'm here to present my dish."

His brow arched in genuine curiosity, but before I could respond, Oliver stepped forward, exuding his usual charm. "Hey, Marco! Good to see you! We just finished our masterpiece. What do you think?"

Marco's eyes flicked between us, and I could feel the tension in the air like a live wire. "You're working together? That's great, really," he said, though the hint of something unspoken lingered beneath his words.

The atmosphere shifted, a subtle crack forming in the foundation of my carefully constructed composure. The moment felt charged, electric, as if the universe was watching, waiting for the next move. Just as I opened my mouth to respond, the sound of a microphone crackling to life interrupted us.

"Welcome, everyone, to the culinary summit! We're thrilled to have you here," the host announced, his voice booming through the hall.

With the attention shifting, I felt a rush of urgency. I had to decide where my loyalties lay. The weight of the moment bore down on me, the choices I'd made cascading through my mind. I glanced at Oliver, who met my gaze with an encouraging nod, and then back at Marco, whose expression was unreadable.

This was it. The summit was about to begin, and with it came the realization that my life was about to change, whether I was ready or not. The choices I'd made, the connections I had formed, all converged in this moment, and I stood on the precipice of something monumental.

The host continued, "Now, let's begin with our first presentation..."

My breath caught in my throat as the words hung in the air, and I braced myself for what was to come, knowing that whatever happened next would alter the course of my journey forever.

Chapter 15: Embracing the Journey

The kitchen hummed with warmth as I prepped for Marco's last evening in town. The scent of garlic and fresh herbs mingled in the air, weaving a tapestry of memories that enveloped me like a favorite blanket. I had arranged a series of dishes, each one a vibrant reflection of our shared moments—colors and flavors that danced like fireflies on a warm summer night. My heart thudded with anticipation, a mix of excitement and melancholy, as I gathered the ingredients, each one a small piece of our story.

I had insisted on doing everything myself, determined to infuse my love into every bite. The truffle pasta, a glorious concoction that had sparked our connection in that dimly lit bistro, was first on the list. I meticulously rolled out the dough, my fingers dusted with flour, reliving the intoxicating atmosphere of our first date. The gentle laughter, the stolen glances, and the way the world outside faded to nothing but the two of us, lost in conversation over a shared plate. With each swirl of the pasta, I imagined Marco's playful smile, the way his eyes lit up when I revealed my newfound affinity for cooking.

As I prepared the sauce, a rich blend of cream, black truffles, and Parmesan, I couldn't help but chuckle at the way he had dramatically declared it was the best thing he had ever tasted. The thought of that night made me giddy, a rush of nostalgia pouring over me like the sauce I stirred in the pan. It was more than just food; it was a language we spoke fluently, each meal layered with unspoken words and promises.

The sun dipped low, casting a golden hue through the kitchen window as I moved on to the next dish: roasted beet salad topped with goat cheese and candied walnuts. The vibrant reds and purples reminded me of our impromptu picnic in the park, the laughter that echoed around us as we tried to outsmart the squirrels begging for

166

scraps. The salad was as much a reflection of our playful banter as it was of the bold flavors that came together beautifully, much like us—unexpected yet undeniably perfect.

When I finally reached the dessert stage, a tiramisu that echoed our cozy evenings at Il Sogno, I couldn't help but feel a pang of sadness mixed with gratitude. We had spent countless nights there, sipping espresso and sharing stories, our laughter blending with the hum of the café. As I layered the rich mascarpone with coffee-soaked ladyfingers, I recalled the time he'd made a joke that sent coffee shooting from my nose, the very essence of romance in that moment being the sheer absurdity of it all.

"Have you ever tried making tiramisu while being covered in coffee?" I had teased him, and his reply had been, "Only if it comes with a side of your laughter." I had stored that in my heart, a small reminder that even the simplest moments with him were treasured memories in the making.

With the table set, the candles flickering softly against the evening shadows, I dressed in my favorite sundress, the one he always complimented. I stared at my reflection, noting the slight tremor in my hands. Would tonight be as magical as I imagined? Would he realize just how much he meant to me, how the thought of his departure gnawed at my insides like a relentless tide?

The doorbell rang, its chime echoing through the stillness of my home. I took a deep breath, a mix of excitement and anxiety churning in my stomach as I opened the door. Marco stood there, his usual charm wrapped in a navy blazer that hinted at the man he was destined to be. His eyes, deep and soulful, searched mine, and a smile crept across his face that sent warmth flooding through me.

"Wow, you look amazing!" he said, stepping inside, his voice rich and inviting.

"Only the best for tonight," I replied, feigning casualness even as my heart raced. "You're going to love what I've prepared."

He raised an eyebrow, feigning skepticism, but I could see the glimmer of intrigue in his eyes. "You've got me curious. What's on the menu?"

I led him to the dining room, where the table was adorned with flickering candles and a bouquet of fresh wildflowers that I had picked from the farmer's market earlier that day. "I thought we'd take a little trip down memory lane," I said, gesturing to the elegantly arranged plates. "Each dish represents a moment we've shared."

He looked at the setup, a blend of surprise and delight washing over his features. "You've really outdone yourself. This looks incredible."

We settled in, and with each bite, I watched as the layers of memories unfolded in his eyes. The truffle pasta brought a delighted laugh, the salad prompted a story about the time we had nearly lost our blanket to the wind, and the tiramisu stirred a deeper connection—a shared understanding of how fleeting time could be.

"Why does this feel so significant?" Marco asked between bites, his gaze locked onto mine, as if searching for answers in the depths of my soul.

"It's just food," I said, trying to play it down, but the weight of my words hung heavy in the air. "But it's also everything we've built together. It's a reminder that even when you're gone, these moments will always be part of us."

He set down his fork, an intensity brewing in his eyes that made my breath hitch. "You know I'll carry you with me, right? No matter the distance, no matter the city."

The silence that followed was charged, our unspoken fears and hopes swirling like the aromas of the dishes surrounding us. For the first time that evening, the truth loomed large between us, beautiful yet terrifying. The future was uncertain, and yet, there we were, anchored in the present, a poignant blend of what was and what could be.

As the last bite of tiramisu lingered on our tongues, the tension between us danced like candlelight, flickering and alive. I wiped my hands on a linen napkin, stealing glances at Marco, who sat across the table, his expression a blend of satisfaction and something deeper—a weightiness that echoed my own unease.

"You've truly outdone yourself," he finally said, his voice low, savoring each word like the last morsel of dessert. "I knew you could cook, but this... this is art."

"Stop it," I replied, waving a hand dismissively while warmth spread across my cheeks. "I just followed a few recipes. It's not like I painted the Mona Lisa or anything."

"True, but the Mona Lisa doesn't make me feel like this," he countered, leaning back in his chair with a thoughtful smile. "It doesn't taste like love."

The compliment hung in the air, thick and heady, mingling with the remnants of espresso on our plates. For a moment, I felt like we were trapped in our own little world, where the outside noises faded into a soft hum. Just as I opened my mouth to respond, the piercing ring of my phone shattered the bubble, startling us both.

"Perfect timing," I muttered, rolling my eyes as I glanced at the screen. It was my sister, Anna, her name flashing like an unwelcome neon sign. I hesitated, unsure whether to answer, but she had a knack for demanding attention, even from the other side of the city.

"Are you going to get that?" Marco asked, the corner of his mouth twitching in amusement.

"Yeah, unfortunately," I sighed, my fingers hovering over the screen. "I'll be right back."

I walked into the adjacent room, trying to suppress the urgency bubbling up inside me. "Hey, Anna!" I chirped, forcing a cheerful tone into my voice.

"Finally! I thought I'd have to send out a search party," she shot back, a teasing lilt in her voice. "You still alive? Or has Marco charmed you into culinary oblivion?"

I chuckled, leaning against the wall. "Barely clinging to life, but it was worth it. I made a tasting menu. You should've seen his face!"

"Wow, a tasting menu? I knew you were capable of wooing a man, but this? This is next level. You're turning into a total gourmet goddess."

"Don't get ahead of yourself," I said, glancing back toward the dining room. I could see Marco still seated at the table, a playful smile tugging at his lips as he sipped from his wine glass. "I just wanted to make our last night special before he leaves."

"Speaking of which, how are you holding up? I know it's only for a few months, but still..." There was a sincerity in her tone that grounded me, reminding me of the emotional weight that was tethered to this night.

"I'm okay, I think. Just...trying not to overthink everything. It's just a few months, and he'll be back. It's not like he's moving to Mars." My attempt at humor fell flat, and I heard the slight crack in my voice.

"Yeah, but it might as well be," Anna replied gently. "You know how these things can go. People change. It's hard enough to keep a friendship alive when there's distance, let alone something deeper."

"Thanks for the vote of confidence," I retorted, a mix of frustration and affection bubbling to the surface. "I know, but I'm choosing to believe in us. He's worth it. We're worth it."

"Just promise me you'll keep your heart intact. Okay? I don't want you turning into a sad song by the end of this."

"I promise," I said, the resolve bolstering my spirits. "Now, if you'll excuse me, I have a romantic dinner to return to. He might eat all the tiramisu if I'm gone too long."

"Go, lovebird. And remember, I'm only a call away if you need to scream into the void."

I hung up and took a moment to collect my thoughts, the soft glow of the dining room beckoning me back. I stepped inside, determined to shift the energy back to something lighter. Marco looked up, his eyes dancing with curiosity.

"What was that all about? Did you have to call for backup?"

I laughed, shaking my head. "Just my sister being dramatic, as always. She worries too much."

"Ah, the classic sibling dynamic," he said, his smile widening. "I wouldn't know much about it. I'm an only child."

"Really? I would have guessed you were the youngest in a family of five. You have that charmingly spoiled vibe."

He raised an eyebrow, feigning offense. "Excuse me? I'll have you know I was the epitome of self-sufficiency. I had to fend for myself against my parents' expectations!"

"Sure, buddy. Self-sufficiency looks a lot like that last slice of tiramisu I see you eyeing."

He feigned innocence, placing a hand dramatically over his heart. "Me? I would never!"

"Right, because you definitely haven't been stealing glances at it since we started dinner." I crossed my arms, trying to suppress a grin as I watched him squirm.

"Fine, you got me! But can you blame me? It's your fault for making it look so good."

I laughed and leaned back in my chair, the weight of the evening lifting slightly. The rhythm of our banter felt like home, and for a moment, the looming departure faded into the background.

"Tell me something," he said, a sudden seriousness settling in his voice. "What's one thing you'll miss most about me when I'm gone?"

It felt like a trap, but I couldn't resist the glimmer of vulnerability that flickered in his eyes. "Your constant need to discuss every conspiracy theory you've ever heard," I shot back, unable to keep the teasing edge from my tone.

He chuckled, but then his expression shifted, becoming more earnest. "Okay, but really. What will you miss?"

I took a deep breath, the moment stretching like taffy between us. "Your laugh," I said finally, my voice softening. "You make everything feel lighter. Even the most mundane things suddenly become an adventure."

He nodded, his gaze steady. "And I'll miss the way you turn a simple meal into an experience. You've made me appreciate food in a whole new way."

As the laughter subsided, the air thickened with unsaid words, a weight that lingered as the last slivers of the evening light began to fade outside. In that charged silence, I felt the unshakeable truth settle between us: that this night was both an ending and a beginning, woven intricately together like the threads of our lives. It was a reminder that even as we faced the distance ahead, we were still two pieces of a puzzle that, somehow, always found a way to fit together.

The soft glow of candlelight cast shadows on the walls as the night deepened, wrapping us in a cocoon of warmth and nostalgia. I watched Marco as he leaned back in his chair, fingers toying with the stem of his wine glass, the remnants of our meal lingering like echoes of laughter. I could see his mind working, contemplating something more profound than the delightful food we had just devoured.

"Okay, so hypothetically," he began, his tone teasing yet tinged with seriousness, "if you could pick anywhere in the world to travel, where would it be? And why?"

The question hung in the air, a gentle challenge that beckoned me to delve deeper. My mind whirled through a myriad of destinations—the beaches of Bali, the art-filled streets of Florence, or perhaps the bright lights of Tokyo. But I knew the answer I wanted to share, one that held more weight than just a destination.

"I think I'd go to Paris," I said, allowing the thought to unfurl like a well-loved map in my mind. "There's something magical about it. The food, the culture... the way everything feels so alive. And it's the city where I feel I could find myself, or lose myself, depending on the day."

He nodded, a knowing smile creeping onto his face. "Paris, huh? I can see it. You'd thrive there, nibbling croissants and arguing about art with pretentious gallery owners."

"Exactly!" I laughed, leaning forward, my elbows resting on the table. "And I'd find a quaint little café where the waiter pretends to be annoyed by my terrible French, but deep down, he secretly loves it."

"What if I told you that I've always wanted to go to Paris too?" Marco leaned in, mirroring my enthusiasm. "You know, to stroll down the Seine, hold hands while dodging the pigeon army... I mean, I don't think I'd survive without a solid strategy."

"Ah, the strategic pigeon dodging. A fine art indeed. You'd be a natural."

Our laughter bubbled like the remnants of the sparkling wine in our glasses. For a moment, the looming departure faded, leaving only the joyous threads of our conversation weaving tighter around us.

But just as I began to let my guard down, a slight flicker of movement outside caught my eye. My heart raced as I turned my head toward the window, where shadows danced in the moonlight. A figure stood there, shrouded in darkness, just beyond the reach of the warm glow from inside. My stomach twisted, instinctively sensing something was off.

"Do you see that?" I whispered, my voice barely above a breath, suddenly feeling very small in our cozy dining room.

Marco turned, his playful demeanor shifting to one of concern as he squinted toward the window. "What are you talking about?"

"There's someone outside." My heart thudded in my chest, the playful mood of the evening evaporating like steam from a freshly brewed cup of coffee.

He stood, moving closer to the window, and I joined him, both of us peering into the night as the figure shifted slightly, illuminated momentarily by the glow of the streetlight. My breath hitched as I recognized the silhouette—a familiar outline that sent a chill racing down my spine.

"It can't be..." I murmured, my thoughts spinning in disbelief.

"Who is it?" Marco's voice was firm, his gaze still focused outside.

"David," I breathed, the name slipping from my lips like a ghost. David, my ex-boyfriend, stood just outside my home, his hands shoved deep in his pockets, an expression of uncertainty etched on his face. Memories surged forward, tainted with the bittersweet aftertaste of a relationship that had been as intense as it was tumultuous.

"Why is he here?" I asked, half to myself, half to Marco, who stepped back slightly, gauging my reaction.

"Should we let him in?" Marco asked, a hint of protective concern shading his voice. I could sense the tension rising, the air crackling like the calm before a storm.

I hesitated, emotions swirling like a tempest within me. David and I had parted ways on shaky ground, our love affair riddled with misunderstandings and miscommunications, leading to an explosive breakup that still felt raw. The thought of confronting that history sent a jolt of anxiety racing through me.

"Maybe he just wants to talk," I said, but even I could hear the uncertainty in my own voice.

"Or maybe he's here to stir the pot," Marco replied, his tone sharp with concern. "You don't owe him anything, you know that, right?"

"Yeah, but…" I trailed off, caught in a web of conflicting feelings. On one hand, I knew I had moved on; I was happy with Marco, and the thought of David intruding on our evening felt like a distant thunderclap in an otherwise serene sky. On the other hand, the unresolved threads of my past tugged insistently at my heart.

"I can go talk to him if you want," Marco suggested, his expression earnest and determined. "I'll keep it cool. Just to see what he wants."

"No, I should handle this." I felt a surge of determination, though my heart raced at the thought of facing David again. "It's my past, and I need to confront it. I won't let him control my narrative anymore."

"Alright," Marco said, but I could see the concern etched on his face. "Just… be careful, okay?"

Taking a steadying breath, I nodded. "I will."

I moved to the door, the hardwood floor creaking beneath my feet as I approached the figure standing outside. My hand lingered on the doorknob, a mix of dread and anticipation swirling in my gut. What was David doing here after all this time? Hadn't he gotten the memo that I had moved on?

With a deep breath, I swung the door open, bracing myself against the cool night air. David stood there, his expression a blend of uncertainty and something that looked like regret.

"Hey," he said, his voice catching slightly, as if the weight of the moment was pressing down on him as much as it was on me.

"Why are you here?" The question fell from my lips like a lead balloon, heavy and laden with unspoken history.

"I came to talk," he said, his eyes searching mine. "I know it's been a while, and I know I messed up, but I need to explain…"

Before he could finish, I felt Marco's presence at my back, a steady force that reminded me I was not alone in this moment.

"Not without a proper introduction," Marco interjected, stepping beside me, his posture protective. "Who are you, and what do you want?"

I glanced at Marco, a surge of gratitude warming me despite the chill in the air. This was my choice, and I would not allow the shadows of my past to overpower the light I had built with Marco.

"David," he said, extending a hand, but the introduction felt hollow, as if the very act of naming himself was an inadequate defense against the waves of emotion crashing around us. "I used to... well, I'm her ex."

"I know who you are," Marco replied, his voice steady. "What's so important that it couldn't wait?"

David hesitated, glancing at me, and in that moment, a thousand questions hung heavy in the air between us. The night felt thick with tension, as if the universe itself was holding its breath, waiting for the next twist in our tangled fates.

"I need to tell you both the truth," David finally said, his voice barely above a whisper. "And it's something that might change everything."

The weight of his words settled around us, heavy and ominous, as I sensed the ground shifting beneath my feet. In that instant, I understood that whatever came next, the night was far from over, and the path ahead was fraught with unexpected revelations that could reshape our lives in ways I could hardly fathom.

Chapter 16: A Distance Apart

The air was thick with the scent of cinnamon and fresh coffee as I sat at my favorite café, a cozy nook nestled between the artisan bakery and a local bookstore, both of which were unwittingly complicit in my attempt to distract myself from the aching absence of Marco. The vibrant chatter around me faded into a comforting hum, like a familiar melody played softly in the background. The barista, a perpetually upbeat woman with a talent for crafting intricate latte art, placed my drink before me with a flourish. "One caramel macchiato, extra foam, just how you like it," she said, winking as if she could sense my turmoil.

"Thanks, Clara. You're a lifesaver," I replied, attempting a smile that felt more like a grimace. I wrapped my hands around the warm cup, drawing in the aroma, hoping to absorb some of its warmth and cheerfulness. As I watched the steam curl into the air, I let my mind wander, chasing after elusive thoughts of Marco and his new life in San Francisco, where he was living out his culinary dreams. I imagined him bustling through the chaotic kitchen of a high-end restaurant, surrounded by fresh ingredients and creative minds, every sizzling pan a testament to his passion.

With each call we shared, his tales of culinary adventures felt like a double-edged sword. I was so proud of him, yet I couldn't help but feel a pang of envy. Marco had always been the bright star, radiating confidence and charisma. I was the grounding element in his orbit, but now I felt like a forgotten planet, my gravitational pull too weak to keep him close. The world he described was a tantalizing playground of flavors and experiences that I couldn't touch, a place where he thrived and I merely existed.

The phone vibrated on the table, shattering my reverie. A text from Marco flashed on the screen, and my heart skipped a beat. I read it twice, needing to absorb his words fully: "Just finished a tasting menu prep for a big event. Can't wait to tell you about it later! Miss you."

Miss you. The words echoed in my mind, filled with both comfort and despair. I took a sip of my macchiato, the sweetness mingling with the bitterness of my thoughts. We had set up this routine, nightly calls that stretched into the early hours, filled with laughter and stories. Yet, despite the warmth of those conversations, the growing distance was palpable, stretching between us like an unbridgeable chasm.

I glanced outside, watching the autumn leaves dance on the breeze, their vibrant hues a stark contrast to my mood. Asheville was beautiful this time of year, but I felt disconnected from its charm, as if I were merely an observer rather than a participant. The cobblestone streets, lined with quaint shops and vibrant art installations, seemed to mock my inability to find joy in the familiar.

That afternoon, I decided to visit the local farmers' market. Perhaps immersing myself in the vibrant colors and lively atmosphere would offer a distraction from my melancholy. As I wandered through the stalls, the air filled with the rich scents of spices, freshly baked bread, and ripe fruit, I felt a flicker of my old self returning. I sampled heirloom tomatoes bursting with flavor, their sweetness reminding me of summers spent with my grandmother, her laughter echoing through her sun-soaked garden.

"Looking for inspiration for a new dish?" A voice pulled me from my reverie, and I turned to find Max, the charming chef who ran the food truck I frequented. His sandy hair was tousled, and he wore an apron splattered with a rainbow of sauces. "You look like you could use a taste of something amazing."

"Just browsing," I replied, attempting to mask the bittersweet undertones in my voice.

"You know, you could join me in the truck sometime. I've been working on a new fall menu, and I could use a fresh perspective," he offered with a grin, his blue eyes sparkling with mischief.

"I don't know about that," I replied, laughter mingling with uncertainty. "I'm more of an enthusiastic eater than a cook."

"Then let's start with that! You can taste-test my creations. I promise it'll be a good time."

Max's enthusiasm was contagious, and I felt a flutter of excitement as he continued to chat, sharing his own dreams of culinary innovation and travel. Yet, as he spoke, I found myself grappling with a mix of guilt and longing. I loved Marco, but here was a spark of camaraderie that reminded me of the joy I used to find in the kitchen, before my own insecurities began to cloud my passion.

"Okay, you've convinced me," I said, surprising myself. "I'll come by tomorrow. But only to taste!"

"Deal. I'll make it worth your while," he replied, winking.

As I left the market, a smile crept onto my face, the promise of tomorrow offering a glimmer of hope amidst the gray clouds hovering over my heart. Maybe engaging with the local culinary scene would help bridge the distance that Marco's ambitions were creating. I needed to rediscover my own passion for food, to remind myself that I, too, could thrive outside the shadow of his brilliance.

Back home, I settled into my favorite armchair, the familiar fabric enveloping me like a hug. I pulled out my notebook, filled with half-baked ideas and scattered thoughts. The blank page beckoned, a canvas for my creativity, and I found myself jotting down notes inspired by Max's enthusiasm and the vibrant flavors I had tasted that day. The more I wrote, the more I felt the heaviness in my chest begin to lift, revealing flickers of excitement and possibility.

Perhaps I didn't need to compete with Marco's world; instead, I could carve out my own space in it. And who knew? Maybe this new venture would open doors I never thought possible, bringing me back to life in ways I had long forgotten.

With my heart cautiously optimistic, I reached for my phone, ready to send Marco a message filled with the day's highlights, the promise of new beginnings, and the lingering hope that we could find a way to bridge the distance that threatened to pull us apart.

The next morning, I woke to the crisp bite of autumn air filtering through my open window, carrying with it the earthy scent of fallen leaves and distant woodsmoke. The sun streamed in, casting warm patches of light across my room, and for the first time in weeks, I felt the spark of inspiration igniting within me. My heart raced with a blend of excitement and trepidation as I remembered my commitment to Max and his food truck. It wasn't just an invitation; it felt like a lifeline tossed into turbulent waters.

As I threw on a cozy sweater, I couldn't shake the thought that this could be my chance to rediscover my passion for cooking, a passion that had languished under the weight of my insecurities. I caught a glimpse of myself in the mirror, tousled hair and a hint of morning fog in my eyes. It was time to shake off the remnants of doubt. I grabbed my notebook, tucking it into my bag, determined to capture every flavorful idea that would come my way.

The sun hung high as I made my way to the food truck, a kaleidoscope of colors lining the streets. As I approached, the vibrant blue of the truck was a welcoming sight, adorned with hand-painted designs that reflected the energy of its owner. Max was already there, a whirlwind of activity, chopping vegetables and tossing ingredients with a flair that suggested both experience and joy.

"Hey there, culinary superstar!" he called out, his grin as bright as the sun overhead. "Ready to taste some magic?"

"I'm just hoping I don't ruin your culinary dreams," I replied, stepping up to the truck's counter, suddenly conscious of how seriously I had taken the whole thing.

"Trust me, I'm more worried about you ruining your taste buds," he teased, placing a small bowl of vibrant salsa in front of me. "This is a fresh tomatillo salsa, perfect for tacos or just eating straight from the bowl."

I dipped my finger in and brought it to my lips, the tangy explosion of flavor igniting my senses. "Okay, wow. This is incredible! How did you come up with this?"

"Ah, the secret ingredient is love," he said, winking. "And a bit of desperation. I had to find something to make my food truck stand out in this bustling market. But it's really about the freshness of the ingredients. It's all about bringing out what nature already provides."

"Nature providing is great and all, but I'm still waiting for my 'nature moment' to inspire me," I replied, my voice tinged with self-deprecation.

"Don't sell yourself short. You're already here, aren't you? That's the first step. Plus, you've got the best raw ingredient of all," he said, gesturing to my notebook. "Ideas! Let's brainstorm a dish together. What's your favorite thing to eat?"

I hesitated, a wave of self-doubt washing over me. My mind raced through a plethora of choices, each one more mundane than the last. "I mean, I love a good risotto, but..."

"No 'buts' allowed!" he interrupted. "Let's work with that. Risotto has so much potential for creativity. We could infuse it with seasonal ingredients, maybe some roasted squash or mushrooms. What do you think?"

A spark of excitement lit within me. "That sounds delicious. And we could finish it with a drizzle of truffle oil—just to elevate it a bit!"

"Now you're speaking my language!" Max exclaimed, jotting down ideas on a notepad. "Let's get cooking."

As we moved through the preparations, the rhythm of our collaboration began to flow seamlessly. We chopped, stirred, and laughed, my confidence building with each moment. I had forgotten how exhilarating it felt to create something with my hands, to transform simple ingredients into a dish that could tell a story.

"Tell me about Asheville," Max asked, wiping sweat from his brow as we sautéed garlic and onions in a pan, their fragrant aroma filling the air.

"It's a small town, but it has this vibrant community of artists and food lovers. People are passionate about their craft, whether it's pottery or brewing beer. It's magical, really," I said, allowing myself to reminisce. "But sometimes, I feel like I'm stuck in a rut. It's like I'm the town's best-kept secret, but no one's looking for me."

"Sounds like you need a new audience," Max replied, a knowing glint in his eyes. "You need to share your talent with the world. What's stopping you?"

My stomach twisted at the thought. "Fear, mostly. What if I fail? What if it's not good enough? What if I just can't keep up with the rest of the world?"

He paused, placing a hand on my shoulder. "Listen, every chef has to start somewhere. What makes a dish memorable isn't just the ingredients; it's the heart behind it. If you put your soul into it, people will feel that. And you're not alone; you have your own community cheering for you."

His words hung in the air, a gentle reminder that I had roots to anchor me, a network of support that could bolster my courage. I felt an unexpected warmth bloom in my chest, pushing back against the shadows of doubt.

As the risotto simmered to perfection, we plated our creation with care, garnishing it with herbs and a flourish of truffle oil. The sight of our culinary creation made my heart swell with pride. "This looks amazing, Max! I can't believe we made this together."

"Let's get some feedback," he suggested, a mischievous grin creeping across his face. He called over a couple of customers who had been waiting nearby, their eyes lighting up at the sight of the steaming risotto. "We have a special dish for you. Free of charge. All I ask is your honest opinion."

With hesitant smiles, they accepted the plates, their forks diving in with curiosity. The seconds stretched out, each tick of the clock feeling like a small eternity. I exchanged nervous glances with Max, my heart racing.

Then came the first sounds of delight—a soft moan from one of the tasters, followed by the inevitable chorus of approval. "This is incredible!" one of them exclaimed. "What's in it?"

Max and I exchanged triumphant looks, the kind that said we had done something meaningful together. The tension that had coiled tightly around my heart began to unravel, replaced by exhilaration. Maybe I wasn't just a spectator in Marco's world; maybe I could carve out a space for myself in this bustling culinary landscape.

As the compliments flowed, I realized this was what I had been missing. A community, an audience, and a connection to something greater than myself. I felt alive, not just for the sake of creation, but for the promise that my own story was still being written. Perhaps, just perhaps, the distance between Marco and me could be bridged by my newfound passion, turning a space of uncertainty into a foundation of possibility.

The exhilaration of our impromptu culinary creation lingered in the air like the sweet scent of caramelized onions. Customers continued to gather around the food truck, their faces lit with delight as they tasted the risotto we had conjured up together. With each bite, I felt a sense of validation wash over me, the weight of my insecurities lifting, if only momentarily. The laughter and chatter enveloped us, forming an invisible bond that wove through the vibrant market, and for the first time in what felt like an eternity, I felt like I belonged.

"Alright, Chef Extraordinaire," Max said, leaning against the truck with a satisfied grin. "What's next on your agenda? More dishes, or are you going to sit back and let me take all the glory?"

I chuckled, feeling a mischievous spark within. "I'm not one to let someone else hog the spotlight. Let's get to work on something else—how about a dessert?"

"A dessert! Now we're talking," he exclaimed, his eyes twinkling with enthusiasm. "I've got some fresh berries and a recipe for a lemon tart that will make anyone swoon."

As we delved into the art of pastry, I couldn't help but reflect on how far I had come in just a day. The kitchen was a sanctuary, and it felt as if each stir of the batter was sweeping away my worries. We whipped cream, folded in zest, and combined ingredients like a painter mixing colors, all while exchanging playful banter.

"Is it true what they say?" I asked, casually rolling out the dough. "That a chef's love life is as complicated as a soufflé?"

Max laughed, shaking his head. "Complicated is an understatement. I once dated a fellow chef who thought adding sriracha to everything was 'culinary genius.' I almost couldn't eat anything without thinking of her."

I snorted. "Sriracha? That's like trying to put fireworks in a symphony."

"Exactly! It was a disaster waiting to happen," he replied, and we both dissolved into laughter, the sound intertwining with the cheerful chatter of customers around us.

Just then, the familiar chime of my phone broke the moment, vibrating insistently against the countertop. It was Marco. My heart fluttered, a mix of excitement and trepidation. I glanced at Max, whose expression shifted from playful to slightly serious as he caught my eye.

"Go ahead, answer it," he encouraged, giving me a supportive nod.

I inhaled deeply, swiping to answer. "Hey! Marco!"

"Hey, you," he replied, his voice warm but tinged with something that set my heart racing—a subtle shift I couldn't quite place. "How's everything in Asheville?"

"It's been... surprisingly good," I said, glancing over at Max, who was busy preparing the lemon tart. "I've been working with Max at his food truck, creating some dishes, and it's been a lot of fun."

"Sounds like you're keeping busy," Marco said, his tone uncharacteristically flat. "How are you holding up? You know, with me being gone and everything."

The question hung in the air like a lead weight. "I'm doing okay, really. Just trying to find my footing while you're off conquering the culinary world."

"Are you sure? Because I've sensed some distance between us," he replied, a note of concern creeping into his voice. "It's like we're living in two different worlds now."

"I know, and I—" I started, but the words caught in my throat. How could I explain the whirlwind of emotions I was feeling, the rising tide of self-doubt coupled with newfound passion?

Before I could respond, Max approached with two plates, adorned with the finished lemon tart. "Ready for a taste test?" he asked, winking. I quickly turned back to Marco, hoping he hadn't noticed my momentary distraction.

"Listen, Marco, I'll call you back later, okay? I really need to focus on this," I said, trying to keep my voice steady.

"Okay... just don't forget about me. I miss you, you know?"

"I miss you too," I said, my voice softer now. "I'll call you later. I promise."

I hung up, trying to shake off the remnants of unease that clung to me. Max handed me a fork, the tart gleaming in the afternoon light, its lemony aroma intoxicating. "You okay?" he asked, his tone gentle but probing.

"Yeah, I just... I don't know. Marco and I have been talking about everything, but it feels like there's this invisible wall between us now," I admitted, my heart heavy.

"Relationships are tough, especially when one person is off living their dreams while the other is left to figure things out," he said, thoughtfully. "But that doesn't mean you can't find your own way too. It's not a competition; it's about support. You should be able to have your own journey."

I took a bite of the tart, the tartness of the lemon melding with the sweetness of the cream, exploding in a burst of flavor that was both refreshing and comforting. "This is incredible, by the way. You really know how to hit all the right notes."

"Thanks! But you know, if you ever need a taste of what it's like to be in the culinary spotlight, I can always use a sous chef," Max offered, his expression earnest.

"I'll keep that in mind," I said, smiling genuinely now.

The afternoon turned into a whirlwind of laughter, creativity, and mouthwatering food. As we plated our creations for the market, I felt a sense of belonging, like I was finally finding my place within the culinary community. Customers raved about our desserts, and I reveled in the feedback, my heart swelling with pride.

But just as I was beginning to feel at home, a shadow fell over the joy of the moment. My phone buzzed again, the screen lighting up with an unfamiliar number. Curiosity mixed with anxiety as I answered.

"Hello?"

"Is this Emily Bennett?" The voice on the other end was smooth yet edged with urgency.

"Yes, who's this?"

"I'm calling regarding Marco. We need to talk."

The words sent a chill coursing through me, an instinctual wave of dread rising in my chest. "What do you mean? Is something wrong?"

"Please, just meet me. I can't discuss this over the phone."

Before I could respond, the line went dead. My heart raced, confusion spiraling into panic. I looked over at Max, whose brow was furrowed with concern as he wiped his hands on a towel. "What was that about?"

"I don't know," I said, my voice trembling. "But it sounded serious."

"Do you want me to go with you?" he asked, his gaze intense.

I hesitated, the uncertainty swirling in my mind like the autumn leaves outside. "I don't know. I have to find out what's going on with Marco first."

As I stood there, the air thick with tension and unsaid words, I felt a growing sense of dread settle in my stomach. The world around me spun in vivid colors, but an unsettling shadow loomed on the horizon, threatening to pull me back into the darkness I had fought so hard to escape.

Chapter 17: An Unexpected Visitor

The doorbell chimed like a sweet, unexpected melody, pulling me from the fog of my solitude. I hesitated for a moment, peering through the peephole, half-expecting it to be another delivery or a stray cat. Instead, there was Lily, a whirlwind of vibrant energy that could only be compared to a summer storm. Her hair was a cascade of curls, bouncing in rhythm with her animated gestures as she stood on my doorstep, arms overflowing with artisanal treats and a glinting bottle of wine.

I swung the door open, and a rush of laughter erupted as she nearly toppled into my living room, catching her balance just in time. "Surprise! I come bearing gifts," she declared, her grin infectious enough to light up the dimmest corners of my apartment. The glow of her presence chased away the remnants of gloom that had draped over me like a heavy blanket since Marco left.

"Gourmet cheese and wine? You're spoiling me," I chuckled, gesturing for her to step inside. As she set the bounty down on the coffee table, I could feel the warmth of her enthusiasm suffusing the air. "I was just contemplating a cheese-less existence," I added, half-jokingly.

"Not on my watch!" she shot back, plopping onto the couch as though it were a throne. "We need to celebrate your culinary prowess, not sulk about unworthy exes." She punctuated her point with a playful roll of her eyes, and I couldn't help but laugh. Lily had always possessed an uncanny ability to dismantle my more morose thoughts with her sharp wit and unyielding support.

As she expertly arranged the cheeses on a wooden board—each slice a masterpiece in its own right—I settled beside her, the soft fabric of the couch a comforting reminder of how cozy companionship could be. "Do you remember that time in school when we accidentally mixed up the salt with the sugar in the soufflé?" she asked, her eyes dancing with mischief.

I groaned, the memory surfacing with all its delicious embarrassment. "How could I forget? We turned a delicate dessert into something that could only be described as a savory disaster. The instructors were horrified."

"Ah, but it was hilarious! And then we saved it with that ridiculous garnish of edible flowers," she cackled, her laughter brightening the space between us. "At least we learned the importance of labels. And always tasting before serving!"

The warmth of nostalgia wrapped around me, and I let it carry me away from the heaviness that had anchored me for weeks. With every bite of cheese and sip of the rich, velvety wine, I felt a little more of the weight lift from my shoulders.

"You know, I was thinking," Lily began, her tone shifting slightly as she plucked a particularly pungent cheese from the board, "it's time for you to shake things up. Stop lingering in the past, even if it's the tastiest cheese platter. Have you considered entering that cooking competition we talked about?"

The question hung in the air, a golden thread woven into the fabric of our evening. I hesitated, swirling the wine in my glass as if seeking answers in the deep crimson hue. "I don't know, Lil. It feels like a leap when I'm still picking up the pieces. What if I fail?"

"Failing is just another way to find out what doesn't work," she retorted, her voice firm but kind. "You're a brilliant chef! Don't let Marco's shadow loom over your talents. You're not defined by anyone else's journey."

Her words echoed in the back of my mind like the vibrant notes of a song that wouldn't fade. But the sting of doubt lingered, a ghost of insecurity that whispered just loud enough to be heard. "But what if it's not good enough?" I murmured, the words tasting bitter on my tongue.

Lily leaned in, her expression softening. "Remember when we tackled that wild mushroom risotto? It was a complete mess at first, but we turned it into something incredible. Just like you, it needs a little love and patience."

A wry smile tugged at my lips, thinking back to our chaotic experiments. The laughter and stress, the overwhelming sense of triumph when we finally plated something beautiful. "You really think I could do it? Compete?"

"Absolutely! You've got the passion, the skills, and—most importantly—the creativity that will blow the judges away. Just imagine—your unique flair could really stand out. Besides, who wouldn't want a taste of your culinary dreams?"

As her words sank in, a glimmer of hope began to unfurl within me. Maybe it was time to rise from the ashes of my past, to whip up something new and unexpected, like a soufflé reclaiming its rise. I took a deep breath, imagining the vibrant colors of a well-executed dish, the flavors dancing on the palate, and the thrill of the competition ahead.

"Okay, you've convinced me. I'll at least think about it," I replied, my heart racing at the prospect.

"Thinking is a start, but I expect you to be all in! We're in this together, right?"

She nudged me playfully, her eyes alight with excitement, and for the first time in what felt like ages, I didn't just feel alive; I felt inspired.

With our plates emptied and the laughter still echoing off the walls, I realized how essential it was to have friends like Lily, who could cut through the loneliness with their humor and unwavering support. And just like that, the shadows in my heart began to recede, making way for something much brighter—possibilities, flavors, and a renewed sense of self that I thought I had lost forever.

With the echoes of our laughter still warming the air, I felt a surge of determination blooming within me. The weight of Marco's departure seemed to lessen, replaced by the fragrant promise of cheese, wine, and the flickering candlelight that cast playful shadows across the room. The world felt a little less daunting with Lily by my side, like the sun peeking through the clouds after a long storm.

"So, what's next on your culinary bucket list?" Lily asked, her eyes sparkling with mischief as she leaned back against the couch, a satisfied smile on her face. "I mean, beyond conquering your fear of competition."

I pondered for a moment, savoring the rich aftertaste of the wine. The idea of re-entering the world of cooking competitions had ignited a small flame of excitement. "I've been thinking about experimenting with some fusion dishes. You know, blending different cuisines to create something unexpected. Maybe a Mediterranean twist on classic American comfort food?"

Lily clapped her hands together, practically bouncing in her seat. "Yes! I can see it now: cheesy, gooey mac and cheese with roasted tomatoes and a hint of basil. Or maybe a falafel burger with a tangy tzatziki sauce. The world needs to taste that!"

Her enthusiasm was contagious, and I couldn't help but envision the plates I could create. Each dish could tell a story, a testament to my journey that didn't just revolve around Marco but also celebrated my individuality.

The evening wore on, our conversation flowing as smoothly as the wine. I recounted stories of culinary mishaps and triumphs, while Lily shared tales from her bustling job at the city's trendiest bistro, where the chefs never slept and creativity was an all-consuming beast. "It's a bit like a reality show in the kitchen, except we don't have to worry about elimination rounds—just the constant threat of our soufflés collapsing," she quipped, rolling her eyes theatrically.

"Sounds intense. Do you have any behind-the-scenes secrets?" I leaned in, intrigued.

"Oh, tons! Like how Chef Paul insists on wearing that ridiculous hat as if it gives him some kind of magical authority. Honestly, I think it just makes him look like a circus performer." She chuckled, her voice a conspiratorial whisper. "But in all seriousness, he's brilliant. Watching him work is like watching a master conductor lead an orchestra."

Our banter flowed effortlessly, and as the clock ticked on, I realized how desperately I'd missed this—someone who truly understood my passion for food and the life that came with it.

"Let's do a cooking challenge," Lily suggested, her eyes narrowing playfully. "I'll come over next week, and we can create our own fusion masterpieces. Winner gets bragging rights, and the loser has to do the dishes."

"Deal! But fair warning: I'm going to channel my inner chef-goddess," I shot back, a smirk playing on my lips.

"Bring it on! Just don't cry when I steal your thunder," she laughed, and in that moment, I felt a surge of resolve. I wanted to take this leap, to craft dishes that were more than mere sustenance but expressions of my growth, my resilience, and my voice.

After what felt like hours of laughter and food, Lily leaned back, her face turning serious for a moment. "But seriously, how are you holding up? I know we've been joking around, but I don't want to ignore the fact that you're still processing everything with Marco."

The air shifted, and I took a moment to gather my thoughts. "I thought I'd be okay after he left. You know, just move on and carry on with life. But there are days when I feel completely lost, like a ship without a sail."

She nodded, her expression softening as she took my hand in hers. "You're not alone in this, and you don't have to rush the healing process. It's okay to feel like you're drifting sometimes. Just don't forget to anchor yourself in the things you love—like cooking, your art. They'll guide you back."

Her words wrapped around me like a warm blanket. It was comforting to know that I didn't have to be strong all the time, that it was acceptable to feel vulnerable.

A sudden knock at the door interrupted the moment, and my heart jolted. "Who could that be?" I wondered aloud, glancing at Lily with curiosity and a hint of apprehension.

"Maybe it's another unexpected visitor?" she teased, but there was a slight tremor of uncertainty in her voice as I made my way to the door.

I opened it cautiously, my heart racing. Standing there, drenched in the soft glow of the hallway light, was Marco. My breath hitched in my throat, a mix of surprise and confusion swirling within me.

"Can I come in?" he asked, his voice steady yet tinged with an emotion I couldn't quite place.

I glanced back at Lily, who was watching with wide eyes, clearly caught off guard. "Uh, sure," I replied, stepping aside to let him in. The moment he crossed the threshold, the familiar scent of his cologne washed over me, igniting a cascade of memories I had tucked away in the recesses of my mind.

"Hey, Lily," he nodded, his gaze flickering between us, as if gauging the atmosphere.

"Marco," she responded, her tone a mix of surprise and neutrality, reminding me of an overcooked soufflé—puffed up but with a hint of collapse.

"Can we talk?" he asked, his tone softer, almost vulnerable, as he gestured toward the couch.

My heart raced. Here was the man who had been my world, the one who had left me feeling adrift, now standing in my space with a request that felt loaded. "Sure," I managed, forcing a calmness into my voice that I didn't quite feel.

Lily stood, sensing the weight of the moment. "I'll just... give you two some space," she said, a knowing look passing between us before she quietly exited the room.

As the door clicked shut behind her, the air thickened with unspoken words. Marco settled onto the edge of the couch, an unfamiliar tension radiating from him. "I've missed you," he finally said, his voice barely above a whisper, and suddenly, the world felt both impossibly small and overwhelmingly vast.

"Missed me?" I echoed, disbelief lacing my words. "You left, Marco."

"I know. I've been a total idiot, and I don't expect you to just forget that. But I've done some thinking." His eyes searched mine, desperation lacing his tone. "I realized that I still care about you. I want to make things right."

The sincerity in his voice clashed violently with the memories of heartache and confusion he had left in his wake. My pulse quickened, torn between the longing that still flickered within me and the reality of what had been.

"Why now?" I managed, struggling to find my footing amidst the chaos of emotions.

"Because I couldn't keep running from what we had. It's like I've been in this fog, and I finally see clearly. I want to try again, to be the partner you deserve."

Every word hung in the air, heavy with implication and possibility. I felt the tug of my heart, grappling with the fear of being hurt again. And as I opened my mouth to respond, I realized that this moment, much like a well-executed dish, would require careful balancing of flavors—courage, vulnerability, and perhaps a dash of hope.

The moment hung between us like the delicate pause before the first note of a symphony, charged with unspoken words and lingering emotions. I could feel the tension rising, thick and palpable, while

Marco's gaze bore into mine with an intensity that both thrilled and terrified me. Here was the man who had crafted a tapestry of memories with me, now threading through my mind like an errant strand of pasta—overcooked and tangled, yet strangely familiar.

"Why now?" I asked again, my voice steadier than I felt. "What's changed?"

He inhaled sharply, as if the air itself was heavy with his hesitation. "I spent some time away, and I realized that running from us didn't make the feelings go away. I thought distancing myself would help, but it only made things worse." His hands clenched together, fingers intertwined in a show of vulnerability that surprised me. "I know I hurt you. I know that I was selfish. But I can't pretend I don't want you in my life anymore."

My heart fluttered uneasily, caught between the nostalgia of what had been and the painful reminder of why it ended. "Marco, it's not that simple. You just waltz back in after weeks of silence and expect me to embrace you? You can't just expect me to ignore the hurt."

He leaned forward, earnestness etched into every line of his face. "I don't expect you to forgive me right away. I just want a chance to prove that I can be better, that I can be the partner you deserve. I've been working on myself—therapy, self-reflection, all that cliché stuff. But it's true."

I couldn't help but raise an eyebrow, skepticism curling around my heart like a vine, prickling with doubt. "Therapy? Wow, look who's evolved. Do I get a trophy for surviving this relationship?"

A faint smile broke through his serious demeanor, and for a moment, the tension lessened. "If there were trophies for surviving emotional disasters, you'd have a whole shelf by now."

The humor in his response tugged at my lips, but I quickly masked it with a frown, the storm inside me still raging. "I appreciate the effort, but that doesn't erase the past. Trust isn't something you just demand back, Marco."

"Then let me earn it," he said, his voice barely above a whisper. "I'll do whatever it takes. Just tell me what you need."

As I searched his eyes, I felt a whirlwind of emotions—anger, longing, and an unexpected flicker of hope. Could he really mean it? A part of me wanted to believe him, wanted to bask in the comfort of his presence and forget the pain. But the more rational side of my mind screamed in protest, reminding me of the countless promises that had come before, now echoing hollowly in the spaces between us.

"I need time," I finally said, steeling myself against the vulnerability that threatened to spill out. "I need to figure out what I want—what I truly want. And right now, I'm not sure what that looks like."

Marco nodded slowly, his expression softening as if he understood the weight of my words. "Time is all I can give you. But please, don't shut me out. I want to be part of your life again, whether as a friend or something more. I just want a chance to show you I can be better."

His sincerity warmed the air between us, but the shadows of our shared history lingered, reminding me that the past was not so easily brushed aside. I let out a shaky breath, torn between the longing for connection and the need for caution.

"Can we just... start slow?" I proposed, the words tumbling out like flour from a poorly sealed bag. "You know, meet for coffee or something? No pressure."

"Slow sounds perfect," he agreed, relief washing over his features. "Just let me know when you're ready."

Before I could respond, a loud knock reverberated through the apartment, startling both of us. I glanced toward the door, my heart sinking as an all-too-familiar sense of foreboding crept in.

"Do you expect someone?" Marco asked, a hint of confusion breaking through his calm facade.

"No, I—" I began, but before I could finish, the door swung open, revealing a figure I hadn't seen in ages—Alana, my ex-roommate from culinary school, her hair wild and a wild spark in her eyes.

"Surprise! I'm back in town!" she exclaimed, her voice bright and loud, as if she were announcing her arrival to a bustling crowd instead of a tense reunion.

"Alana!" I gasped, caught off guard as I scrambled to find my footing in the chaos. "What are you doing here?"

"I just got in from New Orleans! Thought I'd drop by and see my favorite people! I brought beignets and some gumbo from my favorite place." She stepped inside, her arms brimming with takeout boxes, and I could only stare, torn between shock and the warmth that her infectious enthusiasm always brought.

"Uh, we were in the middle of something," I stammered, throwing a glance at Marco, whose expression was now a mix of confusion and curiosity.

"Oh, don't mind me! I love a good drama," Alana chimed, plopping the boxes onto the coffee table, her eyes sparkling with mischief. "Besides, I live for a romantic reunion. Do you need a referee?"

I shot her a warning look, but she just winked, completely unfazed by the charged atmosphere. "Look, I've got a ton of stories from New Orleans that will knock your socks off. You two can sort out your feelings later."

"Right, because nothing says 'let's talk about our complicated relationship' like a plate of beignets," I muttered under my breath, struggling to suppress the swell of laughter bubbling beneath the surface.

But as Alana launched into a tale about a culinary mishap involving alligator and a stubborn sous-chef, the tension in the room began to ebb away, replaced by the familiar warmth of camaraderie. I found myself leaning into the moment, allowing the weight of what had just transpired to drift into the background, if only for a little while.

Yet, just as I started to relax, Marco cleared his throat, his eyes darting between me and Alana. "This is a... surprise," he said, the edge of awkwardness creeping back into his voice. "Didn't realize I'd be sharing this moment with an audience."

"Oh please, you've been on my radar since culinary school. I can't let you two have an emotional moment without my expert commentary," Alana quipped, her grin wide.

"Emotional moment? Is that what you'd call this?" Marco shot back, a hint of a smile playing on his lips despite the tension still crackling in the air.

I rolled my eyes, a smile breaking free against my better judgment. "Just don't mess this up for me, okay? I'm trying to navigate the minefield of my feelings here."

"Minefield? Honey, this is more like a gourmet buffet. Enjoy every dish and see what you like!" Alana chimed, clearly unfazed by the undercurrents between Marco and me.

With her infectious energy filling the room, I found myself laughing along, but beneath the laughter lay the residue of the conversation with Marco, a thread of uncertainty weaving through my thoughts.

As the evening wore on, Alana's stories swirled around us, peppered with laughter and nostalgia, but every time I glanced at Marco, the weight of our unresolved emotions lurked just below the surface.

Just as I thought I could breathe easily, the doorbell rang again, a jarring interruption that sent my heart racing. "Seriously? Who else could possibly show up?" I exclaimed, both exasperated and curious.

Alana shot me a knowing look. "At this rate, we're going to need a reality show. Let's see what chaos this brings!"

I approached the door, my heart pounding as I opened it, fully unprepared for what lay beyond. Standing there, framed by the dim light of the hallway, was someone I hadn't seen in years—someone who, without a doubt, could turn this evening upside down in an instant.

"Surprise," the figure said, their voice low and smooth, sending a chill racing down my spine. "I've come to settle some unfinished business."

Chapter 18: Secrets Unraveled

The air was thick with the scent of sizzling garlic and freshly baked bread, a kaleidoscope of colors painting the festival grounds as vendors flaunted their culinary masterpieces. I clutched a small paper cup filled with fragrant truffle-infused risotto, my senses dancing with each bite. The laughter of children echoed, mingling with the soft strumming of a nearby guitarist, creating an ambiance that felt almost magical. This was my escape, a moment of delicious normalcy in a life that had become a whirlwind of rumors and accusations.

As I wandered through the maze of booths, my heart raced with excitement, each stall a new adventure. A beaming chef handed me a delicate pastry, its crust flaky and warm, promising to melt in my mouth. I bit into it, savoring the way the sweet cream filled my senses, and for a moment, I forgot about the scandal that loomed over me like a dark cloud. It was a bittersweet distraction, a reminder that the world outside could still hold beauty even when chaos threatened to tear it apart.

"Now that's a bite worth savoring!" I exclaimed, my voice rising above the chatter. A nearby vendor glanced over, a smile tugging at his lips as he caught my enthusiasm. Just as I turned to grab another sample, my eyes locked onto a familiar figure making his way through the crowd. James, the food critic whose name had recently become synonymous with scandal, moved with an air of confident charm. His dark hair, tousled and inviting, framed a face that was both striking and unnerving.

Despite my instinct to turn away, something pulled me closer, like a moth to a flame. I had read his reviews, enjoyed his keen insights, yet knew well the danger that lurked behind his polished exterior. It felt reckless to approach him, but curiosity gnawed at me, urging me to explore the man behind the headlines.

"Isn't it a lovely day for culinary chaos?" he said, his voice smooth as caramel. He leaned against the stall, a glass of sparkling water in hand, those warm, deep-set eyes glimmering with mischief.

"Chaos is one way to put it," I replied, arching an eyebrow. "It seems every dish is trying to outshine the last."

James chuckled, the sound rich and warm, wrapping around me like a comfortable blanket. "And isn't that the beauty of it? The creativity, the passion? It's what makes this industry so thrilling, yet so perilous. Just like any story, it's all about perspective."

I could feel the tension in my stomach tighten at his words, his perspective undeniably captivating. But in the back of my mind, Lily's warning echoed like a persistent reminder. "You're right, but with every chef trying to make their mark, there's bound to be some unfortunate casualties along the way."

"Ah, you must be referring to the latest scandal," he replied, his gaze intense, as if gauging my reaction. "It's a messy affair, one that could tarnish reputations overnight."

"Or create a feeding frenzy," I shot back, crossing my arms. "I suppose you thrive in such chaos, don't you?"

He smirked, an amused glint lighting up his expression. "You could say that. But there's a fine line between reveling in the drama and exploiting it for personal gain. Not everyone is motivated by ambition; some genuinely seek to elevate the culinary experience."

I pondered his words, the weight of his truth clashing with my doubts. "Is that what you're after, James? Elevation, or something more?"

"Touché," he said, tilting his head. "I can't deny I enjoy the thrill of discovery, the rush of unearthing hidden gems. But I also believe in integrity. There's a lot at stake for those who dare to dream."

"Integrity," I echoed, glancing away as the word settled uneasily between us. "A word that seems to have lost its meaning lately."

As the conversation deepened, I found myself torn between my fascination with him and the lingering warning from Lily. Just as I was about to let my guard down, I caught sight of Lily striding toward us, her expression a mix of concern and determination.

"Can we talk?" she said, her voice low but firm, her eyes darting between us with an intensity that made my pulse quicken.

"Of course," I replied, but the protest was already bubbling in my throat. I wasn't done with this conversation, not yet. James offered a small, enigmatic smile, as if he relished the unfolding drama, a glimmer of mischief dancing behind his dark eyes.

Lily pulled me aside, her protective instincts igniting a spark of doubt in my heart. "You can't trust him, Emma. He's part of the problem, not the solution."

"Is he?" I challenged, an unexpected edge to my voice. "He's passionate about food, just like us. He could help us understand the bigger picture."

"Or lead you right into a trap," she countered, her brow furrowing with concern. "The world of food critics is treacherous. You can't be too naive in a business like this."

I swallowed hard, torn between my desire to explore this new connection and the weight of the warning in my friend's voice. James had a magnetic quality that drew me in, yet I could feel the shadows of doubt creeping back. The line between ambition and integrity had never felt so fragile, and with every glance at James, I could sense the stakes were rising higher than I had ever anticipated.

As the festival buzzed around us, I felt the thrill of unpredictability sparking in the air, a reminder that sometimes the most delicious discoveries come wrapped in layers of tension, unexpected twists, and tantalizing secrets waiting to be unraveled.

Lily's hand clutched my arm, her grip a mixture of urgency and fear. "You need to be careful, Emma. I know he seems charming, but there's more to him than meets the eye." Her voice was a low hiss, meant only for my ears, but I could feel a dozen eyes curiously glancing in our direction.

"Why are you so quick to judge him?" I shot back, my tone sharper than I intended. It felt unfair to dismiss someone based solely on whispers and headlines. "What if he's not the villain everyone makes him out to be?"

"Because I've seen how he operates," Lily replied, her eyes narrowing. "He'll charm you, and then you won't see it coming until it's too late. You know how the media spins stories. They'll twist everything. You don't want to be part of that narrative."

I couldn't shake the tension that settled like a thick fog around us. As I looked over at James, still leaning casually against the stall, his laughter ringing like soft bells, I wondered if maybe Lily was right. Yet, a part of me felt drawn to him, as if his very presence beckoned me into a world filled with possibility.

"Lily, I appreciate your concern, but I can handle myself," I said, adopting a more placating tone. "I just want to hear him out. There might be more to this whole scandal than we realize."

Her eyes softened slightly, but her expression remained resolute. "Just promise me you won't get too close. This could blow up in your face."

"Sure, I promise," I replied, though my heart didn't fully align with my words. The festival buzzed with activity around us, laughter and shouts intertwining like a lively dance, but my focus was drawn back to James. It was like watching a magician perform tricks—his words seemed enchanting, each one pulling me deeper into the spell.

"Emma! Lily! There you are!" A cheery voice interrupted, breaking the spell. It was Marcus, the culinary school friend I hadn't seen in ages, his bright smile infectious. "You won't believe the dishes I've just tried. It's like a flavor explosion in every bite! You've got to come see—"

"Not right now, Marcus," Lily interrupted, glancing nervously between him and James. "We were just—"

"Talking to Mr. Scandal himself?" Marcus said, his brow arching as he caught sight of James. "You've got guts, Emma. That guy is trouble wrapped in a bow tie. What's he trying to sell you? A bad review?"

James, who had been observing us with an amused expression, chimed in, "I assure you, my reviews are generally more appetizing than that." He flashed a disarming smile, one that could likely charm a snake.

"Didn't you get into some hot water recently, James?" Marcus asked, crossing his arms with a bemused look. "The headlines were quite the page-turner."

James's smile faltered for just a moment, replaced by a flicker of something that felt almost vulnerable. "Ah, yes. The unfortunate consequences of being too honest in a world that often prefers sugarcoated truths."

Lily's grip on my arm tightened, and I sensed her frustration simmering just beneath the surface. "You're here to sample food, not get embroiled in the drama of a critic's failures," she said, her tone firm.

"Drama is often the best seasoning," James replied, his gaze settling on me. "It keeps the taste buds alive, wouldn't you agree, Emma?"

I met his eyes, feeling the pull of curiosity deepening. "Maybe, but too much spice can ruin a dish."

"True," he mused, his expression thoughtful. "But isn't the risk worth taking? After all, who doesn't love a little adventure with their meal?"

Marcus interjected, trying to deflect the tension. "Speaking of adventure, you should check out the booth over there. They're serving something called 'Fusion Tacos'—a blend of flavors you'd never expect!"

As he pulled me away, I couldn't help but glance back at James. The playful spark in his eye had shifted to something deeper, almost contemplative. There was more to him than just the headlines, I was sure of it. Yet, the weight of Lily's caution loomed large.

At the taco booth, I indulged in the vibrant array of flavors, the spicy kick mingling with hints of mango and cilantro. Each bite was a delightful surprise, a testament to the culinary creativity surrounding me. I found myself sharing laughter with Marcus, the worries of the world momentarily fading as he recounted his latest culinary escapades at school.

But James lingered in my thoughts, a specter just beyond the stalls. I couldn't shake the feeling that there was a connection, an understanding waiting to unfold if only I dared to peel back the layers.

"I think you're making a mistake, Emma," Lily said suddenly, her tone sharp, cutting through my reverie. "You're getting too wrapped up in this."

"Wrapped up in what? Exploring new ideas? Learning?" I shot back, my voice rising slightly. "You can't expect me to cower away just because of rumors."

"Emma, I'm just trying to protect you! He's the type who'll sink his teeth into you and then use you as a stepping stone for his next big piece," she countered, frustration spilling over.

I took a deep breath, trying to calm the growing tension. "Maybe I want to be part of something bigger than just a food festival. Maybe I want to understand this industry, even if it means getting close to someone like him."

"Getting close could lead to a disaster," she warned. "I don't want to see you hurt."

Just then, a loud cheer erupted from a nearby booth, pulling our attention. A chef was presenting his signature dish, and the crowd surged, eager to taste his creation. The excitement was palpable, yet it felt like a stark contrast to the heaviness of our conversation.

"Let's go check it out," I said, hoping to lighten the mood. "We can have fun without worrying about scandal."

Lily hesitated, but eventually nodded, her brows still furrowed. "Fine. But I'm not letting my guard down."

We moved toward the crowd, and as I stood in line, I caught sight of James again, speaking animatedly with a couple of fellow critics. There was a confidence about him that was both alluring and intimidating, and I couldn't shake the feeling that my world was about to shift dramatically. The festival, with all its tantalizing flavors and vibrant energy, felt like the perfect backdrop for secrets to be revealed and alliances forged.

Each moment felt charged, the air crackling with potential, as I found myself caught in the thrilling whirlwind of ambition and integrity, waiting for the next delicious twist to unfold.

The atmosphere of the festival pulsated with life, a vibrant tapestry woven from the aromas of grilled meats and sweet pastries. People drifted from stall to stall, their laughter mingling with the occasional burst of music from a nearby stage. Yet amid this joyous chaos, my thoughts were ensnared by the nagging tension of the conversation with Lily.

"Let's just enjoy this, okay?" I said, forcing a smile as we stepped toward the next booth, where a chef was flambéing something in a grand display of culinary showmanship. The flames danced wildly, igniting the faces around us with flickers of orange and gold. "I want to savor this moment without dwelling on what might happen."

Lily shrugged, her expression still troubled, but she was trying, and that was something. "Fine. But if I see him cornering you, I'm stepping in."

I rolled my eyes, half-amused. "As if you're my bodyguard now. Do you want a whistle to blow or a baton to wave?"

"Don't tempt me," she shot back, though the corner of her mouth twitched in a suppressed grin.

The chef, with a flourish that could rival a magician, tossed a sprig of rosemary into the flaming pan, and the crowd erupted in cheers. The flames licked the air, sending a wave of heat that felt both invigorating and intimidating. "Who knew cooking could be so dramatic?" I mused aloud, my heart racing from the spectacle.

"Just like life," Lily replied, her tone unexpectedly philosophical. "A little heat, a lot of flavor, and who knows what might burn."

As the chef plated his creation, a smoky aroma wafted toward us. "You have to try this," I said, nudging Lily forward. "After all, drama is best enjoyed with good food."

She hesitated for a moment, then stepped up, her eyes darting around as if anticipating an ambush. "Okay, but only if you promise to stay vigilant."

"Scout's honor," I said, raising my hand in mock salute before ordering a small serving of the flambéed delight. As I took my first bite, the explosion of flavors sent my senses into overdrive. Sweet, smoky, and just the right amount of heat enveloped my tongue. "This is amazing!"

Lily watched me with a bemused expression, half-proud, half-anxious. "You really get excited about food."

"Can you blame me?" I said, grinning. "In a world full of chaos, these moments remind me that pleasure exists. I want to enjoy it while I can."

"Just promise me that enjoyment won't lead to reckless choices," she replied, her voice slightly softer now.

Before I could answer, the crowd erupted again, this time in applause as James made his way toward us. "I see you've discovered the flambéed sensation! It's a crowd favorite for a reason," he said, his eyes sparkling with excitement.

"I'll say!" I replied, my heart quickening. "This chef knows how to put on a show."

"Much like myself," he grinned, gesturing with mock grandeur. "But seriously, have you had a chance to try the fusion tacos yet? They're a revelation."

"Fusion tacos? What's next, sushi burritos?" I quipped, not ready to let him charm me so easily.

"Don't knock it until you've tried it," he replied, an amused glint in his eye. "Besides, it's all about pushing boundaries. The best dishes come from taking risks, don't you think?"

I glanced at Lily, who looked ready to intervene at any moment. "I suppose you could say that," I replied, a hint of sarcasm in my tone. "But there's a fine line between risk and recklessness."

James chuckled, the sound smooth and rich, like the finest chocolate. "Touché. But isn't that what makes life worth living? Navigating that line can lead to the most delicious surprises."

"Or disasters," I shot back, crossing my arms. "You're not selling me on your philosophy just yet, Mr. Food Critic."

He leaned closer, a conspiratorial whisper playing on his lips. "But imagine the stories you could tell, the flavors you could experience! Life is too short to play it safe."

I felt a flutter of excitement at the thought of adventure—of stepping into the unknown. But then Lily cleared her throat, breaking the spell. "Emma, maybe we should grab those tacos. You know, explore the festival as a whole?" Her tone was subtly pointed, and I could feel her nerves tingle in the air.

"Absolutely, let's go," I agreed, but the thrill of potential adventure danced just out of reach, leaving a tantalizing aftertaste.

As we moved toward the taco stall, James fell into step beside me. "I get it," he said, his voice low. "Lily looks out for you. But I'm not here to cause trouble. I'm merely a guide to the culinary landscape, and it's a wild ride."

"Wild ride, huh?" I raised an eyebrow, skeptical. "Is that how you justify your reputation?"

He paused, his expression shifting into something more serious. "Reputation is a fickle thing. It's crafted from stories, often incomplete. I'm more than just the headlines, you know. I have a vision."

"Sounds poetic, but visions can be misleading," I replied, my skepticism rising again.

"Perhaps," he conceded, but the spark in his eye didn't dim. "But that doesn't mean I'm not worth listening to."

The line for the tacos was long, and as we stood waiting, the crowd around us swelled, voices merging into a harmonious din of laughter and chatter. Yet, my attention was riveted on James. He had a way of weaving himself into my thoughts like a finely crafted dish, each layer more complex than the last.

Suddenly, a commotion erupted to our right—a burst of raised voices and a sudden shove sent a nearby couple tumbling into the crowd. "Hey!" one of them yelled, their face flushed with anger. "Watch where you're going!"

"What's going on?" Lily asked, her eyes wide.

Before I could respond, a figure broke through the crowd, a familiar silhouette that made my heart sink. It was Derek, the executive chef embroiled in the scandal that had sent shockwaves through the culinary community. His face was flushed, his hands clenched at his sides.

"What are you doing here, James?" Derek growled, eyes narrowing, his voice dripping with venom.

"Looks like we're both here to enjoy the festival, Derek," James replied smoothly, his demeanor unchanged, though I could sense the tension crackling between them.

"I don't want to see your face at my event," Derek spat, stepping closer, his aura dark and threatening.

The crowd around us began to murmur, glancing between the two men, tension palpable in the air like a taut string ready to snap. I could feel my heart racing, the festive atmosphere suddenly feeling ominous.

"What's the issue here?" I asked, stepping forward instinctively, my voice shaking but determined. "We're all just trying to enjoy the food."

Derek turned his glare toward me, and for a moment, I felt the weight of his anger, like a heavy fog settling around us. "You shouldn't be associating with him, Emma. He's poison."

"Or maybe he's the antidote," I shot back, surprised at my own boldness. "You don't get to decide who I talk to."

James glanced at me, surprise flickering across his features, but I couldn't focus on him, my attention locked onto Derek.

"Stay out of this," Derek hissed, his voice low, but the crowd was thickening around us, a charged atmosphere of excitement and danger.

But before I could retort, a loud crash sounded from behind us, followed by a series of gasps. I turned just in time to see a table laden with food toppling over, dishes crashing to the ground like shattered dreams.

And then came the unmistakable sound of a phone camera clicking. The weight of the moment hung heavy in the air, and as I looked back at James and Derek, I knew things were about to spiral out of control in a way I couldn't have anticipated.

In the chaos, the truth lurked just beneath the surface, waiting to be revealed, and I was caught right in the middle of it, teetering on the edge of discovery—and disaster.

Chapter 19: Flavors of Doubt

The sun dipped low in the sky, casting an orange glow that melted into the crimson hues of dusk. I found myself ensconced in the chaotic embrace of the festival, where laughter and the tantalizing aroma of sizzling street food mingled in the air like an intoxicating potion. Each booth beckoned with the promise of flavors—smoky, sweet, tangy—like sirens calling to me from the shores of culinary paradise. I moved through the throngs of people, each step an echo of uncertainty, my heart a restless bird fluttering against the cage of my ribs.

James hovered near me, his presence both comforting and suffocating. He had a way of slipping into conversations effortlessly, his words drizzling like honey, sweet but thick with the risk of getting stuck. "You know," he said, leaning slightly closer, his voice low enough to blend with the ambient noise, "your prose has a certain bite to it. Like a well-seasoned dish." The compliment rolled off his tongue, but there was an undertone that felt more like a jab than an accolade.

"Bite, huh?" I replied, my brows knitting together as I sidestepped a group of giggling teenagers. "I didn't realize I was writing food criticism." The sarcasm was a shield, though I knew I should be grateful for his attention. After all, James had connections that could help launch my career. But beneath the surface of my gratitude bubbled a sense of wariness, like the simmering oil in the fryer just waiting to spill over.

The laughter of a nearby couple drew my gaze, and I caught a glimpse of Marco across the fairgrounds, standing confidently at his booth. The sight of him was both a balm and a thorn, reminding me of the joy and heartache we shared like a complicated recipe. His charm was magnetic, drawing patrons like moths to a flame, and I couldn't help but envy the ease with which he engaged with everyone. Marco was an artist in his element, while I felt like an imposter in a costume two sizes too big.

"Are you going to just stare at him all day, or are you planning to join the party?" James's tone shifted, a blend of amusement and challenge that irked me.

"Maybe I prefer the view from the sidelines," I snapped, the bite of my words surprising even myself. James raised an eyebrow, a half-smirk playing on his lips.

"Your writing would suggest otherwise. You seem to have a penchant for diving headfirst into the deep end."

"Writing is one thing; living is another," I retorted, my cheeks warming.

"Touché," he conceded, holding up his hands in mock surrender. But beneath the banter, I sensed an unspoken question hanging between us: why was I hesitating? The festival pulsed around us, a kaleidoscope of flavors and sounds, yet I felt marooned in my indecision, the vibrant world too loud for my quiet fears.

I pulled away, seeking refuge in the bustle, navigating through stalls adorned with colorful banners and the tantalizing allure of exotic dishes. Each vendor had a story to tell, and the air buzzed with the promise of new tastes and adventures. The sizzle of skewers being tossed on the grill mingled with the soft strumming of a guitar in the distance, creating a backdrop that felt alive with possibility.

As I wandered, my thoughts flickered back to the moment I had decided to attend this festival, this opportunity to showcase my culinary narratives. A chance to carve my own niche amid a world that thrived on competition and comparison. But now, the weight of my aspirations felt heavier than the tantalizing aromas that surrounded me. I'd spent countless nights pouring over my drafts, spinning tales that intertwined the culinary and the emotional, yet here I was, questioning every word.

"Hey! You're not escaping me that easily," James called, catching up to my side. The determination in his voice was hard to ignore, and I wondered if he sensed my spiraling thoughts. "Let's grab a bite. You can't let fear of competition ruin the flavors of this festival."

"Easy for you to say, Mr. Charming," I shot back, my voice light but tinged with a hint of bitterness. "You thrive on this. I'm still trying to find my footing."

"Finding your footing is part of the dance," he replied, his eyes gleaming with mischief. "And trust me, you're a far better dancer than you give yourself credit for. Now, let's eat before I starve and lose all semblance of charm."

I couldn't suppress a smile, despite my simmering doubts. The rhythm of our exchange flowed smoothly, like a perfectly executed dish, each word building upon the last. We approached a vibrant stall adorned with a tapestry of spices. The vendor, a jovial woman with laughter lines etched into her sun-kissed skin, beckoned us closer.

"Try this!" she exclaimed, thrusting a small cup of golden saffron-infused rice at us. "A taste of sunshine in every bite!"

James took a spoonful first, his eyes lighting up with surprise and delight. "Wow, this is incredible!" he exclaimed, and I couldn't help but feel a flicker of envy at his unabashed enjoyment.

I hesitated before taking my own bite, letting the flavors wash over me—a delicate dance of spice and warmth, like a comforting hug after a long day. "Okay, I'll admit it, this is good," I said, trying to mask the vulnerability creeping into my tone.

"See?" James said, nudging my shoulder playfully. "You're already tasting the success."

Success felt like a distant shore, its glimmer fading in the midst of my self-doubt. I could see the island of my dreams, but the waves of competition crashed around me, threatening to pull me under. James's playful banter, however, lightened the heaviness in my heart, reminding me of the passion that had brought me here in the first place.

I resolved to shake off the shadows of doubt. This festival was more than just a battleground; it was a celebration of flavors, of stories, of dreams being realized. And while I still felt the weight of my choices, I knew I had to embrace the chaos, the flavors of doubt that mingled with the sweet promise of possibility. After all, every dish tells a story, and mine was just beginning to simmer.

The sun began to retreat behind the horizon, casting long shadows that intertwined with the flickering lights strung across the festival grounds. The golden hour wrapped everything in a soft, warm glow, yet I felt anything but at ease. I could see vendors adjusting their colorful displays as they prepared for the night crowd, each booth pulsating with life and laughter, but my mind was a whirlpool of doubts that threatened to drown me in the tide of insecurity.

"Do you think Marco has any idea what he's doing?" I asked, my voice carrying a hint of bitterness. We stood in front of a stall where a man was grilling skewers of marinated chicken, the scent wafting through the air and mingling with the sugary aroma of funnel cakes. The vendor smiled at me, urging me to sample a piece, but my focus was elsewhere.

James took a deliberate sip of his iced tea, his expression oddly contemplative. "What do you mean? Like, does he know how to cook?"

I rolled my eyes. "No, I mean in life. He seems so... effortless, you know? Like he's just sailing along while I'm over here trying not to capsize every five minutes."

"Effortless is just a well-practiced illusion," James replied, his tone surprisingly serious. "Behind every calm facade is a tempest waiting to break free. Trust me, I've been on the receiving end of that storm a time or two."

I shot him a sideways glance, intrigued despite myself. "So you've had your own moments of turbulence? You always seem so composed."

He chuckled, shaking his head. "Composed? Oh, darling, that's just me pretending to have my life together. If you saw the chaos in my mind, you'd run screaming."

That made me laugh. The tension in my chest eased, if only for a moment. "I guess we're all just fumbling through, then?"

"Pretty much. But some of us do it with style." He leaned closer, lowering his voice as if sharing a secret. "And a good pair of shoes."

"Ah, the shoes," I said, my spirits lifting slightly. "A worthy defense against life's disasters."

Just as I started to feel lighter, I caught a glimpse of Marco in the distance, his laughter echoing through the crowd. I felt a pang of something—jealousy? Longing? I couldn't quite pin it down. He was surrounded by admirers, their faces illuminated by the flickering lanterns, and for a fleeting moment, I wondered if I'd ever be able to share in that kind of effortless charm.

"Why are you looking at him like he just invented chocolate?" James nudged me playfully, pulling me from my reverie. "If you're going to stare, at least do it with the admiration of a critic ready to pen a rave review."

"Maybe I'm just wondering what it's like to be that carefree," I confessed, my voice barely above a whisper. "He doesn't seem to care about anything other than his food. And I used to think I could have that, too."

"Or maybe he's just better at hiding his anxieties," James suggested, eyeing Marco as he chatted with a group of festival-goers. "You should try talking to him. You might find he's just a guy in a chef's jacket, not some culinary demigod."

"Easier said than done," I muttered, tracing patterns in the condensation on my drink. The thought of confronting Marco felt like trying to climb a mountain in flip-flops. "I'd need a good dose of liquid courage, preferably spiked."

"Let's remedy that," he said, grabbing my hand and pulling me toward a nearby booth. "There's a place that serves the best spiked lemonade. If we're going to tackle your feelings, we might as well do it with style."

"Isn't that your motto?" I teased, following him through the crowd, the laughter and chatter swirling around us like a festive whirlwind.

"Absolutely. Style and substance," he shot back, a grin spreading across his face. "Though, mostly style. Substance requires a lot of introspection, and I'm not ready for that level of commitment."

By the time we reached the booth, I felt the warmth of the evening seep into my bones, the camaraderie between us rekindling my spirit. The vendor, an older woman with a twinkle in her eye, handed us two cups brimming with icy yellow liquid. The first sip was tart and sweet, a burst of brightness that invigorated my senses.

"See? We're practically warriors now," James declared, holding up his cup in a mock toast.

"Cheers to that," I replied, clinking my cup against his, the sound reverberating with a promise of adventure.

We stood for a moment, soaking in the festival ambiance, the kaleidoscope of colors and sounds wrapping around us like a cozy blanket. The faint strumming of a guitar played nearby, blending with the clamor of laughter, creating a melody of joy that made my heart ache with longing.

"Okay," I said, feeling bolder with each sip. "Let's do this. I'll go talk to Marco."

James raised an eyebrow, his smile widening. "Now that's the spirit! Just remember, if it goes horribly wrong, I'll be right here, ready to rescue you with our spiked lemonade."

With a deep breath, I squared my shoulders and made my way through the crowd, the chatter buzzing around me like a hive of bees. I could see Marco clearer now, his laughter infectious, a light that drew people in. But as I approached, the laughter faded, replaced by a gnawing doubt. What if he didn't remember me? What if this was just another chance for him to showcase his talent while I stood there like a faded backdrop?

"Hey, Marco!" I called out, my voice steady despite the fluttering in my stomach. He turned, and the world shrank to just the two of us, the festival fading into a blur of colors and sounds.

His smile was genuine, disarming in its warmth. "Well, if it isn't the writer with a taste for trouble," he replied, his tone playful. "What brings you to my corner of culinary paradise?"

"Just taking in the sights—and flavors," I replied, forcing a casualness I didn't quite feel. "Thought I'd see how the competition was faring."

"Oh, you know me," he said with a mock flourish. "Just out here trying to steal all the awards and crush my enemies with my impeccable seasoning."

"Very ambitious. Is there room for more chaos in your kingdom?" I teased, feeling the ice of my doubts start to crack.

"Always," he replied, leaning against the booth, a mischievous glint in his eyes. "Chaos makes the best recipes. So, what's on your mind? I can practically see the gears turning."

His directness caught me off guard, and I almost faltered. "Honestly? Just the usual existential dread about whether I'll ever find my footing in this world. You know how it is."

"Ah, yes, the dreaded culinary existential crisis. It's a classic," he said, his tone laced with humor. "But I think you're closer than you realize."

My heart raced, not just from his words but from the way he was looking at me, as if I were more than just a mere writer vying for attention. Maybe, just maybe, I could navigate this storm of emotions and emerge with more than just bruised pride. As the festival around us came alive with music and laughter, I felt the surge of possibility blooming like the fireflies that danced above our heads.

The laughter around us blended seamlessly with the distant strumming of a guitar, the notes weaving through the evening air like a gentle caress. Marco's gaze held mine, a flicker of something unspoken passing between us, and I felt my heart thrum against my ribcage, each beat a reminder of the stakes. The festival, alive with color and sound, faded to a mere backdrop as his presence pulled me into a universe of shared dreams and culinary passion.

"Are you still trying to find your voice?" he asked, his eyes narrowing slightly as if he were peering into my very soul. "Or have you already discovered it?"

"More like I'm still looking for the right recipe," I replied, forcing a lightness into my tone that didn't quite match the weight of my heart. "I thought I had it figured out, but every time I think I'm on the right track, life throws in an unexpected ingredient. I mean, who even knows what cumin does in a cake?"

Marco laughed, a rich, melodious sound that wrapped around me like a warm blanket. "Cumin in a cake? That sounds like a culinary crime against humanity. But seriously, it's all part of the process. Sometimes the strangest combinations lead to the most unforgettable flavors." He paused, leaning in slightly. "And sometimes, they lead to complete disasters."

I could see the glint of mischief in his eyes, and despite my swirling doubts, a smile crept onto my face. "I suppose there's beauty in the chaos," I admitted, my voice softer now. "But I can't help feeling like I'm stumbling around in the dark, trying to find a light switch that doesn't exist."

"Then stop stumbling. Turn on the lights," he challenged, his gaze steady. "Your words are your own—light them up. Write for you, not for anyone else. The right audience will find you."

I took a sip of my spiked lemonade, letting the coolness wash over me, mingling with the warmth of his presence. "What if I don't even know what I want to say?"

"That's the fun part," he said, an infectious grin spreading across his face. "Just start somewhere. Write about the food, the festival, your struggles—just write. It doesn't have to be perfect. In fact, I'm convinced that the messy drafts often taste the best."

His encouragement felt like a lifeline, the tension in my chest slowly loosening. "Easy for you to say, Chef Marco," I shot back, "but you're the one whose dishes have won awards. I'm just trying not to drop my pen in the frying pan."

"You know, I dropped my first few pans more times than I can count," he said, laughter dancing in his eyes. "You should've seen my kitchen back then. Chaos doesn't just create flavor; it also creates character."

"Character, huh? Sounds like a fancy way of saying 'failed experiment.'"

"Maybe," he replied, the laughter fading into something more serious. "But failure is just the seasoning of success. You learn, adapt, and then try again. Plus, if you don't make mistakes, how will you know what doesn't work?"

I felt a rush of something—was it inspiration? I leaned in, intrigued by the possibilities that lay ahead. "So you're saying I should embrace my messiness?"

"Exactly! Let the world see your culinary misadventures. Trust me, they'll relate. It's like the best stories—they're rarely flawless, but they're always memorable."

In that moment, the doubt that had shadowed me began to dissipate like fog under the morning sun. Perhaps embracing my messiness wasn't just a strategy; it could be the key to unlocking my true voice. I wanted to share my journey, to weave my experiences into something meaningful, something real.

"Thanks, Marco," I said, sincerity lacing my words. "You might just be the inspiration I needed."

His expression softened, a flicker of vulnerability crossing his face. "And you might just be the reminder I need that not everything has to be perfect."

Before I could respond, a commotion erupted nearby, shattering our moment. A crowd had gathered around a booth, animated voices rising in excitement and confusion. My heart raced with curiosity, and I turned to Marco, who wore a look of intrigue.

"What's going on over there?" I asked, nodding toward the crowd.

"Let's find out!" he exclaimed, his curiosity piqued. We weaved our way through the throng, the excited buzz growing louder with each step. As we drew closer, I could see a large man gesticulating wildly, his voice booming above the din.

"Ladies and gentlemen! Prepare yourselves for a taste test of epic proportions! I'm offering a challenge—try my fiery chili, and if you can handle it, you'll win a dinner for two at my restaurant!"

The crowd erupted into cheers, and Marco looked at me, an expression of mischief dancing in his eyes. "You in?"

"Me? Compete in a chili challenge? I'm still trying to decide if I want mild or medium in my own kitchen!"

"Oh, come on! Where's your sense of adventure? It's just a little spice."

"Little? What are you trying to do, burn my taste buds off?"

He laughed, and in that moment, the challenge felt less daunting. "Just think of it as an exploration of flavor. Besides, if you win, I'll treat you to a dessert of your choice."

"Now you're speaking my language."

The crowd had gathered around a table where the vendor was setting out small bowls of a deep red chili, steam rising in fragrant curls. "Alright!" he shouted. "Who dares to try?"

Marco nudged me forward, and I found myself at the front, a rush of adrenaline surging through me. The crowd parted, their eyes on me, and I suddenly felt the weight of their expectations. Was I ready for this?

"Here we go," I murmured to myself as I accepted a bowl from the vendor. The chili was thick and rich, flecked with spices that danced invitingly across the surface. I could feel the heat radiating from it, and the smell—oh, the smell! It was intoxicating, a heady blend of smokiness and spice that teased at my senses.

With a deep breath, I lifted the spoon to my lips, the chili shimmering in the fading light. "Here goes nothing," I whispered, taking a generous bite. The heat exploded on my tongue, fire mingling with flavor, sending a shockwave of sensation that made my eyes water.

The crowd erupted into cheers and laughter as I struggled to keep my composure, my mouth on fire yet somehow exhilarating. Marco laughed, clapping me on the back. "You're doing great! Just breathe!"

But just as I thought I might manage to keep my cool, I felt a presence behind me. I turned slightly to see James, arms crossed, a knowing smirk plastered across his face. "Ah, look at you, embracing the chaos. Are you sure you're ready for this?"

Before I could respond, the heat of the chili surged through me, and I coughed, sputtering in a fit of laughter. The world spun for a moment, and I felt myself teetering on the edge of something—something thrilling yet terrifying.

Suddenly, the crowd gasped, and I followed their gaze to see Marco, his expression shifting from amusement to something darker. "What is it?" I asked, the laughter dying on my lips.

"Look," James said, pointing toward the entrance of the festival. My heart sank as I saw a figure standing there, silhouetted against the last rays of sunlight.

It was a tall man with a commanding presence, the air around him heavy with authority. My pulse quickened as I recognized him—a figure from my past I thought I'd left behind.

"Why is he here?" I whispered, dread pooling in my stomach.

And in that moment, surrounded by laughter and the scent of spices, I felt the ground beneath me shift, the festival transformed into a stage for an unfolding drama I wasn't prepared for.

Chapter 20: Recipe for Disaster

The kitchen felt like a sanctuary as I sliced through vibrant bell peppers, their bright colors dancing under the warm glow of the overhead lights. Each chop echoed the rhythm of my thoughts, a steady metronome that played a symphony of confusion and excitement. The aroma of sautéing garlic and onions wafted through the air, mingling with the earthy scent of fresh basil, wrapping me in a comforting embrace. It was familiar territory, where I could lose myself in the cadence of culinary creation and forget, if only for a moment, the tempest brewing in my heart over Marco's new venture.

I had spent the last week wrestling with my emotions, tossing and turning between the exhilaration of watching someone I cared for ascend to new heights and the suffocating dread of being eclipsed by his success. The culinary summit had rekindled my own aspirations, igniting a flame of ambition within me that I thought had long been extinguished. However, with Marco's name now in lights, I couldn't help but feel like a mere shadow flitting across the stage of his newfound fame.

As I stirred the bubbling sauce, the sound of simmering tomatoes and spices provided a soothing backdrop to my inner turmoil. I paused to catch my breath, leaning against the counter, gazing out of the window. The world outside was bathed in the golden hues of sunset, a breathtaking canvas painted with streaks of pink and orange, but it did little to lift the weight pressing down on my chest.

"What's the matter, chef? You look like you're trying to decipher the meaning of life from a bottle of balsamic," a teasing voice interrupted my reverie.

I turned to find Lily, my closest friend, leaning against the doorframe with a smirk. Her arms were crossed, and her playful expression was all too familiar. "Do you need me to break out my best motivational speech? Because I'm pretty sure I can convince you that a pot roast will solve all your problems."

I rolled my eyes, the corners of my lips twitching in a reluctant smile. "No, thanks. I think I'd prefer to keep my problems on the plate rather than serve them alongside dinner."

"Fine, fine. But you can't avoid talking about it forever. Marco's off competing in a national competition, and here you are, trying to simmer away your feelings in a pot of marinara. Spill it. What's really bothering you?"

With a heavy sigh, I abandoned the spatula and leaned against the counter, crossing my arms as I met her gaze. "I'm proud of him, really. He deserves this chance. But what if this is just the beginning for him? What if he becomes a culinary superstar and I'm left here, a footnote in his story?"

Lily's eyes softened, and she stepped closer, resting a hand on my shoulder. "You're not a footnote, you know that, right? You have your own story, your own talents. Just because he's in the spotlight doesn't mean you have to fade away. It's not a competition."

"But it feels like one," I admitted, feeling vulnerable as the words spilled from my lips. "I thought I was ready to support him, to embrace his success, but now I'm just scared. Scared of being overshadowed, scared of losing what we had. I don't want to be the person who holds him back, but I also don't want to feel small next to him."

"Have you talked to him?" Lily asked, her tone gentle yet insistent.

"No, I... I didn't want to burden him with my insecurities. He's already juggling so much, and I don't want to add to his stress."

Lily rolled her eyes dramatically. "You really think Marco wouldn't want to know how you're feeling? He's not some aloof celebrity; he's your best friend. He'd probably want to help you feel better, even if it's just to hear you say you're proud of him."

With a deep breath, I contemplated her words. She was right, as much as it stung to admit it. My resolve began to solidify, taking the form of a dish I could serve—a culinary metaphor for my emotions, something tangible to share with him.

"I think I need to cook something for him," I mused, the idea igniting a spark within me. "Something that represents what we've built together, a way to remind both of us that even if his star is rising, I'm still here."

"Now we're talking! What do you have in mind?" Lily's enthusiasm was infectious, and I felt the weight of my fears begin to lift as I dove into brainstorming.

"What about a tasting menu?" I suggested, my imagination taking flight. "A small plate of our shared memories—dishes that tell the story of us. Each one a chapter in our friendship."

"Now you're cooking with gas! What would be on the menu?"

"Definitely that spicy shrimp pasta we made that summer in Florence," I replied, a smile creeping onto my face as I recalled the laughter and chaos of our impromptu cooking sessions. "And the chocolate lava cake we perfected after a dozen failed attempts."

"Sounds perfect. But you'll need to add a twist—something new to show him that you're still evolving, just like he is," Lily encouraged, her eyes sparkling with excitement.

"What if I create a dish that symbolizes the journey we've taken together? Something that combines his flair with my roots," I pondered aloud. "Maybe a fusion of flavors that tells our story—a homage to our past while looking forward to the future."

"Now that's the spirit! Let's get you cooking, chef. I'll help you gather the ingredients. This is going to be epic," she said, practically bouncing on her toes.

As we bustled around the kitchen, collecting fresh produce and spices, I felt a renewed sense of purpose blossoming inside me. I was no longer just a spectator in Marco's life; I was an active participant in my own story, ready to carve my path alongside his. The simmering sauce took on a new meaning, transforming from a simple meal into a heartfelt declaration of my support and love for him.

I knew that whatever lay ahead, I would embrace the chaos of it all. The festival may have ended, but this was just the beginning—an opportunity to not only showcase my culinary talent but also to reaffirm the bond that had always tied Marco and me together.

The clatter of pots and pans filled the kitchen, a symphony of culinary chaos that somehow felt soothing. Lily had transformed from a casual observer to my sous-chef, her infectious energy propelling me forward. We gathered ingredients, laughing and bickering like an old married couple over the best way to chop garlic. She insisted on using the "smash and chop" method, claiming it released more flavor, while I preferred my trusty chef's knife, precise and controlled.

"Listen, chef," she said, brandishing a clove of garlic as if it were a trophy, "if we're making a dish that represents us, it has to be a little messy. Just like our cooking adventures!"

"Messy is definitely one word for it," I shot back, trying to suppress a laugh. "But let's keep the kitchen intact, shall we? My landlord is still fuming over that time we set off the fire alarm with the chili."

"Ah, yes. The infamous chili incident. I still maintain it was a culinary masterpiece, just with an unexpected smokiness," she replied with a smirk.

As we prepped, I felt an undeniable thrill, a familiar spark igniting within me. Cooking had always been my form of expression, my art, and with each ingredient I measured and mixed, I felt more in tune with myself. Memories flooded my mind—the afternoons spent in my grandmother's kitchen, the tantalizing scent of her famous rosemary chicken enveloping us like a warm hug, the way she'd hum old songs as she kneaded dough, instilling love into every bite. Those moments had shaped me, crafting not only my palate but also my heart.

"Okay, what's next?" Lily interrupted my reverie, tossing diced tomatoes into the sizzling pan with a flourish. "I need to know how you plan to wow the great Marco with your culinary skills."

I paused, my mind racing. "We need something bold, something that will make him feel the weight of our shared history while reminding him that we're both on our own journeys. What about a seafood risotto with a twist? We can use the flavors from that beachside café in Sicily we loved so much—rich saffron, fresh seafood, and a drizzle of lemon oil."

"Now you're talking! But what's the twist?" Lily's eyes glinted with mischief.

"Maybe we could infuse it with a little something unexpected," I mused. "How about adding a hint of spice to the dish? Something like chili flakes or a touch of harissa to surprise him."

"Spicy seafood risotto? Now we're playing with fire! I love it!" Lily clapped her hands together, clearly pleased with the direction we were headed.

As we moved on to the next steps, the atmosphere crackled with anticipation, the kitchen filled with a medley of sizzling, chopping, and laughter. Each moment felt charged with purpose, weaving the fabric of our friendship tighter as we navigated this culinary adventure together. I poured a glass of white wine, both for the risotto and for us, raising my glass to toast. "To friendship, and to whatever this madness turns into!"

Lily giggled, clinking her glass against mine. "And to the disaster we'll inevitably create along the way!"

The risotto bubbled gently as we stirred, its creamy consistency becoming the canvas for our culinary creativity. As I added the final touches—fresh parsley and a sprinkle of grated Parmigiano—I felt a wave of pride wash over me. This dish was not just about food; it was a declaration of resilience and a celebration of growth, both for Marco and myself.

Just as I was about to serve, my phone buzzed on the counter, vibrating with a ferocity that made it dance across the surface. I glanced at the screen and felt my heart leap. It was Marco.

"Answer it! Go on!" Lily urged, her voice laced with excitement.

I hesitated, a swirl of nerves knotting in my stomach. What would I say? Should I tell him about the dish I was making? Would he sense my insecurity beneath my bravado? But before I could overthink it, I swiped to answer, bringing the phone to my ear.

"Hey, Marco!"

"Hey, you! How are you?" His voice radiated warmth and enthusiasm, instantly soothing my frazzled nerves.

"I'm good! Just... cooking," I replied, trying to sound casual, but I could hear the tremor in my voice.

"Cooking? What are you making? You know I'll probably be too busy to eat for weeks with this competition coming up," he joked, but I could hear the genuine curiosity behind his words.

"Something special," I said, a smile creeping onto my face. "A little seafood risotto with a twist. Thought I'd surprise you when you're back."

"Now I'm really intrigued. I can't wait to taste it! You always have the best ideas."

The sincerity in his voice sent a rush of warmth through me. "Thanks, Marco. That means a lot," I said, the knot of insecurity loosening slightly.

"Anyway, I've been thinking about our talk at the festival," he continued, his tone shifting. "I know things are changing for both of us, and I just wanted to say that you're a huge part of my journey. Whatever happens with this competition, I hope you know you'll always have a place in my kitchen, and in my life."

The words hung between us like a delicate tapestry, weaving together my fears and his reassurances. "I appreciate that, really. I just... I want you to succeed, but I also want to feel like I'm succeeding too, you know?"

"I get it," he replied, his voice softening. "But I don't want you to measure your worth against my success. You're talented and passionate in your own right. Just remember, I'm rooting for you as much as you're rooting for me."

A wave of gratitude washed over me, and I couldn't help but smile. "Thanks, Marco. I'll keep that in mind. Now go win that competition, so I can brag about you to everyone!"

"Deal! But don't forget to save me a plate of that risotto. I'm counting on it!"

As we exchanged goodbyes, I hung up, feeling lighter than I had in days. The tension that had settled in my chest began to dissipate, replaced by a newfound determination. I turned to Lily, who was grinning ear to ear, clearly eavesdropping.

"What was that all about?" she asked, waggling her eyebrows playfully.

"Just a little pep talk," I said, a sense of clarity washing over me. "I think I'm ready to embrace this new chapter, no matter where it takes us."

Lily raised her glass again, her expression proud. "To new beginnings, then! And to the culinary magic we're about to create!"

With the warm glow of friendship surrounding us and the risotto bubbling softly in the pot, I felt invigorated. This wasn't just a dish; it was a bridge connecting my past and future, a canvas where our stories intertwined. I was ready to step into the unknown, fully prepared to savor every moment, every flavor, and every possibility.

The aroma of garlic and saffron hung in the air, weaving through the kitchen like a fragrant tapestry, binding together memories of summer sunsets and laughter-laden conversations. The risotto was finally simmering to perfection, its creamy texture whispering promises of comfort and familiarity. Lily and I danced around the kitchen, an unspoken rhythm guiding us as we prepared for the evening ahead. The anticipation crackled like static electricity, charging the atmosphere with a sense of impending excitement.

"You know," Lily said, stirring the pot with a flourish that sent a splash of broth nearly over the edge, "I'm not sure what's more delicious: the risotto or the prospect of watching Marco's face when he tastes it."

"Definitely the risotto," I replied, trying to sound authoritative. But even I had to admit that the thought of Marco's reaction sent butterflies flitting in my stomach. "I want him to realize that he isn't just soaring above me; he can still find joy in what we created together."

As the final touches came together—fresh herbs and a drizzle of lemon oil—the doorbell rang, interrupting our culinary symphony. I exchanged a glance with Lily, who raised an eyebrow, her playful smirk hinting at a thousand possibilities.

"Who could that be?" I asked, wiping my hands on a kitchen towel as I approached the door.

"Maybe it's Marco, desperate for a sneak peek of his own surprise," she quipped, but I could hear the twinge of hope in her voice.

I opened the door, and to my shock, standing on the threshold was Marco himself, his disheveled hair and worn apron hinting at the chaos of the day. "Surprise!" he said, an exuberant grin plastered across his face. "I finished up early and figured I'd pop by to check on you. What are you cooking?"

"Uh, just a little something," I said, trying to keep my voice steady, my heart racing at the unexpected sight of him. "I didn't know you'd be here so soon."

"Neither did I!" he replied, stepping into the kitchen, the warmth of his presence instantly filling the space. "I'm starving, and judging by that smell, I'd bet it's something amazing."

Lily slipped out of sight, an evident smirk tugging at her lips as she busied herself in the corner of the kitchen, likely hiding her delight at Marco's sudden arrival. I shot her a grateful look, appreciating her discretion as I battled the flush creeping up my cheeks.

"Is that risotto I smell?" he asked, his eyes lighting up like a kid in a candy store. "You always knew how to make it so perfectly creamy."

"Only because I had a very patient teacher," I replied, trying to sound nonchalant as I ladled the risotto into bowls. "But tonight's special. It's infused with a little extra something."

Marco leaned against the counter, his gaze fixed on me with an intensity that made my heart skip a beat. "Extra something? Now I'm even more intrigued. Did you get a secret ingredient from a mystical cooking oracle?"

"Something like that," I said, my voice teasing as I dished out the bright saffron-hued rice. "Let's just say it's meant to be a surprise. But I hope it'll evoke some nostalgia for you."

He raised an eyebrow, a playful challenge in his expression. "You're on! If it's anything like the culinary magic we whipped up in Florence, I'm sure it'll blow my mind."

We settled at the small dining table, the warmth of the kitchen wrapping around us like a comforting blanket. I served the risotto, watching as he took his first bite, anticipation hanging thick in the air.

His eyes widened, the burst of flavor seemingly taking him by surprise. "This is incredible! The spice... it's like a dance party in my mouth! Why didn't I think of this before?"

"Because you were too busy becoming a culinary star," I teased, unable to hide my grin.

"Speaking of which," he said, his expression growing serious, "I'm a little nervous about the competition. There's so much pressure to perform well, and I can't help but feel like I'm up against the best of the best."

"You are the best," I said, trying to reassure him, but my voice wavered slightly. "But remember, it's okay to be a little scared. It means you care."

He nodded, absorbing my words, and for a moment, the atmosphere felt charged with something more profound than our usual banter. "What about you? I know I've been wrapped up in my own whirlwind, but how are you doing with everything?"

My stomach twisted at the question, a surge of vulnerability rushing over me. "Honestly? I'm scared too. Watching you chase your dreams is amazing, but it makes me wonder where I fit into all of this. I want to be supportive, but there's this nagging fear of being left behind."

"Hey," he said softly, reaching across the table to squeeze my hand. "You are not a supporting character in my story; you're a leading lady in your own. I mean it. You have your own talent, your own journey. Just because I'm on this path doesn't mean you can't shine on yours."

His words, while meant to comfort, ignited a spark of both determination and frustration within me. "That's the thing," I replied, pulling my hand away, "I've been trying to figure out what my path is, but it feels like I'm standing still while you're sprinting ahead."

"Then let's find it together," Marco suggested, his tone earnest. "What if we teamed up? I could use a sous-chef, and you could share your magic with the world. Imagine the chaos we could create! We could blend our flavors, take on the culinary world side by side."

The idea swirled in my mind, both exhilarating and terrifying. What would it mean to share the spotlight? To risk our friendship for the sake of ambition? "I don't know, Marco. What if it doesn't work out?"

"Then we'll go back to being best friends, and I'll make it up to you with endless risotto." He grinned, the lightness of his tone attempting to deflect the weight of my hesitation.

Before I could respond, my phone buzzed on the table, cutting through the moment. I glanced down and felt a chill wash over me as I read the message. It was from a number I didn't recognize, but the words made my heart race:

"You need to be careful. I know things you don't."

"Who is it?" Marco asked, noticing the change in my demeanor.

"I... I don't know," I stammered, my pulse quickening. "It's a strange message."

He leaned closer, curiosity etched on his face, but I hesitated to share. Was this the moment everything shifted? What if my fears of being left behind were just the beginning of something more sinister?

Just then, my phone buzzed again, a second message appearing on the screen, and I couldn't help but feel the weight of the unknown pressing down on me.

"Stay away from Marco. It's for your own good."

My breath hitched, the words cutting through the warmth of the moment like ice. I met Marco's gaze, his brow furrowed in confusion. "What's going on?"

I swallowed hard, trying to mask the panic rising in my chest. "I don't know, but I think something's happening that I didn't see coming."

The room felt suddenly charged with tension, the shadows of uncertainty creeping in as I gripped my phone tightly. My heart raced, but before I could voice my fears, the doorbell rang again, more insistent this time.

"Who could that be?" Marco asked, standing up as I remained rooted in place, caught between the thrill of the moment and the cold grip of dread tightening around my heart.

With a quick glance at the messages still glowing on my screen, I felt the world around me tilt, uncertainty blooming in the pit of my stomach. Something was off, and I had a feeling that whatever lay behind that door could change everything.

Chapter 21: Whispers of Change

The sun dipped below the horizon, casting a golden glow over the cobblestone streets of Monteluce. It was the kind of evening that wrapped around you like a warm embrace, laced with the heady scent of blooming lavender and the faint promise of rain. I perched on the edge of my stool at Café Nocciole, where the gentle hum of conversation mingled with the clinking of glasses and the hiss of the espresso machine. My laptop flickered in front of me, a portal to the world of words and narratives that I adored, but tonight, my focus was elsewhere.

James sauntered in, a devil-may-care grin plastered across his face, as if he'd just uncovered the secret to eternal youth. I had noticed him at various gatherings over the past few weeks, his presence more pervasive than the aroma of fresh pastries that seemed to cling to the air. At first, I thought nothing of it. He was just another critic, caught in the whirlwind of our town's burgeoning culinary scene, eager to join the chorus of voices that sang praises or issued critiques. But now, as he approached my table, the hairs on the back of my neck prickled with unease.

"Mind if I join you?" he asked, his tone light, almost teasing.

I offered a noncommittal shrug, aware that saying no would only invite further scrutiny. "Sure, but I'm deep in thought," I replied, flashing a smile that didn't quite reach my eyes.

"Ah, the tortured artist routine. I know it well," he quipped, plopping down without waiting for an invitation. His eyes, sharp and probing, danced around the café, scanning the room as if assessing each patron for their relevance. "What's the article about this time? Something juicy, I hope?"

I kept my tone steady, aware of the predatory glint in his gaze. "Just a piece on the seasonal menu at Il Sogno. Marco's been experimenting with some new flavors."

His eyebrows shot up, genuine interest flickering across his features for a fleeting moment before it was masked by that devilish charm again. "Marco's a genius in the kitchen. But you know, there's always more beneath the surface."

There it was—the not-so-subtle insinuation that there was some hidden scandal lurking behind the scenes. I felt a swell of protectiveness for Marco, my heart thrumming with the rhythm of my loyalty to him and his restaurant. "Not everything needs to be sensationalized, James. Sometimes a dish is just a dish."

He leaned in closer, a conspiratorial gleam in his eye. "Ah, but where's the fun in that? You're a writer. You thrive on the drama, the tension. Surely you must see the potential for a deeper story? The pressures, the artistry, the... desperation that comes with running a place like Il Sogno."

The barista, a wiry man with tattoos spiraling up his arms, interrupted our exchange, sliding a cappuccino toward me. I took a sip, the froth warm and inviting against my lips, grounding me in the moment. "Marco's not desperate, James. He's passionate. That's what makes his food special."

"Passion can be a double-edged sword, my friend," he replied, his tone slipping into something more serious. "And you might want to be careful. The critics have been sharpening their knives, ready to pounce on any weakness."

A chill crept up my spine at the veiled warning, but I kept my composure. "I appreciate your concern, but I'm not worried. Marco can handle himself."

James chuckled, a low sound that set my teeth on edge. "Oh, I'm sure he can. But what about you? In this game, sometimes it's not just about the food but the people behind it. Relationships matter. Connections. You wouldn't want to end up as collateral damage, would you?"

His words hung in the air, heavy with implication. I set my cup down, the clatter breaking the tension. "I'm not interested in the politics of this world, James. I write about what I love, and right now, that's Marco and Il Sogno."

His grin widened, though it didn't reach his eyes. "Ah, love. A dangerous game in itself. Just remember, the bigger the love, the bigger the fall."

I felt my cheeks flush with indignation. How dare he twist my feelings for Marco into some twisted parable about heartbreak? I was about to retort when the door swung open, allowing a rush of cool air to flood the café, accompanied by a figure that made my heart race. Marco stepped inside, his presence lighting up the dim room like a summer storm. His dark hair tousled, a flour-dusted apron clinging to his waist, he was a vision of chaotic artistry.

"Sorry I'm late!" he called out, scanning the room until his eyes landed on me. A smile broke across his face, banishing the shadows of my earlier discomfort.

"Marco!" I exclaimed, feeling the warmth of his gaze wrap around me like a familiar blanket. "I was just talking about your new menu."

"Oh? I hope it was all good things," he said, swaggering over, the tension in my shoulders easing as he approached.

"Just the usual speculations about your kitchen secrets," I replied, trying to keep my tone light, even as James's presence loomed like a dark cloud above us.

"Secrets?" Marco chuckled, shaking his head. "I thought I shared everything with you." He winked, the familiar flirtation dancing in the air between us.

"Not all of it," I shot back, my heart fluttering, momentarily forgetting the unease from earlier. But as I glanced at James, who was now watching us with an inscrutable expression, I couldn't shake the feeling that the peace I found in Marco's company was fragile, teetering on the edge of something darker.

I steeled myself, unwilling to let James's words intrude on this moment. "What did I miss?" I asked Marco, my voice bright, determined to steer the conversation away from the undercurrents swirling around us.

"Just the usual chaos of service," he replied, leaning against the table, his eyes twinkling. "But it's always worth it when I see you."

Yet, as I watched James's smirk deepen, the sense of impending change hung in the air, a silent storm brewing just beyond the horizon. And though I clung to the warmth of Marco's presence, I could feel the winds shifting, threatening to sweep away the security we'd built.

The evening air crackled with a mix of excitement and tension, the atmosphere in Café Nocciole thickening with the unspoken words hanging between us. As Marco settled into the chair across from me, the weight of James's scrutiny pressed down like a summer storm cloud, but I forced a smile, determined not to let it spoil the warmth blooming in my chest.

"So, what's the scoop?" Marco asked, his eyes alight with curiosity. He always had a way of making me feel like the most important person in the room, as if every word I spoke held the key to a hidden world.

"Just the usual—food, flavor profiles, a sprinkle of drama," I replied, leaning into the banter. "You know, the kind that makes the critics swoon."

"Ah, yes. The critics," he mused, his expression darkening momentarily. "Always eager to find flaws where none exist."

I could feel the tension in his shoulders, a flicker of frustration flashing in his gaze. "What's bothering you? Is it the reviews?"

"Not just the reviews," he sighed, rubbing the back of his neck as though trying to soothe away a persistent ache. "It's the pressure, the constant expectation. I love what I do, but some days, it feels like I'm balancing on a tightrope with a hungry crowd below."

"Who needs a crowd when you have a loyal audience?" I quipped, trying to lighten the mood. "You've got me, the world's most devoted food critic."

His laugh was a balm, soothing the frayed edges of the evening. "Devoted? More like an enthusiastic collaborator. You're like my culinary muse, if we're being dramatic about it."

We exchanged playful jabs, lost in our own bubble of warmth until James's voice sliced through like a knife. "It must be nice to have such unwavering support," he said, a casual arrogance lacing his words. He leaned back, arms crossed, observing us with an unsettling intensity.

I shot him a look that would have silenced lesser men. "Support isn't a luxury; it's a necessity, especially in this business."

James raised an eyebrow, clearly unfazed. "Isn't that the truth. But I'd argue that it's also a bit of a crutch. What happens when your muse decides to take a vacation?"

"Then I'll just have to find a new one," Marco replied, his voice steady. "But that's the beauty of creativity. It's a well that never truly runs dry."

The conversation swirled, the air thick with the contrast between Marco's optimism and James's skepticism. I could sense the tension building again, like the pressure before a storm. I took a deep breath, pushing aside my discomfort. "How was service tonight, Marco?" I asked, eager to redirect the conversation.

"Challenging, as always," he admitted, a hint of a smile tugging at his lips. "We had a table of six who all ordered different dishes, and somehow, I managed to mix up the sauces."

My heart raced, not just from the image of a chaotic kitchen but from the way he brought life into every story. "And? What happened next?"

"Let's just say the table got a taste of my improvisational skills. You should've seen their faces when they tried my 'surprise' take on the classic carbonara," he said, rolling his eyes with exaggerated flair. "It was either going to be a culinary masterpiece or a disaster."

"And?" I leaned in, eager for the juicy details.

"Let's just say I'm still breathing, so it must have been the former," he said, his laughter infectious.

Yet, even as we bantered, I couldn't shake the sensation of James lurking in the shadows, his interest less about the art of cooking and more about the secrets he believed lay hidden in the kitchen's depths. As if sensing my discomfort, Marco reached across the table, his hand warm against mine. "Hey, don't let him get to you. This is about passion, not politics."

"I know," I replied softly, the warmth of his touch igniting a spark of courage within me. "But he keeps asking questions that seem... pointed."

Marco's gaze hardened slightly. "He's probably looking for dirt, something to sensationalize. Don't let his charm fool you."

Just then, the door swung open again, a gust of chilly air cutting through our cozy haven. A couple of food bloggers, their phones at the ready, burst in, chattering animatedly about the latest trends. I could feel the dynamic shift, a ripple of energy dancing through the café. The barista slid over another round of cappuccinos, steam rising like miniature clouds above the cups.

"Look who it is!" one of the bloggers exclaimed, spotting Marco. "The culinary genius himself!"

"Seems like your fan club has arrived," I teased, feeling the atmosphere shift yet again.

"Great," he muttered with a wry smile, rolling his eyes in mock exasperation. "Now I can't even enjoy my coffee in peace."

They swarmed him, eager to snap pictures and praise his culinary prowess, and for a moment, I stepped back, watching the scene unfold. The warmth of Marco's charisma drew people in, while the sharpness of James's commentary lurked like a shadow, waiting for its moment to strike.

I took a sip of my cappuccino, the frothy milk mingling with the rich espresso, grounding me in the moment. "You know, sometimes I think they love you more than the food," I said to Marco, nudging him lightly.

"Oh, please," he said, feigning modesty. "It's all about the food. I'm just the guy who happens to be in charge of it."

As I watched him navigate the crowd with ease, I felt a swell of pride. Here was a man who turned chaos into art, who faced the pressure of expectations with a smile, who could transform an ordinary evening into something magical with a flick of his wrist and a dash of creativity. But as the evening unfolded, I sensed that James's presence was more than just a lingering annoyance; it was a threat, one I needed to guard against.

The café pulsed with life around us, laughter and chatter filling the air, yet my thoughts spiraled back to the mounting pressures Marco faced. There was a sense of fragility beneath the surface of his easy laughter, a tension that made my heart ache.

As I excused myself to the restroom, I caught a glimpse of James through the window, leaning against the café wall, his expression unreadable. The chill of foreboding washed over me, and I felt a tug of concern for Marco. Was he aware of the whispers circling like vultures, waiting for an opportunity to swoop down?

Returning to the table, I found Marco deep in conversation with the bloggers, his laughter ringing bright amidst their praise. But my mind buzzed with worry, the need to protect both my work and his growing stronger. I joined in the conversation, throwing in playful quips and stories, but I could feel the tension tightening around me, like a noose slowly pulling tighter.

Just as I was about to excuse myself for a moment of air, James strode over, his demeanor polished but insidious. "I hope you don't mind if I steal Marco for a moment. I'd love to get his thoughts on the upcoming food festival."

"Of course not," I said, though the words felt like a lie.

As James led Marco away, I couldn't shake the sense that shadows were gathering, waiting for the right moment to strike. The warmth of the café began to fade, replaced by a chill that seeped into my bones. I leaned back, forcing myself to relax, even as worry gnawed at the edges of my mind. It was a delicate dance we were engaged in, one that could pivot at any moment, and I knew I had to be ready for whatever came next.

The café pulsed with life, but the energy had shifted ever so slightly, the laughter of the patrons weaving together with a tension that felt almost palpable. I leaned against the back of my chair, trying to catch glimpses of Marco and James as they huddled in conversation at the far corner. Marco's expression, usually so open and inviting, had taken on a wariness that set my heart racing. I could tell that whatever James was saying had crossed the threshold from casual interest to something far more serious.

The bloggers, oblivious to the undercurrents swirling around them, were still buzzing with excitement, snapping pictures and lavishing praise on Marco's culinary genius. Yet, as their compliments bounced around the café, I could see Marco's eyes darting toward James, concern lurking just beneath his playful demeanor. It was like watching a flower bloom in slow motion, only to realize the sun was slipping behind the clouds, threatening the very vibrancy of that moment.

"Do you think he's trying to pull something?" one of the bloggers asked, her voice bubbling with enthusiasm as she gestured animatedly.

I forced a smile, a practiced mask to conceal the growing knot of anxiety in my stomach. "Who, James? No, he's just... enthusiastic. Always fishing for the next big story."

"Fishing? More like he's setting a trap," the other blogger chimed in, her brow furrowing. "He's got a reputation, you know."

My heart sank at that, a cold realization threading through my thoughts. If James was after something, it wasn't just a story. It was leverage, an angle that could twist Marco's world upside down. I needed to intervene, to pull Marco back into the safe harbor of our shared laughter and late-night kitchen experiments.

Pushing through the throng of patrons, I made my way to the table, each step echoing with the urgency of my thoughts. I reached them just as James leaned in, a conspiratorial smile curling his lips. "You're making waves, Marco. I've heard some interesting whispers about your new dish. Care to share?"

I sensed the tension crackling like static in the air, and before Marco could respond, I interjected. "You know how it is, James. A chef never reveals his secrets."

He turned his piercing gaze toward me, the corners of his mouth twitching in amusement. "Ah, but isn't the reveal what keeps us all engaged? The anticipation of what's to come?"

"Isn't that what your column is for?" I shot back, trying to deflect his probing. "Your readers must be dying to know about the latest food trends, not every little detail from a busy kitchen."

"True, but sometimes the real stories are hidden in the cracks, aren't they?" He leaned back, fingers steepled beneath his chin, an almost predatory look in his eyes.

Marco's jaw tightened, and I could see him wrestle with how to handle the situation. "I appreciate your enthusiasm, James, but I'm just focusing on the food right now. I have enough on my plate."

"Of course, but don't you want to share your journey? The challenges, the triumphs? That's what captivates an audience."

"Maybe I'm just not ready to share," Marco replied, his tone flat, the warmth dissipating as if a chill had swept through our little corner of the café.

James, undeterred, leaned closer, a sly smile creeping across his face. "You know, people are always looking for authenticity. They love the juicy details—the ups and downs. It's what makes the food world so vibrant."

At that moment, the air felt thick with tension, and I could sense the walls closing in. "Is that what you're really after, James? To find a crack and expose it to the world?" I asked, my voice sharper than I intended.

"Exposure is merely a byproduct of good storytelling," he replied, his eyes glinting with mischief. "But sometimes it's about the people involved. After all, aren't you two more than just chef and writer? There's a whole story there, isn't there?"

Marco stiffened, and I could feel the heat radiating off him as if the tension was a living thing, wrapping around us both. "We're just colleagues," he said, his voice taut.

"Colleagues who share a passion," I added, the instinct to defend our connection pushing me forward. "That's where the magic happens."

James chuckled, the sound laced with an undercurrent of mockery. "Magic, indeed. But let's not pretend that passion is always sunshine and rainbows. What about the darker side? The sacrifices? Those are the stories that sell."

"Why do you think you need to delve into that?" I challenged, frustration bubbling beneath the surface. "Why not celebrate the good instead of digging for dirt?"

"Because, my dear, that's where the real story lies," he said, a smile lingering on his lips like a wolf watching its prey. "And I'm not just talking about the food. Relationships can be the most delicious drama of all."

Marco shifted in his seat, his expression flickering between discomfort and anger. I felt the weight of his gaze, as though he were silently pleading for me to step in and divert the conversation. I stepped closer, feeling a surge of protectiveness. "You don't get to twist our friendship into some sensational narrative, James. It's about the work, the food, the art—"

"Ah, yes, the art," he interrupted smoothly, his tone suddenly earnest, almost teasing. "But isn't it a little disingenuous to ignore the human element? The emotions? The potential heartbreak?"

"Leave it alone, James," Marco said sharply, his voice low but firm. "We're not your story."

A flicker of something dark passed across James's face, momentarily stripping away his charming facade. "Not yet, perhaps," he replied, his voice a whisper that sent a shiver down my spine.

I could feel the atmosphere thickening, tension wrapping around us like a vice. "Why don't you stick to reviewing restaurants and leave personal matters out of it?" I shot back, my voice low, yet fierce.

"Where's the fun in that?" he replied, a smirk on his lips that sent a wave of revulsion through me. "But fine, let's talk about the food. What's your secret ingredient, Marco? What keeps you awake at night when you're dreaming up those culinary masterpieces?"

The café, once buzzing with laughter and camaraderie, now felt like a stage where we were the unwilling players. I could sense Marco's unease growing, and as I looked around, I realized the patrons were starting to tune into our conversation, eyes darting between us like spectators at a thrilling match.

"Let's change the subject," Marco said, his voice strained. "I'd rather not discuss my 'secret ingredient' with you, James."

"Then how about we talk about the food festival?" James suggested, a calculated glint in his eye. "Everyone's eager to see what you'll bring this year. I can already hear the whispers."

The knot in my stomach tightened as Marco's gaze hardened. "The festival is not the time or place for this conversation," he said firmly.

"Oh, but it's the perfect place, my friend," James insisted, his tone dripping with sarcasm. "An audience, a stage, and all those hungry mouths ready for the truth."

I glanced around the café, feeling the prickle of attention as more faces turned our way, their curiosity piqued. A slight tremor of panic surged through me. The more we engaged with James, the more we fed into his narrative, and I could feel the trap closing around us.

"Let's just enjoy the moment," I said, trying to rally some lightness into the air, but the weight of James's presence bore down on us like a looming storm cloud.

Suddenly, the door swung open, allowing a gust of wind to blow through, carrying with it the promise of impending rain. I turned to look, half-expecting some form of salvation in the form of distraction. But what I saw instead sent chills racing down my spine.

A figure stood framed in the doorway, silhouetted against the fading light, their features obscured. But even from a distance, I could feel the unsettling aura they radiated. A palpable tension enveloped the café, the kind that hinted at secrets long buried and truths about to be revealed.

"Is that—" I started, but the figure stepped forward, revealing a familiar face that sent a jolt through me.

"Why are you talking about the festival?" the newcomer asked, their voice slicing through the air like a knife, cutting through the carefully woven threads of the moment.

In that instant, the atmosphere shifted once again, and I could feel the undercurrent of impending change swell around us, the fragile web we'd spun threatening to unravel. All eyes turned toward the newcomer, and my heart raced as I realized we were standing on the precipice of something monumental, a storm brewing just out of sight, ready to break.

Chapter 22: A Flavorful Escape

The sun hung low in the sky, casting a warm golden glow across the bustling streets of Charleston, creating a picturesque backdrop that felt almost too perfect to be real. As I stepped out of my car, the salty breeze greeted me like an old friend, ruffling my hair and lifting my spirits. I was instantly drawn in by the vibrant colors of the historic buildings lining the streets, each facade a testament to a story untold. It was as if the city itself was a canvas, painted with hues of pastel greens, pinks, and yellows, accented by the lush greens of the hanging moss that draped from the ancient oaks like a Southern fairy tale come to life.

I wandered aimlessly at first, letting the rhythm of the city guide my steps. My senses were assaulted by a cacophony of sounds: laughter spilling from open windows, the clink of glasses from nearby bistros, and the distant cadence of jazz wafting through the air. The aroma of rich spices and freshly caught seafood curled around me, teasing my senses and tugging at my heartstrings like a familiar melody. I realized how much I had missed this—how much I craved the vibrant energy of a city that was alive and breathing with possibility.

Before I knew it, I found myself drawn to a modest seafood shack nestled between two towering brick buildings. Its sign, faded yet charming, read "Gull's Nest," and I could see the faint outline of a fishing net draped haphazardly from the entrance. I hesitated for just a moment, the reality of my spontaneous trip settling in—was this really where I wanted to be? But the aroma wafting from within was irresistible, a warm embrace of smoked paprika, garlic, and something distinctly coastal that made my stomach rumble in agreement.

Inside, the atmosphere was alive with chatter, the sound of shuffling feet, and the sizzle of something delicious cooking in the kitchen. The decor was charmingly eclectic, with fishing rods adorning the walls and wooden tables that had seen a thousand meals shared over laughter and stories. I slid onto a bar stool and placed my order for shrimp and grits, hoping to absorb as much of this culinary haven as possible.

While waiting, I let my eyes roam over the scene. An elderly couple shared a plate of fried calamari, their faces lit with the glow of nostalgia as they reminisced about past summers spent by the sea. A young family, the children giggling with unabashed delight, shared a platter of hushpuppies, their laughter infectious. I felt a warmth spread within me, a reminder that food was more than sustenance; it was a conduit for connection, a bridge that could link strangers in a moment of joy.

When my dish arrived, it was nothing short of a masterpiece. The shrimp glistened with a buttery sheen, nestled on a bed of creamy, dreamy grits that looked almost too good to touch. I lifted my fork, taking in the vibrant colors—swirls of green from fresh herbs mingling with the golden hue of the grits, a sprinkle of red pepper flakes adding a hint of warmth. The first bite was an explosion of flavors, the kind that made my eyes roll back in pure bliss. The shrimp danced on my palate, the grit's creaminess a perfect counterbalance, and I couldn't help but let out a small, satisfied sigh.

Between bites, I struck up a conversation with the chef, a burly man with a salt-and-pepper beard and a laugh that resonated like a warm summer night. His name was Earl, and he had been running the Gull's Nest for over twenty years. He shared stories of his early days, of fishermen bringing in the catch of the day and how he had built relationships with local suppliers who understood the rhythm of the tides. There was a fire in his eyes as he spoke about his craft, a passion that ignited something deep within me. It was a reminder of why I had fallen in love with cooking in the first place—the thrill of creating, the joy of sharing.

"So, what brings you to Charleston?" he asked, wiping his hands on his apron.

I hesitated, the truth hanging in the air like the scent of fried fish. "Just needed a change, I guess. Life felt... overwhelming back home."

Earl nodded, understanding etched in the lines of his face. "Sometimes you just need to step away, let the salt air fill your lungs and clear your head. You can find inspiration in the most unexpected places."

His words resonated, echoing in my heart. I had come to Charleston seeking escape, but here, amidst the laughter, the food, and the stories, I was rediscovering my own passion. I began to share my own experiences—my struggles in the culinary world, the pressures that had dimmed my spark. Earl listened intently, nodding along, his presence both grounding and inspiring.

As the evening wore on and the sun dipped below the horizon, I felt a shift within me, a lightness I hadn't realized I was missing. It was as if the vibrant colors of Charleston had seeped into my very being, reigniting the fire that had dimmed over the years. I could see the world through a new lens, one where flavors and experiences danced together in harmony.

With the sun setting and the streets of Charleston alive with evening energy, I made my way back outside, ready to explore further. The city whispered promises of adventure, and for the first time in a long time, I felt hopeful. Each step was a celebration of my newfound resolve, a promise to myself to embrace whatever came next. As I strolled along the waterfront, the shimmering water reflecting the soft glow of streetlights, I couldn't help but smile. The flavors of Charleston had awakened something within me, and I was determined to chase that inspiration wherever it led.

As the evening descended upon Charleston, the streets came alive with a different kind of energy. The soft glow of lanterns illuminated the sidewalks, casting playful shadows that danced with the rhythm of the night. My senses were still tingling from the flavors of Earl's cooking, but there was something else—a spark of curiosity pulling me deeper into the city's embrace. I wandered toward the historic district, the air thick with the promise of secrets just waiting to be uncovered.

The sounds of laughter and music drifted through the air, pulling me toward an open courtyard where a small group had gathered for an impromptu concert. Musicians strummed their guitars, and a man with an infectious grin played the accordion, filling the air with a lively tune that seemed to encapsulate the very essence of Charleston. I leaned against a nearby wall, tapping my foot to the beat, feeling my worries dissolve with each note. It was in these moments of spontaneity that I felt most alive.

As the song ended, the crowd erupted into applause, and I couldn't help but join in, clapping enthusiastically. A girl next to me, her curls bouncing with the rhythm of the music, turned to me with a mischievous glint in her eye. "You've got some moves there! You should join us on stage!" she shouted over the fading notes.

I chuckled, shaking my head. "Oh no, I'm more of a kitchen dancer. You know, the kind that busts a move while stirring a pot of something delicious."

"Kitchen dancing? I love it!" she exclaimed, throwing her head back in laughter. "I'm Lyla, by the way. I run a little bakery not too far from here. You might say I have a bit of a sweet tooth, which—spoiler alert—makes me really popular at parties."

"Popular? I can imagine," I replied, intrigued by her bubbly personality. "What do you bake? Cupcakes? Cookies?"

"Both, and everything in between! Last week, I made this ginormous cake that looked like a fishing boat. It was for a kid's birthday, and it was epic—until the whole thing slid off the table during the 'happy birthday' song. Just... total chaos. But at least it made for a great story!" Her eyes sparkled with mischief as she recounted the tale, and I found myself laughing alongside her, drawn into the warmth of her exuberance.

We chatted for a while, sharing our respective culinary passions. Lyla's excitement was infectious; every word she spoke dripped with enthusiasm and dreams. As the crowd began to disperse, I hesitated, not quite ready to say goodbye to the newfound camaraderie.

"Hey, you should swing by my bakery tomorrow! I'm trying out a new recipe for peach cobbler, and I could use a taste tester. It's all part of my official 'baking research.'" She winked, her tone lighthearted yet sincere.

"Peach cobbler? Count me in," I replied, already anticipating the flaky crust and sweet, cinnamon-infused filling. "I can't turn down dessert, especially when it sounds like a delicious adventure."

With plans for the following day set, I made my way back to my car, feeling the pull of the night's energy still coursing through me. My mind buzzed with thoughts of Earl's wisdom, Lyla's enthusiasm, and the vibrant city that felt like it was wrapping me in a cozy embrace. I was, dare I say it, beginning to feel at home.

The next morning, I woke up early, the sun streaming through my hotel room window like an eager friend ready to greet the day. I stretched, a smile creeping onto my face as I remembered the sweet promise of peach cobbler. After a quick shower, I dressed casually, feeling a mix of excitement and nervousness. What if Lyla was as talented as she claimed? What if I couldn't help her in the kitchen as much as I wanted?

As I strolled toward the bakery, the streets were bathed in morning light, the air filled with the mouthwatering scents of fresh pastries and coffee wafting from nearby cafes. I found myself humming an upbeat tune, letting the anticipation of the day propel me forward. Lyla's bakery was a charming little spot with a bright blue door and whimsical signs hanging in the window, proclaiming the day's specials in cheerful lettering.

The bell above the door jingled as I entered, the warmth of the bakery enveloping me like a soft blanket. The walls were painted in warm hues, adorned with photographs of mouthwatering treats and happy customers. The sweet aroma of baked goods filled the air, making my stomach rumble in agreement.

"Welcome to Lyla's Little Bakery!" a voice called out from behind the counter. There she was, a vision of sunshine in a bright yellow apron, flour dusting her cheeks. "You made it! Come in, come in!"

I stepped inside, absorbing the cozy atmosphere and the sight of racks filled with baked goods that looked almost too beautiful to eat. "Wow, it smells incredible in here. What's your secret?" I grinned, already knowing the answer.

"Love, and maybe a dash of chaos," she replied, her eyes sparkling with mischief. "Now, let's get started on that cobbler. It's peach season, and we're going to make it legendary."

We dove right in, Lyla guiding me through the process with the finesse of someone who had baked countless cobblers before. As we chopped, mixed, and rolled dough, the conversation flowed easily, punctuated by bursts of laughter. I found myself enjoying every minute, the rhythmic motion of baking soothing my soul in a way I hadn't anticipated.

"Here's the trick," Lyla said, handing me a bowl of sliced peaches. "You have to talk to them. Tell them they're going to be delicious."

"Seriously? You're joking, right?" I laughed, but she remained deadpan.

"Absolutely not. Watch." She leaned in, whispering sweet nothings to the peaches, her expression earnest. "Now you try."

I picked up a slice, holding it up dramatically. "Oh, peachy, you're going to be the star of the show!" I declared, my tone exaggerated and theatrical.

Lyla burst into laughter, doubling over. "That's perfect! You have a real knack for peach-flattering!"

As we continued baking, I realized that this spontaneous road trip was turning out to be much more than a mere escape; it was a revelation. I was rediscovering my passion for cooking in the company of someone whose enthusiasm matched my own. The cobbler came together beautifully, and as we slid the pan into the oven, the sweet anticipation of the finished product mingled with the floury chaos of our kitchen adventures.

We spent the next hour chatting about everything from culinary dreams to personal quirks, the laughter bridging the gap between two strangers who had found an unexpected connection. Each story revealed layers of our lives, the conversation punctuated by a comfortable rhythm that felt both refreshing and exhilarating.

When the timer finally beeped, signaling the cobbler's readiness, we rushed to the oven like children on Christmas morning. The sight that met us was nothing short of glorious: a bubbling, golden crust that emitted an aroma so intoxicating I could hardly contain my excitement.

With a flourish, Lyla pulled the cobbler from the oven, and we stood side by side, grinning like two kids who had just completed a secret mission. "This, my friend, is what magic looks like!" she declared, her eyes alight with triumph.

As we sliced into the warm cobbler, the first bite was pure bliss—a heavenly blend of sweetness and spice that danced on my tongue. I closed my eyes, savoring the moment, feeling as if I had found a piece of myself I thought I had lost. With Lyla by my side, the world felt full of flavor and possibility, and I couldn't wait to see where this journey would lead next.

The cobbler was still warm as we savored the last bites, the sweet tang of peaches mingling with the buttery crust like an unspoken promise of more delicious adventures to come. Lyla leaned back against the counter, her hair tousled and her cheeks flushed with excitement. "This, my friend, is what I call a culinary triumph! We should definitely take this on the road—'The Peachy Duo's Bakery Extravaganza.' What do you think?"

I laughed, picturing us pulling a whimsical little food truck adorned with twinkling lights and colorful murals of fruit. "I can see it now. We'd be the queens of peach cobbler, with a following that rivals rock stars. Just imagine the Instagram stories!"

"Oh, don't even get me started on the hashtags! CobblerQueens, PeachyKeen," she grinned, her eyes sparkling with mischief. "We'd have fans camping out for our next creation."

"Right? But I feel like we need a catchy slogan. Something like... 'We bring the peaches, you bring the dreams!'" I suggested, channeling all the enthusiasm of a late-night infomercial.

Lyla clapped her hands, laughing. "You're onto something! We could have merchandise. T-shirts, mugs—maybe even a cookbook!"

Just then, a chime interrupted our banter, and the bell above the bakery door jingled as it swung open. A tall figure stepped inside, his silhouette striking against the sunlight pouring through the door. The man looked around, his dark hair tousled and his attire casually cool—distressed jeans and a fitted T-shirt that hinted at a well-built frame. He caught my gaze and flashed a smile that could light up the gloomiest of days.

"Hey there! Is this the famous bakery everyone's been raving about?" he called, his voice smooth and confident, like a favorite song you hadn't realized you'd missed.

"That would be us!" Lyla answered, her voice tinged with excitement. "I'm Lyla, and this is my partner in crime, the future peach cobbler superstar."

I waved awkwardly, feeling slightly self-conscious. "Hi! I'm just here for the sugar rush and maybe to plot our world domination through dessert."

The stranger chuckled, stepping further into the bakery. "I'm Alex. Just moved to Charleston and I've been hearing whispers about this place. Thought I'd check it out." His gaze swept over the bakery, a hint of admiration playing on his lips. "You've definitely got the charm down."

I felt a blush creep up my cheeks as Lyla flashed a knowing grin. "You should try our peach cobbler—it's a game changer. We made it just now, and I can guarantee it's going to blow your mind."

"Count me in!" he said, grinning as he approached the counter, his curiosity evident. I could see the ease in his movements, the confidence of someone who knew how to navigate a room—something I admired, especially given my tendency to feel out of place.

As Lyla dished out a generous slice of cobbler and handed it to him, the tension in the air shifted subtly. I couldn't ignore the quickened beat of my heart or the way my skin prickled with anticipation. This man, with his easy smile and laid-back demeanor, was a breath of fresh air. But as I watched him take his first bite, I caught a glimpse of something deeper in his gaze—a kind of longing that mirrored my own.

"Wow. This is incredible," he said, his eyes widening in surprise. "I've never tasted anything like it."

"Welcome to my world!" Lyla exclaimed, beaming with pride. "We're here to turn every dessert into an experience. Isn't that right, partner?"

I nodded, still slightly mesmerized by Alex. "Absolutely. Dessert should never just be dessert; it should be an adventure."

He leaned against the counter, his demeanor relaxed but his eyes intensely focused on me. "So, what's your adventure story? You look like someone who's just escaped from a whirlwind."

I hesitated, my mouth suddenly dry. There was something about his gaze that made me want to spill everything—the struggles, the tension, the sense of being lost. But I had just met him. Instead, I opted for a lighter approach. "Let's just say I needed a change of scenery. A little salt air and some good food can work wonders."

"That it can," he replied, nodding thoughtfully. "I moved here to shake things up too. Needed to get away from the same old routine."

"What's your story?" Lyla asked, her curiosity piqued as she leaned against the counter, her attention fully on Alex.

He chuckled softly, a hint of vulnerability flashing across his features. "Well, I was working in finance—pretty typical, right? But I realized I wasn't living for myself; I was just going through the motions. So, I decided to take a leap of faith and pursue something I actually love."

"Like what?" I asked, intrigued.

"Photography," he said, a spark igniting in his eyes. "I've always loved capturing moments. I figured if I could do that while exploring new places, then why not?"

"That's amazing! Charleston is the perfect backdrop for that," Lyla said, her enthusiasm infectious. "You must have some incredible ideas brewing already."

"Oh, I do," he replied, his smile widening. "But I'm still figuring out how to make it work. It's a bit daunting, to be honest."

I nodded, feeling a strange connection to his uncertainty. "Starting over can be intimidating. But the best adventures often come with a side of fear, right?"

"Exactly!" he replied, his expression earnest. "If we're not a little scared, then are we really pushing ourselves?"

Just then, a sudden commotion erupted outside the bakery—a series of loud shouts and the sound of something crashing. The three of us exchanged worried glances. "What was that?" I asked, my heart racing.

"Let's check it out!" Lyla said, jumping up from her spot. "Stay right here; I'll grab the door."

We moved toward the entrance as Lyla opened the door, the ruckus outside growing louder. The street was filled with people gathering in a cluster, a mix of confusion and excitement rippling through the crowd. I felt the unease creeping in, an instinctive worry tightening in my stomach.

"Should we…?" I started, but before I could finish, Alex stepped out, his curiosity piqued. He turned back to us, his expression now serious. "I'll be right back. Stay here. Let me see what's going on."

I nodded, watching him disappear into the throng. The atmosphere outside was charged, a blend of anticipation and uncertainty. I felt a rush of anxiety that made me fidget, the unexpected shift in the day casting a shadow over the vibrant morning we had just enjoyed.

Moments later, Alex returned, his face pale. "You're not going to believe this," he said, breathless. "A street artist is in trouble! Someone just accused him of vandalism—there's a huge crowd forming, and it looks like it could get ugly."

"Vandalism?" Lyla echoed, a frown creasing her brow. "But artists are supposed to create, right?"

"Exactly. But apparently, he's painted something on a building that didn't sit well with the owners," Alex explained, glancing back outside. "I think we should help him. It could be a big misunderstanding."

My heart raced as I exchanged looks with Lyla. The warmth of our earlier laughter felt distant now, replaced by a sense of urgency. "You're right. We can't just stand by while someone's in trouble."

We moved toward the door, a shared determination driving us forward. The moment we stepped outside, the noise enveloped us—a mix of raised voices, anxious chatter, and the low murmur of the crowd. But then, as if the universe decided to test our resolve, we spotted the artist standing at the center of it all, paint-splattered and visibly shaken, facing a group of agitated onlookers.

"Okay," I murmured, taking a deep breath. "Let's see what we can do."

As we pushed through the crowd, a feeling of uncertainty washed over me. Would our intervention make a difference, or were we stepping into a situation that could spiral out of control?

But just as we reached the front, the crowd erupted, and I felt a chill race down my spine. A figure emerged from the shadows, their face obscured, yet something about their presence sent a shiver of dread through me. In that instant, I realized that this moment, this very decision to step forward, would alter the course of the day—and perhaps, our lives—forever.

Chapter 23: The Crossing of Paths

The aroma of garlic and fresh basil enveloped me as I stepped into Il Sogno, an unassuming Italian eatery tucked between a vintage record shop and a quirky bookstore. The air was thick with laughter and the rhythmic clinking of glasses, each sound vibrating with the palpable energy of a bustling kitchen. I inhaled deeply, allowing the savory scents to wash over me, momentarily distracting me from the knot of anxiety tightening in my stomach. It felt good to be back in Asheville, the vibrant streets alive with familiar faces and the intoxicating promise of connection.

As I rounded the corner toward the kitchen, I spotted Marco, his hands gesturing animatedly as he spoke to James, who stood with his arms crossed, leaning back against the counter with a smug grin that instantly set my teeth on edge. I hesitated, leaning against the doorway, half-hidden in the shadows. The soft light cast a warm glow on Marco's tousled hair, and my heart raced at the sight of him—so alive, so engrossed in whatever culinary plans were bubbling up between them.

"Come on, Marco," James chuckled, his tone dripping with false camaraderie. "You know I've got the edge in this competition. Those pasta recipes are practically legendary." He puffed out his chest, the way a peacock might flaunt its feathers, and I could practically see the pride radiating from him.

"Legendary or just a lot of hype?" Marco shot back, his eyes sparkling with mischief. "You think anyone's going to care about your carbonara when they taste my risotto?"

I couldn't help but smile at Marco's quick wit. The way he defended his passion made my heart swell, but that joy was marred by the tightness in my chest, the sudden realization that I was on the outside looking in. Was this how it felt to watch someone you cared for navigate new friendships while you remained tethered to your insecurities?

"Don't be too sure, my friend," James replied, flashing a grin that could only be described as predatory. "After all, winning isn't just about the food. It's also about the showmanship. You've got to put on a good face for the judges." He winked, as if he were imparting some great secret of the culinary world.

I pushed myself forward, stepping into the warm light of the kitchen, determined to interrupt their little tête-à-tête. "Is that so?" I quipped, my voice light, though my heart pounded in my chest. "Should I prepare my best judge's face, then? I'd hate to disappoint."

Marco turned, and his expression shifted from surprise to delight in an instant, as if I had flipped a switch. "Jess! You're back!" His voice was warm, full of that comforting inflection that made me feel like the most cherished person in the room. "I didn't know you were coming by today."

"I thought I'd see how the competition preparations are going. I missed you," I said, forcing a smile, hoping it would mask the uncertainty bubbling beneath my bravado.

James shifted his weight, a flicker of annoyance crossing his features. "Oh, just discussing some strategies for the competition," he said, feigning nonchalance. "Nothing too serious. Marco's trying to figure out how to impress the judges without giving away all his secrets."

"Is that what he's doing?" I raised an eyebrow, refusing to let James derail my mood. "Maybe he just needs to add a little more flair to his plating. I mean, who doesn't love a good garnish?"

"Hey now," Marco said, his laughter brightening the space. "I'll have you know my plating is impeccable. Just ask my last three dinner guests."

"Three?" I feigned surprise, placing a hand on my chest. "Wow, I didn't realize you had an entire fan club!"

"More like an eager test kitchen," he replied, his grin infectious, and I felt my heart lift a little.

But James, ever the opportunist, seized the moment. "I wouldn't underestimate the competition, Jess. You might think it's just food, but you know how cutthroat it can get. You don't want to be the one left in the dust, do you?" His smile was cool, sharp as the knives on the countertop, and I could sense the challenge in his tone.

I shrugged, summoning all the nonchalance I could muster. "I'm just here to enjoy the culinary chaos. Besides, I trust Marco knows what he's doing."

"Thanks for the vote of confidence," Marco said, his eyes shining with warmth.

We settled into a rhythm, and as we prepared ingredients, I felt the earlier tension ebb away. Chopping vegetables and whisking sauces became a shared language, the silence punctuated by the occasional banter. The kitchen was alive, a living entity, with sizzling pans and the soft hum of music in the background, creating an ambiance that felt like home.

As I worked beside Marco, I couldn't shake the feeling that the dynamic between us was shifting, that I was straddling a line I didn't quite understand. The way he brushed his arm against mine sent shivers racing up my spine, leaving me acutely aware of every movement. I could almost hear the unspoken words hanging in the air between us, a delicate tension that crackled like static before a storm.

Then, just as the moment reached its peak, James cleared his throat, and the air shifted again. "Don't forget, Marco, it's not just about cooking. It's about who you know. Connections can get you places."

The implication was thick and heavy, and I felt the weight of it settle on my shoulders like a shroud. My heart raced as I glanced at Marco, searching his face for a flicker of doubt, but his expression remained firm, a mask of determination that both comforted and unsettled me.

"Right, and hard work and talent?" Marco shot back, his voice steady. "Those might count for something too."

James chuckled, an insincere sound that sent my instincts into overdrive. "Sure, but don't be naïve. You can cook the best meal of your life and still get overlooked. It's the game you play."

With a wink, he turned and sauntered off, leaving me standing in the warm glow of the kitchen, the lingering aroma of simmering sauces filling the space with a false sense of security. I glanced at Marco, his brow furrowed in thought, and suddenly I was afraid of the game he was being drawn into—one I wasn't sure I could navigate with him. The lively chatter faded as the tension thickened, wrapping around us like the fading light of day, leaving uncertainty in its wake.

The kitchen buzzed with a frenetic energy, the kind that seemed to envelop everyone in an intoxicating haze of ambition and dreams. I turned back to my task, immersing myself in the rhythm of chopping and stirring, my hands finding solace in the familiar movements. Still, I could feel the weight of James's words lingering in the air, twisting around my thoughts like an overcooked spaghetti strand.

"Jess, can you hand me that basil?" Marco's voice broke through my internal monologue, drawing me back into the present. I reached for the fresh leaves, their earthy scent a welcome distraction. I loved how the tiniest elements could change a dish, a life—so much potential in the simplest of ingredients. I tossed the basil into the pot, watching as it wilted and released its fragrant oils, and for a moment, I felt like I was doing the same: absorbing what I could and blending into something greater.

"Thanks," he said, his gaze locking onto mine, and for a heartbeat, the world outside fell away. It was just us in that kitchen, the warmth of the stove and the promise of culinary success mingling in the air. I couldn't help but smile, my heart fluttering as if the intensity of his focus might melt away my insecurities.

"Is this the secret ingredient to winning the competition?" I teased, waving my hand over the bubbling pot. "A handful of charm mixed with a dash of desperation?"

"Hey, charm is essential!" Marco laughed, that sound echoing in the tight space, warming me from the inside out. "And as for desperation, well, you've got to spice it up a bit, don't you? Besides," he leaned in conspiratorially, "it's not like I'm the only one who's desperate here. I saw you practically drooling over the pasta during my last demo."

I raised an eyebrow, playfully feigning shock. "Drooling? Me? You must have mistaken me for someone with no self-control." I couldn't help but picture the gleaming strands of fettuccine, rich with a creamy alfredo sauce, and my stomach rumbled in agreement.

Just then, the door swung open with a loud creak, and in strode an imposing figure—Luciana, the owner of Il Sogno, her presence filling the room like the aroma of garlic sizzling in olive oil. "Boys! I need you both to focus! The competition is looming, and we can't afford any distractions," she announced, her tone a blend of authority and warmth.

"Did someone say 'distractions'?" I asked with a grin, pretending to scan the room for any potential interlopers. "Because I could list a few right now."

"Do not encourage him," Marco interjected, shooting me a mock glare. "You'll only make it worse."

Luciana raised an eyebrow at Marco, her lips curving into an amused smirk. "You're not wrong. But Jess, darling, if you have any secrets to keep Marco focused, now's the time to share."

"I'm afraid my secrets are locked away tighter than a canister of saffron in a high-end kitchen," I replied, crossing my arms with mock seriousness. "But I can offer motivational quotes if that helps."

"Only if they rhyme," Marco chimed in, a teasing light in his eyes.

The banter flowed easily between us, lightening the tension that had been hanging like smoke in the air. Yet, even as I laughed, a part of me remained aware of the shifting landscape of our friendship. I was desperately trying to keep the walls around my heart intact, but the cracks were beginning to show.

The rhythm of the kitchen continued, and I lost myself in the tasks at hand, my hands moving with precision as we chopped, stirred, and tasted. With every scoop of sauce and sprinkle of seasoning, I was reminded of how good it felt to be a part of something so dynamic. Yet, even in the warmth of the moment, I felt the prick of vulnerability.

"Jess, can you help me with this?" Marco asked, breaking my reverie as he gestured toward a stack of beautifully arranged plates, each more artistic than the last. They were meant for a trial run—a preview of what would be presented to the judges.

I nodded and joined him, our shoulders brushing as we worked side by side. The closeness stirred a familiar warmth in my chest, the kind that felt both exhilarating and terrifying. As I carefully poured the sauce onto the plate, Marco's gaze caught mine again, and the air shifted once more, crackling with unspoken words.

"What's going on in that head of yours?" he asked, his tone softer now, as if he were peeling back the layers I had so carefully constructed.

"Just contemplating the philosophical implications of pasta," I replied with a smirk, hoping to deflect his inquiry. "You know, the meaning of life might very well be hidden in a well-cooked lasagna."

"Or maybe it's just an excuse to eat carbs," he countered, laughter dancing in his voice. "But seriously, you've been a bit quiet since you came back. What gives?"

I hesitated, the weight of my insecurities pressing down. "I guess I just feel... different. Like I don't quite fit in anymore. Everything feels so much bigger now, you know? Like everyone's in on a joke I missed."

He paused, his expression shifting to one of understanding. "It's normal to feel that way when things are changing. You're in a new place in your life, and it's okay to take a minute to catch up."

His words were a balm, soothing the anxious whirlwind inside me. I appreciated his perspective, but still, the gnawing jealousy simmered beneath the surface. "Yeah, I just... I don't want to be an afterthought. I don't want to lose what we have."

"Jess," Marco said, reaching out to touch my arm gently, "you won't lose me. We're in this together. You and me. That's never going to change."

Before I could respond, James reappeared, his voice slicing through the moment like a hot knife through butter. "Hey, Marco, got a minute? We need to talk strategy." He leaned against the counter, his presence suddenly suffocating, a stark reminder of the competition that lurked around us like a predator.

Marco glanced at me, a flash of apology in his eyes, and I forced a smile, even as disappointment welled up inside me. "Yeah, sure," he said, stepping back and directing his focus toward James, who wore an insufferable grin.

I watched them, a knot of unease tightening in my stomach. The energy shifted, and just like that, the warmth of our moment vanished, leaving me in the cool shadow of uncertainty. It was a reminder of how quickly things could change, how one conversation could unravel everything I thought I understood about our friendship.

As they began discussing competition tactics, I busied myself with the plates, arranging garnishes with meticulous care. My thoughts spiraled, caught in a web of jealousy and fear. What if James was right? What if connections truly meant more than passion? I was determined not to let those thoughts consume me, but they nibbled at the edges of my resolve.

Marco's laughter echoed through the kitchen, mingling with the sounds of sizzling pans and clattering utensils, and for a fleeting moment, I found solace in the chaos around me. Perhaps I could weather this storm. Perhaps there was still a way to bridge the growing distance without sacrificing what we had. The challenge was set, and I couldn't back down—not when there was so much at stake.

The kitchen hummed with a symphony of activity, the sounds of sizzling pans and clattering utensils a soundtrack to my growing unease. I busied myself with arranging the plates, attempting to focus on the intricate patterns of herbs and sauces, but my mind felt like a runaway train, derailing at every thought of Marco and James. The shift in energy had been palpable, and I was left teetering on the precipice of uncertainty, feeling less like an integral part of the team and more like a decorative garnish that had lost its flavor.

"Jess, can you come over here?" Marco called, his voice cutting through the haze of my thoughts like a hot knife through butter. I turned to find him standing at the counter, his brow furrowed in concentration as he measured out flour for the dough. "I need a second set of eyes. This recipe requires finesse, and I'm more of a 'throw it all together and see what sticks' kind of guy."

"Finesse? Are you sure you want my help?" I shot back, trying to mask my nerves with humor. "I'm known for my unconventional techniques, like flambéing pizza. Just ask my smoke alarm."

He chuckled, a sound that felt like sunshine breaking through clouds. "That's exactly what I need! Let's set fire to mediocrity, shall we?"

As I moved to his side, the tension from earlier began to dissipate, replaced by the familiar camaraderie that had drawn me to him in the first place. The way he tossed flour in the air, allowing it to drift like confetti, made me laugh, and soon we were both lost in the rhythm of kneading dough and sharing our culinary dreams.

"Have you thought about what you want to cook for the competition?" I asked, my curiosity piqued. "You mentioned that risotto, but is there something else you're keeping up your sleeve?"

Marco's eyes sparkled with mischief. "Well, I've been toying with a dessert idea—something unconventional, a twist on a classic. Imagine tiramisu, but instead of coffee, it's infused with matcha and layered with a citrus cream. It's bold, a bit risky. I love that."

I raised an eyebrow. "A bold dessert? What are you trying to do, confuse the judges?"

"Exactly! They'll be sitting there, expecting something traditional, and then—bam!—a burst of flavor. Surprise is half the battle, right?"

His enthusiasm was infectious, and I found myself caught up in his vision. "You could call it 'tiramisu with a twist.' What do you think? Or maybe 'green tea dreams'?"

He laughed, shaking his head. "That's the best you could come up with? You're the creative one here, Jess!"

"Hey, I'm a work in progress," I said, rolling my eyes playfully. "I'm still figuring out my own culinary identity."

"Which is exactly why you should be in the competition too," he said, his tone suddenly serious. "You have a knack for flavors that surprises even me."

"Sure, but you know my idea of competition is more along the lines of a baking marathon in pajamas, not dazzling judges with culinary artistry," I replied, wishing I could shake off the heaviness that lingered in the air.

Just then, James swooped in again, his voice slicing through our moment like a poorly timed cue in a bad play. "Hey, Marco! Don't forget we need to finalize our game plan for the competition. The judges will be looking for innovation, and I think we should stick to tried-and-true favorites instead of going rogue." His tone was condescending, as if he were explaining the basics of cooking to a child.

Marco's expression hardened, a flicker of annoyance passing over his features. "Thanks for your input, James, but I think it's important to stand out. Innovation can't just be sidelined."

"Sure, but there's a difference between standing out and crashing and burning. Remember, we're not just cooking for ourselves; we're cooking to win." James smirked, clearly reveling in his role as the self-appointed authority.

"Right. And winning is about creativity, not just safe bets," Marco countered, a hint of defiance lacing his words.

Feeling the tension rising, I chimed in, "Why not do both? Blend a classic with something unexpected? Show them that you're versatile."

James rolled his eyes. "That's all well and good, but we don't have time for this. We need to focus." His words hit me like an unwanted slap, and I could feel my frustration bubbling to the surface.

"Focus on what? Following a formula? That doesn't sound very exciting," I said, crossing my arms. "Food is supposed to evoke emotions, not just satisfy the palate."

Marco's gaze shifted between us, and in that brief moment, I could see the conflict reflected in his eyes. "Let's just take a step back," he suggested, attempting to diffuse the brewing storm. "James, I appreciate your input, but Jess is right. We need to bring our personalities to the plate."

"Your personalities? That's what you think will get you through?" James scoffed. "Fine, good luck with that. Just don't come crying to me when you're not getting called back for the next round."

As he walked away, the air felt charged with unspoken tension. "I hate that guy," I said, releasing a breath I hadn't realized I was holding. "He just has a way of sucking the joy out of everything."

Marco nodded, his expression serious. "I know. But don't let him get to you. You have a way of inspiring me, of reminding me why I started cooking in the first place. That's what matters."

I felt a warmth spread through me at his words, a surge of appreciation that temporarily chased away the unease. "Thanks, Marco. That means a lot."

But just as I thought the moment was healing the rift between us, the door swung open again, revealing Luciana, her expression intense as she surveyed the chaos of the kitchen. "Marco! Jess! We need to talk. Now."

The urgency in her tone sent a chill down my spine. "What's wrong?" Marco asked, his brow furrowing.

"There's been a change in the competition rules, and I need you both to listen carefully," she said, her voice unwavering. "It's not just about the cooking anymore. There's a twist, and it could impact everything."

"What kind of twist?" I asked, my heart racing as I felt the ground shift beneath me.

Luciana hesitated, her gaze darting to the side, as if weighing the implications of her words. "You'll have to pair up with someone—two chefs working as one. It's a team challenge."

The implications hung in the air like smoke from a extinguished fire. My breath caught in my throat as my mind raced. Who would Marco choose? Who would I choose? I shot a glance at him, and in that moment, I could see the tension building once more, the lines drawn not just between teams but in the delicate fabric of our friendship.

"Luciana, you can't be serious," Marco said, disbelief etched on his features. "We've been preparing individually."

"I know, but the competition is evolving. It's not just about culinary skill; it's about collaboration, and it's time to step outside your comfort zone."

James appeared at the doorway, his eyes gleaming with unspoken victory. "Looks like the cards are being shuffled. Good luck, Marco. You'll need it."

My pulse quickened, a rush of anxiety flooding through me as I turned to Marco, whose gaze was now locked on me, the weight of unspoken decisions heavy between us. Would we still be able to navigate this shift together, or would the competition tear us apart?

The world around me began to blur, and as Marco opened his mouth to speak, a sudden crash echoed through the kitchen, followed by an explosion of glass. My heart raced, and just as I turned to see what had happened, everything went dark, plunging us into an unexpected chaos that left me gripping the edge of the countertop, suspended between fear and uncertainty.

Chapter 24: Secrets and Shadows

The kitchen was alive with the scent of garlic and olive oil, the rich aroma clinging to the air like a lover's embrace. As I stepped inside, the soft glow of overhead lights reflected off the stainless-steel appliances, casting a warm hue across Marco's workspace. He stood at the counter, hands deftly chopping fresh herbs, the rhythm of his knife punctuating the silence. My heart raced—not just from the excitement of seeing him but also from the unfamiliar tension that hung like a thick fog, suffocating the joyful anticipation I had expected.

"Hey," I said, my voice barely above a whisper, as if speaking louder would shatter the fragile atmosphere. Marco glanced up, a smile breaking through the stormy clouds that had settled on his face. But it faded almost as quickly as it had come, replaced by a hint of worry that knotted my stomach.

"Thanks for coming," he replied, his tone strained. "I could really use your help tonight." He motioned toward the array of ingredients laid out before him: vibrant tomatoes, delicate basil, and a slab of fresh mozzarella that looked almost too beautiful to slice. I had always adored the way he transformed simple ingredients into something magical, but tonight, the magic felt elusive, like the spark had dimmed.

As I moved closer, I couldn't shake the feeling of James's looming presence. He leaned against the refrigerator, arms crossed, a self-satisfied smirk tugging at the corners of his mouth. His critiques floated through the air like toxic smoke, suffocating Marco's creativity. "You need to show more finesse with that knife, Marco. It's about precision, not just speed," James droned, his tone dripping with condescension.

I felt a flash of irritation, a fire igniting in my chest. "Maybe you should just let him cook," I snapped, surprising even myself. The room fell silent, tension crackling like static. Marco's eyes widened, caught between my defiance and James's silent judgment.

"Rachel, it's fine," he said quickly, trying to ease the mounting friction. "I've been working on my speed for the competition. I want to impress the judges."

I crossed my arms, mimicking James's posture but without the same air of superiority. "Impress them by being you, not some version of you that James thinks you should be." The words tumbled out before I could second-guess them. I had been trying to keep my mouth shut, to let Marco find his own footing in this chaotic whirl of competition, but seeing him flounder beneath James's watchful eye was too much to bear.

James scoffed, the sound harsh and cutting. "It's easy to say that when you're not the one on the line, Rachel. This is a high-stakes competition, not a bake sale."

My fists clenched at my sides, the urge to defend Marco swelling inside me. But I knew I couldn't let myself get pulled into a fight with him—not tonight. "You might want to remember that your approach isn't the only one that matters," I replied, my voice steady despite the adrenaline thrumming through my veins. "You're not the judge of what will impress them."

Marco took a deep breath, a flicker of gratitude in his eyes as he looked between us. "Okay, how about we all take a step back?" he suggested, trying to defuse the tension. "Rachel, I really appreciate your support. Maybe you can help me with a new dish I've been thinking about?"

I nodded, eager to shift the focus back to him. "Of course! What do you have in mind?"

He began explaining his vision—a tomato basil tart that would highlight the freshness of the ingredients and showcase his skills without losing his authentic style. As he spoke, his passion ignited the space around us, transforming the earlier unease into an electric buzz of creativity. I leaned in, captivated by the way his eyes sparkled when he discussed the flavors, the textures, and the final presentation.

"Okay, let's get started," I said, clapping my hands together as if to chase away the lingering shadows of doubt. The kitchen buzzed to life as we gathered ingredients, my heart swelling with pride for Marco. He was so talented, so close to finding his rhythm again, and I was determined to help him see it.

As we worked side by side, our laughter mingled with the sounds of sizzling pans and the occasional clatter of utensils. I snuck glances at him, admiring the way his brow furrowed in concentration, the way his lips curved into a grin when I made a joke about his less-than-perfect herb chopping. Each moment felt precious, like threads weaving a tapestry of memories that I would cherish long after the night had ended.

But the specter of James lingered like a dark cloud, a reminder that our sanctuary was fragile. He stood to the side, arms crossed, the smirk replaced by a contemplative expression that left me uneasy. He interjected occasionally, his remarks sharp enough to cut through the lightness we were building. I could feel Marco's shoulders tighten each time he spoke, the weight of expectation pressing down like a lead blanket.

"Maybe add a bit of lemon zest to brighten the flavor," James suggested, and I bristled. "You know, something to elevate it for the judges."

"Or maybe we just let the ingredients speak for themselves?" I countered, frustration spilling over. The atmosphere thickened again, and Marco's face fell, caught between the two of us.

"Why don't we just make it the way I envision it?" he said, the tension in his voice palpable. "I appreciate your input, James, but this is my dish."

A silence enveloped the kitchen, each breath feeling monumental. James's mouth tightened into a thin line, and I could almost see the gears turning in his head as he processed Marco's words. Would this spark a confrontation, or would he slink away, wounded but unwilling to show it?

In that moment, I realized something crucial. Marco needed to reclaim his voice, to stand up for his culinary vision not just for this competition but for himself. And if it took a little confrontation to make that happen, so be it. I shot him a supportive smile, silently urging him to find his strength amid the chaos.

"Let's just cook," I said, breaking the tension like a spark igniting dry tinder. "Marco, show us what you can do."

His shoulders relaxed just a fraction, and for the first time that night, I saw a flicker of confidence return to his eyes. He nodded, the tension loosening its grip as we dove back into our work, the kitchen humming with the sound of knives chopping and pans sizzling, the symphony of culinary creation drowning out the shadows that had threatened to suffocate us.

The sizzle of onions in a hot pan filled the air, a sound that usually brought me comfort, but tonight, it added to the weight pressing down on my chest. As Marco and I chopped and stirred, I felt the unshakeable presence of James, who loomed like a storm cloud ready to unleash thunder. With each passing moment, the tension coiled tighter around us, a living thing that threatened to choke out the creativity and joy we had ignited just moments before.

"Do you think you can manage the heat better?" James offered, his tone casual but sharp, as if slicing through the steam rising from the stove. "Cooking is all about control, Marco. You can't let it slip away, or you'll end up with a burnt mess."

Marco's hands paused mid-chop, the knife hovering just above the cutting board. I could see the struggle etched across his features, a battle between frustration and his ingrained desire to please. "I think

I've got it under control," he replied, his voice steady but laced with an edge that hinted at his growing impatience.

I stepped forward, reclaiming my space in this kitchen that felt more like a battlefield than a haven. "James, maybe you could take a break from the commentary? I think Marco knows how to not set fire to his own kitchen." The words came out sharper than I intended, but the thought of him undermining Marco's confidence sparked something fierce in me.

James arched an eyebrow, amusement flickering across his face. "Is that supposed to be a joke? Because if it is, it's not very funny."

"Just trying to lighten the mood," I shot back, crossing my arms defiantly. "Or are you just too serious for that?"

"Seriousness is often what distinguishes a good cook from a great one," he replied smoothly, his condescension coating his words like a thick layer of butter.

I turned to Marco, his eyes darting between us, an open book of worry and confusion. "Let's refocus," I suggested, nudging a bowl of vibrant cherry tomatoes closer to him. "How about we prep the sauce for that tart? We need to showcase your talent, not just your ability to listen to someone else."

He gave me a small, grateful smile, and I felt a flicker of hope that we could push past the discord. "Right. Let's do this," he said, his voice gaining strength as he began to chop again, the rhythmic sound of his knife striking the board punctuating the space between us.

As we worked together, the initial tension slowly began to ebb. I focused on the tomatoes, their bright red skins glistening under the light, while Marco immersed himself in his task, the weight of James's comments gradually lifting like a fog. The warmth of the kitchen wrapped around us, a cocoon that momentarily shielded us from the outside world.

But just as I began to believe we could find our groove, the door swung open, and in strode Leah, one of the other competitors, her laughter bright and infectious. "What's cooking, good looking?" she teased, her playful tone piercing through the simmering atmosphere. She leaned against the doorframe, arms crossed, taking in the scene with a knowing smirk.

"Just trying to survive this," I replied, gesturing at the kitchen chaos with a smile that felt forced. Leah was a fierce competitor, one who could charm the judges as easily as she could slice through the competition. She had a knack for deflecting attention away from herself, always ready with a quip or a witty remark.

"What? You're not going to invite me to join this culinary masterpiece?" Leah said, her eyes sparkling with mischief.

Marco, his relief palpable, responded with a genuine smile. "Of course, we could use a hand. It's getting a bit crowded in here, though."

"I thrive in chaos," Leah declared, stepping further into the kitchen, her confidence filling the space. "Besides, I have some secret techniques I'd be more than happy to share."

"Secret techniques?" James's tone turned skeptical, and he leaned forward, interest piqued despite himself. "Like what? Handing out recipes? That's hardly a technique."

Leah laughed, unfazed by his jibe. "Oh, I have a few tricks up my sleeve, but it's more about flair than following the rules. Want me to show you how to infuse that sauce with some personality?"

I caught Marco's eye, a spark of excitement passing between us. He needed this infusion of joy, a reminder that cooking was more than just a competition; it was about passion and creativity. "What's your idea?" I asked, eager to redirect the energy in the room.

"Lemon zest and a splash of balsamic reduction," Leah said, her hands animatedly gesturing as if she were conducting an orchestra.

"It'll elevate your sauce from basic to brilliant. Plus, who doesn't love a little zing?"

James scoffed, but I could see Marco's curiosity piquing. "Maybe we could try it," he said tentatively, glancing at Leah, who nodded encouragingly.

"Exactly! Cooking is all about taking risks, right?" she replied, her enthusiasm infectious. "Let's shake things up a bit."

With a newfound sense of camaraderie, we dove into the cooking. Leah joined me at the counter, and we worked side by side, the tension easing as laughter filled the kitchen. Marco focused on the sauce, his confidence rebuilding with every stir and splash. James hovered nearby, his critiques becoming less frequent, replaced by a watchful curiosity.

"See? You're getting into it now," I said to Marco, who was stirring the sauce with a newfound vigor. "This is what it's all about."

He smiled, a genuine, wide grin that lit up his entire face. "Thanks, Rachel. I think I needed that push."

"And who knew I'd need to recruit a secret weapon like Leah?" I quipped, throwing her a teasing glance. "It's like the Avengers of the kitchen!"

"More like the dysfunctional family of chefs," Leah shot back with a wink.

As we layered flavors into the sauce, the kitchen became a sanctuary, a space where creativity could flourish amid the chaos. Each stir, each addition felt like a brushstroke on a canvas, transforming our humble ingredients into something extraordinary. The sense of competition melted away, replaced by a shared joy that wrapped around us like a warm embrace.

But just as we reached a rhythm, a sudden sound interrupted our harmony—a loud crash echoed from the other room. We all froze, the kitchen air thickening with anticipation. My heart raced as I exchanged worried glances with Marco and Leah, each of us caught in a moment of uncertainty. James's expression shifted from amused to alert, his eyes narrowing as he turned toward the source of the noise.

"What was that?" Marco asked, his voice barely a whisper, the spark of creativity dimming in the face of the unknown.

"I have no idea," I replied, a sense of dread creeping in. "But it sounded like it came from the pantry."

James pushed himself off the counter, his curiosity piqued. "Let's check it out. It could be anything."

As we moved cautiously toward the pantry door, a strange energy filled the air, a tension that spoke of secrets waiting to be unveiled. The world outside our kitchen had just reminded us that not everything could be neatly contained. And whatever lay beyond the door was about to change everything.

The pantry door loomed before us like a gateway to the unknown, the faint light from the kitchen spilling across its threshold. My heart raced as I exchanged wary glances with Marco and Leah. James, the supposed professional, seemed unfazed, his curiosity burning in his narrowed eyes. I wondered if he'd ever encountered a crash he didn't think could be turned into an opportunity to lecture us.

"What do you think it was?" Leah asked, her voice barely above a whisper.

"Something fell? Or someone fell?" I replied, my imagination spiraling. "Maybe it's the ghost of bad cooking past."

James rolled his eyes, but I caught a hint of a smile tugging at his lips. "We should probably investigate. If it's someone getting hurt, it's best to know."

With a nod, we approached the door cautiously. My fingers brushed against the handle, cold and unyielding, as if the door itself knew the secrets waiting on the other side. I turned to Marco, whose expression wavered between determination and dread. "You ready?"

He took a deep breath, and I could see the flicker of resolve igniting within him. "Let's do this."

With a swift motion, I flung open the door, and we peered inside. The pantry was dim, shadows playing across the walls like whispers of past culinary disasters. Shelves filled with various spices and ingredients lined the walls, and in the far corner, a massive sack of flour lay toppled, its contents spilling across the floor like a white dusting of snow.

"What the—" Leah began, but her words trailed off as we stepped inside, revealing the true chaos. The source of the crash was now apparent: a stack of heavy pots and pans lay scattered, some precariously balanced on the edge of a shelf.

As we surveyed the scene, a soft rustling echoed from the back of the pantry, a sound that sent a chill down my spine. "Is anyone there?" I called out, my voice trembling slightly. "It's just us! We heard a crash."

Silence greeted us, thick and foreboding. I exchanged a glance with Marco, whose expression mirrored my own trepidation.

"Maybe it's just a raccoon that wandered in for a late-night snack," Leah joked, but her voice was laced with unease. "Though I'm pretty sure raccoons don't typically enjoy garlic and rosemary."

Suddenly, a figure stepped out from the shadows at the back of the pantry, and I gasped, instinctively moving closer to Marco. It was Claire, another competitor whose talent was only overshadowed by her enigmatic nature. Her hair was disheveled, and her eyes wide with a mix of fear and determination.

"What are you doing in here?" I blurted, my voice a mix of surprise and relief. "We thought something was wrong!"

"I thought I heard voices," Claire replied, brushing flour off her shirt with a nervous laugh. "I was just...looking for inspiration."

"Inspiration or not, you could have warned us before you toppled a whole shelf!" Leah exclaimed, hands on her hips, though

I could see the corners of her mouth twitching, trying to suppress a smile.

"Believe me, it wasn't intentional," Claire shot back, a glimmer of mischief sparkling in her eyes. "Just trying to gather my thoughts for the competition. Things have been so chaotic lately."

"Chaotic is an understatement," I muttered, stepping over the fallen pots. "I'm not sure how anyone is supposed to focus with all the pressure piling up."

"Pressure?" Claire echoed, raising an eyebrow. "You think you have pressure? I just overheard James telling some of the judges that he's looking to make the ultimate culinary discovery with one of you."

"What does that even mean?" Marco asked, his brows furrowing in confusion.

Claire shrugged, a smirk playing on her lips. "I have no idea. But it sounds ominous, doesn't it? Like a culinary sacrifice is in order."

The room fell silent again, the air thickening as the implications sank in. James's ambition had always been evident, but this? "You think he's trying to pit us against each other?" I asked, my voice barely above a whisper.

"Could be," Claire replied, her eyes darting toward the door. "He's been acting a little too...overzealous, if you ask me. And not just with Marco."

"I've felt it too," I confessed, glancing at Marco. "Like he's using our competition as a way to boost his own ego."

"Or to push someone off the pedestal," Leah added, crossing her arms. "Isn't that what the culinary world thrives on? One chef rising while another falls?"

Just then, the lights in the pantry flickered, casting eerie shadows across the shelves. A sudden thought struck me, icy and unwelcome. "Do you think he's doing this to get us to sabotage each other?"

Marco's jaw tightened, and I could see the gears turning in his mind. "We can't let that happen. Not now, not when I'm finally finding my voice."

"Exactly," Leah said, her earlier bravado returning. "We're not going to be pawns in his game."

"Let's keep an eye on him, then," Claire suggested, her tone conspiratorial. "But for now, maybe we should just get back to work and put some distance between ourselves and the drama."

"Agreed," Marco replied, stepping out of the pantry and gesturing for us to follow. "I need to finish that sauce."

As we filed back into the kitchen, the tension of the pantry still clung to us, but the flicker of camaraderie had returned. I started to prepare more ingredients, determined to keep the atmosphere light. "So, what's next? A little dance party while we cook?"

Leah snorted. "Only if you promise to do the robot."

"I don't think anyone wants to see that," I laughed, shaking my head.

Marco's laughter joined ours, a welcome sound that helped ease the lingering unease. As we resumed our culinary creation, I glanced at the clock on the wall. Time was slipping away, and the competition loomed just over the horizon, waiting to test our resolve.

Suddenly, a loud bang echoed from the other room, startling us into silence once again. My stomach dropped as I glanced at Marco, whose face had gone pale.

"What was that?" he whispered, dread creeping into his voice.

Before I could respond, the kitchen door swung open, and in strode a figure—someone I had not expected to see at this hour. It was James, but something was different. His eyes were wide, wild with a fervor that sent a chill racing down my spine.

"You all need to see this," he said, breathless, urgency pouring from his every word. "It's about the competition... and it could change everything."

My heart raced as I exchanged worried glances with Marco and Leah. Whatever James had to say felt like the prelude to something much darker, and I couldn't shake the feeling that we were about to plunge into the depths of chaos.

Chapter 25: Confrontation in the Kitchen

The kitchen was alive, a symphony of sizzling pans and the fragrant dance of spices weaving through the air, wrapping around me like an old, familiar blanket. As I leaned against the cool marble countertop, I watched Marco, his hands deftly slicing through a vibrant red bell pepper, the knife gliding with the precision of a well-tuned machine. The morning light poured in through the wide windows, illuminating the bustling scene—steam rising from pots, laughter mingling with the rhythmic chopping, and the distant sound of clattering dishes. Yet beneath this bustling exterior, an undercurrent of tension lurked, thick enough to slice through.

"Marco," I started, my voice soft yet unyielding as I broke the spell of culinary chaos. He paused, glancing up with those deep brown eyes that held both warmth and a flicker of something distant, perhaps a storm brewing just beneath the surface. "We need to talk about James."

He sighed, an audible release of air that seemed to carry more than just exhaustion; it was laden with unspoken words, doubts, and something I could only describe as the shadow of competition. "What about him?" He resumed his chopping, the rhythmic thud of the knife against the cutting board echoing the tumult in my heart.

"Look," I leaned closer, my voice dropping to a whisper. "I know you appreciate his help, but it feels like he's overshadowing you. You're not just another chef in this kitchen, Marco. You're the heart of it." My words hung in the air, suspended between us as the sounds of the kitchen faded into a dull hum.

He paused again, the knife still in hand, and I could see the struggle within him. "You don't understand," he said, a hint of frustration lacing his tone. "James brings ideas that I never even considered. He challenges me, but it's... it's becoming too much. I feel like I'm losing myself in all of this."

"Then don't let him take over! You have to find a way to balance it all. Remember why you started this in the first place?" I pressed, willing him to see the truth through the fog of ambition and pressure. "It was about your passion, your vision—not just winning a competition."

A flicker of something—hope? Resentment?—crossed his face before he hardened again. "And what if my vision isn't enough? What if he's right about everything? Maybe I need to adapt, or else..."

"Or else what?" I interjected, my voice rising slightly, causing a few heads to turn in our direction. "Lose yourself? Drown in someone else's dreams? You're an artist, Marco! Your food is your voice, and it's beautiful. Don't let anyone else speak for you."

He dropped the knife onto the board with a thud that seemed to resonate through the room, echoing my desperation. "It's not that simple, Sam! You think it's easy to just push him aside when he's got all these great ideas? Everyone loves what he's bringing to the table."

"Everyone?" I scoffed lightly, the bitterness creeping into my voice. "What about what you want? You're not here to please everyone, Marco. This is your dream, and I'm tired of watching you tiptoe around it just to keep the peace."

His expression shifted, a mix of anger and sorrow, as if I had cracked open a door to something he was too afraid to confront. "You don't get it! I'm not just a chef; I'm a competitor now. It's about survival in this industry. It's cutthroat."

"Is it really? Or are you just letting it cut you?" The words escaped my lips before I could stop them, sharp and pointed, and I watched as they landed heavily between us. "You're letting fear dictate your choices. You're scared of losing to someone you think is better, but you have something he doesn't—your heart."

For a moment, the kitchen fell silent around us, the sizzling pans and the laughter of our colleagues fading into the background as Marco's gaze locked onto mine. The flicker of vulnerability in his eyes made my chest tighten, but I pressed on. "You're losing sight of who you are in this rush for validation. You're amazing, Marco. Don't you see that?"

He looked down, his brow furrowed, fingers gripping the edge of the counter like a lifeline. "What if I don't know who I am anymore?" His voice dropped to a whisper, raw and open, a question that cut deeper than any knife.

"Then let me help you find out," I offered gently, stepping closer. "Let's talk about what you want. What you really want. You've poured so much into this place, into the people here. Don't throw it all away just to compete. I'm here for you, but you have to let me in."

Marco looked up, his expression softening as the tension in his shoulders began to ease. "I'm just... afraid. I thought competition would be thrilling, but it's suffocating. I'm trying to balance what I love with what everyone expects."

The words hung heavy in the air, resonating like the lingering scent of fresh basil and garlic wafting through the kitchen. "It's okay to be afraid. But you can't let fear be the thing that defines you. You've got to chase your own dreams, not someone else's. You're more than just a chef in a competition."

I reached out, my hand resting over his, grounding him in the moment. "Let's remember who you are. The flavors you create are a part of you. Don't let them drown in someone else's idea of what success looks like."

In that moment, something shifted. The barrier he had constructed around himself began to crack, and I saw the flicker of recognition in his eyes. Perhaps it was the realization that he was not alone in this, that there was someone willing to fight for his vision alongside him. The world around us faded, leaving just the two of us amid the bustling kitchen, the heart of a dream hanging in the balance, waiting for him to choose his own path forward.

The sun hung low in the sky, casting a warm golden hue across the bustling street outside. As I stepped out of the kitchen, the aromas of roasting garlic and fresh herbs still clung to my clothes, a reminder of the intensity that had unfolded just hours earlier. I needed to take a breath, to clear the clutter from my mind, so I wandered down to the little café around the corner, the kind that looked like it had been plucked from a postcard with its weathered wooden exterior and mismatched chairs.

Inside, the café buzzed with the casual chatter of locals, the clinking of cups, and the soft hum of a guitar playing somewhere in the background. The barista, a sprightly woman with curls that danced around her face, greeted me with a bright smile. "The usual?" she asked, her voice warm and inviting.

"Actually, make it a chai latte today," I replied, wanting something soothing to balance the tumult I felt swirling within me.

I settled at a small table by the window, my mind still racing with thoughts of Marco. Watching the world outside, I could see the rhythm of life continuing unabated—joggers gliding past, children racing after each other, and a couple sharing a laugh over their pastries. A part of me longed for that simplicity, for the lightness that comes from being unencumbered by ambition's heavy cloak.

Moments later, the barista returned, placing my drink in front of me with a flourish, the steam curling up like the tendrils of my thoughts. "Everything okay?" she asked, sensing my distraction.

"Just navigating a bit of a storm," I replied with a wry smile, holding the warm mug between my hands, letting its heat seep into me.

"Ah, the classic kitchen drama," she said knowingly. "Remember, even the best chefs need to stir the pot, not just let it simmer."

I chuckled, appreciating her insight. "That's a good way to put it. I guess I just don't want the pot to boil over."

With a nod, she moved to serve another table, and I found myself gazing out the window, my thoughts circling back to Marco. The weight of our earlier conversation hung like a thick fog, clouding my mind. It was as if the vibrant life outside was mocking the tension inside my heart.

As I sipped my chai, I replayed his expression—the flicker of vulnerability amidst his frustration. I wondered if I had pushed too hard or if I had finally managed to break through the defenses he had so carefully constructed. The thought that he might be feeling lost gnawed at me, a jagged edge that cut deeper than I had anticipated.

Just then, my phone buzzed on the table, the screen lighting up with Marco's name. My heart raced, a mix of anticipation and dread. I picked it up, half-expecting another outburst, but instead, a message popped up: Can we talk later? Need to figure some things out.

I let out a breath I didn't realize I was holding, relief washing over me. There was a chance for clarity, a moment to sift through the chaos together. I quickly typed back, Absolutely. Whenever you're ready.

Setting my phone down, I took another sip of my latte, the warmth enveloping me like a soft hug. In that moment, I felt a sense of determination solidify within me. Whatever was happening with Marco, I wouldn't shy away from the storm. Instead, I would stand by him, even if it meant navigating uncomfortable conversations or confronting the demons that lurked in the shadows of his ambition.

The café began to fill, the air growing rich with the sound of laughter and the clatter of cups. I looked around, taking in the scene, when I noticed a familiar figure at the far corner table—James, the very embodiment of charisma with his tousled hair and effortless charm. He was deep in conversation with a group of aspiring chefs, their eyes glued to him as if he were the sun itself, and they were mere planets orbiting his brilliance. A pang of unease twisted in my stomach.

What if he was the very embodiment of everything Marco feared? The thoughts raced through my mind like wildfire. I considered the competition that had once been invigorating for Marco, now serving as a potent source of stress. What if James didn't just challenge Marco but threatened to eclipse him entirely?

In a fit of uncharacteristic boldness, I stood up, leaving my half-finished latte on the table, and made my way over to him. As I approached, I could hear snippets of his laughter, the lightness in his voice wrapping around the room. I cleared my throat, making my presence known. He turned, that effortless smile widening as he recognized me.

"Sam! Fancy running into you here. I was just telling them about this incredible dish I created—" he began, but I cut him off, my tone sharper than I intended.

"James, can we talk?" I asked, forcing a smile that felt a little too tight around the edges.

"Sure, what's up?" He stood, and I led him a few steps away from the cluster of eager listeners, hoping to gain some semblance of privacy.

"Look, I know things have been intense in the kitchen, and I wanted to get your perspective on it all." The words felt clumsy, like they were tripping over each other as I spoke.

"Perspective?" he repeated, his brow arching in curiosity, a hint of mischief flickering in his eyes. "Are you worried I might steal your boyfriend's thunder? Because if you are, you should know that I'm more interested in collaboration than competition."

That sharpness in my tone faltered as I processed his words. "It's not just that. Marco is feeling overwhelmed, and I can't help but feel that you're part of the reason. He admires your talent, but it's like he's trying to match you instead of being himself."

James leaned back, a thoughtful expression crossing his face. "I get that. But have you considered that maybe he's got to step up? It's not just about admiring talent; it's about growing from it."

"Growing?" I echoed, the word rolling off my tongue as if it were foreign. "Or losing himself in the process?"

"Sometimes growth is uncomfortable, Sam. He can't just coast on nostalgia. If he wants to be great, he needs to embrace that discomfort."

His words stirred something in me, a cocktail of frustration and understanding swirling in my chest. "But there's a difference between growth and losing sight of who you are. If he's only trying to be like you, what happens to his vision?"

James met my gaze, his expression shifting from playful to earnest. "You care about him, don't you?"

"More than I can put into words," I confessed, the honesty spilling out. "But I can't watch him drown in the expectations of everyone else, especially yours."

A pause enveloped us, thick and heavy, before he nodded, an unexpected warmth in his demeanor. "Okay, I'll back off. Just tell him to lean into who he is. That's what he needs right now."

As I walked back to my table, the swirling doubts and fears I had carried felt a little lighter. The conversation with James hadn't been what I expected, but it had offered a glimpse of understanding—a reminder that even amidst competition, there was room for compassion and clarity. I returned to my chai latte, taking a deep breath, readying myself for the next round of this emotional culinary battle.

The café had become a sanctuary, a brief escape from the whirlwind of the kitchen, but as I left, the lingering warmth of the chai was quickly replaced by a chill that slithered through the streets.

A brisk wind tugged at my hair, and I tucked my scarf tighter around my neck, steeling myself against the elements as I headed back to the restaurant. I could sense the energy shifting around me, the anticipation thickening in the air like the aroma of simmering stock, and I knew the intensity that awaited would be palpable.

As I stepped inside, the kitchen was a flurry of activity, a kaleidoscope of movement and sound. Marco stood at the center, his back to me, hands dancing over ingredients with the frenetic energy of someone trying to outpace a ticking clock. I watched for a moment, my heart swelling with both admiration and concern. This was the man I had fought for earlier, the artist who breathed life into every dish, yet the shadows of doubt still clung to him like a second skin.

"Hey," I called, injecting as much warmth into my voice as I could muster, hoping to cut through the tension that felt almost electric. He turned, his expression shifting as he caught sight of me—relief mixed with a flicker of anxiety.

"Hey," he replied, forcing a smile that didn't quite reach his eyes. "I've been... busy."

"Looks like it," I said, glancing around the kitchen where James was leaning against the counter, arms crossed and a smug expression plastered across his face. The sight of him sent a twinge of unease through me, but I pushed it down, focusing instead on Marco. "I spoke with James earlier. He agreed to tone down his ideas a bit."

Marco's brow furrowed, his hands momentarily stalling. "Did he now? That's... unexpected."

"Yeah, well, maybe he actually listened. I told him how overwhelmed you've been feeling," I admitted, my heart pounding in my chest, unsure if I had overstepped. "I thought it might help you focus on what you want."

His gaze hardened for a moment, the muscles in his jaw tightening. "I don't need anyone to listen to me out of pity. If I can't keep up, then maybe I don't belong here."

The words cut deep, echoing the fears I had tried to quell. "That's not true, Marco! You belong here because of who you are, not because of James or anyone else. You have to believe that."

He turned back to his station, and the momentary connection between us felt frayed, like a tapestry unraveling at the edges. I wanted to reach out, to pull him back into our shared space, but he was enveloped in his own storm.

Just then, James broke in, his tone playful yet dripping with challenge. "Hey, Marco, don't let her sweet talk you into mediocrity. This is about pushing boundaries, remember? You can't be afraid to take risks."

"Risk is one thing, but losing yourself in someone else's vision is another," I shot back, my tone sharper than I intended.

Marco turned, eyes narrowing. "You think I'm trying to be someone else? You think I want to lose my identity?"

"I don't know what you want!" I exclaimed, frustration boiling over. "I just want to see you thrive, but you're acting like you're on a treadmill, just running to keep up."

The kitchen quieted, the tension palpable as everyone stopped to watch our exchange, and I felt the heat creep into my cheeks. James leaned against the counter, a smirk dancing on his lips, clearly enjoying the spectacle.

"I'll figure it out," Marco said finally, turning back to his work with a flick of his wrist, dismissing my concerns like one might shoo away a bothersome fly.

I felt my heart sink. This wasn't the breakthrough I had hoped for; it felt like a wall was being built between us, and I was powerless to stop it. With a heavy sigh, I stepped away, giving him space while trying to compose myself. The kitchen continued to buzz around me, but the laughter and chatter seemed distant, muted against the storm brewing in my chest.

Hours passed, and the dinner rush settled in, a chaotic ballet of orders and frantic movements. I slipped into the rhythm, finding solace in the familiar tasks—plating dishes, pouring sauces, and listening to the symphony of clanging pots. But Marco remained an enigma, distant and absorbed, his focus zeroed in on his work while James flitted around like a moth drawn to the flame of his own ego.

As the night wore on, a sense of dread coiled in my stomach. I glanced up to find Marco deep in conversation with James, their voices low and intense, and I could feel the tension crackling in the air like static before a storm. I approached, determined to reclaim a moment of connection, when I overheard a fragment of their conversation that stopped me cold.

"You can't keep relying on her to boost your confidence, Marco," James said, his voice smooth but edged with something darker. "If you want to succeed, you need to push her out of your mind and focus on what really matters—winning."

My heart raced as I registered the meaning behind his words. Was James trying to turn Marco against me? To strip away the very foundation of our partnership? Anger surged through me, hot and sharp. I stepped closer, ready to confront the manipulation, when Marco's eyes caught mine, a fleeting expression of uncertainty crossing his features before he masked it with a smile directed at James.

"I appreciate your input, James. I just—" he started, but I couldn't hold back any longer.

"Is this what you really want?" I interjected, my voice steady despite the tempest swirling within. "To let him dictate your worth? To throw away everything you've built because of some competition?"

Marco opened his mouth to respond, but before he could utter a word, the door swung open, and in walked a group of diners who immediately demanded attention. The moment evaporated, leaving us suspended in a world of chaos and unresolved tension.

I felt my frustration boiling as I took a step back, my heart racing with anger and concern. I wanted to scream, to shake some sense into him, but the energy in the kitchen shifted again, pulling me into the urgency of service.

Hours passed, the adrenaline keeping me afloat, but as the final plates were cleared and the last guests departed, I found Marco alone, his back turned to me as he cleaned the counter. I approached quietly, the weight of the unspoken heavy in the air.

"Marco," I began, but he held up a hand, not turning around.

"Not now, Sam. I'm tired," he replied, the weariness in his voice masking the emotions that danced just beneath the surface.

My frustration erupted. "You can't keep shutting me out! I'm here for you, and you need to decide what you want. Not what James wants, not what the competition demands—what you want."

Finally, he turned to face me, his eyes dark pools of conflict. "I don't know what I want, okay? Maybe you're right, maybe I've been trying to impress everyone else. But you can't just come in here and demand clarity when I'm still figuring things out."

I took a deep breath, the air thick with tension. "Then let me help you. Please."

In that moment, as silence enveloped us, I felt the ground shift beneath my feet, a tremor of uncertainty passing between us. Just as he opened his mouth to respond, the kitchen door swung open again, and in walked a tall figure—unexpected and uninvited.

My heart sank as I recognized the silhouette. James stood there, a glint of triumph in his eyes, and the world around us seemed to freeze. "Hope I'm not interrupting," he said, a sly grin creeping across his face. "I just came to check on my favorite chef."

I exchanged a quick glance with Marco, and in that fleeting moment, I could see the cracks widening. The storm was far from over, and with James stepping into our fragile space, I felt the weight of impending chaos settle heavily on my chest, a cliffhanger poised on the edge of our fragile connection.

Chapter 26: A Recipe for Trust

The sun hung low in the sky, casting a golden hue over Asheville, illuminating the cobblestone streets and eclectic storefronts. I had planned our day meticulously, each stop a carefully selected homage to Marco's culinary past, hoping to unlock memories buried beneath layers of disappointment. As we drove through the winding roads, I glanced over at him. His brow furrowed, a subtle reminder of the conflict that still clung to him like a stubborn shadow. Today was about rekindling his passion, and I had an arsenal of culinary wonders ready to ignite that spark.

Our first destination was a small, family-run farm nestled on the outskirts of town. As we parked and stepped out, the scent of fresh earth mixed with the sweet perfume of blooming herbs enveloped us. Marco inhaled deeply, and I could almost see the gears in his mind shifting. The farmer, a jovial man with hands like tree trunks, greeted us with a wide grin. "Welcome to Green Thumb Acres! You two here for the harvest?"

"Yes, we are!" I beamed, glancing sideways at Marco, who had begun to loosen up, his lips curling into a faint smile.

The farmer led us through rows of vibrant vegetables and fragrant herbs, each plant bursting with life. Marco knelt beside a bed of heirloom tomatoes, their skins glistening like jewels in the sunlight. "You know, tomatoes are like people," he mused, plucking one gently. "Some are sweet, some are sour, but all of them have their own story."

I chuckled, a lightness settling in my chest. "And I suppose you think you're the sweet one?"

He shot me a mock glare, the corners of his mouth twitching in amusement. "I was thinking more like the heirloom variety—complex and rich in flavor, thank you very much."

Our banter carried us through the farm, where we filled our baskets with vibrant produce, our laughter mingling with the sounds of rustling leaves and chirping birds. Marco began to share snippets of his childhood, tales of summers spent in his grandmother's kitchen, the vibrant flavors of her dishes dancing in his memories. "She always said the secret to good food was love. I never understood that until I started cooking," he admitted, his eyes softening as he spoke.

"I think you've got that part down," I replied, nudging him playfully. "What you need now is a dash of adventure."

With our baskets full, we returned to the car, the sun dipping lower, painting the horizon in shades of orange and pink. As we drove back toward the city, I could sense the energy shifting between us. The tension from our earlier confrontation felt like a distant storm cloud, dissipating under the warmth of shared laughter and memories.

Our next stop was a quaint café renowned for its artisanal bread and local cheeses. The air was rich with the smell of freshly baked goods, and the sound of laughter and clinking cutlery enveloped us as we stepped inside. Marco's eyes lit up, the familiar warmth of the café wrapping around him like a favorite old sweater.

"Do you remember coming here?" I asked, nudging him toward a rustic wooden table.

He glanced around, nostalgia evident in his gaze. "This was my refuge. I'd spend hours here, sketching recipes while savoring their pain au levain. They made me feel like I belonged."

I smiled, knowing this was exactly the kind of place that could reignite his love for cooking. We ordered an array of items, from buttery croissants to a charcuterie board adorned with local meats and cheeses. Each bite transported him further into the past, his laughter growing louder with each taste.

"Okay, here's a challenge," I said, leaning in conspiratorially. "We need to create a new dish tonight using everything we picked up today. No pressure, right?"

His eyes sparkled with a mix of mischief and intrigue. "You think I can just whip something up out of thin air?"

"Absolutely. You're a culinary magician. Just think of it as cooking therapy."

We spent the rest of our afternoon sampling pastries and concocting absurd culinary theories. Marco confidently explained how a sprinkle of thyme could elevate a dish, while I insisted that an unexpected splash of balsamic would do the trick. Our playful arguments echoed the harmony of a kitchen in full swing, a rhythm that felt natural and freeing.

As the evening approached, we returned to my apartment, the bags of fresh produce and baked goods spilling across the counter. Marco took charge, his demeanor shifting from hesitant to confident, as if the day had stripped away the doubts that clung to him. He rolled up his sleeves, an excited grin spreading across his face.

"Alright, chef," he said, eyeing the ingredients as though they were puzzle pieces waiting to be assembled. "What's our plan?"

I watched, spellbound, as he sliced and diced, his hands moving with a precision that had me captivated. "Let's start with a fresh tomato salad," he declared, his brow furrowing in concentration. "We'll roast the heirlooms with a touch of olive oil and sprinkle them with basil."

As he cooked, I found myself caught in the magic of the moment, the air thick with the smell of garlic and olive oil, the sound of sizzling filling the space between us. Laughter punctuated our conversation, like notes in a well-composed symphony. Each playful jab he threw my way was met with a quick retort, a dance of witticisms that set my heart racing.

I marveled at the transformation before me. The man who had walked into my life with walls built from past failures was now blending flavors, infusing our kitchen with the vibrancy of his dreams. With every chop, every sizzle, I could see him reclaiming his passion, piece by piece, like a sculptor chiseling away at a block of stone.

"Here, taste this," he said, holding a spoonful of the dressing he'd just concocted, his expression a mixture of eagerness and nervousness.

I leaned forward, savoring the blend of tangy vinegar and sweet herbs. "This is incredible! You're onto something," I replied, my eyes wide with enthusiasm.

A flush crept up his neck, the corners of his mouth lifting into a satisfied grin. "You really think so?"

"Absolutely! Just wait until we serve it. It'll be a hit."

The evening unfolded like a beautifully written narrative, rich with flavors and the warmth of connection. As we plated our creation, I could feel the remnants of doubt fade, replaced by a deep sense of trust and camaraderie. Cooking together had become more than just a way to pass the time; it was a reaffirmation of our bond, an unspoken promise that we would weather any storm together.

In that kitchen, amidst the clattering pots and sizzling pans, I found myself not just rooting for Marco but falling deeper into a world of shared dreams and aspirations. Each moment solidified the truth that love, much like a well-crafted dish, required care, patience, and an abundance of flavors. The recipe for trust was evolving, and I was savoring every bite.

The evening unfolded like the first pages of a well-loved novel, and as we savored our creation, the kitchen filled with the comforting aroma of roasted tomatoes and fresh herbs. The dining table, draped in a simple linen cloth, held our masterpiece alongside a bottle of local wine that caught the fading light in its glass. It was a picture of warmth and intimacy, a moment that felt both effortless and earned.

I poured us each a glass, my heart fluttering with a mixture of excitement and apprehension. "To new beginnings," I toasted, raising my glass with a flourish.

Marco clinked his against mine, his gaze steady. "And to old flavors," he added with a smirk, settling into the easy camaraderie we'd begun to rebuild.

As we took our first bites, the flavors exploded in my mouth—sweet, tangy, and savory, a harmonious dance of ingredients that made my taste buds sing. I closed my eyes for a brief second, allowing the moment to wash over me. "This is incredible, Marco. You've really outdone yourself."

He leaned back, a flicker of pride lighting up his features. "Maybe I should quit my job and become a full-time chef," he mused, his tone half-serious, half-teasing. "What do you think? Would you still want to date me if I was covered in flour and wearing a chef's hat all day?"

"Only if you promise to cook for me every night," I shot back, grinning. "But let's be real, you'd just end up being a grumpy chef, barking orders at me. I don't know if I could handle that."

"Me, grumpy? Never!" he replied, feigning indignation, his laughter filling the space between us.

As we enjoyed our meal, the light conversation wove deeper threads between us. We shared stories, dreams, and even fears that slipped out unbidden between bites of food. I learned that Marco had always wanted to travel the world, experiencing different cultures through their cuisines. "I've got this dream of opening a restaurant that showcases the flavors of the world," he confessed, his eyes sparkling with unrestrained ambition. "But every time I try to take a step forward, I get so tangled in my own head."

"Why not start small?" I suggested, feeling the weight of his vulnerability draw me closer. "You could do pop-up dinners or collaborate with local businesses. Your food deserves to be shared."

He nodded, a flicker of hope igniting behind his uncertainty. "That could work. I guess I just need to find the right moment to dive in. But what if I fail again?"

"Then you learn from it," I said, leaning forward, our conversation bubbling with an electric intimacy. "And besides, failing is just a fancy way of saying you're on the path to something greater."

The tension that had once held him captive began to ebb, replaced by a sense of shared purpose. But as the evening wore on, a shadow of doubt crossed his face, momentarily dimming the light in his eyes. I could see that a part of him was still wrestling with the fear of inadequacy, a specter that haunted him despite the joyful rediscovery of his love for cooking.

I decided to lighten the mood, hoping to dispel the gloom. "Okay, let's make a pact," I said dramatically, placing my hand over my heart. "I promise to always remind you of how amazing you are, and you promise to let me taste test every new dish you create."

He chuckled, the corner of his mouth lifting in amusement. "Deal. But only if you promise to stop stealing my fries."

"Only if you promise not to judge my ketchup-to-fries ratio," I shot back, grinning.

With our laughter echoing through the kitchen, I felt a warm glow of connection envelop us. The evening wore on, and as the last light of day slipped away, I caught Marco's gaze lingering on me, a softness settling into his features.

"Thanks for today," he said quietly, sincerity in his voice. "I didn't realize how much I needed this—how much I needed you."

I felt my heart flutter at his words, but before I could respond, the sudden shrill ring of my phone shattered the moment. My fingers fumbled to silence it, the screen lighting up with an unfamiliar name. A jolt of apprehension coursed through me. It was my mother.

"Sorry, I should—"

"Answer it," Marco said, waving his hand dismissively. "Family first. I'll clean up here."

Reluctantly, I took the call, the warmth of the moment evaporating as I stepped into the living room. "Mom?"

"Sweetheart, we need to talk," her voice was laced with urgency, as if she were standing on the edge of a precipice, ready to plunge into a turbulent sea.

"Is everything okay?" I asked, my heart quickening.

"It's your father," she began, and suddenly, the world felt like it was tilting beneath my feet.

"What happened?" Panic clawed at my throat, each syllable tinged with dread.

"He's... he's had an accident. He's at the hospital," she said, each word heavy with unshed tears.

I felt my stomach drop, the bubbling joy of the evening replaced by a gnawing uncertainty. "How bad is it?"

"They're still assessing his condition, but it's serious. I need you to come home."

The weight of her words hung heavily in the air, my mind racing as I tried to process the enormity of the situation. "I'll be there as soon as I can," I managed to say, feeling a deep chasm open within me, swallowing all my thoughts of food and laughter.

"Please hurry," she said softly, the tremor in her voice echoing the fear that gripped my heart.

I hung up, my pulse racing, and turned back to the kitchen. Marco was wiping down the counter, his movements steady, but the moment I stepped into view, his expression shifted. "What's wrong?"

I swallowed hard, the heaviness in my chest almost too much to bear. "It's my dad. He's had an accident. I need to go home."

The realization struck him like a bolt of lightning, and for a moment, the air was thick with unspoken words. "When do you leave?"

"I need to get my things together," I replied, my voice trembling as I fought to maintain composure.

"Can I come with you?" His offer hung between us, earnest and sincere.

"No, I don't want to burden you with this. You've already helped me so much today," I said, though my heart ached at the thought of leaving him behind.

"Do you really think I'd let you go through this alone?" he asked, stepping closer, his eyes filled with unwavering determination. "I'm not going anywhere."

I took a shaky breath, feeling the warmth of his presence wrapping around me like a protective shield. In that moment, I realized that even in the face of uncertainty, the bond we were forging had the strength to withstand the storms. As I gathered my things, Marco's quiet confidence steadied my racing heart, igniting a flicker of hope amidst the chaos.

As I hastily packed a small bag, my thoughts raced like wild horses in a storm. I grabbed a few essentials, but my mind kept drifting back to Marco. His presence had been a soothing balm, and the prospect of leaving him behind felt as foreign as stepping onto another planet. I could still hear his voice—steady and resolute—offering support when I had felt utterly lost. "I'm not going anywhere." Those words echoed in my mind, a lifeline tethering me to a moment of strength in the face of my family's turmoil.

"Okay, I think I've got everything," I said, zipping up my bag and trying to sound more composed than I felt. Marco stood by the door, his expression a mix of concern and determination. The earlier glow of our shared meal felt distant now, replaced by the stark reality of the situation.

"Do you need anything? Snacks for the road?" he asked, his voice calm but laced with an underlying worry.

"Honestly, I just need... I need you." The words slipped out before I could second-guess myself, and I felt a surge of vulnerability. "You've been my anchor today."

His brow furrowed, and he stepped closer, wrapping an arm around my shoulders. "Then I'm coming with you. We'll figure this out together."

I wanted to protest, to tell him this was my family's emergency, but as I looked into his earnest eyes, I felt my resolve waver. Having him beside me could ease the tight knot of anxiety in my stomach. "Okay, but promise not to judge my road trip playlist," I said, attempting to lighten the mood.

"Deal. But if you play any more show tunes, I'm throwing you out of the car," he teased, a playful smirk gracing his lips.

As we stepped into the cool evening air, the sky had deepened into a rich indigo, the stars beginning to twinkle like scattered diamonds. The drive felt surreal, the blend of city lights and the rush of trees zipping past reminding me how quickly life could shift. With Marco by my side, we navigated the winding roads, and the soothing hum of the engine created a cocoon of comfort amidst the chaos.

"What's the first thing you want to do when we get there?" Marco asked, glancing at me with a mixture of curiosity and concern.

"I guess I just want to see my mom and make sure she's okay. It's strange how things can change in an instant," I said, my voice barely above a whisper. The weight of unspoken worries settled heavily on my heart.

"I know. Just remember, whatever happens, you're not alone," he assured me, reaching over to squeeze my hand. The warmth of his touch sent a wave of reassurance through me.

After a few hours of driving, we finally arrived at the hospital. The fluorescent lights buzzed overhead as we stepped through the sliding glass doors, the antiseptic scent mingling with the underlying hum of medical equipment. My heart raced as we walked down the stark white hallway, the walls lined with framed photos of smiling patients and families.

My mother was seated in the waiting area, her shoulders hunched, eyes glued to the floor as though the weight of the world rested on them. When she looked up and saw me, her expression shifted from anxiety to relief, her face lighting up like the first rays of dawn breaking through a long night. "You made it," she said, rushing forward to envelop me in a tight hug.

"Mom, what happened? How's Dad?"

She pulled back, her eyes glistening with unshed tears. "He's stable, but they're keeping him overnight for observation. He took a bad fall while working on the roof."

I felt a mixture of relief and guilt wash over me. A fall sounded so trivial compared to the ominous tone in her voice, yet I could see the worry etched into her features. "Can I see him?"

"Of course, but only for a moment. He's still sedated," she said, leading me down the corridor toward his room.

As we approached, my heart thudded in my chest. The sterile smell of disinfectant and the muted beeping of machines surrounded us, and I paused outside the door, the reality of the situation crashing over me. "What if he doesn't recognize me?"

"He will," Marco chimed in, standing close enough for me to feel his reassuring presence. "You're his daughter. He'll feel that love even through the haze of the medication."

With a deep breath, I pushed the door open. My father lay in the hospital bed, a stark contrast to the strong figure I had always known. He was pale and fragile, a tangle of wires and machines surrounding him. But as I stepped closer, I saw a flicker of familiarity in his features.

"Dad?" I whispered, my voice catching in my throat.

He stirred slightly, eyes fluttering open. "Is that you, sweetheart?" His voice was hoarse but filled with warmth, grounding me in the moment.

"Yeah, it's me." I leaned closer, holding his hand, the familiar roughness of his palm bringing back a rush of memories.

"I'm sorry for worrying you," he murmured, a weak smile playing at the corners of his lips.

"You've always worried me, Dad," I joked, my heart swelling with relief. "But seriously, what were you thinking climbing on the roof?"

"Just trying to fix a leak," he replied, his eyes shimmering with mischief. "You know me—always the handyman."

I couldn't help but chuckle, a comforting laughter amidst the worry. "Just promise me you'll let someone else handle the repairs next time."

As we spoke, I noticed Marco standing quietly by the door, giving us space but still present. I felt an overwhelming gratitude for him, for his unwavering support.

"Who's that?" my dad asked, squinting to see Marco better.

"This is Marco. He's... well, he's been a great friend," I said, glancing back at Marco, who offered a friendly wave.

"Nice to meet you, sir," Marco said, his tone respectful yet light. "Just here to make sure she doesn't lose her mind."

"Good luck with that," my father replied, a glint of humor in his eyes.

I turned to Marco, a warmth blooming in my chest at the easy exchange. But before I could say anything more, the door swung open, and a nurse stepped in, her face serious.

"Excuse me, but I need to check on Mr. Thompson," she said, her voice clipped. "If you could step out for a moment."

My heart sank at the abruptness of her words. "Is everything okay?"

The nurse paused, glancing between my father and me, and for a fleeting moment, uncertainty flickered across her face. "Just a routine examination," she replied, but her eyes told a different story, an unspoken worry lurking beneath her professional facade.

As we stepped back into the hallway, a creeping sense of unease filled the space around us. Marco's hand found mine, squeezing gently. "What do you think she meant?" he asked quietly, concern etching his brow.

"I don't know," I said, anxiety knotting in my stomach. "But something feels off."

Just then, the lights flickered overhead, and a faint alarm sounded in the distance. My heart raced as I exchanged a worried glance with Marco. "This doesn't feel good," I murmured, panic rising within me.

Suddenly, the nurse hurried past us, a look of urgency on her face. My instincts kicked in, and I followed her down the hall, Marco right beside me. "What's happening?" I called out, my voice echoing against the sterile walls.

"Ma'am, you need to stay back!" the nurse called over her shoulder, but I refused to stop.

We rounded the corner, and there it was—an open door to my father's room, the machines beeping erratically, lights flashing in a chaotic rhythm. My heart dropped into my stomach as I took in the scene. Medical staff swarmed around my father, their expressions grave, the room pulsing with a sense of urgency that twisted my insides.

"Dad!" I screamed, the word tearing from my throat as I rushed forward, but Marco's grip on my arm stopped me.

"Wait!" he urged, his voice laced with panic.

But the sound of my father's name hung in the air, unanswered, as the world around me spiraled into chaos.

Chapter 27: The Calm Before the Storm

The sun dipped low on the horizon, casting a golden glow over the sprawling vineyards that surrounded the competition grounds. I stood at the edge of the field, inhaling deeply, the scent of ripening grapes mingling with the crisp autumn air. It was a fragrant promise of something beautiful, yet the weight of uncertainty hung heavy on my heart. Tomorrow would mark the culmination of months of hard work, and the air vibrated with palpable energy—anticipation, nerves, and a dash of something sinister. I was acutely aware of the stakes, each heartbeat echoing the unrelenting tension building inside me.

Marco, with his tousled hair and infectious smile, radiated confidence as he prepared for the event. He was everything I admired—passionate, driven, and undeniably talented. I watched him from a distance, moving with a grace that seemed to defy the gravity of the situation. He adjusted the collar of his crisp white shirt, his brow furrowed in concentration as he reviewed his notes. I wanted to reach out, to reassure him that everything would be okay, but my own anxiety twisted my stomach into knots.

In my pocket, my phone buzzed ominously, pulling my attention away from the vineyard's beauty. I fished it out and stared at the screen, the anonymous message burning a hole into my brain. "James is planning something. Be careful." It felt like a jigsaw puzzle missing crucial pieces, the image distorted and barely recognizable. I had thought James was a ghost from my past, something I could safely ignore, but the message clung to me like the lingering taste of burnt toast, unpleasant and unshakeable.

I thought I had put distance between us, but it seemed he had an uncanny ability to infiltrate my life even when I wished he wouldn't. I tapped my fingers against the screen, contemplating whether I should share the message with Marco. I could already envision his eyes narrowing, the momentary flash of fear passing across his face, quickly replaced by the steadfast determination I had come to love. But what good would it do to worry him before such a pivotal moment? Still, the idea of James lurking in the shadows, concocting plans to sabotage Marco, sent an icy chill coursing through my veins.

"Are you just going to stand there daydreaming, or do you plan to help me?" Marco's voice jolted me back to the present. His laughter danced in the air, warm and inviting, like sunlight spilling over freshly mown grass. I couldn't help but smile, despite the chaos swirling in my mind.

"Right! I'm here, I swear," I replied, forcing my thoughts to the backburner. "What do you need?"

He gestured to a table laden with tasting glasses, each one filled with rich, dark liquid that shimmered under the setting sun. "Help me set these up. I want everything to be perfect for the judges."

I moved closer, the familiar rhythm of his energy pulling me in like a magnet. As I arranged the glasses, the cool crystal felt reassuring in my hands. It was grounding, a reminder of the tangible beauty that surrounded us amidst the storm of uncertainty brewing in my heart. "Do you think the judges will like the blend?" I asked, glancing sideways at him.

"They'll love it," he replied, a mischievous grin spreading across his face. "But if they don't, I have a backup plan involving a show-stopping monologue on the artistry of winemaking. Who could resist that?"

I laughed, the sound echoing around us. "Is that how you plan to win their hearts? Through theatrical performance?"

"Absolutely," he said, feigning seriousness as he placed his hands on his hips, his eyes sparkling with mischief. "And if that fails, I'll dazzle them with my winning smile. Works every time."

"Oh, you're incorrigible." I nudged him playfully, but my smile faded as I recalled the dark shadow of James. "Marco, can we talk about something?"

He paused, his expression shifting to one of concern. "What's wrong? You look like you've seen a ghost."

"Not quite a ghost," I said, trying to choose my words carefully. "More like a bad omen. I got a message... about James."

His brow furrowed. "What about him?"

I hesitated, weighing the implications of my revelation. "It said he's planning something that could hurt you, your career. I don't want you to worry, but I think we need to be cautious."

For a moment, silence enveloped us, thick with tension. The playful light in Marco's eyes dimmed, replaced by a steely resolve. "James again? I thought we were done with him."

"We were, but he seems to have other plans." I bit my lip, torn between my instinct to protect him and the fear of igniting a confrontation that could spiral out of control.

"Let's not let him ruin this," Marco said, his voice firm. "I've worked too hard to let anyone take that away from me."

His determination sparked a flicker of hope within me, mingling with the anxiety coiling tightly around my chest. "You're right. We can't let him win."

As the last rays of sunlight faded, painting the sky with hues of orange and purple, I made a silent vow to uncover the truth behind James's intentions. My thoughts churned, plotting a path forward, but I knew one thing for certain: we were not facing this alone. Together, we would expose whatever darkness lay ahead. And in that moment, surrounded by laughter and the scent of the vineyards, I felt an indomitable spark ignite within me, a fierce protectiveness that promised to shield Marco from the storm.

The competition loomed like a storm cloud on the horizon, heavy and foreboding, yet filled with the possibility of rain. As dusk settled over the vineyard, I stood amidst the rows of grapevines, the twilight air alive with the chirping of crickets and the distant laughter of competitors setting up for the next day. The ambiance was electric, but beneath it all lay a current of tension that had wrapped itself around my heart like a vine, twisting tighter with every thought of James. I refused to let him shatter the moment, especially not with Marco's dream hanging in the balance.

"Okay, are you ready for the tasting notes?" Marco's voice broke through my musings, warm and teasing, as he approached with a clipboard in hand. His eyes sparkled with mischief, and despite my worries, a smile tugged at my lips.

"Do I have a choice?" I quipped, taking the clipboard and pretending to scrutinize it with utmost seriousness. "Let me see... 'Fruity, aromatic, and just the right amount of pretentiousness'—how's that for a review?"

"Hey, that's not even on the notes!" He laughed, stepping closer, his shoulder brushing against mine. I could feel the heat radiating from him, grounding me in this moment of levity. "But I'll take that as a compliment."

We stood side by side, the anticipation of the event bubbling between us like the sparkling wine we had shared on many evenings. The distant glow of lanterns strung between the trees illuminated the path ahead, and I found myself lost in the flickering light. It felt like a moment suspended in time, a brief escape from the tumultuous thoughts that swirled in my mind.

"Listen, what if we do something fun tonight?" Marco suggested, his voice dropping to a conspiratorial whisper. "A distraction before the storm. How about a late-night vineyard tour? I know the best spots."

My heart quickened at the thought. "You mean the places where you sneak off to drink wine when you're supposed to be working?"

"Exactly," he replied, his eyes gleaming with mischief. "Plus, it's a great chance for you to see my secret winemaking techniques. I promise it won't involve any grape stomping, unless you're into that sort of thing."

"I'm not sure I want my feet stained purple," I replied, but the idea of escaping into the night, away from the looming threat of James, was undeniably appealing. "Alright, lead the way."

As we wandered deeper into the vineyard, the air grew cooler, and the stars began to blanket the sky, twinkling like diamonds scattered across velvet. Marco guided me to a secluded grove where the vines were heavy with fruit, their leaves rustling gently in the evening breeze. The moon cast a silvery glow over everything, transforming the familiar landscape into a dreamscape.

"This is one of my favorite spots," he said, gesturing around. "It feels like the world disappears, doesn't it?"

I nodded, absorbing the beauty around us. "It's perfect. Almost magical."

"Just like my wine," he teased, raising an imaginary glass in a toast. "To the perfect blend of life and laughter."

"To life and laughter," I echoed, allowing myself to relax, if only for a moment. Yet, the gnawing anxiety lingered in the back of my mind, a persistent shadow threatening to eclipse our joy.

Marco began recounting stories from his early days of winemaking—how he had once accidentally added salt instead of sugar to a batch of wine, resulting in a memorable (and horrifying) tasting event. His animated recounting, complete with exaggerated gestures and dramatic flair, made me laugh until tears streamed down my cheeks. For a fleeting moment, I was able to forget the complications waiting for us at dawn.

But as his laughter faded, an unexpected silence settled between us, and I could feel the weight of the unspoken pressing against us.

"What's really bothering you?" he asked, breaking the stillness. His gaze pierced through the facade I had carefully constructed.

"Marco, I—" I hesitated, torn between honesty and the desire to shield him from the impending storm. "It's just... James."

"James again?" He frowned, running a hand through his hair in frustration. "Why does he keep coming back into our lives? He's like a bad penny."

"Maybe it's not that simple," I said, feeling the knot in my stomach tighten. "He's been... watching us, and I got this message. It's like he's waiting for the perfect moment to strike."

His expression shifted to one of concern. "What do you mean 'watching'? Are you serious?"

"Yes," I replied, my voice low. "I don't know how else to say it. I just have this feeling that he's planning something, something that could hurt you."

Marco stepped closer, his body radiating warmth against the cool night air. "We can't let him do that. Not when you're this close to achieving everything you've worked for."

I marveled at his determination, but I felt a tremor of doubt echoing in my heart. "What if he has information that could damage your reputation? Something we don't see coming?"

He took a deep breath, the tension in his shoulders visibly easing. "Look, I can't promise that everything will be perfect. But I won't let him take this away from me. We've come too far. Besides, I have you in my corner, and that's enough to make me feel invincible."

The warmth of his words wrapped around me like a cozy blanket, but the lingering dread in my gut warned me that this fight was far from over. Just then, a distant shout shattered the tranquility of the night, the sound echoing through the vineyard like an ominous bell tolling.

"What was that?" I asked, instinctively moving closer to Marco.

"I don't know, but it didn't sound good," he replied, his voice low and tense. The playfulness of our earlier moments faded, replaced by an urgency that gripped my heart.

As we turned to investigate, the air seemed to thicken, the once-familiar landscape morphing into something menacing. A surge of adrenaline coursed through me as I felt the threat of James looming, a shadow stretching longer as the night deepened. We had to get back, to protect what we had fought so hard to build.

"Let's go check it out," Marco suggested, his resolve unyielding. I nodded, knowing that whatever awaited us, we would face it together, armed with the fire of determination that had ignited between us. With each step, I could feel the storm gathering strength, but so too did my resolve to shield Marco from whatever chaos James had planned.

As we hurried toward the source of the shout, the moonlit path felt more like a tightrope than a way forward. Each step seemed to pull the earth beneath me tighter, a stretching tension that mirrored the turmoil in my chest. Marco moved with purpose, his determination evident in the way his jaw clenched and his shoulders squared. The laughter from the party we had left behind faded into the distance, replaced by the crackling energy of the night, heavy with uncertainty.

"What do you think it was?" I asked, trying to keep my voice steady despite the rising anxiety. I could hear the rhythmic thump of my heart echoing in my ears, each beat syncing with the distant commotion.

"Not sure, but it sounded like it came from the main tent," Marco replied, glancing back at me with a mixture of concern and determination. "Let's check it out."

As we approached the vibrant glow of the main tent, a sense of foreboding washed over me. The soft rustle of leaves turned into a cacophony of raised voices, panic lacing their tones. I exchanged a worried glance with Marco, and in that instant, we both understood that something was wrong. We pushed through the canvas flap, stepping into a world of chaos.

Inside, the atmosphere buzzed with tension. A group of competitors was huddled together, their faces pale as they whispered frantically. Judges hovered at the edge, their expressions a mixture of confusion and alarm. The long tables that had once been adorned with shimmering glasses and elegant arrangements now lay in disarray, evidence of a struggle.

"What happened?" Marco demanded, his voice rising above the clamor.

A tall woman with tousled hair turned to us, her eyes wide. "James! He... he just stormed in and accused one of the competitors of cheating. It's chaos! He says he has proof."

The words hit me like a cold splash of water, shock coursing through my veins. James, the specter of my fears, had materialized into a real threat. "What kind of proof?" I asked, my voice barely above a whisper.

The woman shook her head. "I don't know! But he was waving around a flash drive, and he seemed certain it would ruin someone's career."

Marco exchanged a worried glance with me, his expression darkening. "This is exactly what I was afraid of. If he's targeting anyone, it could easily spiral out of control."

"Especially if he's got something on you," I added, the weight of those words settling between us like an anchor.

"Let's find him," Marco said, determination burning in his eyes. "We can't let him manipulate this situation."

We pushed our way through the crowd, the chaos swirling around us like a storm. I felt the air thicken with anxiety, each heartbeat resonating like a drum in the silence that followed Marco's declaration. The competitors, once brimming with excitement, now wore expressions of disbelief and fear, as if they were caught in the eye of a hurricane.

Just then, I spotted him—James stood at the far end of the tent, his presence commanding attention. His slicked-back hair and tailored suit made him look like a snake dressed in silk, a predator feasting on the panic he'd created. He was animated, gesturing wildly as he spoke to a small group, the flash drive clutched in his hand like a trophy.

"Let's go," Marco whispered, pulling me along as we edged closer, careful to stay out of sight. The tension between us was palpable; I could feel the heat radiating from him, the resolve in his movements pushing me forward, urging me to act.

As we crept nearer, I could catch snippets of James's voice, dripping with venom. "The competition is rigged! I have undeniable evidence that shows collusion among the finalists. If anyone deserves to win, it's not them!"

Anger surged within me, a wild flame igniting at the thought of James tearing down everything Marco had worked for. "What a coward," I muttered, glancing at Marco. "He's trying to incite chaos just to make himself feel powerful."

"Exactly," Marco replied, his eyes narrowing. "But we need to figure out what he has before it's too late. If it's real, it could destroy everything."

We maneuvered through the throng, the air thick with tension and unspoken dread. James's voice rose, echoing against the tent walls, and I could see the faces of competitors turning to him, drawn in by his theatrics.

"What if we distract him?" I suggested, glancing around for anything that could help us. "Create a scene to pull the attention away?"

Marco nodded, a spark of mischief lighting up his features. "Good idea. Just give me a signal."

Before I could respond, a commotion broke out as someone bumped into a table, sending glasses clattering to the ground. The noise was deafening, and for a moment, everyone turned to see what had happened. It was the opening I needed.

"Now!" I hissed, nudging Marco forward as I stepped back to create some space. He shot me a quick grin, then turned to the crowd, raising his arms theatrically.

"Ladies and gentlemen!" he boomed, his voice cutting through the chaos. "We have a surprise guest! A celebrity judge has arrived to witness this event!"

Eyes widened, and heads turned, curiosity piqued. The moment was electric, a breath of hope in the chaos. James, caught off guard, spun around, disbelief etched across his face. The crowd murmured, confused yet intrigued.

"Who?" someone shouted.

"Why, it's the one and only—" Marco began, but before he could finish, a shadow loomed over us. I turned, my stomach dropping as I found myself face-to-face with a figure I hadn't expected.

"Is that really how you're going to play this, Marco?" James interrupted, a smirk curling at the corners of his lips. "Didn't your mother teach you to never play with fire?"

The room fell silent, tension crackling like static in the air. My heart raced as I caught Marco's eye, a silent understanding passing between us.

"We need to end this, once and for all," he said, determination etched in every line of his face.

But before we could respond, James raised the flash drive high, his voice booming over the stunned crowd. "I'll reveal the truth, and it will burn your precious dreams to ashes!"

In that moment, everything shifted, and I felt the world tilt on its axis, the ground beneath us quaking with the impending storm. The stakes had never been higher, and as the realization settled in, a single thought reverberated through my mind: we were standing on the edge of chaos, and whatever came next could change everything.

Chapter 28: Unmasking the Truth

The sound of clinking glasses and the distant hum of laughter spilled from the restaurant's open patio, a lively backdrop to my turmoil as I perched on a weathered stool at the bar. Each sip of my half-hearted cocktail felt like I was swallowing razor blades, the tangy citrus fighting against the bitter realization that I had stumbled into a labyrinth of deception. The air was thick with the aroma of grilled herbs and smoked meats, each whiff a reminder of what I had devoted my life to—food. Yet, at that moment, all I could think about was how the very essence of my passion was tainted by the shadow of James's ambition.

My heart raced with each tick of the clock, the seconds dragging like a thick syrup across the counter. Just days ago, James had charmed his way into my life, disarming me with that disarming smile, full of promises wrapped in golden words. But as I uncovered more about him, that smile transformed into a sinister mask, revealing a man who wielded his culinary talent like a weapon, using it to manipulate those around him. The thought made me want to hurl my drink at the wall, shattering the crystal facade he had built. Instead, I took a deep breath, channeling my frustration into clarity.

"Hey, you alright there?" A voice pulled me from my thoughts, soft yet carrying an edge of curiosity. I turned to find a familiar face—Marco, my steadfast ally, leaning against the bar with his arms crossed, concern etched into his features.

"Just peachy," I replied, forcing a smile that felt as real as a plastic fruit. "You know, drowning my sorrows in overpriced cocktails."

Marco chuckled, the sound warm and inviting. "You know they're just as expensive at the bottom of the glass, right?" He motioned for the bartender, a tall guy with tousled hair and an easy grin, who nodded in recognition. "Two margaritas, please. On the rocks. Extra salt."

I watched him, the way his confidence lit up the space around him, even as my insides twisted like a pretzel. "You didn't have to—"

"Consider it a bribe to get you to open up," he said, his eyes narrowing playfully. "I've seen that look before. It's not a good one."

I scoffed lightly, shaking my head, but the playful banter fell flat against the heavy truth I was carrying. The drink was placed in front of me, vibrant and inviting, but it felt like another veil to the brewing storm.

"Alright," I finally relented, leaning closer, my voice barely a whisper amidst the clinking and chatter. "I've been digging into James's past. It's... not what I expected." The words slipped out like marbles tumbling from a jar, uncontainable and chaotic.

Marco's brow furrowed, his teasing demeanor shifting into something more serious. "What do you mean?"

"His history in the culinary world—it's rife with manipulation and sabotage. He's been using chefs as stepping stones. Those who don't play by his rules? He destroys them." The confession felt like lifting a boulder off my chest, but the weight of my revelation remained, heavy and oppressive.

Marco's expression shifted from concern to incredulity. "You can't be serious. James? The man who whips up magic in the kitchen?"

"Exactly," I said, my voice a mixture of disbelief and frustration. "That's what makes it so twisted. He's a culinary genius, but he wields his talent like a sword. I found testimonials from chefs he's worked with, all singing his praises until you peel back the layers. It's like a horror story wrapped in a Michelin star."

He took a long sip of his drink, pondering my words, his eyes narrowing as he processed the information. "So, what are you going to do? This isn't just some kitchen gossip; this is serious."

The reality of the situation settled like a fog in the pit of my stomach. "I have to confront him," I said, determination rising in my voice. "Before he can do any more damage. But what if I'm wrong? What if I'm just seeing shadows where there are none?"

"Then you'll be a culinary detective, and we'll laugh about it later over a good meal," Marco replied with a grin, his attempt at lightening the mood only deepening my unease. "But if you're right, then you're not just saving your career; you're protecting others from his influence."

"You make it sound so simple," I replied, a bitter laugh escaping my lips. "Just march right up to him and demand the truth. I wish it were that easy."

"Isn't it?" He raised an eyebrow, challenging me. "You're stronger than you think. Trust your instincts. Besides, you're not alone in this. You have me, remember?"

The sincerity in his voice cut through my anxiety, reminding me that I had a partner in this battle. The camaraderie between us always felt like an unbreakable bond, yet there was an undercurrent of tension that I couldn't ignore, a spark that seemed to dance just below the surface every time our eyes met.

As I stirred my drink absentmindedly, the citrusy scent mixed with a hint of salt reminded me of brighter days, culinary adventures shared with friends, laughter ringing through the air. It was a world I was determined to reclaim, but first, I had to face the dark reality lurking in the shadows.

"Okay," I said, my voice steadying. "I'll talk to him. But if he tries to twist the narrative or deflect blame, I won't back down. I'm done letting fear dictate my choices."

Marco grinned, the infectious energy filling the space between us. "That's the spirit! You've got this, and when you do—"

"Let's not jump ahead," I interrupted, a teasing smile creeping across my face. "I still have to survive the encounter first."

"True, but I have a good feeling about this," he said, his confidence buoying me. "Just remember, even the most skilled chefs burn a dish now and then. It's how they salvage it that defines them."

As we clinked our glasses together, the familiar weight of resolve settled in my stomach. I wasn't just facing a chef with questionable ethics; I was standing up for my passion, for those who had fallen victim to James's dark schemes, and for the integrity of a culinary world that had given me everything.

With a newfound sense of purpose coursing through me, I took a deep breath, ready to unmask the truth and take back the narrative that had begun to slip through my fingers like grains of sand.

The sun dipped below the horizon, casting a golden glow across the kitchen as I slipped through the door of the bustling restaurant. The familiar clatter of pots and pans mixed with the sizzle of meat hitting the grill, an orchestra of chaos that usually made my heart swell with excitement. Tonight, however, the melody felt off-key. I was caught in the grip of anticipation and dread, the atmosphere thick with the unsaid words hanging between me and James.

As I approached the pass, I caught sight of him. He was orchestrating his team with the practiced ease of a conductor, his hands slicing through the air like blades as he barked orders. I paused for a moment, my breath catching as I took in the sight. In the midst of the frenetic energy, he looked effortlessly in control, and I felt a wave of unease wash over me. The person who had charmed me just days ago now seemed to be a stranger cloaked in authority.

"Hey, you're back! I was just about to send out a search party," James called, a grin spreading across his face as he caught sight of me. The warmth of his smile almost made me forget the turmoil churning within. Almost.

"I thought you might need a hand," I replied, forcing cheerfulness into my tone, my stomach twisting at the thought of the confrontation to come. I stepped closer, trying to ignore the nagging voice in my head urging me to turn and run.

He raised an eyebrow, his interest piqued. "You? In my kitchen? Now that's a plot twist. I'd have to warn the staff to keep their knives close."

I smirked, attempting to inject humor into the tension. "Don't worry, I'm not here to usurp your throne. Just doing my civic duty as a fellow chef."

"Oh, is that what you call it now?" He leaned against the counter, arms crossed, his demeanor shifting slightly. "I could have sworn I heard you plotting world domination last night."

A flicker of uncertainty darted through me, but I couldn't let it show. "Only if world domination involves perfecting the soufflé," I shot back, the banter a thin shield against the storm brewing in my mind.

"Now that's a goal I can get behind." His laughter filled the air, but as I watched him, that mirth felt like a facade, a mask he wore to hide the ruthless ambition lurking beneath. The realization was unsettling, the line between friend and foe blurring with each passing moment.

I busied myself with a stack of fresh herbs, chopping them with a precision that belied the chaos in my heart. Each slice felt like a countdown to the inevitable moment I had to confront him. The fragrant scent wafted through the air, a brief respite that distracted me from the reality closing in. I couldn't keep pretending everything was fine. I needed to speak up.

"James," I began, my voice steady despite the quiver in my stomach. He looked up, his expression shifting to one of curiosity. "Can we talk?"

"Sure! Just let me wrap up this order." He waved dismissively, but I could see the flicker of uncertainty in his eyes. It was a glimpse of the man behind the mask, and I seized it.

I nodded, watching him dart around the kitchen, a flurry of motion and chaos that masked his growing apprehension. With each passing second, my resolve solidified. I would unearth the truth, even if it meant dismantling the very foundation of the camaraderie we had built.

Finally, after what felt like an eternity, James wiped his hands on a kitchen towel and turned to me, his smile faltering slightly. "What's on your mind?"

"About your past," I said, the words tumbling out with an urgency that surprised me. "I've been doing some digging. You know, just curious chef stuff."

His expression darkened, the jovial atmosphere evaporating like mist in the morning sun. "Digging? What exactly did you find?" The question hung in the air, heavy and charged.

"Let's just say your reputation precedes you," I replied, a tremor of defiance punctuating my words. "I've heard things, seen things that don't add up. You've hurt people, James. Chefs who trusted you."

He stiffened, the light in his eyes dimming. "Is that what you think? That I'm some sort of monster?" His voice was low, laced with a hint of incredulity.

"I think you've played a dangerous game, and now the stakes are higher than ever." I leaned closer, emboldened by the righteous anger bubbling within me. "People's lives are at risk. Their dreams—"

"Enough!" He interrupted, his voice rising, cutting through the tension like a hot knife through butter. The kitchen fell silent, all eyes on us. The camaraderie of our team faded, leaving only the two of us in a charged standoff.

I took a breath, unwilling to back down. "You can't silence me. This isn't just about you anymore. It's about everyone who's suffered because of your actions."

His eyes narrowed, the darkness within them swirling like storm clouds. "You think you understand me? You don't know anything about the sacrifices I've made to get where I am." The pain in his voice felt genuine, yet I couldn't let it sway me.

"Sacrifices? Or manipulations?" I shot back, the words sharper than I intended. "You've exploited the very people who looked up to you. That's not sacrifice; that's betrayal."

The silence stretched between us, a taut wire ready to snap. I could see the walls rising around him, the vulnerable facade crumbling, revealing the raw emotion beneath. "You're wrong," he said finally, his voice barely above a whisper. "I did what I had to do to survive in this industry."

"Survival shouldn't come at the cost of others' dreams," I countered, my heart racing. I was standing on the edge of a precipice, and the view was dizzying.

Just then, Marco stepped into the kitchen, a storm of concern etched on his face. "What's going on here?" His presence felt like a lifeline, a grounding force in the midst of chaos.

"Nothing we can't handle," James replied, his tone flat, but I could see the flicker of uncertainty in his eyes as he turned back to me.

I shot Marco a glance, the unspoken understanding passing between us. "This isn't just a personal issue, Marco. This is bigger than all of us. I can't let James continue this way."

Marco nodded, his expression resolute. "You're right. We have to take a stand, for everyone who's been affected."

James's face twisted into a mask of anger, and for a moment, I feared he might lash out. But instead, he took a step back, as if the weight of our accusations bore down on him like an anchor.

"Do you really think you can take me down?" he said, a bitter smile creeping across his lips. "This isn't just a kitchen; it's my empire."

I met his gaze, unflinching. "An empire built on the ruins of others. It's time to dismantle it."

The air crackled with tension, the stakes higher than ever. I could feel the battle lines being drawn, the fragile balance of power shifting with every word spoken. It was no longer just a confrontation; it was a declaration of war, and I was ready to fight for what was right.

The tension in the kitchen was so thick it felt like a tangible force, a wall of uncertainty looming over us as I stood my ground. James's presence, usually a source of warmth, now felt like the chill of a winter wind—sharp and biting. The silence stretched like a taut wire, and for a moment, it seemed we were all holding our breath, waiting for the next move.

"Do you think you can just threaten me and walk away?" James challenged, his tone icy, but there was a flicker of something else in his eyes—fear? Perhaps the shadow of regret? "You have no idea who you're dealing with."

"Oh, I think I have a pretty good idea," I shot back, crossing my arms defiantly. "You're a man who hides behind charisma and culinary genius to mask your manipulation. But that charade is ending now."

"Watch it," he said, stepping closer, the space between us shrinking. "You might want to remember who has the upper hand in this kitchen."

"That's just it, isn't it?" I pressed on, the fire in my belly igniting as I met his steely gaze. "You think power is about control, but it's really about respect. You've turned this place into a battleground, and I refuse to be one of your casualties."

Marco moved closer, his expression a blend of concern and determination. "This isn't just about you two anymore. We have a team that deserves to know the truth," he said, raising his voice to cut through the tension.

James's eyes darted between us, calculating, as if weighing his options. "And what makes you think they'll believe you?"

"They'll believe me because I have the truth on my side," I replied, feeling the adrenaline surging through me. "This isn't just personal; it's about the integrity of our craft."

The air crackled with electricity, and I could sense the collective heartbeat of the kitchen staff as they eavesdropped, their curiosity piqued. The flames of the grill flickered, sending shadows dancing across the walls, adding an unsettling ambiance to our confrontation.

"Let's not forget," James said, his voice lowering to a menacing whisper, "that I've built this kitchen from the ground up. I made every one of you what you are today."

"By stepping on us?" I challenged, refusing to be intimidated. "You think loyalty can be bought with a chef's coat? That's not how this works."

He smirked, but there was something darker lurking behind it. "You should be careful who you provoke, especially when you don't know the whole story."

"What do you mean?" I shot back, my heart racing.

"Let's just say there are reasons I've had to play the game the way I do," he replied cryptically, his gaze growing distant as if he were recalling something painful.

Marco interjected, "Enough with the riddles, James. If you have something to say, say it."

For a moment, the kitchen was steeped in a profound silence, and then James took a deep breath, almost as if he were gathering his strength. "You think I enjoy this? That I revel in the drama and the backstabbing? This industry is unforgiving. You either adapt or you get left behind. I've had to make choices—hard choices—to survive. But you wouldn't understand."

"Try me," I said, my voice firm, defiant. "I might surprise you."

James hesitated, and I could see the internal struggle in his eyes. The mask of confidence he wore cracked just enough for me to glimpse the turmoil beneath. "You think you're so different, don't you? You think you can save the world with your ideals. But the truth is, everyone is out for themselves. You'll see."

I stepped forward, feeling the heat radiating off the grill behind me. "Not if we band together. We can change things, James. But not if you keep operating like this."

His expression shifted, a flash of vulnerability breaking through. "Change is a dangerous game, and not everyone gets to play."

"Maybe not, but I refuse to be one of your pawns anymore," I declared, my pulse racing.

The tension hung heavy, thickening the air between us, and then, as if the universe were trying to intervene, the door swung open with a loud bang, making everyone jump. A figure burst into the kitchen, their eyes wide with urgency. It was Clara, our head pastry chef, her apron dusted with flour and a frantic expression etched on her face.

"Guys! You need to see this!" she shouted, breathless and wide-eyed, completely oblivious to the charged atmosphere.

"What is it?" I asked, the adrenaline still surging through my veins as I turned my attention to her.

"Social media is blowing up! There's a video... it's about James," she gasped, her words spilling out in a rush.

"What kind of video?" James asked, the panic barely concealed in his voice.

"It's someone filming inside the kitchen—behind the scenes! And it's not flattering. They caught some... uh, interesting moments of you, James."

"Interesting how?" I pressed, my curiosity piqued.

Clara shook her head, her voice trembling. "You need to see it. It's all over Instagram, and people are starting to connect the dots. It looks like... like you're not who you say you are."

James's face paled, the bravado he had just displayed evaporating like steam in the air. "This can't be happening," he muttered, more to himself than to anyone else.

I exchanged a glance with Marco, a shared understanding settling between us. Whatever was on that video could change everything.

"Let's go," Marco said, urgency creeping into his tone.

As we filed out of the kitchen, following Clara, I could feel the weight of the moment pressing down on me. This was it—everything I had feared was about to come to light, and there was no turning back.

The dining room was bustling, the sound of forks clinking against plates filling the air as we made our way to the back where Clara's phone was propped up against a wall, streaming the chaos unfolding online.

"What are they saying?" I asked, my voice tight with anticipation.

She tapped the screen, and the video began to play. A shaky hand recorded the inner workings of our kitchen, catching snippets of James barking orders, the staff exchanging worried glances, and the atmosphere thick with tension. But then, as the camera panned, it zoomed in on a moment that made my stomach drop.

James was seen in a heated argument with one of the line cooks, and I could see the anger on his face, the way he leaned in, looming over the young chef like a predator. The sound was muffled, but the context was clear. He was belittling him, tearing down his confidence with sharp, cutting words.

"No..." I whispered, feeling my heart race. This was worse than I had imagined.

The comments flooded in, the chat buzzing with disbelief and outrage as viewers reacted in real time.

"Is this what you meant by survival, James?" I whispered, turning to him, but the mask had completely shattered. His eyes were wild, and I could see the cracks forming in his facade.

"I... I didn't mean for this to happen," he stammered, looking at the screen as if it were a mirror reflecting his deepest fears.

The chat exploded, more videos surfacing, capturing moments of tension, dishonesty, and manipulation. The air thickened with the palpable sense of betrayal, and I could feel the eyes of the restaurant staff on us, their murmurs rising in crescendo.

And just as I was about to speak, the screen flickered with a new notification, the headline bold and glaring: "Chef James Exposed: A Culinary Tyrant?"

I turned back to him, my breath catching. "What now, James? This is your moment of truth."

But just then, the front door swung open again, and the figure that stepped inside sent a jolt of shock through me—a reporter, camera in hand, with a knowing grin that promised trouble.

"Excuse me, Chef," they called out, eyes scanning the room as if they were already crafting a story. "Can you comment on the allegations against you?"

Panic flickered across James's face, and in that instant, I knew this was far from over. The storm was just beginning, and as chaos erupted around us, I braced myself for the whirlwind of consequences that was about to follow, a feeling of dread creeping in as the gravity of our situation settled like a stone in my gut.

Chapter 29: The Competition Begins

The kitchen was alive with an electric energy, each station a small universe of sizzling pans and clattering utensils. I could feel the warmth emanating from the ovens, mingling with the fragrant spices that danced in the air like whispers of inspiration. A kaleidoscope of colors spilled across the countertops, from vibrant green herbs to ruby-red tomatoes, each ingredient waiting to play its part in the unfolding drama. Chefs darted about like fireflies, their expressions a blend of fierce concentration and simmering anxiety.

I spotted Marco, his tall frame leaning over a gleaming countertop, meticulously arranging his ingredients with the precision of an artist at work. The way he wielded his knife reminded me of a conductor leading an orchestra, each slice and dice harmonizing into the symphony of his dish. Yet, behind that confidence, I noticed the flicker of worry in his eyes, a silent battle against the shadows of self-doubt that threatened to overtake him. I had seen that look too often lately, and it made my heart ache.

As I approached him, the hum of the kitchen faded into the background, and I felt the weight of my news pressing down on me like a heavy cloak. "Marco," I started, my voice barely above a whisper yet laced with urgency. His eyes met mine, and for a brief moment, I thought I could see the world shift in his gaze.

"What's wrong?" he asked, his brow furrowing.

I took a deep breath, steeling myself for the confession. "It's about James. I found out something you need to know before you compete today."

The air around us thickened, and I could feel the tension rise as I revealed the truth. The way James had been sabotaging not just Marco's dishes but also spreading lies to undermine his confidence—it all poured out in a rush. "He thinks he can play dirty and take you down. But you can't let him. You have to rise above this."

As I spoke, I watched the emotions play across Marco's face: hurt, anger, and finally a flicker of gratitude. "Why didn't you tell me sooner?" he asked, a note of disbelief creeping into his voice.

"I needed to gather the evidence first. I didn't want to accuse him without proof. But seeing you here, I couldn't keep it to myself any longer. You deserve to compete fairly."

Marco ran a hand through his tousled hair, a mixture of frustration and admiration evident in his features. "I should have known. He's been acting strange lately. I thought it was just the pressure of the competition getting to him."

"But you can't let that define you. You have to stand tall, show everyone the kind of chef you are. It's about your talent, Marco, not the games he's trying to play."

His jaw set, and I saw the determination spark back to life in his eyes. "You're right. I won't let him win. I'm going to show everyone what I can do, and I won't let him take that from me."

The moment hung between us, charged with unspoken promises and the bond we had forged through late-night conversations and shared dreams. It was as if the world outside faded away, leaving just the two of us standing against the backdrop of the bustling kitchen.

As the clock ticked down toward the competition's start, I leaned in closer. "Just remember, you're not alone in this. I'll be right here cheering for you."

With a small smile, he nodded, and I felt a warmth spread through me, a reassurance that our partnership was solid, built on trust and mutual respect. But as he turned back to his station, a twinge of doubt lingered at the edges of my mind. Was I truly prepared to face James when the time came? Would he retaliate in ways I couldn't foresee?

The competition was about more than just cooking; it was a battlefield where egos clashed and aspirations were tested. The judges, an imposing trio with discerning palates, were taking their seats, and the murmurs of anticipation rippled through the crowd like the first stirrings of a storm. Each chef looked poised and ready, but beneath their calm exteriors, I sensed the undercurrents of anxiety, the fear of failure that clung to them like a second skin.

I took my place near the front, a spectator in this grand culinary showdown, my heart racing with a mixture of pride and concern. As Marco's first dish was plated, a vibrant seafood risotto that shimmered under the lights, I couldn't help but feel a surge of hope. He had poured his heart and soul into that dish, and it showed.

When the judges tasted his creation, their faces morphed into expressions of surprise and delight. I could hardly breathe, my heart pounding in sync with the drumroll of excitement echoing in my chest. They nodded appreciatively, and for a moment, the world around us dimmed, leaving just the glow of Marco's triumph in the spotlight.

But then I caught a glimpse of James in the corner of my eye, lurking like a storm cloud, his expression twisted into something I couldn't quite decipher—was it envy or malice? I felt a shiver run down my spine, a premonition that this was just the calm before the storm.

With each dish that followed, Marco continued to impress, his confidence blossoming like a flower breaking through the frost. Yet, I remained acutely aware of James's shadow, a dark reminder that this battle was far from over. As the final rounds approached, I couldn't shake the feeling that the competition held more than just culinary feats; it was a test of character, integrity, and the strength to rise above the fray.

With the stakes higher than ever, I vowed to stand by Marco, even as the tension thickened in the air, each moment pregnant with uncertainty and anticipation.

The judges' table loomed ahead, a fortress of stern faces and notepads poised to capture every nuance of the culinary performance. The atmosphere crackled with tension, a symphony of bubbling sauces and the hiss of pans filling the air. I shifted on my feet, my palms clammy against my apron. Watching Marco work was like watching a magician at his craft; he moved fluidly, hands deftly assembling flavors and textures into a cohesive masterpiece, his concentration as palpable as the steam rising from his pots.

I leaned against a nearby counter, trying to soak up the energy around me, but I could hardly focus. My mind was an unending loop of concern about James and what he might pull next. He was a coiled spring, waiting for the perfect moment to strike. Just then, I spotted him at his station, grinning at his reflection in a polished knife. The smile didn't quite reach his eyes, which glittered with something far more sinister than friendly competition. My gut twisted. It was a reminder that this was more than a culinary showdown; it was a stage for egos and ambition.

"Is it just me, or is that guy giving off serious 'villain' vibes?" I muttered to myself, eyeing James like he was an unexpected ingredient in an otherwise perfect recipe.

From behind me, a voice chimed in, smooth as butter and just as slippery. "If looks could kill, I'd be a goner." It was Lila, Marco's sous chef, her hair pulled back in a tight bun that made her look both fierce and slightly frazzled. "But we're not here to dwell on him, right? Let's focus on what really matters."

I turned, trying to muster a grin. "Right! The food! Delicious, soul-nourishing food!"

"Exactly. You know, like a solid risotto that could make anyone forget about their nemeses."

I laughed, the tension in my chest easing slightly. "If only we could cook up a winning attitude for Marco as easily as he makes that risotto."

Lila's eyes sparkled with mischief. "Maybe we should sprinkle some motivational quotes into his next batch. 'You're better than James' would fit right in, don't you think?"

As we chuckled, I caught sight of Marco's station again, and my smile faded. He was plating his second dish: a stunning herb-crusted lamb with a side of roasted vegetables. I could see him nervously eyeing the judges, the weight of their scrutiny pressing down on him like a heavy blanket. My heart ached for him; I wanted to reach out and tell him how incredible he was, how talented, how deserving of this moment.

Then came the first round of critiques. The judges tasted Marco's risotto, and I could see the tension in his shoulders relax slightly when their expressions shifted to delight. It was a small victory, but I could feel the surge of confidence that followed him into his next dish. I allowed myself a moment of relief, hoping that momentum would carry him through the day.

Yet, the specter of James loomed large. During the next presentation, I watched him saunter over to Marco's station, a casualness that sent chills down my spine. "Nice presentation," James said, voice dripping with feigned sweetness. "You know, I'd hate to see anyone ruin a dish over a little... accident."

Marco clenched his jaw, refusing to engage, and I could see the effort it took for him to maintain his composure. "I'm not worried about accidents, James," he replied, a tightness in his tone. "I'm focused on cooking."

James chuckled, a sound that set my teeth on edge. "Good to hear. But you know how it is—pressure makes diamonds, and sometimes it just makes a mess."

Before I could shout out a warning or jump to Marco's defense, Lila stepped in. "Why don't you focus on your own dish, James? I hear the judges love a good show. Or was that just a rumor?"

With that, she flashed a brilliant smile that was equal parts charming and lethal. James's expression soured slightly, and he took a step back, clearly taken aback by her audacity. "Careful, Lila. You might just find yourself in the line of fire."

"Oh, I'm always in the line of fire. It's where the magic happens."

The banter hung in the air like a fine mist, swirling with the scents of herbs and spices, as I tried to ground myself in the moment. James retreated, muttering something under his breath that I couldn't quite catch.

"Who knew Lila had a flair for theatrics?" I whispered to her, my heart racing.

"Just doing my part to keep the drama on stage, not off it," she replied with a wink.

The rounds continued, each dish pushing Marco closer to the climax of his dreams. I watched as he transformed ordinary ingredients into extraordinary flavors, his passion infusing every bite. The judges responded, praising him with thoughtful critiques that felt like warm sunlight breaking through a cloudy day. I could see the confidence blooming in him, his initial nerves melting away like butter on a hot skillet.

Yet, as the final dishes were presented, the air grew thicker with anticipation. Marco was up again, and this time he was going big: a stunning duck confit with a cherry reduction that looked like art on a plate. My heart swelled with pride as he plated it with the finesse of a painter, but just as he turned to face the judges, I felt a chill wash over me.

James was nearby, leaning against a countertop, arms crossed, an almost predatory gleam in his eye. I could sense that he was preparing to strike at the very moment Marco shined the brightest.

My instincts screamed at me to intervene, but before I could take a step forward, the head judge approached Marco's station.

"Let's see what you've got," she said, her voice booming and authoritative, echoing in the charged air.

As the judge took a bite, I held my breath, a mix of hope and dread coiling tightly in my stomach. I could see the moment she closed her eyes, savoring the taste, and my heart lifted—until I heard a loud crash from James's station.

In a split second, the atmosphere shifted from anticipation to chaos as a pan slipped from James's hands, its contents splattering across the floor like a culinary crime scene. "Oops!" he exclaimed, feigning innocence, but I saw the glimmer of satisfaction in his eyes.

The commotion drew attention, and in that instant, Marco's focus faltered. I could see the doubt creeping back in, and it broke my heart. "No, Marco! Stay strong!" I whispered under my breath, desperate for him to remain unfazed.

But as the judge's attention diverted, I sensed a fracture forming in the confidence that had taken root in Marco's heart. The stakes had escalated, and with them came the peril of distraction. As I took a step closer, determination washed over me. I had to protect his vision, to keep the integrity of this moment intact, even if it meant stepping directly into the fray.

With the judge's focus momentarily diverted by the chaos erupting at James's station, I seized the opportunity. "Marco!" I called out, my voice slicing through the tension. "Focus on your dish! Don't let him get to you!"

His eyes flicked toward me, and for a heartbeat, I could see the confusion cross his face, as if the surrounding turmoil had momentarily clouded his thoughts. But then, something ignited in his gaze—a flicker of resolve. He took a deep breath, returning his attention to the judge, who was wiping sauce from her chin with a look of appreciation that made my heart flutter.

"Delicious! The duck is perfectly cooked, and the reduction is rich without being overwhelming," the judge praised, and I felt the tension in my shoulders ease slightly. But my relief was short-lived as I turned back to James, who had just been caught red-handed scraping the remnants of his own failed dish off the floor.

"Need a hand, James?" I shouted, my voice dripping with faux concern. "Or perhaps a lesson in basic kitchen hygiene?"

The tension around his mouth twitched as he glared back at me, but before he could respond, a fellow competitor chimed in, "Better keep that attitude in check, James. We wouldn't want you to spill anything else, would we?"

The laughter that rippled through the nearby stations bolstered my confidence, but I could still feel James's eyes on me like a predator waiting for the right moment to pounce. Marco finished his presentation, the judge's nod of approval feeling like a lifeline thrown into turbulent waters.

But just as the wave of success began to crest, James leaned in, his voice low and menacing. "You're playing a dangerous game, you know. You might want to watch your back."

The threat hung in the air like an ominous cloud, but I brushed it off. "You think I'm worried about your petty threats? I've got more spice in my life than you can handle."

As the competition progressed, I kept my eye on both Marco and James, each interaction between them becoming a delicate dance of tension and resolve. Marco had just completed another dish, an exquisite paella bursting with color, the saffron weaving through the ingredients like golden threads. The judges praised his creativity, and I felt a swell of pride that was only slightly tempered by the ever-present shadow of James.

But just as I allowed myself to believe that maybe, just maybe, Marco was on the path to victory, disaster struck. A high-pitched scream erupted from the crowd as one of the competitors, a woman I barely knew, stumbled backward, a large pot of boiling water spilling onto the floor. Chaos ensued, and in the ensuing frenzy, James saw his moment to create further mayhem.

In a flash, he snatched up an empty bowl from Marco's station, slipping it into his own, a move so slick it sent chills racing down my spine. "Whoops! Sorry, Marco!" he called out with feigned innocence, but the malice behind his eyes was unmistakable.

"James, what are you doing?" Marco's voice rose, a blend of confusion and anger.

"I'm just... borrowing. I'm sure you have plenty more," James retorted, but the mischief in his tone was laced with a hint of something darker.

I darted toward them, feeling the pulse of adrenaline heighten my senses. "You need to stop this right now," I said firmly, my voice unwavering as I squared my shoulders against James. "This is a competition, not a playground for your childish antics."

"Childish?" he echoed, mock surprise dancing in his eyes. "This is survival of the fittest. You wouldn't understand; you're not even a competitor."

"Maybe not, but I'm not about to let you ruin Marco's chances with your games. You're playing with fire."

James leaned in closer, the scent of burnt garlic wafting off his clothes, mingling with the tension. "And what are you going to do about it? You're not the one holding the spatula."

The confrontation simmered, thickening the air between us until it felt like a physical barrier. Before I could muster a sharp retort, the head judge called for attention, demanding silence as she prepared to announce the next round. I turned to Marco, who looked more determined than ever, his focus unwavering despite the chaos surrounding him.

"Just keep your head in the game, Marco. Ignore him," I whispered, the urgency in my tone evident. "You can't let him distract you."

"Yeah, I got this," he replied, but his voice held a hint of uncertainty that twisted my stomach.

The judges announced the next challenge: a mystery basket filled with a variety of unconventional ingredients. I watched as Marco's eyes lit up, his creativity bubbling to the surface. It was a beautiful thing to witness, but as the competitors scrambled to gather their ingredients, James's smirk returned, his demeanor shifting from playful to predatory.

"Let's see if you can handle the heat, Marco," he taunted, snatching a particularly exotic ingredient from the basket before Marco could reach it.

"Seriously, James? Grow up," Marco shot back, the irritation in his voice barely masking his frustration.

With the clock ticking down, I knew I had to intervene. "James, if you're so desperate for attention, why don't you show us all what you're capable of instead of sabotaging others?"

"Desperate? Hardly," he replied, his eyes narrowing. "I'm just ensuring the competition is... interesting."

"Interesting? Or unethical?"

But he brushed off my words, refocusing on his own station, the tension thickening around us like a dense fog. As the countdown began, Marco shifted into overdrive, whipping together flavors and techniques that made my heart race with anticipation.

Just as I thought James would fade into the background, he sneered and threw down his final dish, a messy pile of ingredients that barely resembled a meal. The judges frowned at it, and I felt a rush of vindication. But then, with a gleam in his eye, James whispered something to Marco, too low for anyone else to hear.

"I've got a secret ingredient you'll never see coming."

I felt the blood drain from my face. Was he really trying to play mind games now? And what could he possibly mean?

Before I could process it, the judges approached Marco's station for the final assessment, and I felt a knot of dread settle deep within me. This was it; the moment that could either lift Marco to soaring heights or drag him into the depths of defeat.

The judges took their time, savoring each bite, the seconds stretching into eternity. Marco stood with bated breath, and I could almost hear the ticking of his heart against the backdrop of the bustling kitchen. Just as the head judge opened her mouth to deliver her verdict, the lights flickered.

The kitchen plunged into darkness. Gasps erupted from the crowd as panic surged through the room. My pulse raced in sync with the frantic shuffling of feet, and I squinted into the void, trying to make sense of the chaos.

"Marco!" I shouted, my voice cutting through the din, but there was no reply.

In the pitch-blackness, everything felt surreal, the only sounds the clattering of pans and muffled whispers. A moment later, the emergency lights flickered on, casting an eerie glow across the chaos. My eyes darted around, searching for Marco. But he was gone.

And in that instant, I realized with dread that the competition had just taken a turn I never saw coming.

Milton Keynes UK
Ingram Content Group UK Ltd.
UKHW041821201024
449814UK00001B/36